One Drop of Blood

By Anne Austin

Originally published in 1932

One Drop of Blood

© 2012 Resurrected Press
www.ResurrectedPress.com

All rights reserved. No part of this book may be used or reproduced in any manner without written permission except for brief quotations for review purposes.

Published by Intrepid Ink, LLC

Intrepid Ink, LLC provides full publishing services to authors of fiction and non-fiction books, eBooks and websites. From editing to formatting, to publishing, to marketing, Intrepid Ink gets your creative works into the hands of the people who want to read them.
Find out more at www.IntrepidInk.com.

ISBN 13: 978-1-937022-53-2

Printed in the United States of America

RESURRECTED PRESS CLASSIC MYSTERY CATALOGUE

Journeys into Mystery
Travel and Mystery in a More Elegant Time

The Edwardian Detectives
Literary Sleuths of the Edwardian Era

Gems of Mystery
Lost Jewels from a More Elegant Age

Anne Austin
One Drop of Blood
The Black Pigeon
Murder at Bridge

E. C. Bentley
Trent's Last Case: The Woman in Black

Ernest Bramah
Max Carrados Resurrected:
The Detective Stories of Max Carrados

Agatha Christie
The Secret Adversary
The Mysterious Affair at Styles

Octavus Roy Cohen
Midnight

Freeman Wills Croft
The Ponson Case
The Pit Prop Syndicate

J. S. Fletcher

The Herapath Property
The Rayner-Slade Amalgamation
The Chestermarke Instinct
The Paradise Mystery
Dead Men's Money
The Middle of Things
Ravensdene Court
Scarhaven Keep
The Orange-Yellow Diamond
The Middle Temple Murder
The Tallyrand Maxim
The Borough Treasurer
In the Mayor's Parlour
The Saftey Pin

R. Austin Freeman

The Mystery of 31 New Inn from the Dr. Thorndyke Series
John Thorndyke's Cases from the Dr. Thorndyke Series
The Red Thumb Mark from The Dr. Thorndyke Series
The Eye of Osiris from The Dr. Thorndyke Series
A Silent Witness from the Dr. John Thorndyke Series
The Cat's Eye from the Dr. John Thorndyke Series
Helen Vardon's Confession: A Dr. John Thorndyke Story
As a Thief in the Night: A Dr. John Thorndyke Story
Mr. Pottermack's Oversight: A Dr. John Thorndyke Story
Dr. Thorndyke Intervenes: A Dr. John Thorndyke Story
The Singing Bone: The Adventures of Dr. Thorndyke
The Stoneware Monkey: A Dr. John Thorndyke Story
The Great Portrait Mystery, and Other Stories: A Collection of Dr. John Thorndyke and Other Stories
The Penrose Mystery: A Dr. John Thorndyke Story
The Uttermost Farthing: A Savant's Vendetta

Arthur Griffiths
The Passenger From Calais
The Rome Express

Fergus Hume
The Mystery of a Hansom Cab
The Green Mummy
The Silent House
The Secret Passage

Edgar Jepson
The Loudwater Mystery

A. E. W. Mason
At the Villa Rose

A. A. Milne
The Red House Mystery
Baroness Emma Orczy
The Old Man in the Corner

Edgar Allan Poe
The Detective Stories of Edgar Allan Poe

Arthur J. Rees
The Hampstead Mystery
The Shrieking Pit
The Hand In The Dark
The Moon Rock
The Mystery of the Downs

Mary Roberts Rinehart
Sight Unseen and The Confession

Dorothy L. Sayers
Whose Body?

Sir William Magnay
The Hunt Ball Mystery

Mabel and Paul Thorne
The Sheridan Road Mystery

Louis Tracy
The Strange Case of Mortimer Fenley
The Albert Gate Mystery
The Bartlett Mystery
The Postmaster's Daughter
The House of Peril
The Sandling Case: What Would You Have Done?

Charles Edmonds Walk
The Paternoster Ruby

John R. Watson
The Mystery of the Downs
The Hampstead Mystery

Edgar Wallace
The Daffodil Mystery
The Crimson Circle

Carolyn Wells
Vicky Van
The Man Who Fell Through the Earth
In the Onyx Lobby
Raspberry Jam
The Clue
The Room with the Tassels
The Vanishing of Betty Varian
The Mystery Girl
The White Alley
The Curved Blades
Anybody but Anne
The Bride of a Moment

Faulkner's Folly
The Diamond Pin
The Gold Bag
The Mystery of the Sycamore
The Come Back

Raoul Whitfield
Death in a Bowl

And much more!
Visit ResurrectedPress.com
for our complete catalogue

FOREWORD

Anne Austin started out her literary career writing romance novels about young women overcoming adversity and finding true love, but within a few years turned to the mystery genre as more rewarding or at least more marketable. Her first mystery was *The Black Pigeon.* She then began writing a series of novels featuring James "Bonnie" Dundee that spanned the decade of the 30's. Dundee was a Special Investigator for the Office of the District Attorney in the town of Hamilton.

The series began with *The Avenging Parrot* in 1930, continued on with *Murder Backstairs*, *Murder at Bridge*, *One Drop of Blood* before ending with *Murdered But Not Dead* in 1939. Several of the early novels also appeared in serial format in various newspapers.

The events in *One Drop of Blood* take place at the Mayfield Sanitarium, a psychiatric hospital that caters to a mostly wealthy and middle class clientel. Rather than an asylum for the criminally insane, Mayfield deals with patients with nerosies, substance abuse problems, or who just feel the need for a "rest cure," a time out from the rigors of modern life.

A sanitarium can provide a fertile ground for a mystery writer. The action is confined to a small locale with a limited number of characters in much the same way that the small English village has served as a setting for so many British mysteries. Also, as many of the residents are by definition, not completely sane, one can deal with imaginary motives as well as real ones. Because of these facts, psuchiatric facilities have featured in a number of mysteries over the years, often with the detective going undercover as one of the patients. The earliest example that I know of is 1912 novel *The Ivory Snuff Box* by Arnold Fredericks (Frederic Arnold Kummer).

The public's fascination with such psychiatry was particularly high in the period when this book was written. Those with mental problems were no longer just being locked away and forgotten in asylums. Advances in medicine and the work of people such as Freud and Jung gave hope of real treatments for various forms of insanity. Mental problems were being seen as a disease, and not just a sign of a weak character or a bad blood line. With the promise of treatment, psychiatric problems were no longer something that had to be hushed up, but could now be discussed openly over dinner of cocktails.

However, along with the advances came the quacks and charlatans promising miracle cures. Some of these practicioners were merely following pet theories with little basis in science, but there were also those who were willing to abuse their patient's trust for profit or fame. There were certainly some questionable practices such as lobotomies that came out of this period.

This is the popular image of an upscale sanitarium which serves as a backdrop for *One Drop of Blood*. When the head doctor at the facility is murdered, the list of suspects includes not only the patients, but some of the staff as well. But Austin forgoes some of the more lurid staples of such environments, and when Dundee goes undercover he is not subject to drugs or other treatments for Mayfield is really quite a pleasant place, except for the murder, of course.

Anne Austin is not well known today, a product of a decade eighty years in the past. Yet her mysteries are not without their charm and interest. It is therefore with pleasure that Resurrected Press brings you this new edition of *One Drop of Blood*.

About the Author

Born in 1895, Anne Austin began by writing romance novels about young women in the mid 1920's but soon turned her talents to producing a string of mysteries through the 1930's, some of which appeared as serials in newspapers.. Many of these mysteries feature as the detective "Bonnie" Dundee, Special Investigator for the District Attorney, including *Murder Backstairs*, *The Avenging Parrot*, *Murder at Bridge*, and *One Drop of Blood.* Several of her mysteries were translated into French, including *Le Pigeon Noir* and *Le Crime Parfume.* Despite her success as a novelist, Anne Austin disappears from the public record after the 1930's.

Greg Fowlkes
Editor-In-Chief
Resurrected Press
www.ResurrectedPress.com

CHAPTER ONE

"SURE you wouldn't be better off in a hospital, Chief?" James F. Dundee rose, to end his call upon the district attorney, who had been laid very flat by an attack of pleurisy.

Sanderson started to chuckle, then clapped a hand to his right side, as a grimace of pain contracted his pleasantly homely, freckled face. "Whoever first described this pain as like the thrust of a knife hit on the only apt simile for it in the English language," he groaned, but his gray eyes twinkled affectionately at his "special investigator." "No, Bonnie me lad, as Captain Strawn calls you, I haven't the heart to cheat my sister of the thrill of playing nurse. She has a passion for thermometers, hot water bottles and in valid trays, that amounts to an obsession. Our mother used to say that Nell would resort to feeding the family small doses of poison, if she couldn't get hold of an invalid in any other way."

"Well, don't let her kill you with kindness," Dundee grinned. "Things are dismally quiet now, but we're just about due for another crime wave."

"Can't kill a husky like me," District Attorney Sander son boasted. "I'll be thirty six in July, but damned if I don't feel more like a colt than I did at twenty one. . . . By the way, what do you hear from—from Penny?"

Dundee stopped halfway to the door of the sickroom. "From Penelope Crain?" he asked, as if it had required a prodigious feat of memory to dig up the full name of his chief's former secretary. "Haven't had a letter for months.

. . . How is she liking law school by this time? A grand little female spellbinder Penny ought to make, that is, if she can keep from bawling out the judge when he makes a decision she doesn't like."

"She *is* a peppery little piece," Sanderson agreed, grinning broadly, but to Dundee's amazement his chief's freckled face was turning a fiery red.

"Are—congratulations in order, Chief?" he managed to ask, with great cheeriness, but his heart contracted sharply with a return of the old pain of which he had thought it cured. Darling little Penny! Clever, quick, thorny little Penny, who had helped him so marvelously, so chummily in the solving of the famous Bridge Murder Mystery.

"I—I thought maybe she'd written you," Sanderson stammered. "You two were great friends, weren't you? I confess I was afraid you'd beaten me to the prize, Bonnie."

"Oh, no! No!" Dundee reassured him, with unnecessary vehemence. "Nothing like that, Chief! I'll have to be making a lot more money and have a more dignified job than that of a common 'dick' before I can ask a girl like Penny Crain to marry me."

"I'm afraid there isn't another girl like Penny Crain," Sanderson smiled almost fatuously. "But you're not a 'common dick,' and you know it. You're an expert criminologist, and I'm damned proud to have you attached to my office. . . . You're not quoting Penny, by any chance?"

"I never gave her a chance to turn me down," Dundee answered, his blue eyes frank and friendly again. "But I don't mind telling you that you're the luckiest man in the world, Mr. Sanderson. . . . When is it to be?"

"Oh, not for another year yet," the district attorney answered, with sudden glumness. "Penny insists on graduating from law school—Now, who the devil can be ringing me at this time of the night?" He stilled the clamor of the telephone bell by lifting the receiver. "Hello!

. . . Yes, this is the district attorney speaking . . . Dr. who? . . . Oh, yes, Dr. Cantrell . . . What's that? . . . *Dr. Koenig!?* My God! ... Yes ... Yes ... How long—? . . . Yes, I see . . . Any idea who—? ... I see ... You have my heartfelt sympathy, Dr. Cantrell. It's a national tragedy. . . . No, Doctor, I'm sorry to say I can't come in person. A nasty attack of pleurisy. But I'll send young Dundee, special investigator attached to my office. I consider him the ablest detective I have ever met. . . . Thanks. By the way, have you notified the police? . . . Then I'll call them for you . . . No, no. I'm quite equal to it. Glad to relieve you of the job. You'll see that nothing is disturbed, of course. . . . Terribly sorry, Doctor. Good bye."

Dundee waited tensely, like a hunter poised to take a fence. Very slowly the district attorney replaced the telephone receiver.

"Dr. Carl Koenig," he began heavily, "was murdered tonight in his office at the Mayfield Sanitarium. Exit a fine man and a great psychiatrist. . . . The back of his head cracked open—God!"

"Who did it?—a loony patient?" Dundee asked.

"That will be the conclusion both police and newspapers will jump at, of course, since it seems to be one of those motiveless, clueless mysteries," Sanderson answered. "That was Dr. Cantrell on the phone—medical head of the sanitarium, and sort of a partner, I believe. . . . Well, hop to it, boy, and keep in touch with me. Why, damn it! Koenig was a *friend* of mine, as well as the finest alienist I ever had on the witness stand."

But Dundee did not "hop" instantly. "Can you give me a line on the sanitarium, Chief? Are most of the patients crazy?"

"Not by any means," Sanderson assured him. "Only a small minority of the patients have been 'committed'—that is, adjudged insane in court. Those are in a locked ward, of course. Then there's quite a large group of more or less mild psychopathic cases, voluntary patients—cases of senility, incipient paresis, epilepsy, manic depression, chronic alcoholism, amnesia, aphasia, and victims of all sorts of complexes, psychoses and neuroses, harmful, usually, to no one but themselves. In addition, the place has become the most fashionable 'rest cure' and convalescent home in the state. Society women go there to indulge in 'nervous prostration' or the luxury of being psychoanalyzed, and rich men to be 'boiled out' after a prolonged spree. A good example of the latter is that handsome scapegrace, young Webster. He's in and out of the place half a dozen times a year—seems to enjoy it."

"Expensive?" Dundee interrupted.

"A big price range, but they've rather gone in for luxury for those that can afford it," Sanderson answered. "Suites of sitting room, bedroom and bath, at a hundred and fifty a week, I believe, and even separate cottages that are pretty darned ultra. Dr. Koenig's reputation as a psychiatrist, neurologist and psychoanalyst is so great that he's been the making of the place from a financial standpoint. It's now considered smart to go to Mayfield for treatment, whereas it used to be considered a disgrace to have to go into a 'mental hospital.' "

"Know anyone else there, sir?"

"I think not. No, wait! Bruce Cantrell found himself a peach of a wife among the patients, one of our society girls who went there to be psychoanalyzed a year or so ago. Claire Hobson, she was; pretty and rich as butter. . . . But you'd better get going, my lad."

"Right, sir! But give me a ten or fifteen minutes start before you notify Captain Strawn, won't you? I'd like to have a few uninterrupted moments on the scene of the crime. By the way, where is the sanitarium?"

Within two minutes Dundee had his roadster headed south, his foot pressing hard upon the accelerator, for there was little traffic in the streets of Hamilton at that hour of the night—a quarter to eleven. The cool June breeze lifted the crisp waves of his Irish black hair, hat-free, and fanned into flame the recently quenched fires of hope and ambition. Life was good, when it could so easily fling one into a big new job, the kind of adventure he liked best in the world. A new job, a new—Good Lord! He caught himself up sharply, half amused and half ashamed. He'd almost said, "A new job, a new girl!" Of course he was miserable. Hadn't he lost precious, funny, peppery little Penny? Ye e es. But Well, he told himself defiantly, every one of his three big jobs heretofore in Hamilton had brought him a new girl. Why not admit it? Hadn't he felt almost as badly over Norma Paige's being disgustingly satisfied with Walter Styles; over Gigi Berkeley's being just a little too young to be taken seriously? And now Penny Crain had broken his heart. . . . But was it really broken? Wasn't it true that, a mystery triumphantly solved, a murderer unmasked, the romantic adventure which had gone hand in hand with the adventure of crime detection always displayed an alarming tendency to write Finis for itself too? Perhaps—and he grinned at the drought—if he ran into an unsolvable crime and a lovable girl at the same time, he'd be permanently intrigued by both. . . .

A new job, a new girl, his blood persisted in singing to the hum of his speeding motor. . . . But that was absurd, his common sense objected. What more unlikely place for romance than a sanitarium for "mental" cases?

Suddenly his handsome young face became grim and purposeful, as, throwing off nonsense, he recalled the first and last time he had seen the famous psychiatrist. Dr. Carl Koenig had been called by District Attorney Sander son as an expert witness, to testify as to the legal sanity of a confessed murderer on trial for his life, and whom brilliant defense attorneys were trying to save on a plea of insanity.

As if he were before him then, in a phantom witness box, Dundee saw the thin, dark, rather small man, with his lean, clever face uplifted in an attitude of patient listening, as a defense attorney read a long hypothetical question requiring the alienist's uncompromising "Yes" or "No." He saw those smoky dark eyes, sad eyes they were, light up for an instant with a gleam of humor, as he uttered an answer which confounded his heckler. The face of a scholar and of an ascetic, a Christlike face, the lips thin but mobile, the swart skin drawn tight over high cheek bones, the nose high bridged and wide nostrilled. Not a man to be greeted as "Doc" and clapped on the back. Not a man for a patient to get chummy with, but a man of such sincere humanitarianism, Dundee believed, that any patient could trust him with any secret, however vile and shameful, and find in his tortured mind a great peace after the telling. . . .

And now the famous healer of sick minds was dead. Murdered. As unjustly dead as was justly dead the murderer against whom he had given expert testimony. Would there be another courtroom battle between alienists, with perhaps the ghost of the great Koenig whispering in a colleague's ear: "Forgive him. He knew not what he did."

His speedometer told Dundee that he had been traveling for nearly five miles along Mirror Lake Road. He slowed down, and began to search for the highway sign that would tell him when he had reached Willow Creek Drive, the turning which would take him, after a hundred yards' or so, to Mayfield Sanitarium.

If he had known the road and had been driving fast he would probably not have noticed, in the darkness which was doubly black in contrast with the light from his head lamps, that which caused him to step so hard and so suddenly upon his footbrake that he was almost catapulted over his own windshield.

And if her dress had not been white– But he did see and he did stop, after swerving his car so that the head lights threw their bright glare across the huddled body of a girl.

For a moment he thought she was dead, her fragile body crushed and flung into the roadside weeds by a hit and run driver. But as he knelt to lift her she moaned faintly, and the largest pair of dark blue eyes he had ever seen fluttered open and gazed upward at him with curious trustfulness, as if she were looking at a very old friend.

"Hello!" he greeted her happily, out of the profound ness of his relief.

"How do you do?" she returned with quaint politeness, lifting a hand feebly to push back the tumbled golden chestnut curls from her childlike forehead. But with the gesture she seemed to remember many things. Fear distorted her delicate, very white face.

"Are you a—a policeman?" she amazed him by asking, as she cowered away from the hands which were extended to help her rise.

"No," Dundee answered, truthfully enough. "Why?"

But she was not satisfied. One fragile, beautifully kept hand fluttered to his coat and turned back the left lapel. Reassured, she sighed and sank back upon her pillow of dusty weeds.

"I think," she said faintly, without answering his question, "I've sprained my ankle. Probably it's broken. It hurts dreadfully. ... I was running away," she explained simply. "Will you help me to run away?"

"We'll discuss that later," Dundee retorted cheerfully. "First, I'm going to take you to Mayfield Sanitarium— "

"No, no! Not there!" she panted, her whole body shrinking away from him. "Any place else—a hospital in Hamilton—anywhere "

"But I'm on my way there myself, and it's the nearest," Dundee reasoned with her gently.

"*You*—going to Mayfield?" she cried in horror.

"You poor kid!" Dundee ejaculated, but he was smiling. "You've got an idea that all the patients there are crazy. Isn't that it?"

"No." She shook her head and closed her eyes with great weariness. "It's—Mayfield I'm running away from."

"And you thought I was a policeman sent to bring you in—dead or alive?" Dundee asked, smiling more broadly. Then a cold chill raced down his spine. Only *insane* patients could fear such an aftermath to running away — those who had been committed. . . . Was this lovely, frail girl—*crazy?*

"Yes, yes!" she answered quickly. "I was afraid they'd —missed me and sent the police after me. I was afraid they'd put me in the locked ward for running away."

"Then you're not a locked ward patient?" he asked tactlessly.

"I—a *locked ward* patient?" she echoed indignantly. "Certainly not! I'm there for—for nerves."

"I see," Dundee said gently, not believing her for an instant. What a terrible pity that one so young, so lovely should be demented. . . . "But I'll really have to take you back, you know, since I have to go there myself "

"It's long past visiting hours," the girl protested. "And you can't be going as a patient. I'm sure you're not nervous, or—or anything queer, and you look awfully healthy "

Dundee made a sudden resolve. "I'm sorry to say I *am* going as a patient. I've been working too hard," he went on, lying gracelessly but convincingly. "My doctor orders rest and regular hours—that sort of thing. You see," and he grinned, making use of his earlier reflections on his susceptibility, "I'm subject to heart attacks. No organic disease; purely—er, functional, but quite distressing at the time."

"Oh!" the girl breathed softly, and stroked his hand with a rose tipped, slim forefinger. "I'm so sorry."

"And I'm afraid," Dundee took advantage of her shamelessly but truthfully, "that I feel an attack coming on now."

"Then—then good bye," she quavered, and lay back on her bed of weeds. "Please don't tell anyone you saw me."

"Silly! Do you think I'm going to leave you here?" And over her hysterical protests Dundee lifted her feather weight but rather long body in his arms and carried her to his roadster.

After the car was bowling along the highway again the girl suddenly ceased to struggle and protest. Dundee had removed the little white sandal from her badly swollen left foot, which she now nursed against her right knee, whimpering softly with pain.

"What's your name?" Dundee asked, partly to divert her. "Mine is Dundee," he added, for he had determined not to resort to the use of an alias. Outside of newspaper and police circles he was known scarcely at all. There was scant probability that any patient at Mayfield Sanitarium woula recognize his name or suspect his connection with the district attorney's office.

"E Enid Rambler," she told him, and Dundee wondered if her "nerves" caused her to stammer.

"That's a pretty name," Dundee commented idly. "I don't think I've ever known any Ramblers except the ancient automobiles of that name."

Oddly enough, the girl shrank from him at that. . . . A queer little thing she was. . . .

Isn't this where we turn?" He slowed the car to scan a highway sign. "Yes. Willow Creek Drive. You were going to let me miss my turn, weren't you?"

Sulking, Dundee decided, as she did not answer. But after he had made the right hand turn, a swift glance told him that she was not sulking. The expression on her rigid face and in her unwinking, staring eyes was that of hope less despair.

"Why were you running away?" he asked, very gently.

She appeared not to have heard.

Suddenly the detective instinct in him asserted itself over the knight to ladies in distress. "*When* did you run away?"

She answered that, dully: "I don't know what time it was. I was nervous. I get that way—hysterical. I can't sit still or lie still. I wandered around, looking for the head nurse, Miss Lacey, or for one of the doctors to give me a bromide. But I couldn't find anyone, so I—I walked about the grounds for a—a long time. Then I ran away. The gates are never locked."

Even if the gates she had referred to had not loomed ahead of him then he would not have dared question her further, for fear of exciting her suspicions as to his business at Mayfield. He swung his roadster between the high stone pillars and drove slowly along the winding, box hedged driveway. On either side lay acres of beautifully kept lawn, studded with formal flower beds and majestic trees, the whole faintly lighted by powerful electric lamps set at intervals along the base of the high wrought iron fence.

"Don't take me to the offices," the girl begged, her hands gripping his right arm with sudden vehemence. "Take me nearly to the door of the cottage I live in, and let me out. Then drive away and I'll call for help. A nurse will be sure to hear me. Please, please! If they know I've run away "

Because of the mounting hysteria in her voice Dundee agreed, silently regretful that he would have to betray her to Captain Strawn, turn her over to him for questioning. For even if she did not know that Dr. Koenig had been murdered, by her own confession she had been "wandering around" either shortly before or shortly after the murder. Probably the girl herself did not have the least idea how long she had lain unconscious after spraining her ankle, but Strawn would certainly pounce upon her. . . .

"Stop here!" the girl commanded. "That's my cottage over there. I'll crawl along on my hands and knees till I get to the steps, and I'll tell Miss Hunter—she's the night attendant—that I sprained my ankle while walking on the grounds "

"Do you have a cottage to yourself?" Dundee asked, as he stopped the car.

"Oh, no. Just a suite. There are six suites in Sunflower Court. They're built around a patio, where we can sit when we don't want to be on the main lawn with the other patients," Enid Rambler explained hurriedly. "There's a vacancy. Maybe they'll assign you to it," she added shyly, but hopefully.

"That would be nice," Dundee agreed, his mind instantly made up to subject the county to that expense, however large it might be. "Sure you'll be all right?—not faint again?"

"Sure," she whispered. "And thank you with all my heart, Mr. Dundee. Only—I wish you hadn't made me come back," she added, terror again stamping her delicate, mobile face. "The main building is straight ahead. It's the biggest building. You can't miss it."

Ruefully aware that the accident of his discovering the crippled runaway had cost him several of the precious minutes by which he had planned to beat Captain Strawn to the scene of the crime, Dundee drove rapidly up the driveway and stopped in a vacant space in a row of several cars parked diagonally in front of the main building. To his vast relief, Captain Strawn's car was not among them, nor was any policeman on guard.

He was walking toward the steps leading to the broad porch of the cream colored brick building when a man stepped from behind one of the white Doric columns, a flashlight and a metal box in his hands.

"I'm the night watchman, sir. Who you want to see?"

"Dr. Cantrell. He's expecting me."

"You're from the district attorney's office, sir?"

"Yes."

"I'll take you in, sir. I was just going to register the hour on my rounds. Eleven o'clock, but—" and the grizzled, heavy bodied man sighed, as he pointed to the dial of the boxed clock he was carrying, "all is not well. . . . It's a sad night for Mayfield, sir, a mighty sad night."

"You check in here every hour?" Dundee asked.

"Yes, sir. And patrol the grounds and buildings all night long."

"Did you see or hear anything at all unusual tonight?"

"No, sir. That is, not until Miss Hunter, who's night attendant over at Sunflower Court told me to look about the grounds for one of her patients—a young lady by the name of Rambler. Rambler by name, and now rambler in fact, it looks like, sir "

"I found her unconscious on the highway. A sprained ankle. I've just set her down at Sunflower Court," Dundee explained impatiently. "And please tell Miss Hunter for me to keep the girl under constant supervision for the rest of the night. . . . Now, outside of Miss Rambler's disappearance ?"

"Nothing, sir, until Dr. Cantrell blew his whistle for me half an hour ago. I was over at Ten'—that's what we call the locked ward, sir—and when I got here Dr. Cantrell told me Dr. Koenig had been killed, and asked me if I'd seen any suspicious characters about, but I told him, with all the comings and goings tonight "

"What's that?" Dundee cut in sharply.

"We have a picture show every Wednesday night, sir, in the O. T. Shop, and nearly all the patients are allowed to invite guests to see the show, so there's always a lot of strangers about of a Wednesday night."

"Where and what is the O. T. Shop?" Dundee asked.

"O. T. stands for Occupational Therapy, sir," the night watchman answered, with a trace of condescension. "Where the patients make baskets and shawls and hooked rugs and pottery. It's good for their nerves, sir. The O. T. Shop is in this building, sir, a big room at the center back. Talking pitchures we have, sir. We spare no expense "

Dundee grinned at the proud use of the personal pronoun, but he made haste to interrupt. "And at what time was the show over tonight?"

"It was an extry long pitchure, a fine new talkie called 'Manslaughter,' all about a girl that gets sent to prison for killing a traffic cop with her automobile "

"Yes, yes, I know! But when was it over?"

"There was a comedy first," the night watchman went on, a little offended, "and then the feature pitchure, and futhermore the operator was nearly an hour late getting here, so it was just turned ten, because it was almost time for me to clock in—"

"And you'd been watching the show, of course?" Dundee pounced.

"Off and on, sir, everything being quiet like," the man admitted.

"So that Dr. Koenig could have been murdered while you were enjoying 'Manslaughter,' " Dundee drove in his point relentlessly. Then: "Are any patients quartered in this building?"

"No," Whalen answered flatly, omitting the "sir." "Some of the staff have apartments on the second floor, and downstairs we have the doctors' offices, and the chartroom where Miss Lacey—she's the head nurse—has her desk, and then there's a big living room with a fireplace for the use of the patients, besides the O. T. Shop. And in the left wing there's the main kitchen, the staffs dining room, and another dining room for the men patients who don't want trays in their rooms."

"We'll go in now," Dundee cut into the watchman's volubility. "Is this door usually closed?"

"No, sir, except in cold weather, and then it's not locked. There's likely to be comings and goings all night, and the night head nurse is on duty in the chartroom. But the other outside doors to the doctors' offices are locked at night, after the secretary, Miss Home, is gone, unless one of the doctors is working late."

"Other outside doors?" Dundee repeated. "How many are there?"

"There's an outside front entrance, sir, just to the right of this porch, leading into the reception room where Miss Home and Dr. Harlow—that's Dr. Koenig's young lady doctor—do their work, and where patients and visitors are received," the night watchman explained, with a returning relish of his importance as guide. "Dr.

Koenig's office is right behind the little reception room, and to the right of his office with a door between is Dr. Cantrell's office. And there's a back outside door to Dr. Cantrell's office. He uses it to go home, sir. His house is about two hundred feet back of the office."

Without comment, Dundee followed the watchman into a large central hall, pleasantly furnished with lamps, chairs and settees.

"This first door on your right opens into the reception room, and that next one into Dr. Koenig's office," Whalen continued, then, shaking his grizzled head lugubriously: "And this is the first time I ever knowed the Big Doctor's door to be shut when he was in his office. Always open it was, sir, no matter how busy he might be "

"Why?" Dundee asked, surprised.

"Because, sir, a lot of our patients are not exactly what you'd call theirselves, in a manner of speaking, and they get so nervous and upset that nothing will do them any good but to speak to Dr. Koenig himself. So they ain't no red tape here, Mister. A patient can—I mean could walk right in on the Big Doctor and have a chin with him any time of the day or night, if he was in his office. I don't know what we'll do without him. Looks to me like the place will go to the dogs "

"I hope not. . . . This is the living room for the patients' use, I suppose?" and Dundee nodded toward the wide, arched doorway on his left, beyond which he could see a piano, a huge sofa, a set up bridge table, smoking stands, overstuffed armchairs, and floor lamps.

"Yes, sir. It's used mostly by the bridge players in the evening after it gets too dark to play on the lawn."

"Was there a game this evening?" Dundee asked hope fully, since players would have a clear view of the doctor's office directly across the hall.

"No, sir, more's the pity," the watchman answered gloomily. "You see, sir, nearly all the patients was attending the pitchure show this evening. Like as not, if the bridge game had been going on as usual the murderer— may he burn in hell!—wouldn't have had a chance to kill the poor doctor and wreck his office without somebody hearing the fuss he made."

"You're probably right," Dundee assured him, then wheeled to face a small, gray haired, pale faced nurse who had entered from the porch. "Good evening. I've come to see Dr. Cantrell. He's expecting me."

"Oh, yes, sir," the nurse gasped. "I'm sorry I wasn't here when you arrived. I was busy giving a hypodermic to a patient in 'Ten.' I'll tell Dr. Cantrell you're here, Mr.—?"

"Dundee, from the district attorney's office. . . . Just a minute, Mr. Whalen," the detective halted the watchman, who was moving on. "I may find it necessary to stay on here for a day or two, and if I do it will be as a patient. You understand? None of the patients is to know what I am here for."

"Yes, sir, yes, sir!" Whalen answered eagerly, gloom giving way to keen relish.

And the nurse smiled at Dundee from tear reddened eyes before scurrying across the hall to knock at the reception room door.

Dundee was not kept waiting. Two men and two women rose to receive him as the night nurse slipped away, closing the door after her. A rather stout man, of perhaps forty, advanced with outstretched hand.

"Mr. Dundee? I'm Dr. Cantrell, medical head of Mayfield Sanitarium."

Burning, deep sunken black eyes under an incongruous thatch of rust colored hair held Dundee's eyes briefly be fore the doctor continued:

"And this is Dr. Harlow—Dr. Justine Harlow, Dr. Koenig's assistant psychiatrist."

He paused impatiently for the small and very girlish, pretty young doctor to shake hands with the detective; then:

"And this is Mr. Baldwin, our business manager, and a partner with Dr. Koenig and myself. . . . And this is Miss Lacey, our head nurse."

Dundee shook hands first with the nurse, whose Irish youthfulness of face was belied by the threads of white in her curling black hair, then gave his attention to the business manager. And he felt a swift, unreasoning dislike of Mr. Baldwin. In the first place, the man was physically most unattractive, with his insignificant, round shouldered body, his glistening, egg shaped head whose bald area was fringed with thin, white hair, his curiously dead looking brown eyes, and his hooked nose pointing to a tightly pursed mouth. But it was something more subtle than physical appearance which repelled Dundee. He fumbled for an explanation and found it before Baldwin's limp hand had quickly released his own firm clasp. There was a complete absence of decent grief in the man. His partner had been brutally murdered, and this man was not grieving. He was angry, disturbed, indignant. But he was not grief stricken. The obvious desolation of the two women and the burning sorrow in the medical doctor's eyes put him to shame. And they were all aware, too, of Baldwin's callousness to the tragedy, for Dundee was positive that they shrank from him, huddled together spiritually for consolation.

As the detective was about to voice his personal grief for the man he had seen only once, but had respected and admired deeply, the business manager cut in sharply:

"Yes, yes. But there is something I must request immediately, sir, immediately! Since you are representing the district attorney, and will therefore have prestige with the reporters who are certain to flock around like vultures, I must insist—" He may have realized that he was going too far, for the pursed lips sucked in a whistling breath before shaping more tactful words. "I must beg of you, Mr. Dundee, to do everything in your power to keep the press from jumping to the conclusion that one of our patients murdered Dr. Koenig!"

"But—if the evidence points to that conclusion?" Dundee asked mildly.

"If it does, I assure you that the murderer faked it very cleverly," Baldwin assured him vehemently. "Wouldn't that be the natural thing for the fiend to do? Not only to throw suspicion from himself, but to bring ruin upon the institution which Dr. Koenig's great skill and outstanding reputation have built up. And I must ask you to help defeat that base intention, Mr. Dundee. Prospective patients will shun us like the plague if they are led to believe that not even the doctors themselves are safe from the violence of demented patients. I tell you, sir, every precaution is taken here—"

"May I see the body, please?" Dundee interrupted curtly. The old fool! Did he think he was making a speech before a jury? And was he so concerned with balance sheets that he would be more than willing to have his partner's death unavenged, if the murderer should indeed be one of his precious and profitable patients? Every precaution indeed! When he—Dundee himself—had found a patient unconscious by the roadside a mile from the sanitarium; when he had been in the hall of the main building for minutes before even a nurse had appeared; when Dr. Koenig's office had been accessible that night from at least three unlocked doors, while visitors and patients had swarmed in and out of the building!

It was Dr. Cantrell who, after a glance of bitter contempt at his partner, was about to lead the way into the small office where the murder had been committed, when the outside door was opened unceremoniously and a very plump, cherubic man bounded into the room.

"Hello, folks! 'Happy' Day is here again!" the man yodeled, his round face one vast smile, which abated some what with embarrassment as his beaming brown eyes encountered Dundee. "Scuse! Didn't know you were busy!"

"It's all right, 'Happy'," Dr. Harlow quavered, as if his joyousness hurt every nerve in her body. "I'm glad you got my message. It's your friend, Archie, this time. He's over in 'Ten.' "

"Thanks, doc! That's swell. Archie's a great kid. Believe me, I'm glad to get another case so soon. I feel like a fish out of Water when I'm not at Mayfield."

Dundee permitted the man to bounce blithely away, before he asked Dr. Harlow: "And who is the happy young man?"

The girl doctor smiled tremulously. "His nickname does suit him, doesn't it? His name is Howard Day, but everyone calls him 'Happy' Day. He is one of our most popular attendants. The case he had been on for a long time was transferred Monday to the State Hospital for Mental Diseases, and he has been 'on call' since."

Because time was pressing, and Strawn was overdue, Dundee forebore to inquire into the popular attendant's new case. His chief interest now lay in the murdered doctor's office. And one sweeping glance sufficed to show Dundee that Business Manager Baldwin had good cause to fear that suspicion would fall upon one of Mayfield's demented patients.

CHAPTER TWO

A CLEANING woman, after one indignant look at Dr. Carl Koenig's office, would have muttered: "Looks like a cyclone had struck it!" And Special Investigator Dundee could think of no better simile. But apparently it had been a cyclone of fury, of unreasoning, destructive rage that had swept through the private sanctum of the great psychiatrist, striking with deadly aim at the doctor himself, then spending itself upon the victim's possessions.

Over a thick, taupe colored rug cluttered with letters and books, finely torn scraps of paper, and an overturned floor lamp and smoking stand, Dundee picked a cautious path to the dead man's desk.

The body, seated in a swivel chair, was so bowed that the forehead of the dead man's face, which was sharply turned to the left, rested upon the big blotter that protected nearly half the surface of the flat topped desk. The left arm was stretched across the desk, but the other arm dangled against the chair, the palm of the hand turned outward with the fingers curled almost to the tip of the thumb.

The cause of death was apparent at a glance. Blows from some ax like instrument upon the back of the head, slightly to the left, had shattered the skull. Dundee quickly averted his eyes from the nauseating spectacle, and sought the weapon.

He did not have far to search. On the rug, almost touching one of the curved legs of the swivel chair, lay a small bronze replica of the famous sculpture, "The Discus Thrower." And it had been the sharp edge of the discus itself which had crashed through the skull of the doctor, for it bore traces of its gruesome use—a few short black hairs matted to the bronze with dried blood.

Inserting the toe of his boot beneath the body of the bronze athlete, Dundee raised the statue an inch or so from the rug, stared thoughtfully for a moment, then let it sink slowly into its former place.

"At what time was the murder discovered?" Dundee asked, as his eyes took in the disorder of the desk: pulled out drawers, a flower vase and an inkwell both over turned upon the blotter, ashes and stubs scattered from a metal cigarette tray and wet from the same fluids which had stained the bowed face of the dead man. The three lovely roses, which almost touched the nose that could no longer inhale their fragrance, had also been stained with ink. Unusual roses they were, too: their gold tipped petals shading into a deep, rosy saffron. Still crisply fresh and only half opened. . . .

"At about ten twenty five," Dr. Cantrell answered. "Miss Lacey—"

"Just a minute. I'll get her story later. When did you view the body?"

"Not more than three minutes after Miss Lacey discovered what had happened. I was at home. She called me on the telephone. My house is only two or three hundred feet back of this suite of offices. I answered the telephone myself and came immediately."

"Did you make any tests to determine how long the doctor had been dead?"

"Yes. I took the body temperature, and tested for rigor mortis, which had not set in to any appreciable extent," Dr. Cantrell replied. "To the best of my ability to calculate, Dr. Koenig had then been dead about forty five minutes."

"Which, you would say, places the murder at approximately nine forty five?"

"Yes. Of course there could well be a leeway of five or ten minutes."

"In your opinion—and of course you understand that all your findings will be checked by the coroner, Dr. Price, when he arrives—was death instantaneous?"

"Not a doubt of that," Dr. Cantrell answered.

"Another thing, doctor," Dundee continued, his eyes again flicking a reluctant glance at the broken head. "Would you say that a person of extraordinary strength struck that blow?"

Dr. Cantrell seemed to weigh his words very carefully before uttering them. Then: "Not necessarily, Mr. Dundee. My examination of the wound shows that Dr. Koenig's skull was rather thinner than the average. The weapon, you will notice, weighs at least fifteen pounds, I should judge "

"Have you touched it?" Dundee interrupted sharply.

"Certainly not. But the statuette is of solid bronze and is more than eighteen inches tall. The pedestal alone—"

"Could a woman have struck that blow?" Dundee interrupted again.

Again the doctor hesitated. "Ye—es, especially if the woman were under terrific mental stress—"

"Yes, I understand that insanity—whether temporary or chronic—lends abnormal strength to a person in a homicidal rage," Dundee cut in.

The medical head of Mayfield Sanitarium was silent, his face rigid, his burning black eyes fixed upon some terrible picture which only he could see.

"Then you, too, are afraid that one of your patients did this thing?" Dundee asked.

He had not heard the door open and he wheeled in surprise as a woman's faltering but very musical voice called from the doorway:

"Please, Mr. Dundee! There's something I *must* say."

"Certainly, Dr. Harlow. . . . Will you come in?"

The small, girlish doctor advanced gingerly, her little low heeled patent leather pumps as careful not to tread upon the litter as the detective's had been. Very pretty, indeed, she was, Dundee observed appreciatively, although amber rimmed spectacles detracted from the beauty of her large, gray green eyes, and her magnificent red hair, which she wore in great coils over her ears, had become sadly disordered in the storm of grief through which she had undoubtedly passed. She was still in uniform—stiffly starched white linen, with only a severe little black crepe de chine jacket and the absence of a cap to distinguish her from the institution's nurses.

"I overheard what you asked Dr. Cantrell," she began as she stood before him, her lovely voice becoming quite steady with the professional authority that sat quaintly upon her smallness and girlishness. "Please remember that I am speaking as a doctor, as a psychiatrist, when I beg you not to voice any such theory to reporters."

"May I ask why?"

"I can't expect you to be in sympathy with our problems here," the little doctor began, a note of despair in her voice. "But if the morning papers print a theory that a patient here is the—the murderer " She flinched at the word, then brought it out bravely—"it will do untold damage here, not only among those who are mentally ill, but throughout the institution. It would simply create a panic. We could not possibly hire enough attendants and special nurses to handle the situation of a sanitarium full of terror stricken patients, each one fearing he or she might be the next victim. And even if we doubled our staff, the patients, believing *we* feared for their safety " The beautiful voice broke, and the girl doctor's small but very firm hands stretched toward the detective appealingly.

"I understand," Dundee assured her gently.

"Oh, I hope you do!" she breathed, almost prayerfully. "But there's still—another angle. I can illustrate by telling you that when one patient commits suicide—and in spite of our vigilance that does happen sometimes—we can count on five attempted suicides when the news gets about. Do you—see what I mean?" she persisted, her gray green eyes wide with a very real terror.

"I think I do," Dundee answered slowly. "You mean—the power of suggestion might bring about other murders, or attempted murders?"

"Yes," the little doctor nodded. "And undoubtedly a flurry of confessions, which would only hinder you in your work."

"I am sure you are right," Dundee assured her, with entirely respectful admiration. "And I'll gladly do all I can, not only because I want to help, but—*because I do not believe Dr. Koenig was murdered by a person in a homicidal rage!"*

Dundee watched her face keenly as he spoke the slow, emphasized words. He saw relief give place to blankness, then—and he was very sure of that—startled fear flickered in those candid eyes and twitched her pretty, rougeless lips.

It was with obvious effort that she spoke again, after a shuddering intake of breath: "Then—you don't think a patient did it?"

"I didn't say that," Dundee reminded her, and he was sure she was again relieved. "Of course I have no power to dictate what Captain Strawn of the Homicide Squad shall say to the press, but, for my part, if I cannot escape the reporters entirely, I shall voice no theories and make no statements as to the murderer unless our investigation tonight succeeds far beyond my expectations. . . . And by the way, I wonder what is detaining the captain so long. The District Attorney was to telephone him—"

"Oh!" Dr. Harlow gasped, flushing. "He's in the reception room now. That's what I came to tell you, but I wanted to enlist your help first. Shall I show him in here? He has been questioning Mr. Whalen, our night watchman."

"Good! I've already talked to Whalen," Dundee said. "Show the Captain in when he's ready."

A moment after the girl doctor had left, Captain John Strawn, Chief of the Homicide Squad, bulked large in the doorway, a reluctant grin pulling downward one corner of his typical policeman's mouth.

"Well, Bonnie me lad, I see you've taken the first trick," the gray haired detective greeted the former member of his squad. "You've beat me to the game by a good half hour, I take it. Sanderson vows he tried that long to reach me. Matter of fact, I took my wife for a drive after a movie."

"Sure it was your wife, Chief?" Dundee gibed affectionately, as he shook hands. "Dr. Cantrell, Captain Strawn."

"Glad to meetcha, Doc, though I wish it was a happier time and place," the old detective boomed, shaking hands with the proper touch of solemnity. "Well, Bonnie! Got your murderer all picked out?"

"I wish it were that easy, Captain."

"What!" Strawn ejaculated, his keen gray eyes again sweeping the disorder of the room and the corpse at the desk. "Here we have a nut hospital, the brain doctor's head bashed in with the handiest weapon, and his office left in one hell of a mess. Plain sailing, Bonnie. Some loony patient comes in to talk with the doc, gets sore, runs amok and kills him. . . . Don't it look that way to you, Dr. Cantrell?"

The medical head of the sanitarium glanced at Dundee, then shrugged helplessly, without answering in words.

"Now, what does he mean by that?" Dundee reflected silently. "Does he agree, along with Dr. Harlow and Baldwin, or—does he just want me to think he agrees?"

"Sure I'm right," Strawn went on emphatically, as if Dr. Cantrell had confirmed his suspicion. "Got a lot of nuts here who could a done it, eh, Doc?"

"I do not feel qualified to answer that question, sir," Dr. Cantrell answered stiffly. "My work is purely medical. I am not a psychiatrist. But I may say that all patients who have shown any tendency to harm themselves or others are kept in a locked ward—Ward Ten, we call it, and are under constant observation when not locked in their rooms. But I suggest you question Dr. Harlow, the assistant psychiatrist, along these lines."

"I'll do that! Don't worry," Strawn retorted, stung by the doctor's attitude. "But I've already had a talk with your night watchman, Whalen, and he tells me there was a picture show in what he calls the O. T. Shop this evening. Moreover, he says that five of the crazy patients out of Ten' attended the show. Saw 'em himself," Strawn added triumphantly.

"If he saw them, then he also saw their attendants," Cantrell retorted coldly.

"It was pretty dark in the O. T. Shop while the pictures was being run, wasn't it? ... Well, then! . . . And by the way, Doctor, it struck me as being kinda funny that a picture called 'Manslaughter' would be picked out to amuse a bunch of nuts and nervous patients."

"I thought of that, too, Captain," Dundee commented approvingly. "I admit I don't know the story, but I have been wondering about—the power of suggestion."

"I saw the picture Monday evening in Hamilton," Dr. Cantrell said, plainly on the defensive. "Certainly it would have no power to suggest the crime that was committed here tonight, since 'Manslaughter' is the story of a girl who kills a traffic policeman who has been chasing her for speeding. Accidental homicide, in other words, though the girl in the case was extremely culpable and deserved the prison sentence she received. I feel sure that there was nothing unduly exciting, even to the very nervous, and that, on the contrary, the punishment of the girl would have a salutary effect on any patient with tendencies to violence. In fact, I feel safe in assuming that our business manager, Mr. Baldwin, had just such an effect in mind when he chose the picture for tonight's run. His choice of pictures is limited, also, since Dr. Koenig had banned the showing of gangster pictures and movies which were decidedly 'sexy.' "

"Why?" Strawn demanded.

"Gangster pictures are full of violence, shooting and sudden death," Cantrell explained impatiently, "and the so called 'sexy' pictures, in Dr. Koenig's opinion, would cause decidedly erotic reactions among the psychopathic patients, as well as create a restlessness among our other patients who are temporarily deprived of the society of their mates or sweethearts."

"You mean the loony patients are apt to be nuts on sex, eh?" Strawn decoded the doctor's academic explanation.

"To put it crudely—yes!"

"Must cost you a lot to rent a popular movie like that," Strawn ruminated.

"Not an excessive amount," Cantrell answered coldly. "One of Dr. Koenig's grateful patients donated the rather expensive machines for the showing of talking pictures, and Mr. Baldwin has made an arrangement with the Hamilton theaters whereby, at a nominal sum in addition to the payment for the operator's services, he secures first class pictures. We usually show a comedy, which is secured from one theater, and a feature picture from another. As you know, the downtown theaters have two hour programs. We arrange for the transportation of the films, picking them up as soon as the theater operators have finished running them, and returning them before they are needed for the next show."

"I see," Strawn admitted. "Now, Doc, you were called in to view the body right after it was discovered, weren't you?"

Dundee, already familiar with the forthcoming questions and answers, began to wander about the room, minutely investigating its disorder. He paused first at the desk, considered it thoughtfully, then concentrated upon the low typewriter table placed near the end of the desk, farthest from the door into the hall, and at right angles to the desk. The table was large enough to hold a telephone of the French type, a stack of typewriter paper, and a portable machine. Nothing here was disarranged, except that the ribbon had been yanked from the typewriter's spools and lay in purple coils upon the keys. But there was something else, Dundee discovered. He had almost missed it, for the torn scrap of paper was nearly hidden under the rubber platen or the typewriter. Someone, whether Dr. Koenig, dissatisfied with what he had written, or his murderer, had snatched from the machine the last sheet of paper upon which the doctor would ever type. And, remembering the quietness and calmness of the alienist upon the witness stand, Dundee could not believe that it was Koenig's hand which had done the violent snatching.

With increasing excitement, the young detective continued his wandering. Kneeling, he examined the over turned floor lamp, carefully scrutinizing the socket, the globe and the decorated parchment shade. Next he paused before the large bookcase, principally devoted to textbooks on mental diseases. The gaps in the rows were accounted for by the books scattered over the floor. Kneeling before the book nearest the case, he lifted it very carefully, then examined the thick pile of the rug in a circle of at least three feet in diameter. He repeated the strange procedure with all the scattered books, then, more than satisfied, turned his attention to the five drawer steel filing cabinet set against the wall between the bookcase and the door leading into the reception room. All the drawers had been pulled approximately halfway out, and a glance was enough to show Dundee that the cabinet contained a well indexed file of patients' case histories, everyone in its own manila folder, labeled with the patient's name. A number of the folders had been partially withdrawn and left sticking out of the file drawers at untidy angles.

With a sharp exclamation below his breath, Dundee grasped a corner of one of the folders, tested it for smoothness and weight, then again dropped to his knees and searched among the finely torn scraps of paper that littered the rug. He found what he was looking for, then hurried back to the filing cabinet, where he further satisfied himself by comparing the fragment with the manila folder he had been fingering.

Slowly he strolled to the room's one window, set almost in the corner of the back wall of the office. The shade was drawn exactly flush with the sill, but the silk pongee curtains were pushed to either end of their rod. By means of its cord, Dundee raised the shade, and. peered out upon a faintly lighted bit of garden, through which a cement path led to the Cantrell home. The window was closed but not locked. . .

After a few moments of deep thought, he wheeled abruptly from the window and pushed wide the partly open door between Dr. Koenig's office and the room beyond. Dr. Cantrell's office was somewhat larger than the psychiatrist's. In addition to the locked door in the back wall, there were three screened windows, all locked and with drawn shades.

It was a typical medical doctor's private office: scales for weighing patients and measuring their height; a long, high, narrow table covered with brown leather, and used in making physical examinations; a white enameled instrument cabinet, which Dundee found to be locked; an instrument sterilizer; a hand basin with running water; two lidded metal hampers; a file cabinet, a large, flat topped desk, a swivel chair, two straight chairs, and a well stocked bookcase, which was topped with a leather framed photograph of a beautiful girl, whose silver blonde hair was in enchanting contrast to large, liquid black eyes. Cantrell's wife, of course. . . .

Here was perfect order, apparently. But Dundee left nothing to chance. He made a thorough tour of the room, looking for any faintest trace of the murderer's visit. And at last he was triumphantly justified.

He had pressed his foot upon the pedal which raised the lid of the smaller of the two white enameled hampers, and had gasped at his discovery.

"Bloodstained swabs!" he gloated. "And rubber gloves. ... Of course he would wear rubber gloves. And what more certain than that he would find a pair in Dr. Cantrell's office!"

Stooping, he fished out the two red rubber gloves, one badly torn at the wrist. But strangely enough Dundee was disappointed with his first examination of the find. Then he swiftly turned the gloves inside out and let his eyes run eagerly over the tips of the thumbs and fingers. And he found what he was looking for.

"Hey, Bonnie! Stealing another march on me?" Captain Strawn boomed from the doorway, his bulk almost hiding the doctor, who stood behind him.

"I'm afraid I am," Dundee assented gravely. "Will you come here a moment, Dr. Cantrell?"

When the doctor had joined him Dundee pointed rather melodramatically to the blood soaked gauze swabs in the hamper. "A tidy murderer, after all, in spite of the mess he made in that other office!"

Dr. Cantrell laughed, a sharp, mirthless bark. "I'm afraid I'm the tidy one, but—not the murderer. I dropped those swabs into that hamper myself. One of the male patients, who has the reputation of being rather an exhibitionist, and given to half hearted attempts at suicide, which he takes good care will not be fatal, slashed his arm from the wrist almost to the elbow this evening, and I dressed it. Miss Caplan, the night nurse, helped me."

Dundee did not seem so dashed as Strawn, broadly grinning, evidently expected him to be.

"And these rubber gloves, doctor?"

"Miss Caplan wore them. There was not time for her to 'scrub up.' She put the gloves on and applied a tourniquet, while I washed my hands with an antiseptic before sewing up the wound," Dr. Cantrell explained.

"Did you notice whether she tore them when she removed the gloves?" Dundee asked. "And whether she discarded them?"

"I didn't notice," Cantrell answered, then caught him self up short. "Yes. I do remember seeing her take them off. But—*she didn't drop them into that hamper!* It's used for waste stuff only, such as the swabs we used in staunching the blood and cleansing the wound. I distinctly remember seeing her drop them into the instrument tray she had got ready for me. Here's the tray on top of the cabinet," he added, frowning slightly. "I see that Miss Caplan did not sterilize the instruments and return them to the cabinet. Called away, I presume."

"Then the gloves she had used were in plain sight and accessible to anyone who wanted to use them?" Dundee persisted.

"Apparently so," Dr. Cantrell admitted. "But I can't see–"

"Where did Miss Caplan get the rubber gloves?"

"Out of the cabinet, of course. It is kept locked, so that no patient with suicidal tendencies can possibly get at a sharp instrument. As an added precaution, the windows and doors of this office are always kept locked when I am not using it."

"Then you locked the door between your office and Dr. Koenig's when you finished in here this evening?" Dundee asked.

"No. Dr. Koenig was in his office, and I left this door ajar in case he might have occasion to use my office," Dr. Cantrell replied. "Naturally he had a key, and I left the door ajar as a courtesy."

"What's all the Sherlocking for, Bonnie?" Strawn interrupted disgustedly. "The case will be as good as closed as soon as Carraway photographs the fingerprints. The nut murderer must have left hundreds of 'em—"

"Not so nutty, I'm afraid," Dundee cut in. "At any rate he had his wits sufficiently about him to don rubber gloves before stepping into the role of 'homicidal maniac.' "

"How do you know he wore the gloves?" Strawn demanded belligerently. "Just because you find a torn pair in a waste hamper "

"Whoa, Captain!" Dundee grinned. "Am I the lad for jumping at conclusions? . . . Dr. Cantrell, is it likely or even possible, in your opinion, that anyone connected with the sanitarium—yourself, Dr. Koenig, or the nurse—used these gloves tonight to keep his or her hands clean while changing or untangling the ribbon on a typewriter?"

"Certainly not! Those gloves were soiled—stained with blood," Dr. Cantrell assured him coldly. "If Dr. Koenig —and he was the only one using a typewriter this evening, to my knowledge—had wanted to wear rubber gloves while changing a ribbon, he would have got a clean pair out of the cabinet. He had a key, of course."

"Just as I thought," Dundee nodded. "The *inside* of the gloves was stained with blood when the murderer put them on "

"The inside?" Strawn repeated, frowning.

"I am assuming that the nurse removed them in the natural way—shucked them off so that they were turned inside out," Dundee explained. "When the murderer pulled them on, he did not see the bloodstains. But when he took them off it was not to clean them tidily of blood spots, but to wash away any possible trace of his finger prints from the inside of the gloves—which was then the *outside*, of course, since he had shucked them off his hands, turning them by doing so. And, unidentifiable, it is true, the towel he spread across his hands while manipulating the washing and drying of the gloves is now in the other hamper. Just my opinion, of course, but it is the obvious thing for him to have done. You see, he was canny enough to take no chances. *Or so he thought!* He forgot to cleanse again what had become the *inside* of the gloves when he shucked them off. Look, Doctor! Don't you agree with me that the forefinger and thumb of this glove, which I turned after I found the pair, are stained with purple typewriter ribbon ink?"

"It looks like it," Dr. Cantrell agreed, furrowing his brows as he studied the glove extended for his inspection. "But how—?"

"Just a little souvenir of the murderer's 'mad rage,' which by the way, was probably the most noiseless, methodical 'mad rage' on record!"

CHAPTER THREE

"Noiseless" ejaculated Captain Strawn, as he stepped back into the dead doctor's office. With this room in the mess it is? Books thrown around, this big lamp and the smoking stand turned over–"

"All of which is exactly what the murderer counted on your saying" Dundee assured his former chief. "But I'll wager only two sounds could have been heard, even faintly outside one cf these closed doors tonight. The first, made before the murderer had put on the rubber gloves, of course was the sound of the blow, or blows, which did the deed. And the second was the much fainter and not at all suspicious sound of paper being torn."

"You're cuckoo, Bonnie!" Strawn was becoming angry. "Why when he flung down the statue—"

"Yes. If he had flung it down. But it just happens that there is proof that he laid it down beside the doctor's chair — very carefully, without any noise whatever, after wiping it clean of his fingerprints."

"You can't know that!" Strawn protested hotly.

"Look. Chief." Dundee urged, as he again inserted the toe of his boot beneath the prone statue of "The Discus Thrower," raising it slightly from its resting place on the rug. "The pile of the rug is mashed down only very slightly. If the statue had been hurled or even dropped from a height of a few feet — say from the hand of the murderer — there would be deep indentations in the pile of the rug, where the sharp edges of the statue struck. After Carraway quite unsuccessfully tests it for finger prints, I can demonstrate my point to you, if you wish. But I can convince you otherwise, I believe. . . . Look at this lamp'"

"Well, what about it? Toppled over, ain't it?" Strawn growled.

"But oh, so gently!" Dundee smiled. "The globe is not broken, you notice, though the lamp standard is a heavy metal one. The socket is not bent even slightly, as invariably happens when I tip over a floor lamp by catching my foot in the cord. And, lastly, the light wire frame of the shade is not bent, either. . . . Now for the books. . . . Dr. Cantrell, will you be good enough to take a book from that bookcase and hurl it across the room?"

Frowning, as if he resented this attack upon his dignity, Dr. Cantrell obeyed, throwing the volume with consider able force. Dundee, with Strawn at his heels, strolled over to where the book lay open, face downward, some of the leaves ruffled and bent, and one of the stiff corners of the binding sadly broken.

"That's the way a thrown book usually looks," Dundee pointed out. "But look at the books our murderer deposited over the room. Two are open, face downward, but quite tidily so, with no leaves crumpled, no corners broken. The other five books are very decorous indeed, showing no signs whatever of having been hurled—not even a strain on the ribs. . . . No, Captain. These books were never thrown. They were very carefully and noiselessly deposited on the floor. . . . But that's not all!"

And Dundee led the way to the psychiatrist's desk. "Here we have an overturned, very fragile crystal vase. It is not broken, you see. Moreover, it was carefully laid on its side *on the blotter,* although, judging by this dust free circle near the back of the desk which fits the size of the base of the vase, the murderer had to move it nearly two feet, before his 'rage' overcame him. ... I wonder," he said softly, "if this was a sardonic touch: the overturning of the vase so that the roses would exude their fragrance directly against a nose which would never smell roses again?"

"Don't go fancy on us, Dundee," Strawn snorted with disgust.

"Sorry!" Dundee apologized, his blue eyes twinkling. "Now for the inkwell. You'll observe that it lies half on, half off the blotter. But there is not even a faint scar on the mahogany, as would have been inevitable if the murderer had picked up the heavy inkwell and dashed it down. Right?"

"Maybe," Strawn conceded grudgingly.

"And here is where the murderer over reached himself," Dundee went on, pointing to the coils of purple ribbon lying across the typewriter keys. "A nice little touch, that. But in adding it, the murderer stained his rubber gloves, and then left faint smudges on the case history he tore into exceedingly fine fragments, as well as on case histories whose folders he touched while searching for the one he wanted to destroy."

"Case histories!" Dr. Cantrell exclaimed. "Good Lord, Dundee! Are you sure? Why, that's a calamity!"

"Calamity?" Strawn boomed. "It's a lucky break for us, you mean. Find the guy whose case history is missing "

"Just what did you mean, Dr. Cantrell?" Dundee asked curiously.

The doctor wiped his forehead with a newly unfolded handkerchief. "Only that case histories are sacred, and guarded above anything else in the institution. If anyone has wantonly destroyed some of them it will be a very serious loss."

"I take it, then, that this filing cabinet is usually kept locked?" Dundee asked.

"Always," the doctor answered emphatically. "And there are only four keys in existence. Dr. Koenig had one, Dr. Harlow has another, Miss Home, the secretary, has the third, and I have the fourth myself. Since the cabinet is open, Dr. Koenig must have been making some additions to a case history this evening."

"Was Dr. Koenig in the habit of typing such things himself?"

"Oh, yes. He was an expert on the typewriter, and he never bothered to wait to dictate, if the secretary wasn't available."

"Then we can assume that Dr. Koenig was typing an addition to a case history on the sheet of paper that the murderer tore from the machine?" Dundee persisted.

"If a sheet of paper *was* torn from the machine—yes!" Dr. Cantrell answered. "Dr. Koenig almost never wrote letters in the evening, but frequently worked on the histories."

"Listen, Doc!" Strawn interrupted excitedly. "Do the nutty patients know their what d' you call it?—their diagnosis? I mean, does the brain doctor tell 'em the technical names for their troubles?"

"Certainly not, as a rule," Dr. Cantrell answered, with great dignity. "Naturally some of the patients are educated enough to know the technical terms without being told, and have enough self knowledge to know their own diagnoses. Epileptics, for instance, and most manic depressives "

"But now looky here!" Strawn interrupted impatiently. "Suppose a guy come in here tonight to have a chin with the brain doctor. The doctor looks up, says wait a minute, and goes on with his typing. But the patient comes close, bends over, sees what the doc is writing, and—*it's all about this patient*, see? With terrible sounding words that the patient don't understand but which sound like an insult to him. . . . See? . . . Well, the patient backs off, the doc keeps on typing, the patient sneaks the statue off that bookcase where you said it was kept, and bangs the doctor over the head. Then he jerks the sheet of paper out of the typewriter, tears it up; finds the rest of the case history open on the doc's desk, tears it up, too—"

"First calming down enough to hunt for and find a pair of rubber gloves, so as to make sure of leaving no finger prints," Dundee interrupted. "Wait, Chief! I'm not saying you aren't right. In fact, there are strong indications that you are "

"Spoken like the sport you are, lad!" Strawn beamed. "Sure I'm right! This bird gets cagey. He says to himself, 'If I tear up only my own case history, they'll pin it on me sure, when they check up on the case history file. So I'll destroy one or two more, just to put 'em off the track!' . . . Which he does."

"Thereby proving himself a very level headed, calculating 'nut' as you call him, Chief," Dundee smiled.

"A great many psychopathic patients are not 'insane' at all, in the sense that the layman understands the term," Dr. Cantrell volunteered. "They are quite capable of sane, sound reasoning. And, at the risk of poaching upon Dr. Harlow's preserves, I may add that we are quite familiar here with the extreme cunning of some of the definitely insane."

"The *legally* insane?" Dundee asked.

"Yes."

"But would not a legally insane patient—and he must know his legal status if he has been committed after having been adjudged insane—*know that he could not be held accountable for his crime*, and therefore not take the trouble to set the stage as this murderer did?"

"That is true," Cantrell admitted. "But it is also true no patient, however insane, would relish the idea of being transferred to an asylum for the criminally insane. I assure you that even our locked ward here is heaven compared to such a place."

"And you have already assured me that your definitely insane patients are kept under constant observation in the locked ward," Dundee reminded him.

"That is true," Cantrell assented shortly. "Every patient who has been committed after being adjudged insane is kept in the locked ward. But we have a few patients who have not been committed, who are here voluntarily or because their relatives have placed them here, and who, because they have shown no disposition toward running away or toward violence, are permitted to live in the cottages, although they *could* be legally committed, if a charge were made."

"Why, looky, my lad!" Strawn became excited again. "That's the ticket, right there! Our friend the murderer is one of these patients who don't even know he's loony, because the family has been protecting him, see? And he sees the doc writing it all out—how crazy he is, and that he ought to be locked up, maybe. . . . Look at it this way, Bonnie! Supposing you're here, with the folks kidding you that you're here for 'nerves.' You're restless, don't like it here much, have come in to ask the doc to let you go home. Well, you take a peep at what the doc's writing, and you find out that he thinks you're bugs; not only that, but a dangerous lunatic. *And you know that what this doc says will be gospel to the lunacy commission!* Not only that, but, being loony, you jump to the conclusion that they're trying to frame you, put you away to get hold of your fortune, or something like that," the Chief of the Homicide Squad ended lamely, aware of the movie melodrama tinge to his last few words.

"Pretty clever, Captain," Dundee applauded. "And of course if his case history is destroyed and the doctor whose word is gospel with the lunacy commission is dead, your theoretical murderer would feel doubly safe."

"Exactly!" Strawn agreed with great satisfaction. "Come in!" he bawled, as he was interrupted by a knock on the door. "What is it, little lady?"

Dr. Harlow, her dignity affronted, tried her best to look three inches taller and ten years older, as she announced: "Dr. Price, the coroner, is here with the morgue ambulance." But her voice broke childishly on the dreadful word.

"Come on in, Price!" Strawn bawled, through the partly opened door, and the coroner obeyed, his thin legs very spry, but a look of real regret on his nice old face.

"Too bad, Captain, too bad! . . . How're ye, Bonnie? . . . Had the pleasure of knowing Dr. Koenig. Fine man! Fine man! . . . Hmm! Death must have been instantaneous. A very nasty blow. Hmm."

"Carraway!" Strawn called. "Bring in your camera, and get busy!"

The fingerprint expert, who was also the police department's official photographer, sauntered into the office, carrying camera and tripod, as well as the box containing his fingerprinting paraphernalia.

"Pictures of the corpse after Doc Price has finished with it," Strawn directed. "Also of the room from all angles. Then pick up any fingerprints you can find on the desk, the flower vase, the inkwell, that statue laying there, the smoking stand, the lamp, the books and the doorknobs. Also, gather up all them scraps of paper on the floor and go over every one of them with your powder. ... By the way, little lady," and he turned to Dr. Harlow, "whose fingerprints would normally be on the case histories?"

"Case histories!" she repeated, the same acute dismay in her voice as had characterized Dr. Cantrell's at the mention of those important documents.

"Sure! The murderer tore up some of 'em, including his own, to my way of thinking!" Strawn told her. "Now, who's been handling them in the ordinary course of duty?"

"Why—" she began, her voice still flat with dismay. Then, more firmly: "Only Dr. Koenig, myself, and the secretary, Miss Home. . . . That is," she amended conscientiously, "we are the only three who have handled the case histories during the last five years, with the exception of temporary stenographers, who have relieved Miss Home when she was on vacation."

"Five years?" Strawn pounced. "Mean to say a kid like you has been a doctor for five years?"

"I'm twenty nine years old," Dr. Harlow informed him, with great dignity. "Dr. Koenig took me on as his assistant when he became head psychiatrist here, five years ago."

"And who was here ahead of him?" Strawn asked.

"Dr. Cyrus Mayfield," the girl doctor answered in a low voice, as she shot a strange glance at Dr. Cantrell. pushing a loose strand of curling red hair off her forehead.

"And where is this Dr. Mayfield now, Dr. Harlow?" Dundee interrupted, since he was sure that that was the one question the diminutive doctor most wished not to hear.

"Why, he—he's " The girl drew a deep breath,

"Dead?" Dundee helped her gently.

"His—*body* is alive," the girl answered, her voice quivering.

CHAPTER FOUR

"JUST what do you mean, Dr. Harlow?" Dundee persisted. "You put it very strangely—'his *body* is alive.' "

Before the girl doctor could answer, Baldwin, the business manager, stepped into the office from the reception room.

"Let me explain, Justine," he commanded curtly. "She means exactly what she says, Dundee. Dr. Mayfield's body is alive, but his mind is practically dead. He is and has been for about six years the victim of senility—or, in medical terms, senile dementia."

"And where is Dr. Mayfield now?" Dundee asked.

"In his apartment upstairs," Baldwin astounded him by announcing calmly. "I may explain that when Dr. Mayfield's condition became painfully apparent, some six years ago, his daughter, Harriet, who is now Madame Arnaud and a resident of Paris, took her father abroad for rest and treatment. He became worse steadily, and when I met them on a ship returning to America, Miss Mayfield told me that it would be necessary to have her father adjudged incompetent, in order to protect his estate and to permit the sanitarium to pass into other hands. Dr. Cantrell was with the party, as Dr. Mayfield's physician, and it was at his suggestion that the two of us conferred on the possibility of a three way partnership—neither of us having money enough to purchase the sanitarium outright."

"That is correct," Dr. Cantrell corroborated him. "But let me add that the original suggestion of such a partnership came from Miss Mayfield, who also suggested that we approach Dr. Koenig, whom she and Dr. Mayfield knew personally, and in whom she had the highest confidence. After the legal steps had been taken here in

Hamilton, the partnership was formed, one of the conditions of sale being that Dr. Mayfield be taken care of here for the rest of his life, retaining his former apartment upstairs, and—" He hesitated and glanced uneasily at Dr. Harlow.

"Yes?" Dundee prompted.

Dr. Harlow obeyed the unspoken appeal in her colleague's eyes. "Miss Mayfield also stipulated that her father never be told that he was no longer head of the sanitarium. . . . It is a characteristic of senility, you know, that the patient believes he is still in his mental prime, and quite capable of managing his own affairs."

"I see," Dundee said slowly, as he pondered frowningly upon what he had heard.

"I say, Bonnie!" Strawn ejaculated. "We're onto some thing, sure as you live! . . . Listen, little doctor!" and he turned to Dr. Harlow. "Dr. Koenig kept a case history on the old doc, same as on any other patient, I take it?"

"Yes," the girl admitted, startled.

"Is this loony old doctor bedridden, by any chance?" Strawn went on, with mounting excitement.

"No. He is quite feeble, and in bed a good many hours of the day, but— "

"He can walk all right, can't he? Get up and downstairs without help?" Strawn persisted.

"Yes. He spends a part of each day, when the weather permits, in a little private garden."

"And where is that?"

"Behind these offices, between here and Dr. Cantrell's house," the girl answered faintly.

"All right!" Strawn struck his hands together triumphantly. "The old doctor thinks he's still the big cheese here and thinks Dr. Koenig is just his hired assistant. . . . That so?"

"Yes," the girl answered, rather defiantly.

"Look, then! Dr. Mayfield wanders downstairs, sees Dr. Koenig in his office, drops in to give him some 'orders', finds him actually writing some additional notes for *his own case history*, tumbles to the deception that's been played on him, and—kills him!"

Dr. Harlow flung back her head. Her cheeks were white and her gray green eyes blazing behind their horn rimmed spectacles. "That's absurd! Dr. Mayfield hasn't the physical strength to strike a blow like that!"

"Do you agree, Dr. Cantrell?" Dundee asked quietly.

"I—don't know," the medical head answered haltingly. "When he's crossed, he shows—surprising strength "

"For instance?" Dundee cut in.

"Well, he refuses to let an attendant stay near him," Dr. Cantrell answered, still very slowly. "Naturally I have convinced him that he is not a well man, physically, and that he mustn't tax his strength by attending to too many 'duties,' and the presence of a nurse is explained in that way. But he drives his male attendant out of the room, whenever he has a lucid interval. Those are becoming increasingly rare, I may add."

"Can either of you tell me when Dr. Koenig last saw Dr. Mayfield professionally?"

Both doctors hesitated, and then it was Dr. Harlow who answered defiantly: "This afternoon. Dr. Koenig was with Dr. Mayfield for only a few minutes, and when he returned to his office he called me in and told me he was thinking of cabling to Madame Arnaud, since, in his opinion, the old doctor had no more than a few months to live. . . . *Senile dementia*," she added in her professional voice, "usually terminates fatally in about five years."

"May I see Dr. Mayfield's case history, Dr. Harlow?" Dundee asked suddenly.

The little doctor again tried to look three inches taller than her five feet one. "The case histories of our patients are sacred, Mr. Dundee," she told him severely. "Only when you can show me a court order—"

"Then," and Dundee smiled at her very winningly, for her dignity and her loyalty aroused both his admiration and his amusement, "will you—just to clear things up a bit—look in the files and see if Dr. May field's history is there?"

"Won't find it," Strawn whispered to Dundee, as the girl obeyed. "Sure as you're alive, the old boy destroyed it."

"Here it is," Dr. Harlow called, her voice very cold.

"Just a minute, doctor!" Dundee sprang across the room. "Was it by any chance in one of the folders that was sticking almost half out of the files?"

"No. It was in its place," she answered triumphantly.

"Then—" and Dundee glanced at Strawn, his eye brows cocked, "will you just glance at it and see if Dr. Koenig made any additions to day?"

The girl turned the loose pages until she came to the last. "Yes," she said. "He has recorded a very brief and very mild attack of *senile delirium*, which was the cause of his visit to Dr. Mayfield this afternoon. The next attack," she explained, "will probably end in death. . . . Dr. Koenig prescribed a sedative, and I feel sure Dr. Mayfield has been sleeping ever since the attack."

"He has an attendant at night, of course?"

"Yes. But the attendant keeps out of sight, sitting just outside the bedroom door, in the sitting room of the suite."

"Let me have a crack at that attendant!" Captain Strawn commanded belligerently. Not easily would he relinquish his pet theory! "Cain!" he bawled, and one of his plain clothes squad appeared almost instantly in the doorway. "Show this man the way, Doctor."

With head high and cheeks scarlet, Dr. Harlow left the room in advance of Detective Cain.

"All finished, Dr. Price?" Dundee asked.

"Some minutes ago, and Carraway has made his pictures of the body," the little old coroner answered testily. "Any questions? . . . Make 'em snappy! I'm getting old and I've got the post mortem ahead of me yet tonight."

"Did you find the skull to be of the usual thickness?" Dundee asked, remembering Dr. Cantrell's opinion.

"No. On the contrary. Very thin skull."

"At approximately what hour do you calculate that death occurred?" Strawn took a hand.

"Somewhere between half past nine and ten o'clock this evening," the coroner answered. "By the way, Doctor," and he turned to Cantrell, "what time did Dr. Koenig dine? That will help me fix the time of death more accu rately, after I've examined the stomach contents."

"At six o'clock promptly, in the staff dining room," Dr. Cantrell replied. "The patients have their dinner between eleven thirty and twelve, and their supper between five and five thirty, but the members of the staff have dinner together at six o'clock."

"Any other wounds or abrasions of any kind, besides the head wound?" Dundee asked, as a matter of form.

"A bruise on the chin, slightly to the right of the mouth," Dr. Price answered laconically.

"What!" Dundee exclaimed. "I don't see how that happened. The head was bowed in such a position that only the forehead struck the desk at all."

"Well, then, you've got something to play sleuth with," Price twinkled. "For the forehead is not bruised, and the chin is. In my opinion—to be verified by the post mortem, of course—the bruise was made *after death*. . . . Would you care to look, Doctor?"

The two medical men returned to the body, consulted together in low tones, then retraced their steps to where Dundee was standing, deep in thought.

"I am inclined to agree with Dr. Price," Cantrell announced tiredly.

"I confess that's a poser," the detective said, frowning, but his reflections were interrupted by the return of Cain and Dr. Harlow, followed by a young man in the white uniform of an attendant.

"Found this bird asleep at the switch, Chief," Cain blurted out. "His patient, a white haired old gent, was reading in bed."

"*Reading*, was he?" Strawn boomed. "Thought you said the old doc was clear gone in the upper story, little lady!"

"He has lucid intervals, and such an interval is likely to follow an attack of senile delirium," Dr. Harlow answered with dignity. "Though I confess I expected the sedative to keep Dr. Mayfield asleep longer than it did."

"So you were snoozing on the job, eh?" Strawn lashed out at the cringing attendant. "What's your name?"

"Peters, sir. I'm afraid I did doze off "

"Doze!" Cain repeated contemptuously. "This baby had to be shook before he opens his peepers "

"You see, sir," the attendant stammered, "my wife is pretty sick, and I didn't get any sleep at all today. But I give you my word I hadn't been dozing more than a few minutes. Dr. Mayfield was sleeping "

"So you thought you'd keep him company in slumberland!" Strawn snarled.

"I'm sorry if any harm's been done " the poor young man began timidly, well aware that he had lost his job.

"Harm?" Strawn snorted. "Just a little matter of murder, that's all. . . . All right, Price. You can take the body away."

While the morgue ambulance crew were busy with the stretcher, Peters cowered, trembling and white faced, against the door leading into the hall.

"Now, young fellow," Strawn began again, when the body had been removed. "Just what were you doing between nine and ten o'clock tonight?"

"Sitting outside Dr. Mayfield's door," the attendant quavered. "I was reading a detective story, but it was hard to keep my mind on the story, because I could hear the voices from the talking picture right under Dr. Mayfleld's apartment."

"So you went down to have a look at the pictures your self?" Strawn pounced.

"No, sir!" the attendant denied emphatically.

"Cain! How close to the bedroom door was this man's chair?"

"About two feet away from it, sir."

"Room for the old man to pass without waking up this bird?"

"Yes, sir."

"Listen, you! Does your patient ever get up and wander around at night?"

"Some—sometimes," Peters stammered. "But I always persuade him to get back to bed."

"Did he get out of bed tonight?"

"No, sir!"

"You mean, if he did, he didn't wake you up!" Strawn corrected contemptuously. "Cain, you go with this baby and keep him company for the rest of the night. And listen hard for anything the old gentleman may say."

"You know, Chief," Dundee began mildly, when the two men had left the room, "I don't really believe that feeble old doctor murdered Koenig. Remember, his case history, with today's addition to it, was left in the files. That fact alone destroys your theory. But there is another point. *Case histories are sacred to a physician!* You have heard both Dr. Harlow and Dr. Cantrell say so, and have seen their dismay at the idea of case histories being destroyed. Dr. Mayfield was, first and last, a doctor, a psychiatrist. To him, too, case histories would be sacred. Granted that he would destroy his own, in a fit of rage, I believe it is psychologically impossible for him to destroy others."

"Tommyrot!" Strawn snorted.

"Am I right, Dr. Harlow?"

"Absolutely!" the girl doctor assured him eagerly. "Even in his present condition, Dr. Mayfield's every lucid and—delusional thought is connected with his work. He was and still is devoted to it. In fact, his devotion is so strong that we have to humor him when he desires to interview patients."

"He actually treats patients?" Dundee asked, in astonishment.

"Oh, yes, or he thinks he does. He questions them quite in his old manner. ... Of course," she added, "we send him only those patients who were here when he was still in charge, and whom he remembers. Sometimes he sends for a patient who is dead or who has left, and we persuade him to talk to another of the old stand bys. They are very kind to him. They understand, and enjoy their visits."

"Very interesting," Dundee commented absently. Then: "Dr. Harlow, have you a list of all the patients who are here at present?"

"Yes, of course. In the chartroom, with the room or suite number opposite the name of each patient, for the convenience of the head nurse."

"Then will you please check the file, and tell us which case histories are missing?"

As Dr. Harlow left the office, Carraway sauntered up to his chief.

"What luck?" Strawn asked the fingerprint expert.

"A world of prints, most of 'em not so new," Carraway answered. "But none at all on the statue. Been wiped clean."

"What about those fine torn scraps of paper?" Dundee asked.

"Four sets of prints, taking the whole heap of scraps," Carraway answered. "A man's fingerprints—I've compared them with the corpse's and they match—and three sets that look like they belong to women. Smaller, with the ridges more delicate and less pronounced, you know."

"Confirming my suspicion that the murderer wore gloves," Dundee commented. "Undoubtedly the women's prints will be found to belong to Dr. Harlow and a couple of stenographers—easy enough to check the correspondence files for similar prints. . . . Anything else, Carraway?"

"A flock of prints that I got from doorknobs and doors and door frames. . . . Say, I supposed you noticed that smear on the desk?"

"What smear?" Dundee was plainly chagrined.

"Looks like where somebody wiped off blood," Carraway answered nonchalantly. "You and the Captain were both busy, and I took the liberty of wiping the spot some more with the damp end of a towel. Dr. Price said it was blood, all right, but he's going to make a report later. . . . Look! You can see where I wiped the desk. I didn't make the smear any bigger."

Both Strawn and Dundee bent over the spot which was easily discernible near the right hand corner of the desk. The dampness of the towel and the original stain had dulled the bright polish of the mahogany.

"That's damned odd," Dundee said slowly. "Look, Chief! Here's something that looks like blood on the blotter, too, which we couldn't have seen without lifting up the head."

"I believe I can explain that stain," Dr. Cantrell interrupted. Uninvited, he had come close. "A blow such as killed Dr. Koenig causes a slow oozing of blood from the ears. As the head was resting, the right ear would have been directly over that spot on the blotter."

"Is that so?" Dundee commented, still frowning. "But —*why the blood on the corner of the desk?* How did it get 'way over there, why should the murderer wipe it up, and what did he wipe it *with?* ... By Jove! Those blood stained swabs in the hamper!"

"I have explained them," Dr. Cantrell reminded him.

"Yes, *but there they were*, some of them not so badly soiled!" Dundee pointed out. "When the murderer discarded the rubber gloves, he must have seen them. All nicely made to order for his purpose! A little more blood on one of those swabs would never be noticed—and blood on the corner of the desk doesn't fit into the picture our murderer is painting. . . . Well, we have a couple of posers, Chief. A bruise that has no business to be on the doctor's chin; blood that couldn't logically be on this corner of the desk—"

"Why should the murderer bother about the blood and whether it could be explained?" Strawn objected.

"That's exactly what I should like to know," Dundee admitted, very thoughtfully. "There's the key to the puzzle—or I'm much mistaken!"

With his hands in his pockets he bent a brooding gaze upon the dead doctor's desk. Nothing there to explain the bruise made *after death*. True, there were the ash tray, the overturned vase, the inkwell, a couple of pencils, and a penholder. But all these objects had been well away from the doctor's bowed face. Granted, for the sake of argument, that the chin had struck one of these objects: why had the murderer removed it?

His puzzled, roving eyes came to rest upon a small, loose leaf desk calendar, which, curiously enough, had not been disturbed by the murderer. The used leaves had been turned back over the metal rings, and the exposed leaf bore the date of the following day, Thursday, June 4th. The doctor had obviously used the calendar as a memory tickler, for, in pencil, were the notations:

Call Morse
Inner spring mattresses
Dr. Sandlin

The last two words were heavily underlined.

"Dr. Harlow!" Dundee called suddenly to the girl who was busy at the case history file. "Who is Dr. Sandlin?"

The little doctor stared blankly then shook her head. It was the business manager, Baldwin, who threw a bomb shell into the quiet room with his answer.

CHAPTER FIVE

"DR. SANDLIN," the business manager announced calmly, "is the psychiatrist whom Dr. Koenig hoped to be able to hire to take Dr. Harlow's place here."

Dr. Cantrell's reaction to the news was apparently blank surprise, but it was to Justine Harlow's vivid little face that Dundee shifted his eyes. She looked as if she had been knocked almost senseless by a blow in the solar plexus. Her small body seemed bent and shrunken in the suddenly too large white uniform. Every scrap of color had left her cheeks, leaving them waxen and drawn. Even her eyes were changed in color, the green being scarcely noticeable now.

"No, no! I—don't believe it," her white lips quivered, the voice so low that Dundee could scarcely distinguish the words.

"This is the first intimation you have had that you were not—giving entire satisfaction?" Dundee asked, and was instantly ashamed of the wording. As if she were a servant girl!

The girl doctor did not answer, except to straighten her small body as if to brace it for the new blow he had dealt her.

"Dr. Koenig was extremely fond of Justine—of Dr. Harlow, I mean," Dr. Cantrell put in, emphatically. "I am afraid Mr. Baldwin misunderstood something our colleague said—"

"Not a chance!" Baldwin denied brusquely. "The doctor and I had a business conference this afternoon—informal, of course, or you would have been included, Bruce. You see, Dundee, Dr. Koenig had returned late Monday, from a three weeks' trip, and there were a number of matters I had to take up with him."

"What was the nature of the trip?" Dundee asked.

"Partly business, partly a lecture tour," Baldwin answered. "Business took him to New York, where he completed negotiations with the principal creditors of a sanitarium at Meridian, about a hundred miles from here, to take over their patients and some of their equipment. A good stroke of business for Mayfield, since we eliminate our only local competition, and increase our prestige enormously. We already have plans under way for the building of one large new cottage."

"And we were agreed that it meant the hiring of another assistant to Dr. Koenig," Dr. Cantrell added curtly. "A male assistant. But I feel absolutely sure that Dr. Koenig had no intention of dispensing with Dr. Harlow's services."

"What makes you feel so certain, Doctor?" Dundee asked, his pitying eyes still fixed on Dr. Harlow's white face.

"Because I know how much Dr. Koenig valued her, both as a friend and as an assistant," the medical man retorted stoutly. "I hope I am not betraying his confidence when I say that his appreciation of Dr. Harlow is amply proved by the terms of Dr. Koenig's will."

"Ah!" Dundee breathed. "And—you know the terms of that will, Doctor?"

"I do, because I was one of the witnesses when it was signed. My wife was another. By the terms of that will, drawn by Clifford Forrest, Dr. Koenig's attorney, Justine Harlow and Norah Lacey, our head nurse, share equally in the estate, which of course includes Dr. Koenig's third interest in Mayfield Sanitarium."

"You mean to say that those two girls are to have an equal say so with you and me?" Baldwin demanded, his lips twisted with anger.

"I'm satisfied!" Cantrell retorted curtly.

Dundee saw the girl draw a deep, quivering breath, which seemed to bring color to her cheeks and a sparkle to her eyes, as well as tears.

"I knew it!" she cried. "I knew he was too big a man to let one little disagreement turn him against me!"

"So you had a quarrel with the Big Doctor, eh?" Strawn pounced, as if to say, "Now we're getting somewhere!"

"Certainly not!" Justine Harlow flared indignantly. "It was only the slightest disagreement—purely professional!"

"So the doctor thought you were getting too big for your britches, eh?" Strawn suggested vulgarly. "When did this quarrel take place?"

The girl's cheeks were scarlet. "I refuse to discuss the matter if you insist upon calling it a quarrel!"

"Easy, Chief!" Dundee warned, in a low voice. "Dr. Harlow," he began, in a friendly, casual voice: "It is natural enough for two physicians to disagree about a diagnosis or the treatment of a case. I take it that you and Dr. Koenig did disagree in regard to some patient?"

"Yes," the girl answered, turning to the young detective and ignoring the older. "It was really too trivial for me even to remember, until—until it appeared that Dr. Koenig wished to replace me. Professional ethics forbid me to go into details, but the disagreement was over a young girl patient who has been almost entirely under my care. I thought her condition much more serious—increasingly serious—than Dr. Koenig, who had been away a good deal since the girl came here, was inclined to regard it."

"Are you, by any chance, referring to a girl named Enid Rambler?" Dundee asked.

The girl's eyes widened. "I am, as a matter of fact, but—"

"Then let me assure you that I believe you were right, and Dr. Koenig wrong for once," Dundee said quietly. "The young lady was in so serious a state tonight that she became hysterical and tried to run away from the sanitarium."

"And got herself arrested for disturbing the peace?" Baldwin cut in.

"No. She was very quiet when I found her—unconscious, in fact. In a ditch by the roadside, with a sprained ankle. I brought her back."

"*Enid Rambler?*" Dr. Harlow asked, incredulity written all over her expressive face. "I can't imagine Enid's *running away*—"

"Why not?" Dundee forestalled Strawn, who was chewing his gray mustache in a way that portended a new theory.

"Because Enid Rambler has consistently refused to leave the grounds, even with other patients or for a drive with me," Dr. Harlow answered, her brows still knit with perplexity, and professional ethics apparently forgotten. "Why, Enid would run like a deer to keep from meeting a stranger! If a patient begged her to meet his visitors, she refused, and hid in her room until the visitors were gone. And the very suggestion that she must try to get well so that she could leave was enough to send her into hysterics."

"Then it's about time I had a go at that young lady!" Strawn interrupted grimly. "If Dundee found her on the roadside, after she'd run away from the sanitarium, and if what Dr. Harlow tells us is true, it's a cinch she had one swell reason for running away this particular night. And say! The Big Doctor was anxious to get rid of her, wasn't he? Wanted to send her away and you said she wasn't able to go—eh, little lady?"

Justine Harlow's cheeks again burned scarlet in resentment of the insinuation behind the old detective's words. "That's not true!" she flashed. "I suggested to Dr. Koenig that the girl should be thoroughly psychoanalyzed, to rid her of two complexes: one a fear of crowds, strangers; the other a very definite claustrophobia."

"Says which?" Strawn frowned at the unfamiliar word.

"Claustrophobia consists of an inability on the part of the patient to remain in a closed space," Dr. Harlow enlightened him crisply. "It also frequently exhibits itself in a desire for unusually large rooms."

"So she hates locked doors and *little rooms*, does she?" Strawn commented grimly. "Wouldn't like prison cells *a tall!* . . . Looky, Bonnie! This girl comes here for the express purpose of *getting Koenig!* He don't know her, or she wouldn't take the chance. But let's say she wants to avenge some wrong done to a member of her family. I'll grant it may have been one of them fancied wrongs you read about in books. But Koenig gets suspicious. He won't treat her himself, but gives the job to Dr. Harlow, and he wants the little doctor here to *hustle her out*. . . . Get me? . . . Well, she gets wind of his intentions some how, and she don't lose any more time. Picks a night when a lot of strangers are coming and going, does the job, plans it to look like the work of one of the nuts, and beats it. What's more, I don't doubt she got this here glostrophobia or whatever you call it. A girl all steamed up to murder a man in cold blood is apt to think a mighty lot about prison cells. And to take every precaution to see that she don't get stuck into one!"

Dundee shook his head. "Somehow—and mind you, I've had quite a talk with the girl, Chief—I can't picture Enid Rambler as the cold blooded murderer who could strike down a man, don rubber gloves, disrupt the room to look as if a homicidal maniac had done the deed, and then —run away. You see, Captain the two sets of characteristics don't jibe. If the murderer lives here, he— or she— didn't lose his or her head and run away! Too cool a head for that! But I grant you that *something* happened to panic the girl, and that that something may very well be connected with the murder."

"I'll say it's connected!" Strawn snorted. "Did you finish checking that file, little lady?"

"Yes. I was just finishing when Mr. Dundee called me."

"Then I'll wager my shield you found this Rambler baby's case history among the missing!" Strawn challenged her triumphantly.

"Then you lose your shield," the young doctor told him coolly. "There are two case histories missing, the patients being Samuel Rowan and Archibald Webster."

The last name rang a bell in Dundee's memory. What was it Sanderson had said?—"rich, handsome scapegrace, young Webster. ... In and out of the place half a dozen times a year—"

But Strawn was crawfishing with ease: "That don't mean nothing, but that the dame is smarter than I give her credit for. Fixed it so's the blame would fall on two other guys—take your choice, or, better still, take the guy who can't give an ironclad alibi."

Dundee smiled. "I'm afraid I'm more interested, at the moment, in the 'two other guys,' Captain, than I am in Miss Rambler. Can any of you tell us whether either or both of these patients attended the movie?"

Baldwin, Cantrell and Dr. Harlow shook their heads. Then the girl doctor suggested: "I feel sure Miss Caplan, the night head nurse, could answer that question. I'll call her." She went to the door leading into the main hall, opened it, and called: "Rose! Rose! . . . Will you come here, please?"

The thin, gray haired, pale faced nurse who had received Dundee came hurrying across the hall, frightened deference in her voice as she answered: "Yes, Dr. Harlow?"

"These gentlemen wish to question you, Rose. Don't be afraid to tell anything you know, or to answer any question whatever."

Strawn waved her to Dundee, as if granting the younger detective's greater ability where the questioning of women was concerned.

"At what time did you come on duty, Miss Caplan?" Dundee asked, accepting the task gladly.

"At seven o'clock," the nurse quavered.

"And at what time did the patients begin to gather for the picture show?"

"About fifteen minutes after I came on duty. Our movies usually start about 7:20, but, due to a misunderstanding on the operator's part, because the downtown theaters had changed their schedules, the first picture did not start until eight o'clock this evening," the nurse answered painstakingly, little gasps punctuating her sentences.

"And did the patients wait in the O. T. Shop all that time?" Dundee continued.

"Some did, laughing and talking together in groups. Some strolled about the grounds until they saw the car arrive with the films."

"Were you in a position to note all arrivals and departures, and returns?"

"Yes, sir, except when the phone rang. And even when I had to talk over the phone I kept an eye on the hall. You see, the door to the chartroom is very close to the door into the O. T. Shop, and I kept a watch because I was afraid something might happen—with the patients getting restless and excitable—"

"I understand," Dundee assured her, as her voice trembled to an uncertain pause. "Now, Miss Caplan, can you tell us whether Mr. Rowan and Mr. Webster attended the show?"

"Mr. Rowan did," the nurse answered more confidently. "I noticed him particularly, because"—and she turned shining, glad eyes upon Dr. Harlow, as if to share her pleasure—"*he talked and laughed* with two of the patients while they were waiting for the films to come!"

"And is that extraordinary^' Dundee asked quickly.

"Very extraordinary," Dr. Harlow replied. "Poor Mr. Rowan has been almost completely silent for two years. No one could reach him, no one could make him talk. But this afternoon he walked into Dr. Koenig's office and voluntarily began to talk. He talked for three hours—until Dr. Koenig had to make him stop. The doctor was jubilant, told me he was sure Rowan could be cured now—"

"What did Rowan talk about?" Dundee asked.

The little doctor stiffened. "I don't know," she answered coldly, "and if I did, professional ethics—"

"Ethics be damned, Doctor—begging your pardon," Strawn interrupted. "Get wise, little lady! This is *murder!*"

"I have told you I don't know. Dr. Koenig did not have an opportunity to go into Rowan's case with me then."

"But in all probability he made some additions to Rowan's case history this evening?" Dundee suggested.

"It is quite likely. He worked steadily all evening."

"Did he tell you—or you " and Dundee turned first to Cantrell and then to Baldwin, "what Rowan talked about? It must have been a rather important unburdening, if it unlocked a silence of two years' duration."

"No," Dr. Cantrell answered flatly.

"No," Baldwin said, too, then: "But he did remark to me that if a psychiatrist chose to, he could give the police plenty to keep them busy!"

"Did he make that remark apropos of Rowan?"

"No. But Rowan had just left. I passed him in the hall, on my way into Dr. Koenig's office. It was just a few minutes before five—supper time for the patients. Dr. Koenig was pretty 'high,' and I took the remark to refer to the last patient he'd been seeing. A success like that always stirred him up, made another man out of him."

"And it was during this same visit that Dr. Koenig mentioned Dr. Sandlin?" Dundee remembered to ask.

"Yes."

"What time does Miss Home, the secretary, leave?"

"At five," Baldwin answered. "She came in to say good night while I was still with the doctor."

"Thanks. . . . Now, Miss Caplan, will you tell us whether Mr. Rowan stayed for the entire showing of the pictures?"

"So far as I know, he did. I saw him come out with the others when the program was over."

"Is there more than one door to the O. T. Shop?" Dundee asked.

"Yes. There are two other doors. One opens out onto the back lawn, and another leads into the storeroom, back of Mr. Baldwin's office."

"Were these doors locked?"

"The door into the storeroom was," the nurse answered. "Mr. Baldwin has one key, and the other is kept in a desk drawer in the chartroom. The storeroom door is always locked. But the other door was open for the sake of coolness—it was a hot night."

"Then it was possible, while the shop was dark for the showing of pictures, for a patient or a patient's visitor to slip out of that back door without being noticed?"

"Possible, of course," the nurse answered hesitantly.

"Very possible to leave—and return unnoticed?"

"I suppose so. But of course some of the other patients would have noticed"

"Engrossed in so thrilling a picture as 'Manslaughter'?" Dundee was skeptical.

"I—"

"Did *you* notice anyone leave in that way?" Strawn pounced.

"No!" the nurse cried, too emphatically, her face turning too pale.

To Strawn's disgust, Dundee seemed to take sides with the nurse, for he assured her soothingly: "I understand, Miss Caplan. You mean to say, don't you, that you were not in a position to observe arrivals and departures *after* the show had started, since you were at your post in the chartroom?"

"Yes!" the girl fell into the trap. "Of course! I was in the chartroom—"

"But," Dundee interrupted»her regretfully, his brows knit as if in great perplexity, "I've just remembered that Miss Rambler said she couldn't find you in the chartroom after she left the O. T. Shop in the middle of the feature picture. She said she was looking for a nurse to give her a sedative. . . . But perhaps," he continued guilefully as the nurse's pale face became ashen, "you were called away on some duty?"

The woman turned hunted eyes from face to face, but in that circle of stern judges there was only one friendly, pitying pair of eyes.

"Don't be frightened, Rose. We all know how conscientious you are. Simply tell the exact truth," Dr. Harlow urged.

"I—I was looking at 'Manslaughter,' too," Miss Caplan gasped. "I—I knew I could hear my phone ring. I was just inside the door to the shop—"

"But, of course," Dundee suggested casually, "the door was closed because the light from the hall would have interfered with the showing of the pictures."

"Yes, sir," the badgered woman admitted in a low voice.

"Another thing is puzzling me," Dundee went on. "Dr. Harlow has told us that Miss Rambler had a complex against encountering strangers, and yet there were a number of visitors who came with patients to see the show this evening."

"Enid—I mean, Miss Rambler, came in when the shop was dark for the showing of the pictures, and she left before 'Manslaughter' ended," Miss Caplan explained in a rush, then clapped her hand to her mouth as she realized, too late, that she had revealed what she had been trying to conceal.

Dundee showed no triumph, as he asked: "Can you tell us approximately the time Miss Rambler arrived for the pictures, and the time she left?"

"The comedy had been on about ten minutes, so it must have been about ten minutes after eight when

Enid—Miss Rambler—slipped in," the nurse answered hopelessly. "It was pretty dark, but I suppose she recognized me standing there by the door when she opened it and let a bit of light in. Anyway, I recognized her, and put out my hand. She—she took it and squeezed it and said, 'Aren't I brave?' Then she edged along the wall till she got to the back of the room, and I saw her hesitate, then creep along in the dark until she found a seat near the back door. I knew she would want to escape before the lights went up, and I didn't think anything about it when I saw her slip out when 'Manslaughter,' the second picture, was about half finished."

"Listen, Doc!" Strawn cut in, turning to Dr. Cantrell. "You said, when you was telling us about that picture, that it was about a girl that got sent to prison, didn't you? . . . Well, then, whereabouts in the fillum do they show her in a cell? *About halfway through it*, eh?"

"There you are, Bonnie!" Strawn spread his hands in a gesture of triumph.

"I—believe so," Cantrell answered coldly.

"But exactly *where* am I?" Dundee grinned. "It seems to me that the sight of another girl in prison would act as a deterrent to a girl who already has claustrophobia—not as an incentive for her to go out and kill a man! . . . What do you think, Dr. Harlow?"

"I think Enid's leaving the picture and subsequently running away was caused by an acute attack of claustrophobia," the little doctor answered emphatically. "It is a well known fact that a girl, viewing a motion picture, puts herself in the place of the heroine, consciously or unconsciously. Temporarily, Enid Rambler was the girl in the picture, and she could not bear the close quarters or the locked door. Her other complex—fear of strangers from the outside world—made her control herself until she was safely out of the shop. Then, I don't doubt, she became hysterical. It is likely, too, that for the first time she visualized the sanitarium as a sort of prison, and the impulse to escape became stronger than her fear of the world."

"I think that is quite clear," Dundee commented respectfully.

"Just a heap of words, if you ask me!" Strawn brushed it aside violently. "A pretty woman could always make you believe black is white, Bonnie me boy! Just let me have a whack at this Rambler dame!"

It was the timid nurse who flared the answer: "She didn't have a thing to do with that awful murder! Enid Rambler is the sweetest, kindest, most lovable—" She stopped suddenly, her voice choked with tears.

"Pretty fond of her, ain't you, sister?" Strawn asked sarcastically.

"I certainly am! But so is nearly everybody else! But why pick on her? She wasn't the only one who left the shop while the pictures were on!"

"Ah!" Dundee said softly, about to reap the harvest of patience and tact. "You saw someone else leave, Miss Caplan?"

"Two others!" she affirmed emphatically. "Archie Webster and a man who was visiting him this evening!"

CHAPTER SIX

"WELL, sister, your eyesight and memory are sure improving fast!" Captain Strawn commended the nurse sarcastically. "Take a good long think and see if you can't conveniently remember a few more patients who strolled out of the *dark* shop tonight."

"Others may have left, but I saw only those three," Miss Caplan retorted angrily. "The phone rang twice and once Mrs. Appleby came over to ask for a sedative for her patient, so I was out of the shop three times while the pictures were being shown."

"But you're sure about Mr. Webster and his visitor, Miss Caplan, in spite of the shop's being dark?" Dundee asked, his voice very gentle.

"I am," she answered earnestly. "You know how your eyes get accustomed to the dark. And the shop is narrow, although it's quite long."

"How did you identify these two men in the gloom?" Dundee persisted.

"Well, Mr. Webster is a very unusual type," the nurse replied confidently. "He's the tallest patient we have here, and very broad shouldered. This evening he was wearing a red and white striped blazer, which showed up clearly. And I noticed his friend very particularly, because he was so awfully fat and short—like a balloon that's been blown up till it's ready to burst. ... I don't know his name."

"They left together, of course?"

"No. The fat man left first, and about five minutes later I saw Mr. Webster leave. They both had seats near the door, in the same row where Enid sat."

"Did Webster speak to the girl before he left?"

"Oh, she'd already left, just a minute or so before the fat man did."

"But Webster knows Miss Rambler, of course?"

"Ye—es," the nurse admitted. "He seems to be terribly in love with Enid, but I don't think she cares especially for him."

"There was no reason why you should have had Mr. Webster followed?"

The nurse flushed and looked toward Dr. Harlow entreatingly. "I—well, it *would* have been safer—"

"What do you mean?" Dundee asked sharply.

"Well, you see," the nurse stammered, "Archie—Mr. Webster—got drunk. We had to—to put him in the locked ward, because he became violently quarrelsome."

"Hmm. . . . So he'd slipped out to do a little intensive drinking with his friend, I suppose?"

"He couldn't have got the whisky any other way," Miss Caplan assured him defiantly. "1 think that fat man was just a bootlegger—"

"When, exactly, was Webster's condition discovered?" Dundee interrupted.

"When the movies were over and the patients and their visitors were leaving the shop," Miss Caplan told him.

"Archie came lurching into the hall from the front porch, and tried to pick a quarrel with Mr. Rowan. Archie is usually the sweetest tempered person in the world, but when he's drinking. . . . Well, he said Mr. Rowan had insulted him yesterday by not speaking to him, and that he could whip ten Rowans with his hands tied behind him. I thought," she added, "that it was too bad he had to pick on Mr. Rowan, because it was the first time the poor man had ever attended one of our movie shows, and I did want him to keep on being happy—"

"What happened?"

"Mr. Rowan simply knocked Archie down with one blow and walked out," the nurse said, with a trace of pride. "Mr. Whalen had just come to 'clock in,' since it was ten o'clock, and he helped two of the attendants to carry Archie off to 'Ten.' Dr. Harlow heard the racket and came down from her apartment upstairs, and she and I went over to 'Ten' with Archie."

"And the fat man?"

"I didn't see him, and Mr. Whalen couldn't find him anywhere on the grounds."

"You observed the patient closely, of course, Dr. Harlow?" Dundee turned deferentially to the little doctor.

"Naturally, but his condition was obvious. He was quite drunk. I administered a sedative, which took effect very rapidly."

"Then he's asleep now, I suppose," Dundee commented regretfully. "No chance to question him before morning?"

"It would be very unwise, and, in my opinion, quite useless to arouse him," Dr. Harlow answered emphatically. "Archie will keep. Besides being in the locked ward, he will be watched every minute by 'Happy' Day, the attendant you saw arrive this evening."

"What is Webster's trouble?"

"Periodic drunkenness. But he is not, medically speaking, a true alcoholic," Dr. Harlow told him. "He's a very rich and idle young man, given to excesses of many sorts, I am afraid. His father persuades him to enter Mayfield voluntarily for hydrotherapy and enforced abstinence. That is all the treatment he needs."

"Too bad the abstinence wasn't enforced this time," Strawn commented sourly.

"It is," the little doctor agreed sturdily. "But it is not entirely our fault. We have told his father that it is unwise for Archie to have visitors, but his father argues that only by dealing very tactfully with the boy and permitting him a degree of liberty here, can he induce him to come for treatment. But I made Mr. Webster agree to his having an attendant if Archie again succeeded in getting liquor while in our charge. He likes Happy—everyone does; so I don't anticipate any trouble on that score."

"Let's return to Miss Rambler for a moment," Dundee suggested. "You may go back to your work, Miss Caplan, and thank you very much. . . . Now, Dr. Harlow, will you tell me frankly what Dr. Koenig thought of Miss Rambler's case?"

The doctor hesitated, then apparently decided to waive professional ethics. "Dr. Koenig was of the opinion that, for some unknown reason, Enid was malingering—that is, faking symptoms and exaggerating her probably natural tendency to hysteria."

"Did he say why he thought so?"

"He—thought she was having so good a time here that she didn't want to leave. I granted that she was extremely popular with our men patients, but I pointed out that so pretty and charming a girl and one who was apparently a rich orphan would be popular anywhere, if it were not for her fear of strangers."

"Then her fear of strangers does not extend to new patients?"

"We—ell, yes," the girl hesitated. "When she first came we could not induce her to leave her suite—the largest in the sanitarium, by the way. But she still avoids new patients, does not make friends until they have taken her unawares and—shown themselves friendly. As I said, she is extremely popular, especially with the men. I am afraid most of our women patients are a little jealous of her beauty and her very smart clothes, but all the nurses and attendants are devoted to her."

"But Dr. Koenig considered her a disturbing influence?" Dundee guessed.

"Yes, for both reasons. I may as well be frank. There have been two or three fights—nothing really serious, of course—among the men who are infatuated with her. And one of the women patients—a former trained nurse who has been a sort of pensioner of Dr. Koenig's since she be came paretic about a year ago—had to be put temporarily in 'Ten' for tearing to pieces three or four of Enid's prettiest dresses."

"But you are still of the opinion that Miss Rambler is definitely ill?" Dundee asked.

"Yes, I am, and I feel sure Dr. Koenig would have agreed with me if he had had more opportunity to observe her," the young doctor answered stoutly. "When I failed to get at the source of her complexes, I suggested to Dr. Koenig that he try to get her consent to psychoanalysis."

"And did he talk with Miss Rambler after you made that suggestion?"

"Not to my knowledge."

"Did Miss Rambler appeal to either of you two doctors for a sedative this evening?"

It was Dr. Cantrell who answered first. "Not to me. I was at home all evening, but was not called and received no visitors."

"I was out from immediately after eight until five minutes to ten," Dr. Harlow told him.

"Alone?" Strawn shot at her.

"Yes!" the girl answered, the gray green eyes flashing angrily. "I was out in my car, taking a long drive for relaxation and fresh air."

"*Worried* about something, and wanted to get off to yourself?" Strawn insinuated.

"Not at all!" the girl flashed. "I am in the habit of taking a drive whenever I have the opportunity, that is, when Dr. Koenig is—was—on hand to take care of any emergency that might arise. It is a confining life."

"Perhaps that is another reason why he planned to take on an additional assistant," Dundee suggested tactfully.

"I tell you Koenig said he was going to *replace* the girl," Baldwin, who had been silent for a long time, burst out.

"Did he give you any reason for his decision to dismiss Dr. Harlow?"

"Yes. He said Justine was too credulous, an impractical idealist, and inclined to let her heart run away with her head," the business manager answered without hesitation. "Then of course there was the question of expense. We didn't feel that we could afford two assistant psychiatrists just yet, and Koenig said a man would be required to handle the batch of new patients we'll be getting. The Meridian Sanitarium has been catering largely to alcoholics and drug addicts, and a doctor who has specialized in those fields as well as in general psychiatry will be badly needed. And I agreed that, what with the expense of new building and furnishing, we would not be in a position to afford two assistants for him, since Dr. Cantrell will also require an assistant in the medical department."

"It's you who are always harping on economy and cutting down expenses!" the girl cried indignantly. "Dr. Koenig never considered expense for a minute when the good of the patients was jeopardized. He had to fight you every inch of the way to put improvements through. . . . Look!" and she pointed a trembling forefinger at the dead doctor's desk calendar. "There's a notation—'inner spring mattresses.' He told me this very morning that, in spite of your opposition, he was going to replace every mattress in the sanitarium with the finest inner spring box mattresses."

"He said the same to me," Dr. Cantrell upheld her. "Baldwin was holding out for having the old mattresses renovated at a nominal cost."

Captain Strawn thrust both hands into his pockets and looked the business manager up and down with narrowed gray eyes.

"So you and Koenig had your *spats*, too, eh?"

"We had differences of opinion—yes!" Baldwin replied defiantly. "The business manager of any institution has a constant fight on his hands to keep down expenses. That's what business managers are for."

"Then I take it there wasn't much love lost between you and the doctor?" Strawn went on, rocking back and forth on his heels.

"That's a nasty crack, but I'll answer it frankly," Baldwin retorted, a glow of anger lighting up his usually cold, emotionless eyes. "I'm not a sentimentalist, like these two!" and he indicated Dr. Harlow and Dr. Cantrell with a contemptuous wave of his claw thin hand. "But I had the highest respect for Dr. Koenig—as a psychiatrist. He made this sanitarium! As its business manager I can tell you that in Dr. Koenig's death Mayfield has suffered the greatest calamity that could happen to it. And as Mayfield's *business manager*, I mourn Dr. Koenig's death with all my heart. But I couldn't be truthful and say that I have lost a bosom friend. We shared a cottage on the grounds and a manservant; we ate most of our meals together when the doctor wasn't away on a lecture trip—every trip being good business, I assure you!—and spent a good many hours in each other's company, in the way of business. But we were not congenial. Now—take that and make the most of it!"

In spite of his instinctive dislike of the man, of his cold bloodedness and obvious mercenariness, Dundee could not help admiring the business manager's fearless frankness. Certainly this man, together with Dr. Cantrell, had every thing to lose and apparently nothing to gain by Dr. Carl Koenig's death.

"And have you any plans for replacing the man who 'made Mayfield'?" Strawn asked, his voice still edged with sarcasm. "Somebody who'll be a little easier for the business office to handle?"

"That question is in pretty bad taste, Captain Strawn," Dr. Cantrell interjected quietly. "For two reasons. First: Dr. Koenig is so recently dead and so tragically dead that none of us has given any thought to his possible successor. Second: the implied insinuation against Mr. Baldwin is unwarranted. It is my experience that an institution's business manager is usually not very popular with the doctors, who are nearly always impractical outside their own particular field. Mr. Baldwin is no exception, but both Dr. Harlow and I can tell you that, in the last analysis, he has the good of Mayfield at heart as much as any of us. ... Isn't that correct, Justine?"

Dundee was sure the "Yes" cost the girl doctor a real effort.

"Thanks!" Baldwin said gruffly, then cleared his throat before going on: "As for a successor to Dr. Koenig, that's entirely out of my line. My only concern is that we get a man of whom Koenig himself would have approved."

"Meaning this Dr. Sandlin, eh?" Strawn caught him up. "Friend of yours, eh?"

"I've never met the man in my life," Baldwin denied scornfully. "Everything in the world that I know of him is what Dr. Koenig told me—and that was precious little. I gathered that Dr. Koenig had a talk with him while he was on this last trip, though I don't even know where Sandlin is located."

"I do," Dr. Harlow said very quietly, but with an almost fanatic light in her eyes. "He's on the staff of a private sanitarium near Chicago. And Dr. Koenig lectured on mental hygiene at the Medical College of Northwestern University while he was on this trip. Doubtless he interviewed Dr. Sandlin when he was in Chicago, and I, for one—if I really have any right to do so—will cast my vote for him. Dr. Koenig's wishes have been and always will be sacred to me!"

"Same here!" Dr. Cantrell said emphatically if inelegantly.

"No use being hasty," Baldwin reminded his two associates. "Dr. Koenig undoubtedly thought this Sandlin would fill the bill of assistant, but as far as being head psychiatrist here is concerned "

"At least, he shall be on the staff," Justine Harlow interrupted stubbornly. "He can—have—my place," she added haltingly, her voice choking. "For if Dr. Koenig really didn't want me to stay, that wish of his is sacred to me, too."

Dr. Cantrell shot a venomous look at Baldwin, as he reached for the girl's small, firm hand and gripped it hard. "I don't believe Carl had the least idea of dismissing you, Justine. Any such idea, I am sure, originated with Mr. Baldwin, as an economy move "

"Are you intimating that I lied, Bruce?" Baldwin interrupted furiously.

"Not at all," Dr. Cantrell assured him coldly. "I merely mink it quite possible that you misunderstood Dr. Koenig."

"It occurs to me," Dundee interrupted what promised to be a quarrel, "that if Dr. Koenig seriously considered dismissing Dr. Harlow, he would first take steps to change his will. Does anyone know Attorney Forrest's telephone number?"

"He is my attorney also," Cantrell told him. "The office number is Main 0300, the residence number Mirror 3421. But it is after midnight now "

"Sorry!" Dundee smiled, and reached for the telephone on the dead man's typewriter table. As he dialed the second number, he kept his eyes on the three most concerned, but observed no expression more incriminating than tense expectancy.

"Hello! I'm sorry to be calling so late, but it is quite important. May I speak with Mr. Forrest, please?" He listened for a moment, disappointment clouding his blue eyes. Then: "I wonder if you could tell me, Mrs. Forrest, whether Dr. Carl Koenig tried to reach his attorney this evening? . . . He *did?* Then did he tell you the nature of the business on which he wished to consult your husband? This is Dundee, of the District Attorney's office. . . . No? ... Oh! I see! . . . Thank you very much, Mrs. Forrest."

He replaced the hand telephone slowly. "I didn't want to spoil her sleep by telling her the news. . . . Mrs. Forrest told me, Captain, that Dr. Koenig telephoned about half past nine this evening, asking for Forrest, who is out of town. Mrs. Forrest told him the lawyer would be back in the morning, and hoped there was nothing urgent that could not wait until then."

"Well?" Strawn prodded, as the young detective paused, frowning.

"Dr. Koenig replied that the matter *was* urgent, and that *he would attend to it himself tonight.'"*

"Well! Well! Well!" and Strawn rocked back and forth on his heels. "Three guesses, my lad, as to what the doctor was writing on that sheet that was torn out of his typewriter! Wants a lawyer quick. Can't wait till morning——"

"I'm afraid you're jumping pretty high to reach that conclusion, Captain," Dundee warned, averting his eyes from the girl doctor's blanching cheeks.

"High, nothing! The Big Doctor tells Baldwin here that he's going to replace the lady doctor. She's down in his will for one half his estate. Believe me, boy, whatever it was that made Koenig determine to get rid of the girl—and I'm sorry to be as blunt as this, little lady!—was serious enough to make him determined to draw up a new will without even waiting until morning! . . . And even then he wasn't quick enough!"

"I—Oh, Bruce!" It was not a dignified doctor, but a desolate girl who clung, shuddering, to the only friend she had in the room.

Cantrell hugged the girl close for a moment, then strode swiftly toward Strawn, his black eyes blazing, his right hand knotted into a powerful fist.

"Just a minute, Doctor!" Dundee commanded, stepping between the two. "I agree with you that Captain Strawn is a bit hasty. It is pure supposition that Koenig wanted to see his lawyer about changing his will, and even if that was his intention, we must not overlook the f act that the will names *two* beneficiaries."

"Norah Lacey is just as much above suspicion as Dr. Harlow is!" Cantrell assured him savagely. "Oh, I can see what you're getting at, all right! Anyone unlucky enough to be named in a murdered man's will is bound to have the police yelling 'Motive!' at him—or her. But it's a damned outrage that the two finest women I've ever known—barring my wife, of course," he amended tardily, "should have to submit to being suspected of killing the greatest man that ever lived!"

To Dundee's amazement, the business manager joined his partner in defending the weeping little doctor.

"I'm no sentimentalist—far from it!" Baldwin began grimly, "but I'm a just man. And I'll frankly confess that, if I'd known the line you were going to take, Captain Strawn, I'd have bitten out my tongue before I should have said what I did of Koenig's intention to replace Dr. Harlow. And don't forget that I'm as anxious as you are—far more so!—to have this nasty business cleaned up. But I repeat I'm just a man. And I can't stand by without a word and hear you try to pin the job on this girl. Carl Koenig was God to her. A blind man or a fool could have seen that she worshiped the ground he walked on. . . . *Kill* him? Not if he'd been a billionaire and had left her every dime of his fortune! *Kill* him because they'd had a disagreement? Bosh! The girl would have let him shave her head, clip her ears and cut off her nose, if he'd wanted to! *Kill* him because he intended to replace her? Bosh, again! If he had told her it was to his best interest to have a man assistant, she'd have kissed his feet when she told him good bye! . . . And what's more, literally the same applies to Norah Lacey! Sentimental fools, but —there you are!"

"You're pretty eloquent, Mr. Baldwin," Dundee commented drily.

"I'm merely being just. And not wholly disinterested either," the business manager retorted savagely. "I have Mayfield's welfare at heart. It's my job to safeguard that welfare. And God knows we're in for enough scandal through the very fact that a murder has been committed here, without it's being broadcast that one of the staff is under suspicion of having killed the Big Doctor."

"Spoken from the heart," Dundee murmured. "At least, Baldwin, you make no bones about being mercenary. It's quite refreshing to find a man so free from hypocrisy."

"Your opinion of me does not interest me in the slight est," Baldwin told him sourly. "Just stick to your job. Find the murderer with the least possible delay, keep your 'theories' out of the papers, and above all, don't waste time barking up the wrong tree."

"Now that we've got our orders, Captain Strawn," Dundee said wryly, "don't you think we'd better see Miss Lacey?"

"Collins!" Strawn bawled, and a plainclothesman almost instantly opened the door between the office and the reception room. "Come on in and shut the door. . . . Now, anything to report?"

"Yes, sir. Pretty soon after you come in here, a nurse by the name of Hunter come and told Miss Lacey that a patient named Rambler was in a pretty bad state, and Miss Lacey beat it with her over to a cottage they call Sunflower Court. I trailed along and waited outside the patient's door. She was taking on something terrible, but this Lacey dame quieted her down. Come out and fixed a shot in the arm for her, and then set with her till she was asleep. Then we come back over here, and that's all."

"All right! Send Miss Lacey in, Collins," Strawn ordered.

The tip of the nurse's little Irish nose was scarlet, and dark circles emphasized the grief in her tear reddened eyes. Her white cap with its black ribbon band sat askew on her gray threaded black curls, a fact of which she was as desolately unconscious as she was of the streaks which tears had left on her freckled cheeks.

She must have been thirty five years old, but she looked curiously like an inconsolable child as she hesitated just inside the door, little hiccoughy sobs breaking up her words:

"You—wanted—to see me?"

Because she had looked straight into his eyes, Dundee took upon himself the duty of questioning her.

"I believe it was you who discovered what had happened here this evening, Miss Lacey," he began very gently. "Will you tell us about it?"

"At ten twenty I went up to my apartment on the second floor to change into my uniform. I always relieve Miss Caplan while she's at supper, if I'm in. She has supper between half past ten and eleven "

"Hold on a minute, sister!" Strawn interrupted rudely. "You say you went upstairs at twenty past ten. Where were you before that time?"

"I was—out," the nurse answered defiantly.

"Out where?" Strawn demanded. "And who were you with?"

"I was alone. I—I went to a movie."

"Yeah? What movie did you see, sister?"

The nurse's eyes widened as she stared at him, then the tear reddened lids hid them for a moment before she answered:

"I went to the Symphony. I saw 'His Wife's Lover.' "

"Just a minute, Captain," Dundee interrupted Strawn's next question.

And very slowly, his eyes on the nurse's paling face, he drew a folded theater program from his inside breast pocket.

CHAPTER SEVEN

"I THINK, Captain Strawn," Dundee said quietly, "that Miss Lacey would like to revise her story as to where she spent the evening. Am I not right, Miss Lacey?"

"No!" the nurse answered dully. "I went to the Symphony. I saw 'His Wife's Lover.' I can tell you everyone that's in it and the story, too, if you don't believe me."

"I'm quite sure you saw the picture, Miss Lacey, but that you did not see it this evening," Dundee contradicted more sternly. "You see, it happens that the Symphony changed its schedule only last Saturday. That is, the programs are changed now on Saturday and Wednesday, instead of Sunday and Thursday. I, too, saw 'His Wife's Lover'—a very poor picture, by the way, one whose story I really couldn't bear to hear again. But because the feature which began its run *today* is one that I'd hate to miss I kept the program with its announcement of future attractions. Would you like to see it, Miss Lacey?"

"No!" The woman repudiated the proffered sheet with a violent gesture.

"But I'm afraid it will be necessary for you to answer Captain Strawn's question as to where you did spend the evening, Miss Lacey. Naturally, if such an answer would tend to—incriminate—"

"Incriminate? *Me?*" The nurse's voice shrilled. "Dr. Koenig was the best friend I ever had, the finest man that ever lived! I'd have *died* for him, and then—you *dare* insinuate that *I*— "

"Please, Miss Lacey! It's your own refusal to tell the truth that is involving you," Dundee assured her curtly.

"All right! I'll tell," the nurse capitulated wearily. "I was lying. I saw that picture Sunday night. I spent this evening with friends. I didn't want to drag them into this–“

"Your friends' names?" Dundee prodded.

Norah Lacey cast a despairing glance at Justine Harlow, then flung up her head defiantly. "I spent the evening, from eight o'clock until ten, with Mrs. Satterlee and her daughter, Mabel."

"Surely that's an innocent diversion," Dundee commented drily. "Their address and—telephone number?"

"They live on Vine Street in Hamilton—5540 Vine Street," the nurse told him reluctantly.

"And the telephone number?" Dundee insisted.

"Can't you take my word for it that I was there?" Norah Lacey protested, almost wailing. "The number is Lakewood 0341, but—" and she sprang forward as if to prevent Dundee by force from using the telephone which he had picked up. "*Please* don't call them now. It's so late. You might wake up the " She gasped, then completed her sentence: "—the old lady."

With his eyes steadily upon her, the young detective called the number. To his surprise the call was completed almost immediately. A girl's voice, which, as the conversation continued, betrayed its owner's Southern origin, drawled "Hel—lo—o—o!"

"I'm speaking from Mayfield Sanitarium, Miss Satterlee. Will you please tell me whether Miss Norah Lacey was there this evening?"

"Oooh!" the soft voice cooed consternation. "Hasn't she got home yet? She left here simply ages ago."

"Can you tell me just when she did leave?" Dundee asked.

"Why, yes, sir." The drawl was becoming anxious. "It was exactly ten o'clock. Miss Lacey said she'd have to be back at the sanitarium in time to change into her uniform before half past ten. She always leaves exactly at ten. I simply can't imagine "

"Don't be alarmed, Miss Satterlee," Dundee interrupted soothingly.

"But I'm simply scared to death," the soft voice mourned. "Won't you please tell her to call up Mabel the very minute she gets back?"

Having given the promise, Dundee said good night, with apologies, and rather thoughtfully relayed the conversation to Strawn.

The Chief of the Homicide Squad was at heart a kindly man. "Looks all right for you, sister," he told the nurse grudgingly, "but I can't see what you made such a to do about. Better call up your friend in a minute or two. . . . Now get along with your story."

Relief made the woman's face almost radiant. "I'm sorry, but I didn't want my friends to be bothered. . . . Well, I changed into my uniform and came downstairs. It lacked about five minutes of half past ten, and I thought I'd get a book out of Dr. Koenig's office. Doctor had shown me a new textbook on psychiatry which the author had autographed and sent to him, and I thought I'd read while I was relieving Miss Caplan, though it wasn't likely that I'd not be interrupted. The patients are apt to be restless after the movies, and I'd been told the pictures lasted late—till ten o'clock—and nine is bedtime here. . . . Well, anyway " and she raised one of her clenched fists to press the knuckles against her trembling lips, "I tried the door that opens into the main hall, and I found it locked, of course, but I didn't know what to think when my key wouldn't work."

"Then you have a key to Dr. Koenig's office?" Strawn cut in.

"Certainly," the nurse answered with a flash of resentment. "So has Miss Caplan, and Miss Home, Doctor's secretary, has one, too, of course. Well, I thought maybe Doctor had turned the bolt on the door—it has a Yale lock—and had forgot about it, so I went through the door that leads from the main hall into the reception room—"

"That door was not locked?" Dundee interrupted.

"No, because patients are brought in at all hours, and that room is kept ready to receive them. I tried the door into this office, and it was locked, as I expected, but my key worked, and I entered. There's a light switch just inside the door "

"Then there was no light on in here when you entered?"

"No, of course not. If there had been, I should have seen it from the transom outside in the hall, and I'd have knocked, supposing Dr. Koenig was still working. I pushed the switch button, and—and I saw him—sitting there " Norah Lacey covered her face with her shaking hands.

"I know it's hard, Miss Lacey," Dundee sympathized. "Did you touch the—touch him?"

"I—no, I could see he—was His head— "

"Just what did you do?"

"I—ran," the nurse confessed miserably. "I ran and unbolted the door and ran on into the chartroom. Miss Caplan, knowing I was ready to relieve her, had gone on to her supper, and I Well, finally I managed to call Dr. Cantrell on the telephone. Then I ran upstairs and told Dr. Harlow. She was just getting into bed, and while she was dressing I ran back downstairs and waited for Dr. Cantrell in the reception room. When I heard him come into Dr. Koenig's office—"

"You came in through your own office, I suppose, Doctor?" Dundee turned to Cantrell.

"Of course! It's the shortest route, and the one I always use. I unlocked the outside door of my office, and found the door between the two offices ajar, just as I had left it shortly after seven o'clock."

"Thank you. . . . Now, Miss Lacey, was this office left exactly as you found it?"

"It was. Except that I unbolted the door into the hall, just as I told you."

"Dr. Cantrell?"

"I disturbed nothing. I even took care not to shift the body in the slightest when I took the temperature, in an effort to decide how long Dr. Koenig had been dead."

"But you used the telephone later to call the district attorney?"

"No. Not the instrument in this office. I used the phone in the chartroom."

"By the way, are your telephones on a switchboard?" Dundee asked.

"No," Cantrell answered. "We have three outside lines. This telephone is on one of them. This instrument and the one on my desk are extensions from the telephone in the reception room. During the day, Miss Home, the secretary, answers the telephone, and notifies either myself or Dr. Koenig of a call by pushing the correct button on her desk. Mr. Baldwin has another of the outside lines, with an extension on his secretary bookkeeper's desk. The third line, which is listed as 'Mayfield Sanitarium (Information),' is in the chartroom. In addition we have an intercommunicating telephone system between all of the cottages, the chartroom, my home, the head nurses' apartment on the second floor, and Dr. Harlow's apartment on the same floor."

"I see," Dundee commented, cocking an amused eye brow at Strawn's impatience. "Where were you when the crime was discovered, Mr. Baldwin?"

"In the cottage I share—did share, rather," the business manager amended without emotion, "with Dr. Koenig. Bruce—Dr. Cantrell—called me on the intercommunicating telephone at ten thirty five. I had not gone to bed, so I came right over. We talked things over a bit, had Whalen in to see if he could tell us anything, then I suggested that we call the district attorney, rather than the police. Dr. Cantrell agreed, and called Sanderson himself."

"And how did you spend the evening, Mr. Baldwin?" Dundee asked.

"Working," Baldwin told him curtly. "Went back to my office directly after dinner. Carl—Dr. Koenig—and I left the dining room together, and parted just outside his door in the main hall. I had some estimates on the new two story building which will be required to house the new patients, and I wanted to go over them in detail. Also, since it's just after the first of the month, I had a flock of sanitarium bills that required my O. K. before the bookkeeper could pay them."

"How late did you work?" Dundee persisted.

"I can't say to the minute," the business manager answered, frowning, "but it must have been about half past nine. My office opens into the main hall just to the left of the staircase, and I pass this door on my way out. It was ajar."

"Did you see Dr. Koenig?" Dundee asked.

"I did. But he did not see me. He was typing, so his back was turned to the door. There was no reason why I should interrupt him, so I passed on through the hall and went straight to our cottage."

"Did you see anyone at all, except Dr. Koenig, in this building?"

"No one at all," Baldwin answered emphatically. "I remember glancing into the patients' living room across the hall, as I passed, but it appeared to be deserted. Naturally I did not give it more than a passing glance."

"And on your way to your cottage?"

"No one at all," came the unequivocal answer. "I still had my mind on the plans for the new building, and I don't remember looking about at all as I walked."

Dundee lapsed into a thoughtful silence, and it was Strawn who took up the burden of the investigation.

"We can take it for granted that the doctor was alive at half past nine or thereabout. Now, speak up! Anybody see him alive after that time?"

There was a throbbing silence.

"How about you, little doctor?" the Chief of the Homicide Squad demanded, pointing a finger at Justine Harlow. "You got home at five minutes to ten, you say, and you must have passed through the main hall. Was the doctor's door open then?"

"No. And there was no light showing through the transom. I was a little surprised, since Dr. Koenig had said he would work until I returned," Dr. Harlow answered.

"But you made no inquiries as to when the doctor had left?" Strawn demanded, accusingly.

The girl flushed, but she answered steadily: "No. I knew he was tired, and I concluded that he had gone to bed. Since he lived on the grounds, he would have been accessible in case of emergency. Shortly after I got in, Miss Caplan called me to help her handle Archie Webster, but there was no reason at all to call Dr. Koenig."

"What about you, Cantrell?" Strawn leveled his forefinger at the medical man.

"I did not see or communicate with Dr. Koenig after about seven fifteen, when I finished sewing up Chester's slashed arm," Cantrell answered positively. "Carl—Dr. Koenig—looked on as I worked, and gave young Chester a good tongue lashing for the trouble he had caused. When I had finished with the boy—"

"Bawled him out, did he?" Strawn pounced. "Kinda funny way for a brain doctor to treat a patient, ain't it?"

"Not at all!" Justine Harlow took up the cudgels spiritedly. "It's exactly the right way to treat a patient like Luke Chester. He hasn't the slightest intention of committing suicide, but because his father has forbidden his marriage with a middle aged adventuress, he has been punishing his family and indulging his own love of excitement and the limelight by very half hearted suicide attempts. His father got tired of the excitement and put him in here. There's nothing actually wrong with the boy mentally, except a perverted desire for sympathy and excitement."

"Not at all!" Dr. Harlow retorted. "He was devoted to Dr. Koenig, as are all our patients. In fact, he was pleased that Dr. Koenig should take time to give him a good, stiff lecture. He voluntarily promised to ask to be put into 'Ten,' the locked ward, the next time the urge came on him to 'commit suicide.' And of course," she smiled, for the first time that evening, "he'll enjoy himself immensely when he does go into 'Ten.' A new and different way of getting into the limelight."

"But the boy got good and sore at the doctor, eh?" Strawn guessed.

"Each to his own fancy!" Strawn growled. "Now, Cantrell! You say you didn't see or communicate with Dr. Koenig after seven fifteen. Where were you from that time on?"

"At home, subject to call. No call came."

"Anyone to back up that alibi?" Strawn demanded crudely.

"Alibi?" Cantrell repeated angrily. "Don't you think, sir, that the use of that word is a little premature?"

"I take it, then, that you are going to say you were alone," Strawn caught him up shrewdly.

"As a matter of fact, I *was* alone after eight o'clock," Cantrell answered, with an obvious effort to control his anger. "That is, I was alone in the living room of my house, my wife having gone to bed very shortly after dinner, with one of her severe neuralgic headaches. Naturally she can not support my 'alibi,' as you call it, since our bedroom is so far separated from the living room that I could have left the house and returned half a dozen times without her hearing me."

"Have you told her the news of the murder?"

"I looked in on her when I left, and found she was asleep. I did not wake her."

'"Then we'd better get hold of her right now, don't you think, Bonnie?" and Strawn turned to the younger detective.

Dundee glanced at the medical man's flushed cheeks and blazing eyes. "Hardly necessary, is it, Chief?" he answered lazily. "The doctor has already admitted that his wife cannot corroborate his story of not having left the house, and if Mrs. Cantrell is ill, it seems rather a shame to disturb her. . . . Your wife was formerly a patient of Dr. Koenig's, I believe?"

"She was," Cantrell answered, more pleasantly. "Not a 'mental' case in the usual sense of the word, Claire was a neurasthenic. Dr. Koenig psychoanalyzed her and she has been a very normal and happy girl ever since."

"You don't say!" Strawn commented. "By the way, Doc, how old are you?"

Again the doctor's eyes blazed wrath, but he answered with savage brevity: "Forty nine!"

"And how old is that pretty little wife of yours?" Strawn grinned.

"Look here!" The doctor almost choked with anger. "I don't know why you're wasting time on damn fool questions My wife is twenty four years old, if that fact concerns you in the least!"

Strawn's advice to the medical man that he keep a civil tongue in his head was interrupted by the appearance of Detective Harmon from the reception room, his heavy face red and damp with perspiration.

"I can't hold off them newspaper boys much longer, Chief!" he protested apologetically. "They're threatenin' to bust down this door if you don't give 'em a story within five minutes, so's they can catch their home edition deadlines."

"Tell 'em to go to hell!" Strawn growled. "I ain't running the Homicide Bureau on newspaper deadlines... . You want to see 'em, Bonnie?"

"No, Captain," Dundee smiled, for he well knew his old chief's love of publicity. "I'm not in the picture officially—at least not yet. Keep my name out of it, will you?"

"Blamed if I know what to tell the boys," Strawn worried, scratching his thick gray hair.

"Personally, I don't think it would be wise to let them see this room," Dundee suggested tactfully. "I think we are agreed that this is merely a well set stage—just a little too well set; but I believe the less said about it in the papers, the better. No use tipping off the murderer that he overplayed his hand."

"How's this, lad?" Strawn was still thoughtfully scratching his scalp. "Owing to the fact that they was a lot of visitors here tonight, on account of the movies, the police have a theory that the murderer sneaked in unnoticed, and killed the doctor to even up some old score. I can hint that we're on the track of the relative of some killer that the doctor, as an alienist in court, helped to hang by testifying he wasn't insane. It's a cinch Koenig made a slew of enemies that way, first and last."

"A good idea!" Dundee applauded sincerely, and Dr. Harlow gave a quick, tremulous sigh of relief.

As Detective Harmon returned to the impatient reporters, Strawn rocked back and forth on his heels, his chest expanded with satisfaction in his own cleverness and Dundee's appreciation of it. "Now, folks," he began pompously, "what I've just said brings up a mighty important question, and I want all of you to think seriously and answer truthfully: did Dr. Koenig have any enemies that any of you know about?"

After a suitably long and solemn pause Dr. Harlow spoke up, her lovely voice very earnest and reasonable: "You yourself, Captain Strawn, have hit upon one class of enemies that any alienist is sure to have. Dr. Koenig was famous as an expert witness on legal insanity, and he has taken the stand in almost every state in the Union. Whether he testified for the prosecution or for the defense, almost every important trial brought its aftermath of death threats for the doctor. Sometimes the relatives of a murderer's victim threatened his life, because he helped to send the murderer to an insane asylum instead of to the death house. More often, of course, the relatives of criminals who received long term sentences or the death penalty swore to be avenged."

"Did the doctor keep those letters?" Dundee asked.

"Not one of them. Nor did he bother to turn them over to the police. He did not have an atom of fear in his make up," the little doctor answered emphatically.

"Any other enemies?" Strawn prodded.

"As an alienist in court and as a member of the lunacy commission," Dr. Harlow answered, "Dr. Koenig some times balked a well planned conspiracy on the part of scheming relatives to have a rich member of the family 'put away,' in order to get control of his or her property. And I should also explain that every patient, at a certain stage in the treatment, hates his psychiatrist, because the doctor forces him to face some bitter truth about himself. But once that truth is faced and understood, and mental healing has begun, it is just as natural to love the psychiatrist with a deep devotion."

"So you admit that a patient could have been at the hating stage in the treatment, and hated the doctor enough to kill him?" Strawn bore down on her.

"I admit the possibility—yes!" the young doctor said quietly. "But I cannot reconcile the scheming and planning *after* the murder with the impulsive act of an enraged patient."

"How about this chap Rowan?" Strawn suggested. "By all accounts, he was the last patient to have an interview with the doctor, and according to Miss Caplan he has a violent temper—took a sock at Webster and knocked him flat."

"Samuel Rowan did have a three hour interview with Dr. Koenig this afternoon," Dr. Harlow admitted. "But when he left this office he was a changed man—relieved, buoyant, sociable, in contrast to two years of almost total silence. Dr. Koenig was jubilant, as Mr. Baldwin has told you. And Rowan was so much a new man that he attended the picture show for the first time since he's been here, and chatted and laughed with the other patients almost as normally as if he'd never been ill. Of course he was, and will be for a time, in a state technically called 'elation'— the pendulum having swung from extreme depression to extreme well being, based on relief. When he is really completely normal again he will be neither depressed nor elated. But I can assure you, from all my past experience, that Samuel Rowan was worshiping Dr. Koenig as his savior this evening."

"Just the same, I'd like to have a little powwow with Mr. Samuel Rowan!" Strawn interrupted her eloquence belligerently. "This is the way I look at it, Bonnie! Here's a bird that's had something pretty fierce on his chest for two years. He spills it to the Big Doctor. Sure he's relieved! Every crook is, when he confesses! Haven't I seen a Bluebeard dance a jig and sing a jazz song, after I'd third degreed him into telling where he'd buried the bodies of his four missing wives? . . . Well, this Rowan, chap feels swell until he sees that movie, 'Manslaughter,' where the girl gets sent to the 'pen.' And he don't feel so good. He gets to worrying, see? That damned doctor knows too much! And Rowan wonders how the hell he happened to go so cuckoo as to spill the beans. Why, the doc can notify the police and it'll be the 'pen' for Sammy Rowan! What does he do? He slips out of the dark shop, and into the doc's office. And the first thing he sees is his case history lying on the doc's desk, and the doc typing it all out—what he'd told him, and what's enough to send him up maybe for the rest of his life. Get it? He don't stop to reason that the doc can't squeal on him, on account of professional ethics. He ain't taking no chances! He kills the doctor, and tears up his case history. But this bird ain't crazy, and he knows he can't get away with it on no insanity plea. So he fixes things up to look like one of the nuts did it, and then strolls away and into the shop again by the back door. . . . Get it, boy?"

Dundee nodded slowly. It really was amazingly convincing. And he had no better theory of his own to offer. None half so good, if he would admit the truth. But still

"Why, boy, it's air tight!" Strawn jubilated. "Mr. Baldwin here has already told us what the doc said to him *after Rowan bad had his powwow!* Just what was the words the doc used, sir?"

Baldwin, answered reluctantly: "Dr. Koenig remarked that, if a psychiatrist chose to, he could give the police plenty to keep them busy. But he did not mention Rowan by name. I admit that your theory sounds very plausible, Captain, but I feel absolutely sure that you are making a mistake—"

"So do I, Roger!" Justine Harlow cut in, her lovely voice warm and rich with gratitude.

The business manager flushed with pleasure at the girl's first use that evening—and Dundee suspected it was the very first—of his Christian name.

"I'm beginning to think," Strawn began savagely, "that nobody around here wants the doctor's murder cleared up! But the police do! And I'll thank you to send for this Rowan bird without any more shillyshallying!"

Dr. Harlow's small face flamed with anger, but her voice was steady with professional dignity and authority:

"I am sorry to have to refuse that request, Captain Strawn! Unless you show me a warrant for Samuel Rowan's arrest you cannot see him tonight!"

CHAPTER EIGHT

DUNDEE grinned his delight in the little doctor's spunk, but Captain Strawn glared at her as if he would love to spank her.

Dr. Harlow continued implacably: "Mr. Rowan has gone through the most exciting day of his life, and to haul him out of his sleep now to question him ruthlessly about a murder would work an injury to his precarious mental condition which I, as his doctor, cannot permit."

"I agree with Dr. Harlow, and stand back of her in that decision!" Bruce Cantrell stated uncompromisingly.

Before the outraged Chief of the Homicide Squad could spit out the words which were almost choking him, Dundee interposed: "Rowan will keep until morning, Chief. I am sure the doctors will see the advisability, however, of having a detective stationed outside his door—"

"Certainly!" Dr. Harlow agreed crisply.

"God! What a case!" Strawn exploded, and stamped out of the office into the reception room, where the reporters were almost ready to tear him limb from limb.

"We are all very tired, Mr. Dundee," Dr. Harlow reminded the detective who remained.

He regarded the little fighter with genuine compassion. She looked wizened and blanched with fatigue. And nervous reaction to the shock of the murder was showing itself now in half a dozen twitching muscles in face and hands. Tardily he remembered the other woman whom Dr. Koenig had left the richer in worldly goods by his tragic death.

Norah Lacey had long since sunk almost out of sight in a huge leather chair in the farthest corner of the room. A crooked arm shielded her face, but Dundee could see slow tears trickling down her wan, freckled cheeks, and dropping with tiny splashes upon the stiffness of her uniform. . . .

"I'm terribly sorry," he said gently, turning back to the girl doctor. "I am sure we shall all be the better for a few hours' rest. I don't believe there is much more that either Captain Strawn or I can do tonight. By the way, I understand that there is a vacant suite in Sunflower Court. If you will permit me "

"We shall be glad to have you as our guest," she assured him with something more than perfunctory polite ness, "for as long"—and she drew a sharp breath—"as it may seem necessary for you to remain on the ground. I'll telephone to Miss Hunter to make you comfortable. . . . Oh, Mr. Dundee! Please believe that we all want to help! You seem so—so understanding, so—kind! You must realize that we who are left must safeguard our patients as *he* would have wished us to—"

"I do understand," Dundee assured her humbly, for he could have knelt before her loyalty and courage. "I'll help you to the very best of my ability. . . . Now, if you will trust me here alone—" he suggested tactfully.

But before the two doctors, the nurse and the business manager had obeyed his suggestion, the girl psychiatrist had locked the precious case history file and had asked for and received from the detective the key to it which lay among the few possessions taken from the murdered man's pockets. Strawn might have considered his yielding a weakness, but Dundee had a profound respect for Justine Harlow's attitude toward the secrets that filing cabinet held. And he felt fairly sure that none of those secrets had any place in the mystery he was investigating.

"You will not try to piece together those tiny scraps of the destroyed case histories?" she had asked him anxiously. "I know they are "evidence," but—"

"I'm afraid that would take many days and a Job's patience," he reassured her, and a singularly sweet smile rewarded him.

When he was alone, awaiting Strawn, who was still busy with the newspaper men, Dundee poked tentatively at the great mound or scraps which Carraway, the fingerprint expert had examined and then left in a glass letter tray upon the dead man's desk.

A superhuman task, indeed, to paste these fragments into two complete case histories! But what a reward for patience it might be! What dark secret had clouded Samuel Rowan's mind and sealed his lips for two long years? If Rowan himself did not choose to tell—and why should he?—was that secret to be locked forever in the dead doctor's brain? And that other case history which the murderer had destroyed. Why had he chosen Archie Webster's record of drinking debauches and probably mild attacks of delirium tremens? Had he chosen hit or miss, as part of his scheme for making this murder look like the work of a demented patient, or had he, as Strawn believed, destroyed his own record, and that of another patient merely as camouflage?

Samuel Rowan. . . . Archibald Webster. . . . Both *current* patients, while the files were crowded with case histories of the dead or departed. And had chance or a diabolical schemer hit upon two patients who could not possibly furnish the police with an unassailable alibi? Had the murderer possibly seen Webster leave the O. T. Shop, just as Miss Caplan had seen him? *And who was Webster's visitor?* If Strawn was right in his theory, Rowan could have seen Webster and his friend leave; could have made use of that knowledge with the cold blooded intention of "framing" the young scapegrace for his crime. Certainly there had been bad blood between the two men. . . . But—and Dundee caught himself up short—if Rowan had actually sneaked out of the shop, committed murder, framed Webster, and crept back into the O. T. Shop while the movie was still on, would he have been so foolhardy as to make himself conspicuous and label him self violent, by knocking young Webster down? But might not a super clever man have done just that? How better to prove that he had stayed in the shop all evening and had left with the crowd, than to make a scene out of what might have passed unnoticed?

Dundee propped his elbows on the dead doctor's desk and rested his head upon his cupped hands, for he too was very tired. He had had a hard day. . . .

"Damn that blood smear!" he groaned, as his heavy eyes rested on the whitish spot on the comer of the desk.

How big had the smear been before Carraway had officiously dabbed at it with a wet towel end, to make sure that it *was* blood? And what the devil was blood doing there, anyway?

It simply did not fit into the picture. He closed his eyes and again visualized the murder drama. The doctor tapping away at the typewriter keys, not hearing the soft, stealthy footsteps, which came from the reception room, on through the open door and across the thick rug to the doctor's very chair.

But wait! If the doctor had been typing, he would have been sitting in such a position that, out of the corner of his eye at least, he would have caught sight of that stealthy, approaching figure. For the typewriter table was at right angles to the desk, which was set against the wall almost directly opposite the door into the reception room.

Dundee frowned. There were two alternatives, of course. Either the doctor was bent over work at his desk, with his back squarely to the door, and the entry had been so noiseless that he had not heard a sound, or he had been typing, and the sight of his visitor had not surprised or alarmed him. Someone he knew! Someone he was accustomed to seeing. Someone who was privileged to walk into that office unannounced! But any member of the staff or any patient in Mayfield could do that!

Dundee again concentrated on visualizing the murderer's movements. The doctor had not been alarmed; had continued with his typing, with perhaps a word to his caller. The murderer had strolled to the doctor's chair, and had glanced over those bowed shoulders at the sheet of paper in the machine. What had he read there? Somewhere in that mound of fine torn scraps was the answer— if Dundee was not guessing wildly. But if he was right, whatever the murderer had read had been so great a shock to his mind or so horrible a menace to his liberty that only by destruction of the writer as well as of the written words could the doctor's caller ever feel safe again. The doctor— Dundee let the imaginary film unwind rapidly—had gone on with his typing, unaware that his visitor had peeked. The murderer had withdrawn a few steps, involuntarily; had backed slowly away in horror, a terrible resolution already forming in his shocked brain. He had backed to the open door leading into the hall, had silently drawn it shut. And if the doctor had heard the click of the lock, he had undoubtedly surmised that his visitor desired privacy for his interview. Then the murderer's eyes had fallen on the heavy bronze statue atop the bookcase so near at hand, in the corner between the two doors. Without pausing for reflection, he had seized the statue, stepped swiftly and silently back to the doctor's chair, and had brought the thing crashing down on that bowed, intent head.

For only by that hypothesis could Dundee account for the bruise upon the murdered psychiatrist's chin. Certainly the blow struck in that way would force the head down so violently that the chin could be bruised upon the frame of the typewriter. And naturally it had been necessary to swing the swivel chair so that the head was no longer jammed against the typewriter, since the incriminating sheet of paper must be removed from the machine and destroyed. But Dundee could picture the Unknown recoiling from the machine, even as his fingers were reaching for the all important paper. Fingerprints!

The statue, which he had carefully and silently laid on the rug beside the swivel chair, could be wiped clean of betraying prints, but he must touch nothing else with uncovered fingers. Gloves! But it was summertime, and he had no gloves with him. But through the half open door into Dr. Cantrell's office he could see the white enamel instrument cabinet. Of course! Doctors always used rubber gloves in making examinations. And silently he had tiptoed into the medical man's office. There, as if Fate were on his side, he had found the soiled rubber gloves which the night nurse had left lying on top of the cabinet in the instrument tray.

No use picturing all that had followed. It was quite obvious how the murderer's mind had worked. This was primarily a sanitarium for the treatment of mental diseases. There, too, Fate had been working for him. What easier than to "wreck" the room, so that police and hospital authorities would jump to the conclusion that one of the psychopathic patients had gone berserk and had murdered in a homicidal rage?

But—how had blood come to be upon the corner of the doctor's desk? The head wound had bled but little, most of the blood matting in the hair and the rest trickling down the neck to disappear beneath the collar. And the blood that had slowly oozed from the right ear had soaked into the blotter. Dundee swung himself in the swivel chair until he faced the typewriter, bent his head until it touched the machine, then raising his head only slightly, he swung the chair until his forehead came to a rest upon the desk. No! The blood *could not* have been flung to the corner of the desk in that way! But how—*how?*

Temporarily abandoning that poser, the detective asked himself *who* the murderer could be. If his reconstruction of the crime was even approximately the truth, Dundee knew certain things about him.

First: the murderer was someone who was privileged to enter that office unceremoniously.

Second: the murderer was probably someone who was occupying the doctor's attention at the very moment he had entered the office. Now, what had the doctor been typing? One of three things, obviously: an addition to a case history; a change in his will; or a letter.

Third: the murderer was quick witted and cold blooded.

Fourth: he was apparently familiar with the names of the current patients. Or had his choice of case histories to be destroyed been hit or miss?

As he made his points, Dundee wrote them on a fresh sheet of paper which he had rolled into the typewriter. Now he paused and stared at the second paragraph, frowning intently. "An addition to a case history." . . . Only patients figured in case histories No, wait! Doctors and nurses must be mentioned in them, too! And the head psychiatrist had been away for three weeks. The mental welfare and the very lives of his patients had been in the hands of Dr. Cantrell, Dr. Harlow, Norah Lacey, Rose Caplan, and a small army of attendants.

After so long an absence Dr. Koenig had undoubtedly been besieged by patients. Was it possible—and Dundee sat up, startled, at the new train of thought—that a patient had complained to the Big Doctor of brutal treatment suffered during his absence? Or of criminal neglect on the part of some member of the staff or of an attendant? And if so, would not Dr. Koenig have recorded the accusation in the patient's case history, labeling it, possibly, as evidence of a "persecution complex" or a delusion? But suppose the accused—attendant, doctor, or trained nurse— had seen the accusation being typed out by the doctor, *and had known it to be true?* Had known that investigation would bring about dismissal or disgrace? And was it not possible, too, that Dr. Koenig had summoned the accused, to confront him or her with the patient's serious charge? Such speculation had endless possibilities. An attendant or a doctor who had criminally assaulted a girl patient. Such a girl as Enid

Rambler, for instance. A subtle drug administered to produce the symptoms of insanity. Criminal malpractice, resulting in the death of a patient during the head doctor's absence. Bribery of a doctor or an attendant or a nurse by the relative of a patient, so that the patient would be kept wrongfully incarcerated. Such things had been done, Dundee knew. Wives of rich old men had been known to put their undesirable husbands away in just such institutions as this, so that they might enjoy the poor devil's money unhampered. With the collusion of a doctor, tempted by a heavy bribe—

Dundee's head swam. He closed his eyes and pressed his fingers into his temples. But he could not drive away the hideous possibility that lurked behind all these speculations. Finally he faced it squarely.

Roger Baldwin, Koenig's partner and certainly in his confidence where business matters were concerned, was authority for the statement that Dr. Koenig had planned to dismiss Justine Harlow and secure another assistant psychiatrist in her place. A sudden decision, undoubtedly, since neither the girl doctor nor the medical head of Mayfield had known of it. But the girl was co legatee with Norah Lacey in his will. That, certainly, was a fact, since Dr. Cantrell and his wife had witnessed the will. And it was as indisputably a fact that Dr. Koenig had been in pressing need of the services of a lawyer, that he had called his attorney that night, and, finding that he was out of town, had told Mrs. Forrest that he would attend to the matter himself, since it could not wait until morning.

And Justine Harlow herself had admitted that she had had a "disagreement" with the Big Doctor on the subject of Enid Rambler. And Enid Rambler was certainly a girl of wealth. Was it possible that the girlish, loyal seeming little doctor had succumbed to the temptation of a huge bribe to aggravate the girl's mental condition until she should finally be a fit subject to be "committed" by a lunacy commission?

No! Dundee surprised himself by crashing his fist upon the dead doctor's desk. It was unthinkable! That girl was all she seemed to be, or he was crazier than any inmate of Mayfield Sanitarium. But—*the doctor had determined to dismiss her.* The doctor had telephoned his lawyer. . . . And the vicious circle began to spin again in the detective's head. Justine Harlow was a graduate of medical school as well as of psychiatry. *She knew drugs.* And some secret anxiety had gnawed at her nerves all evening. . . .

Dundee was so sunk in miserable speculation that he did not hear the door open.

"Well, boy! I've got rid of them damned reporters at last!" Strawn boomed. "And say, one of the boys spun a theory that ain't so dusty."

"Yeah?" Dundee asked wearily, without turning to face his old chief.

"Yeah! Says me!" Strawn retorted. "Creston, of *The News.* His idea is that Doc Koenig was in collusion with some rich woman to keep her hubby shut up here, then go before the lunacy commission and swear he's a nut, so that the wife could get herself appointed the guardian of his person and of his property—"

"I thought of that," Dundee interrupted wearily. "But Koenig was too big a man for that."

"Every man's got his price," Strawn quoted cynically. "And I got a hunch of my own. The Big Doc was away for three weeks. Just got back. This girl doctor probably don't get a whale of a salary, and if a rich dame come along and offered her—"

"Great minds run in the same channel, Chief—to quote another old saw," Dundee interrupted, grinning wryly. "I'd just been going over that very possibility, and—I can't believe it! Not of that girl!"

"Because she's got red hair and green eyes, and a cute way of wrinkling her nose when she grins?" Strawn cut in slyly. "Well, you needn't tear your shirt, lad! I'm thinking it's that Rowan bird, and I'll be after him bright and early in the morning. I'm leaving Harmon and Clinton on guard outside these doors, and shoving off myself. What about you?"

"I now become an inmate of Mayfield Sanitarium," Dundee grinned. "My temporary address is Sunflower Court."

"Next door to the Rambler baby, eh? Gonna sit up with her and hold her little white hand? . . . Well, I'd rather pound my ear. "Night!"

"Just a minute, Captain. I'm taking charge of this trayful of scraps, if you don't mind."

"Sure! Paste 'em up, if you like. I never was any good at jigsaw puzzles, and there ain't a man on the squad I feel like giving a week off to do the job. But don't take any chances with that trash, Bonnie. I'm betting the district attorney can make a rope out of it to hang Rowan with."

"If," Dundee replied slowly, "it's the stuff that hangman's rope is made of, why do you suppose the murderer left it lying about? Why didn't he burn it?"

CHAPTER NINE

UNESCORTED, Special Investigator Dundee crossed the driveway before the main building and struck off across the dew wet, thick grassed lawn toward Sunflower Court. Except for a small cottage in the far corner of the grounds, the building in which he was to be housed was the only structure to the left of the long, U shaped driveway. In the faint light diffused by the powerful lamps set at intervals along the high iron fence Dundee saw, in this segment of the vast grounds, a croquet field, a miniature golf course, a large flower bed encircling a fountain, two huge, colorful umbrellas with their scalloped edges fluttering in the flower scented night air, three iron tables topped with gay oilcloth, and numerous striped canvas chairs, with canopies to protect the patient's eyes from the glare of the summer sun. Truly, these looked like the grounds of a fashionable resort hotel.

And when he had inspected his suite in Sunflower Court he knew that for such luxury and comfort a hotel visitor would pay even more than Mayfield Sanitarium exacted of its wealthy patients.

Miss Hunter, the nurse in charge of Sunflower Court, and whose name had bobbed up frequently during the long hours of the investigation into the murder of Dr. Carl Koenig, greeted the detective as he was crossing the cement floored porch of the stucco building. And she chuckled richly as he was momentarily dumb with astonishment.

"I know I'm big," she laughed, as she extended the largest arm Dundee had ever seen on a woman, "but I wouldn't hurt a fly. You'll get used to me. . . . Come along in, sir, and make yourself at home."

Dundee grinned apologetically and stepped into a pleasant, charmingly furnished room, which jutted out upon the porch. A chart table and a signal board above it were the only features to distinguish the room as in anyway connected with a hospital.

"Everything quiet now, nurse?" he asked in a low voice.

"Yes, thank heaven!" the huge nurse sighed, but she could not make her great, red, freckled face look lugubrious to save her life. "And what a night it's been! Honest, my feet are killing me. . . . Have you found out who did that awful thing, sir? Let me tell you, Mr. Dundee, a finer man and a greater doctor than Dr. Koenig never drew breath of life."

"I'm afraid I don't know any better than you who did the deed, Miss Hunter," Dundee told her regretfully. "How is Miss Rambler? It was I who found her and brought her back, you know."

"Poor lamb! She'd have had a conniption fit if she'd known you were a detective. . . . She's asleep now, bless her heart, but she wouldn't shut an eye till Miss Lacey gave her a hypo and promised to sit with her until it took effect."

"Has she an attendant?" Dundee asked.

"Sure! Crippled like she is with that sprained ankle, poor kid! But she hasn't needed an attendant before this. . . . Would you like to go to your rooms now, sir?"

Dundee followed her into a narrow hall, which, midway its length, gave upon an immaculate kitchen.

"Most of the food is cooked in the main kitchen, and brought over," Miss Hunter explained, "but the trays and extra delicacies are prepared here, as well as the nine o'clock nourishments. . . . This way out, sir."

Dundee found himself facing a long open court, carpeted with grass, bordered and gemmed with flower beds. A narrow, roofed porch hugged the building on all sides, except the far end, which was guarded by a spiked iron fence.

"Nice little private garden, isn't it?" boasted the nurse in charge of Sunflower Court. "The gate at the end is always kept locked, and there's no other way out except through my office, so you see the patients are pretty safe here."

The mountainous, jolly nurse leading the way, they walked softly for a few feet along the left side of the court, before Miss Hunter paused at a door marked with a gleaming brass "B."

There was a tiny hall, and to the right of it a large, luxuriously furnished sitting room, complete with easy chairs, radio cabinet, bookcase, down stuffed couch, coffee table, end tables, and rather good bric a brac and pictures. Gold silk curtains and a golden brown velvet rug gave the room a rich glow of comfort.

"And here's your bedroom," Miss Hunter told him proudly, as she ushered him into a large, exquisitely appointed chamber. The color scheme was daffodil and green, carried out in the painted furniture, the window drapes, bedspread and rug.

"We usually put a woman here," Miss Hunter admitted, as Dundee grinned at the thought of his occupying so feminine a bower. "This is the bathroom. It has a door into the sitting room, too, to make it convenient for the attendant, which you'll not be needing, of course."

The green and yellow bathroom was as luxurious as the rest of the suite.

"There are six apartments in the court, I believe?" Dundee asked, when he had sufficiently praised his quarters.

"That's right. Miss Rambler has Suite C, next to you toward the end of the court. It and Suite F are even larger than this."

"Who are the other patients in the court?"

"Well, a real old lady, by the name of Horton, has A," Miss Hunter began. "That's on the other side of yours. And across the court in D we have a Mrs. Morse– "

"*Morse?*" Dundee repeated. He saw again the two words "Call Morse," which headed the three notations on the dead doctor's calendar.

"Yes. Do you know her? Poor thing! She's been awfully 'queer' for months, but she's much better now. Or, rather, she was until tonight, when she got all upset again."

"What happened to upset her tonight?" Dundee asked sharply. "Did she go to the movie?"

"No. Her husband visited with her from about half past seven until nearly nine, and when he came through my office on his way out he said he had never seen his wife in better spirits," Miss Hunter explained. "He acted just tickled to death, poor man. But it wasn't more'n fifteen minutes before she was taking on something terrible. Her nurse—she has three attendants, on eight hour shifts—had gone to our kitchen to fix her nine o'clock nourishment, and when Miss Macy took her her hot chocolate and toast she found Mrs. Morse moaning and shuddering, her head all covered up with a sheet. She rang for me and I had to get Miss Caplan to come over and give her a strong sedative."

"Did Mrs. Morse say what had upset her?" Dundee asked.

"No. She wouldn't say anything except that she was going to kill herself. . . . And here we'd been singing Hallelujah because she was cured," the fat nurse sighed.

"Cured? You mean a sudden cure?" Dundee asked, startled.

"It was like a miracle!" Miss Hunter assured him solemnly. "You know Dr. Koenig had been gone for three weeks. Well, it seems that he did a lot of studying about Mrs. Morse's case while he was gone, because as soon as he got back—"

"What was wrong with Mrs. Morse?" Dundee interrupted.

"Some kind o' delusion, I guess you'd call it," Miss Hunter answered. "You see, Mr. Dundee, I'm not a trained nurse—just head attendant here; so I don't know all the doctor book names for things. . . . Well, anyway, Mrs. Morse never would say 'I' or 'me' "

"What's that?" Dundee puzzled.

"It was like this, sir," the nurse explained patiently. "If anybody spoke to her, said 'How are you, Mrs. Morse?,' for instance, she'd say, '*She* is very well, thank you,' or, '*She* says she doesn't feel well to day.' It was the same every time she referred to herself. Never did say 'I' until Tuesday, after she'd had a long talk with Dr. Koenig. You could have knocked me down with a feather, big as I am, when I come on duty Tuesday night and she answered me just like anybody else. She spoke right up: Tm feeling fine, Miss Hunter!' she said, and I ain't ashamed to tell you I broke right down and cried, I was so happy to see the poor darling was cured."

"You say she talked with Koenig on Tuesday?" Dundee asked, frowning.

"Yes, sir. You see, Doctor had been psychoanalyzing her for weeks, and the word went round that he'd finally hit on whatever it was that had got her poor mind all kinked up. A complex, they call it. Or maybe it's a psychosis."

"Do you know whether Mr. Morse saw Dr. Koenig this evening, before or after he visited his wife?" Dundee persisted.

"I guess he did," the nurse admitted, her hazel eyes widening. "He said he was going to drop in and speak to the doctor, to ask him when he could take his wife home."

Dundee stared silently into the nurse's apprehensive eyes, his mind buzzing with questions and conjectures.

"Is Mrs. Morse's attendant thoroughly reliable?" he asked at last. "She must not be left alone an instant."

"You—don't think ?" the nurse gasped.

"I don't think anything!" Dundee retorted curtly. "But Mrs. Morse must be guarded every second of the day and night! . . . Now, who are the other patients in the court?"

The nurse looked like a huge child whose feelings had been wounded. "Mr. Salter has E, the suite next to Mrs.

Morse, and Archie Webster is in F. That is, he was until they put him in 'Ten' tonight. I expect he'll be back here in the morning. He's an awfully sweet boy, except when he's drinking– "

"So I've heard," Dundee interrupted drily, for he was a little tired of hearing Archie Webster's praises sung by infatuated nurses. "Who is Mr. Salter? The name sounds familiar."

"Howard Salter, the writer," the nurse explained. "He writes Western novels—the most exciting things! But you don't dare mention them to him. They say he hates his books like poison, but they've made him rich enough to afford Suite F, which is two hundred dollars a week—the same price as Enid's. The rest of these apartments are only a hundred and fifty."

"Did Mr. Salter go to the movies tonight?" Dundee asked.

"No. He hates the movies, too, though I've heard that five or six of his novels have been made into pictures."

"Perhaps that is why Mr. Salter doesn't like the movies," Dundee smiled. "Just what did Mr. Salter do with his evening?"

"Sally Porter, the girl he's going to marry if he ever gets well– "

"And what's wrong with him?" Dundee interrupted.

"He's what they call a manic depressive," Miss Hunter elucidated, obviously proud of her knowledge. "Manic depressives ain't really crazy, you know—just 'mentally sick.' They're in a sort of black despair. They can't bear themselves and they think the whole world's a sink of sin and sorrow, I guess. But they always come out of it, just like Mr. Salter's doing. He's been just fine for four or five days, and his girl friend was mighty happy tonight. I guess they'll be getting married soon."

"How long did Miss Porter stay with Mr. Salter?"

"I don't know exactly," the nurse confessed. "She come about eight and him and her took a little drive in her car, then they sat out on the lawn. Mr. Salter come in alone about five minutes to nine and I gave him his bromide, which he takes at nine every night. All the manic depressives are given bromides at night so they won't lie awake and brood."

"Has Mr. Salter an attendant?"

"Oh, no! Not since he's been getting better. He had an attendant at night as long as there was any danger of him committing suicide, like he threatened to do when he first came here. But I make the rounds every half hour. The patients ain't allowed to lock their bedroom doors, and I peep in to see if them that haven't attendants are all right. Just now Mr. Salter is the only patient I have to keep an eye on, so if you'll excuse me– There's pajamas and a dressing gown on your bed, and a new toothbrush and a shaving kit in your bathroom. Mr. Baldwin brought them over before you got here."

"Decent of him," Dundee said with an effort, for he hated the idea of being under any obligation to the only person he had met that evening whom he did not like. "I'm sure I'll be very comfortable, Miss Hunter. And thanks for everything."

"I'm afraid I've talked too much," the big nurse apologized, but her face was one vast smile of hospitality and genuine friendliness. "Good night, sir. Just ring if you want anything. You'll find the bell cord hanging from the head of your bed."

Tired though he was Dundee found that he could not lay himself down to sleep. He had counted on the warm shower to relax his nerves, but they remained annoyingly taut. At last, clad in the delft blue silk pajamas, black satin dressing gown and dark blue leather slippers which Roger Baldwin had thoughtfully provided for him, the young detective stepped out of his miniature hall into the silent, flower fragrant patio. Perhaps a walk in the balmy June air would help. . . .

He strolled noiselessly, hands deep in the big pockets, his brows knit with perplexed thought. If he only had something to read. . . . The bookcase in his room was empty, awaiting the patient's choice of literature–

"What luck!" he ejaculated to himself, as he saw a book lying open and face down upon one of the iron tables set at intervals along the roofed porch of the patio. There was not light enough from the small electric lanterns which swung from every door along the court, but he thrust the volume into his dressing gown pocket, and continued his stroll to the spiked fence at the rear.

Grinning at the thought that he was as well locked up as any psychopathic resident of the court, Dundee idly shook the heavy iron gate set in the center of the fence. But the grin was wiped off instantly. *The gate was not locked.*

Miss Hunter raised startled eyes from the hooked rug she was working on, as the newcomer she thought asleep confronted her.

"You said that gate at the rear was always kept locked!" he reminded her grimly. "Well, it's not locked now!"

"Not locked?" the nurse repeated blankly. "Oh! Then Frank, the kitchen man, must have forgot to lock it after he brought the supper wagon through. But surely there's no harm done– "

"More harm may have been done than you suspect," Dundee interrupted darkly. "Dr. Koenig was murdered tonight, and Mrs. Morse was mysteriously thrown into a panic. . . . Have you a key to that gate?"

"Yes, sir!" the nurse quavered. "I'll go lock it now. Such a thing has never happened before "

"Who else has a key?"

"There's one in the chartroom in the main building, and Frank has one."

"See that Mrs. Morse's nurse doesn't go to sleep on the job tonight!" the detective warned her, and then left the room as unceremoniously as he had come.

He was strangely disturbed. And his scalp was prickling with the same premonitory unease which had served to warn him of danger so many times in the past. Morse. ... Morse. . . . "Call Morse." . . . The name writhed through his brain. . . . Mrs. Morse had been almost miraculously cured by Dr. Koenig only the day before. Her husband had come to rejoice over her cure, to plan to take her home. But had he really rejoiced? Had the unexpected cure of his wife upset some vile, deep laid scheme? Had Morse stopped in to see the doctor who had wrought the miracle? If so, why had Dr. Koenig not crossed out the notation on his calendar "Call Morse." Had death itself interfered with his meticulous efficiency?

With sudden resolution, Dundee knocked upon the door of Suite D. An elderly woman in nurse's uniform answered his knock, then drew back in startled amazement at sight of her informally dressed caller.

"You are Mrs. Morse's nurse?" Dundee asked curtly, in a low voice.

"Yes, sir. Mrs. Appleby is my name."

"I'm Dundee, of the district attorney's office. I am occupying Suite B, *as a patient*, until the mystery of Dr. Koenig's death is cleared up. You'll remember that, I hope? . . . Very well. Is your patient asleep?"

"Yes, sir," the woman breathed.

"I understand that Mrs. Morse was unaccountably upset this evening after her husband's visit," Dundee went on, keeping his voice very low. "I want you to tell me about it. You were with her while Mr. Morse was here?"

"Not in the sitting room with them—no, sir. I never like to intrude. Part of the time I was in the bedroom, but most of the time I was out in the patio, dose enough to hear if I was called."

"Tell me! When did you first notice that Mrs. Morse was upset?"

"I came in when I saw Mr. Morse leave," the nurse answered, her voice frightened. "I couldn't find Mrs. Morse at first, but then I heard the water running in the bathtub. I called to her and she said she was going to take a hot bath. I thought her voice sounded a little queer, but she never likes to have me help her with her bath, so I turned down the bed, and then went to fix her nine o'clock nourishment. When I got back with it—I was gone about fifteen minutes, making toast and hot chocolate, and having to whip the cream and everything– "

"And gossip with the other nurses, I suppose!" Dundee cut in grimly.

"I had no reason to think Mrs. Morse wasn't quite all right!" the elderly woman flared. "She was in high spirits before Mr. Morse came, seemed to be as well as anybody."

"And what state did you find her in?" Dundee asked more gently.

"She was in bed, with the sheet over her head. And she was crying and moaning– "

"Any words you could distinguish?" Dundee interrupted.

"All she said was 'Too late! Too late!—over and over! But I couldn't make her tell me what she meant. And she was in such a state that I didn't worry her much with questions. I rang for Miss Hunter, and she got Miss Caplan to give Mrs. Morse a strong sedative."

"Is it your opinion that something Mr. Morse said or did to his wife caused this upset, or that it was something that happened while you were in the kitchen?"

"I don't know, sir, since I didn't see her at all until I got back with the nourishment."

Dundee gave it up for then, and, with a word of apology and thanks, departed for his own suite.

Determined to "Call Morse" himself the next morning, and equally as determined to dismiss the matter from his mind for the night, the weary young detective stretched out between the smooth, fresh sheets of his bed. The book he had found in the patio proved to be a mystery story, and, grinning in anticipation of the technical flaws he was very apt to spot in it, he adjusted the bedside lamp for reading.

"Murder Without Motive." . . . Not a bad title, that. And it must be a popular book among the patients, Dundee concluded, after a glance at its dog eared condition. An envelope pasted upon the fly leaf bore the printed words: "Ex libris Mayfield Sanitarium. . . . Guests are kindly requested to return books to the library as soon as they have read them."

He settled himself to read, slightly annoyed by the fact that some previous reader had underlined significant sentences and phrases on almost every page. The story concerned the apparently motiveless, brutal slaying of a housewife at work in her own kitchen. After a crisply sensational first chapter, the story meandered rather dully, Dundee thought, but perhaps that was because a far more baffling mystery in real life persisted in distracting his attention from the printed pages.

Suddenly, however, he uttered a sharp exclamation. No need for the penciled underlining to attract his attention to these words, uttered by the amateur detective whose "brilliant work was putting the police force to shame," as the author assured the reader:

"No, Sergeant. I am afraid you are wrong. Don't waste time looking for a foppishly dressed man, the kind, as you say, who wears gloves in July. Poor Mrs. Stone furnished her murderer with gloves. Look!" And Hartley Jarnegan pointed dramatically at a pair of innocent looking rubber gloves lying atop a bar of yellow soap in the soap dish above the kitchen sink.

Dundee whistled. *Rubber gloves!* Had he stumbled upon an odd coincidence, or had the prospective murderer, reading this very book, stored away in his subconscious mind a fact that had proved to have a sinister usefulness?

Was it his hand—or *her* hand—which had underlined these pages so liberally? The story forgotten, Dundee turned rapidly through the book, searching every page for a scribbled word, a marginal comment or query. But there was nothing upon which a handwriting expert could exercise his craft. Who had read this book? Dozens, apparently, but Dundee determined to have a look at the withdrawal card which undoubtedly reposed this minute in the sanitarium's library card file. Another chore for the morning, which promised to be a very busy one. He ticked off his tasks upon his fingers:

Check up Norah Lacey's alibi. That would necessitate a trip to the Satterlee home in Hamilton.

Call Morse, to find out what had taken place during his visit with his wife, and whether he had called upon Dr. Koenig.

Interview Mrs. Cantrell.

Check the doctor's visitors, including patients, since his return on Monday, with the secretary, Miss Home.

Visit Enid Rambler, in the guise of fellow patient.

Listen in on Strawn's questioning of Rowan and Webster.

Circulate among patients on the lawn, to hear comment on the doctor's murder.

Call on the district attorney, to report progress—or lack of it!

Dundee sighed as wearily as if he had already performed these labors. Then sleep descended upon him so suddenly that he could scarcely arouse himself to turn off his bedside lamp.

A knock startled him into instant wakefulness. He was sure he had just that minute dozed off, but the sun was shining brilliantly through the flowered silk curtains at his bedroom windows.

Miss Hunter's vast bulk filled the door, but over her shoulder Dundee saw the hennaed and marcelled head of a stranger.

"Good morning, Mr. Dundee!" the big nurse greeted him heartily. "I brought Miss Doty—Lurline Doty—in to meet you. She's in charge here during the day.

"My, Mr. Dundee! I won't know how to act with a detective watching me!" the newcomer babbled, a hint of hysteria in her voice and in her rounded blue eyes. "I'm still all of a tremble. I didn't know a blessed thing until I come on duty ten minutes ago– "

"Yes. It's pretty bad," Dundee agreed curtly. "Every thing quiet, Miss Hunter?"

To his astonishment the night nurse flushed darkly behind her freckles and her hazel eyes avoided his. "Everything's quiet—*now*. I wanted to wake you up last night to tell you, seeing as how you're the detective, but Dr. Harlow wouldn't let me– "

Dundee sat bolt upright in bed. "For God's sake, what happened? Is Mrs. Morse– ?"

"No, sir. It was Mr. Salter!"

CHAPTER TEN

"DR. HARLOW, why wasn't I told last night that Howard Salter had tried to commit suicide?"

The little doctor, her coiled red braids gleaming, her uniform crisply immaculate, opened wider the door to her apartment on the second floor of the main building, with a gesture which invited the outraged young detective to enter.

"Why should I have told you?" she countered. Then, with a hint of laughter in her lovely voice: "But how stupid of me! I remember now that it is a crime to commit suicide. Naturally you wanted to arrest him! But isn't it rather early in the morning for you to bully me, Mr. Dundee? I haven't even been fortified by breakfast. . . . By the way, have you?"

"No. I came here as soon as Miss Hunter told me what had happened."

"Charlotte Hunter always did talk too much," the girl reflected with mock sadness. "Pardon me!" and she stepped to a table which held two telephones and a black metal box with perhaps a dozen pairs of push buttons. After a moment of manipulation she spoke into a receiver:

"The kitchen? . . . Joe? . . . Dr. Harlow speaking. Send up two breakfast trays as soon as possible."

"That's kind of you," Dundee admitted, a little less stiffly. "But you must realize, Doctor–"

He was interrupted by the ringing of a telephone bell. Justine Harlow, who still stood by the table, picked up the instrument she had used in her house call.

"Dr. Harlow speaking. . . . Yes, Miss Lacey. . . . Very well." She replaced the receiver and reached for the other instrument, her eyes on Dundee. "Good morning, Captain Strawn. . . . No, not very well, thank you. . . . Yes, I had thought of that, and I've given orders that all morning papers are to be withheld from the patients. . . . I beg your pardon? . . . Why, ye es, I suppose so. ... What time? . . . Very well. Good bye!"

She slowly hung up the receiver and faced Dundee. "Captain Strawn will be here about eight o'clock with the police stenographer, to question every patient in his room. He has asked that no patient be informed of the doctor's death, or permitted to see a newspaper. He will begin the rounds at nine, he says, and until then patients are to be allowed to follow their regular routine. ... I suppose," she concluded dejectedly, "that some sort of examination of the patients is necessary, but—there's a hard day ahead for doctors and nurses. . . . Will you accompany Captain Strawn on his rounds?"

"Remember I'm here as a patient," Dundee reminded her. "But about Salter–"

"Come in! . . . Good morning, Joe. . . . Put the trays on the table between the windows. . . . That's fine. Thanks!"

A minute later Dundee was facing the little doctor across the improvised breakfast table, and was accepting a cup of coffee.

"Now, if you'll let me have just two swallows of coffee," she begged, and raised her own cup to her pretty, unrouged mouth. "Now! I'm beginning to feel human. ... In the first place, I didn't call you last night, or rather at two o'clock this morning, because I was too busy to think of anything or anybody but Howard Salter. In the second place, the poor man was too near dead to be questioned, and you would have been terribly in the way."

"Just what happened?" Dundee asked. "Miss Hunter was called away before she could give me more than the bare fact that he had tried to kill himself."

"He slashed his wrist with a safety razor blade. Fortunately, he neglected to turn off the bathroom light and shut the door, and Miss Hunter, on her two o'clock visit to see if he was resting—she makes the rounds every half hour—saw the light and investigated. She found Mr.

Salter unconscious and soaked with blood. But for a lucky chance I am afraid he would have been dead by now–"

"You mean the bathroom light?" Dundee interrupted.

"No. The lucky chance was that we were able to give a blood transfusion immediately. We make a blood test of every patient who comes in, and also classify his blood according to type. Howard Salter's blood happens to be the rarest type. Of course we have a file of blood donors, classified according to type, but there was no time to send into Hamilton for a registered donor. Mr. Baldwin, whom Miss Lacey had aroused to send on errand into Hamilton, regardless of the apparent hopelessness of the case, volunteered the information that he is what we call a 'universal donor'—that is, his blood can fuse with any other type— and offered his own blood to save Salter's life. Dr. Cantrell and I performed the transfusion operation, and Howard Salter will live."

"Baldwin doesn't look as if he has much blood to spare," Dundee commented with a trace of malice, then, ashamed of himself, he added: "It was decent of him."

"Oh, Roger wouldn't thank you for the compliment!" Justine Harlow laughed. "He'd shut you up by saying it was good business to save a patient who can afford a suite in Sunflower Court. But it was decent of him. Perhaps Roger Baldwin is a much better man than he gives himself credit for being."

"Did Salter talk at all? Give any reason for his act?"

"He cursed us feebly for saving his life," the little doctor twinkled. "And insisted that it was better to be dead than insane. I tried to convince him that he was in no danger of losing his mind, but there's no reasoning with a manic depressive in a suicidal mood."

"And yet Miss Hunter told me last night that Howard Salter was greatly improved—that he'd be able to leave soon and get married," Dundee told her, frowning thoughtfully.

"Yes. I confess I was surprised. Dr. Koenig and I both thought he was almost cured."

"What is the cause of his trouble?" Dundee wanted to know.

"A conviction of personal failure," Dr. Harlow answered succinctly. "He is a writer—very well known for his Western stories. But it seems that for two or three years he has hated the sort of book he writes, and wanted to do 'bigger and better' things—serious novels, as he calls them. I understand from Sally Porter, the girl he is engaged to, that his present breakdown was caused by two things. Every house in the publishing business rejected a 'serious' novel Salter had worked on intermittently for two years, and he could not write even the first chapter of a Western story he had contracted to deliver by May first. He was in speechless, black despair when he came here about the middle of April, but oddly enough this is the first time he had tried to carry out his threats to commit suicide."

"Salter has the rooms next to Mrs. Morse, hasn't he?" Dundee asked thoughtfully.

"Why, yes!"

"Rather odd, isn't it? Yesterday Mrs. Morse was considered cured. And yesterday Howard Salter seemed to be almost normal. A rather strange coincidence, isn't it, that both of them should have a serious relapse last night?"

"I don't know what you're talking about!" the girl cried sharply. "I haven't heard a word about Mrs. Morse's relapse. . . . Wait a minute!" and she sprang up from the breakfast table and ran to the telephone table. In a moment she was giving a curt order: "Miss Lacey, send me up the night reports from Sunflower Court immediately!"

While she was waiting, her small body tense with impatience, Dundee asked: "Did Salter have an interview with Dr. Koenig after the doctor's return from his trip?"

To his surprise the little doctor flushed. "I—don't think so. In fact, I'm fairly sure he did not. You see, our patients are a queer lot. They become unreasoningly attached to the psychiatrist who first gains their confidence, and they resent any interference whatever. It happens that Dr. Koenig was out of town when Howard Salter first came, and that he became so devoted to me that he never sought out Dr. Koenig at all. In fact, he refused to talk at all the one time Dr. Koenig summoned him to his office."

"Have you read Salter's 'serious' novel?" Dundee asked, idly enough.

"No. But Dr. Koenig read it. Sally Porter took charge of the manuscript when Howard came, and just a day or so before Dr. Koenig left on this last trip she brought it in to him and asked his opinion. She hoped it would give the doctor a clew to Howard's mental condition. Doctor read it on the train."

"And his opinion of it?" Dundee asked, strangely eager.

"He said it was terrible," Dr. Harlow answered simply. "Fumbling in style, almost amateurish, erotic and futile."

"I wonder," Dundee said slowly, "if last night, while Sally Porter and Howard Salter were walking on the lawn, they dropped in to ask the doctor his opinion and—he told them what you've told me!"

The girl's eyes widened and she paled, but her voice was quite steady: "If they asked him, he told them the truth. Carl—Dr. Koenig—was almost ruthlessly honest. He found honesty the best medicine in treating manic depressives."

"Strong medicine—in this case!" Dundee commented grimly.

"You don't think—? . . . Come in! ... Thank you, Mary. Yes, that's all."

The gingham frocked girl, who, Dundee guessed, was a maid, handed a sheaf of chart sheets to the little doctor, and scurried out of the room as if terrified.

Dr. Harlow shuffled the sheets until she found the night report on Mrs. Morse. He watched her read, saw her cheeks pale and her lips tighten.

"But—there's something wrong here!" she gasped. "*Mrs. Morse doesn't hear voices!* She never has! It doesn't fit–"

"*Voices?*" Dundee echoed incredulously. "Miss Hunter did not tell me last night that Mrs. Morse claims to have heard voices–"

"Only because Miss Hunter did not know it when she talked with you," the doctor assured him, with a little click of her teeth. "She seems to have told you everything else she ever knew. . . . Mrs. Appleby, Mrs. Morse's night attendant, records that at five o'clock this morning Mrs. Morse awoke, began to cry hysterically, and then confessed that 'the voice of God' had spoken to her; that she had heard His voice quite plainly while Mrs. Appleby was preparing her nine o'clock nourishment. . . . But it's absurd. Mrs. Morse is not subject to auditory hallucinations. Her case was a remarkable one—that of a pseudo split psyche due to a submerged conviction of unpardonable sin. But Dr. Koenig cured her! I tell you, she was absolutely and definitely cured!" she insisted, a note of hysteria in her own voice.

"Will you tell me what, exactly, caused Mrs. Morse's illness?" Dundee asked earnestly. "Believe me, I consider it important that I know."

"A patient's case history is sacred," the girl reminded him in her most professional manner.

"Dr. Harlow, do you want Howard Salter to be cured of his fear that he has suddenly become insane, and Mrs. Morse to be saved from probable insanity?" Dundee demanded very solemnly.

"Of course! But–"

"I'm afraid there is someone who doesn't want one of those patients ever to be able to leave!" Dundee interrupted grimly. "I'm a detective, not a psychiatrist, so it is becoming quite plain to me that Mrs. Morse *did* hear a voice last night. But it was not the 'voice of God'!"

"I don't understand!"

"And I only have a glimmer," Dundee assured her. "Which is why I want you to tell me what brought about Mrs. Morse's 'split psyche.' "

"Very well!" she conceded crisply. "Mrs. Morse was born and reared a Catholic. During adolescence she drifted away from the Church, and fancied herself almost an agnostic. While still in that state of rebellion against religion, she married—by civil ceremony only—a non Catholic, a man who is really an agnostic. They had four children in ten years. The youngest was two years old when Mrs. Morse began to show symptoms of mental derangement. Finally, she repudiated her ego entirely—refused to be herself any longer. She–"

"– referred to herself always in the third person," Dundee completed the sentence for the doctor.

"Oh, that Hunter!" Dr. Harlow smiled, wrinkling her nose in the quaint gesture Dundee was beginning to watch for. "Yes. Subconsciously, you see, she had denied her own identity, *in order to escape the consequences of what she believed to be an unpardonable sin.* That sin, of course, was her marriage, which, to the true Catholic she was at heart, was no marriage, but adultery. Her children born in sin and not baptized–"

"And all this was entirely in the unconscious?" Dundee asked, wonderingly.

"Oh, yes! Dr. Koenig dug deep, in psychoanalysis, before he found the root of the mental evil," Dr. Harlow answered, pride in her dead hero enriching her beautiful voice. "He had a long talk with Mrs. Morse on Tuesday, then sent for Mr. Morse. You see, her cure was in her husband's power. Dr. Koenig asked him if, to save his wife, he would be willing to remarry her, with a priest officiating and blessing the union, and then have his children baptized."

"And what did Morse say?" Dundee demanded tensely.

"He said he would get the Pope himself to marry them, if it would save his wife's mind."

"Then why did Mrs. Morse hear 'the voice of God' crying to her that it was 'Too late! Too late!'?" Dundee leaned close to inquire, his blue eyes gleaming with excitement. "For I'm sure Mrs. Morse will tell you that those are the words she heard. Mrs. Appleby told me last night—even then I was oddly disturbed by Mrs. Morse's strange relapse—that the woman would tell her nothing, would only moan, 'Too late! Too late!' . . . Remember! *Her husband had left her only a few minutes before!"*

"Yes—so the report says," Dr. Harlow agreed, her voice dragging. "But Mr. Morse is a good man—" she protested despairingly.

"I'm afraid Dr. Koenig was right. You're a credulous child, who lets her heart run away with her head," Dundee smiled. "By the way, do you have any idea why Dr. Koenig made the notation, 'Call Morse,' on his desk calendar?"

"Yes. He made the notation yesterday morning when he was talking to me about Mrs. Morse," Dr. Harlow told him, and Dundee saw her cheeks grow paler and the gray green eyes widen behind their spectacles. "You see, the Morse baby has died since Mrs. Morse came here, and she has never been told, because Dr. Koenig feared the effect it might have on her mind. He suddenly remembered about the baby yesterday, and tried to call Mr. Morse then. But his secretary reported that he was out of town on business, and would not return until today. So Dr. Koenig wrote that notation to remind himself to call Mr. Morse today, in order to warn him against telling his wife until she is stronger."

"And Morse visited his wife last night!" Dundee reminded her grimly.

"But what you're thinking is fantastic!" Dr. Harlow protested vehemently. "I tell you, he is a good man, and a devoted husband! It's absolutely criminal of you to accuse him of telling her of the unbaptized baby's death, then of sneaking under her window to wail 'Too late! Too late!,' in order to drive her crazy again! Call me a credulous fool if you like!" and she stamped her foot, "but I know–"

"Do you happen to know *this?*" Dundee interrupted gently but firmly. "Did Mrs. Morse, rich in her own *right*, marry a poor man as well as an agnostic?"

"I do not!" she flared.

"It should be rather easy to find out," Dundee reflected aloud, as he rose to leave.

"But what has all this to do with Howard Salter?" she detained him.

"That, with your permission," Dundee assured her gravely, "is what I am going to find out. As I said before, I am a detective, not a psychiatrist, but I have a hunch that I am going to be the Miracle Man in person this morning."

"Exactly what do you mean?" the girl demanded.

"Only that, as one poor devil of a patient calling on another, I'm going to have a pleasant little visit with Howard Salter. After that visit, you will either find your manic depressive quite cured of his fear of insanity, or—he may be fervently wishing he had succeeded last night!"

"I forbid–" the little doctor began, imperiously.

"I really don't think you'd better," Dundee interrupted gently, and, as she stood staring dumbly after him, he strode from the room.

It was still too early—not yet eight o'clock—for patients to be out and on the grounds. The only persons Dundee encountered, as he left the main building and set off across the lawn to Sunflower Court, were the two plainclothesmen Captain Strawn had left to guard the suite of offices in which the murder had been committed. He had already spoken to both of them, and had learned that the only disturbance during the night had occurred when Dr. Cantrell and Miss Lacey had asked permission to enter the former's office shortly after two o'clock in the morning, for the purpose of getting instruments needed in dealing with the attempted suicide.

His parley with Miss Doty, the day nurse in charge of Sunflower Court, was brief but effective. Very meekly, the henna haired, blue eyed girl led the way to Suite E, the door of which was opened by a male attendant.

"This is Mr. Dundee, Roy," she whispered. "He wants to have a private talk with your patient."

"I'm afraid you'll have to do most of the talking, sir," the attendant deprecated respectfully, aware obviously of Dundee's status. "He ain't said 'Yea,' 'Nay' or 'Go to hell!' since I come on duty."

"How is he physically?"

"Oh, fine! Old Baldwin's pint of blood has put roses in his cheeks. Pulse fine, temperature normal."

And indeed Howard Salter did not look like a man who had been snatched from the jaws of death only a few hours before. His long body was not thin, and there was a faint, natural color in his swarthy, handsome young face. Only his gray eyes, which gazed dully and without surprise, at the detective, gave a hint of the strain through which he had passed.

"Good morning, Mr. Salter," Dundee began, with the winning diffidence he knew so well how to assume. "I'm a new patient here, and sort of restless, so I thought I'd drop in–"

The man in the bed closed his eyes and his nostrils flared, but to Dundee's relief he did not order him out of the room.

"I wouldn't butt in on a sick man like this," Dundee went on, awkwardly and apologetically, "but there's something on my mind, and I hoped you might be able to tell me whether I'm going cuckoo or–"

"What's that?" the sick novelist interrupted sharply, his eyes blazing open.

"Miss Hunter kidded me and said she guessed it was high time I came here," Dundee went on guilelessly. "She said I'd had an 'auditory hallucination' or some rot like that, and got me scared stiff–"

"What the devil are you talking about?" the sick man almost shouted, raising himself upon an elbow. "Are you trying to say you heard something queer last night?"

"Either I actually heard a voice, or I belong in 'Ten,' " Dundee laughed awkwardly. "I thought maybe if I could find somebody else that had heard the same thing–"

"Was it a voice, like a Banshee wail, moaning 'Too late! Too late!'?" the sick man demanded feverishly. "For God's sake, man–"

"By George! You heard it, too, and I'm not crazy!" Dundee pretended to exult, slapping his knee joyously.

The novelist fell back upon his pillows. A brighter color glowed in his cheeks and his eyes lost their dullness, sparkled with new life and hope. "And I'm not crazy, either, it seems!" he gasped. "Man! You're a lifesaver, whoever you are! I heard that damned voice. I'd just gone to sleep. Had a bromide, you know," the writer went on, almost babbling in the blessedness of relief. "It was a long drawn out moan–"

"Would you say it was a man's voice or a woman's?" Dundee interrupted.

"God knows. It sounded like nothing human," the novelist assured him. "Just those two words, over and over, 'Too late! Too late!' I'd hate to tell you what I thought it was–"

" 'The voice of God,' perhaps?" Dundee dared interrupt again.

"Something like that," the other grinned. "I thought it was a message meant for no other ears but mine. 'Too late,' it said to me, "for you to write a great book, Howard Salter. 'Too late,' even, for me to write the popular trash I've been grinding out for years. 'Too late'—because my mind was tottering, was going even as I listened. ... I tried to kill myself. Didn't fancy being a raving lunatic locked up in "Ten,' " he added simply.

"You and me both!" Dundee agreed, still in the role of awkward new patient. "Not even to make an interesting case for the Big Doctor, as they call him. . . . What sort of a chap is Koenig anyway, old man?"

He watched the novelist narrowly, as he put the apparently innocent question, but the now happy gray eyes did not change expression.

"One of the best," Salter assured him heartily. "But I'm Doctor Harlow's patient. She's a peach, and got a head on her like old Socrates himself. I do want to see Koenig today, however, if they'll let me up, and I feel like a million dollars now. Miss Porter, the girl I'm engaged to—you'll be meeting Sally—told me last night that she'd given the Big Doctor my novel to read, and I want to chin with him about it. If he says it's rot, I'll take it standing, and begin over again! . . . Come in often, Dundee. Glad to see you any time."

Dundee shook hands. The man in the bed had answered the one question he had not dared to ask him. Howard Salter had not talked with Dr. Koenig last night. Moreover, Salter did not know that the great psychiatrist was dead. So sure was he of these two things that Dundee unhesitatingly shook hands with the man he had "healed."

CHAPTER ELEVEN

As Dundee stepped into the patio out of the tiny hall of Suite E, he almost bumped into Salter's attendant, carrying a tray which held nothing but a pint bottle of milk and a glass.

"If this is Mr. Salter's breakfast, you'd better add a couple of eggs, some bacon and a stack of toast," the detective advised blithely. "Your patient says he feels like a million dollars now, and he had a hungry gleam in his eye when I left."

"Thought you was a detective, not a doctor," the attend ant chuckled. "Say, mister, Dr. Harlow just phoned over that she wants to see you right away. She's in her private office on the second floor of the main building."

Grinning at this evidence that the little doctor had her share of the feminine vice, curiosity, Dundee set out to obey the summons. But as he crossed the front porch of Sunflower Court he determined to let her wait a bit while he studied the scene of last night's minor mystery—"the voice of God."

Whoever, with fiendish cruelty, had wailed those sinister words in a sepulchral, well disguised voice, must have stood or crouched beneath the windows of the adjoining bedrooms of Suites D and E, the first occupied by Mrs. Morse, the second by Howard Salter. Sunflower Court, he discovered, was enclosed on all sides but the front with a high box hedge. Inside the hedge there was a narrow cement walk, bordered on both sides by grass and flowers. The hedge ended opposite the front corner of Mrs. Morse's bedroom. The nocturnal wailer must have bided his time and slipped inside the hedge; must have crouched beneath the window of the patient chosen to be the victim of his cruel plot. Who was that chosen victim? For surely the plotter had intended that only one person should hear and be terrified into hysteria or into a relapse into insanity. An audience of *two* patients would defeat his purpose— had, in fact, defeated it. For, just as Howard Salter had been "cured" by the assurance that other ears had heard that voice, so would Mrs. Morse, Dundee hoped and believed, be restored to sanity, if not to happiness. Yes, it was quite clear that the plotter had felt sure, before he sent that sepulchral wail floating through open windows, that only *one* patient would hear it. And, logically, that patient was Mrs. Morse. Her light was on. The watcher could see that she was alone; knew, possibly, that her nurse was in the kitchen. On the other hand, Salter's light was out. By his own account, he was asleep when the wailing voice had startled him into wakefulness and the conviction that his mind was tottering. Had that sinister plotter beneath the window seen Salter strolling on the lawn with his fiancee? Had he counted on the fact that Salter was still out? Or had he known merely that a movie was being shown that evening, an attraction that could be counted upon to lure all of Mayfield's guests into the O. T. Shop? All, that is, who were able to attend— *except Mrs. Morse*. How had he known of that exception? And the logical answer to that was: *because he had just left her in her room.*

"I'm getting as acrobatic at jumping to conclusions as Captain Strawn himself," Dundee gibed mentally, but he could find no reason to climb down from the height his speculations had carried him to.

Very softly, professional curiosity being stronger than his reluctance to play eavesdropper, the detective crept along the inside of the hedge until he stood squarely opposite the first of Mrs. Morse's bedroom windows. The shade was up and the silk curtains pushed aside to admit the brilliant morning sun.

His view unobstructed, Dundee gazed eagerly into the luxurious room. The bed was placed along the wall near the window, so that the patient, propped on pillows, presented her profile to the eavesdropper. Dundee caught his breath with admiration and pity, then held it lest he make the slightest sound. It was like looking upon a life size picture representing "The Grieving Madonna." Long, rippling black hair framed a face of extraordinary purity and pallor. The thin, white fingers of the woman's beautiful hands were laced to support her chin, and to receive, like a chalice, the tears that strained slowly through the thick, long, black lashes of her closed eyes. Her eyes would be black, too, Dundee told himself; large, and heavy with sorrow. She seemed neither old nor young— an ageless, heartbreakingly beautiful incarnation of Motherhood and Despair.

When he had escaped without betraying himself, Dundee struck off hurriedly across the lawn. Thank God, part of her burden could be lifted. One of her unbaptized children was dead, but soon Dr. Harlow could convince her that God had not spoken out of the night to condemn her.

Three or four of the patients, ignorant of the tragedy, had come out for early morning air and sunshine. An extremely thin, gray haired woman was idly slashing at croquet balls with a mallet. A young man, who seemed to be partially paralyzed, was staggering along on tiptoe, eyes bulging out of a drawn, distorted face. A very large, hideously ugly woman, with thin, greasy blonde hair, crimson cheeks and thick, wet lips, was squatting before a flower bed, wantonly tearing the blooms from their stalks. As Dundee passed near, she looked up and laughed—a horrible peal of shrill notes that made the detective's scalp tingle.

"She ain't laughing at you, Buddy! She's laughing at life. . . . Ain't you, Rosie?"

It was a blithe voice, and a vaguely familiar one. Dundee turned toward the driveway, and saw two men crossing it. He paused until they had almost reached him, then took a step or two to meet them.

"Mr. Day, isn't it? I believe I saw you last night."

"Sure. 'Happy' Day in person. I've even got a theme song all my own. . . . Say, Buddy, I didn't catch your name. . . . Dundee? Scotch Irish, ain't you? . . . Meet my pal, Archie Webster."

Turning from the plump, jolly attendant, Dundee shook hands with the man he had heard so much about the night before, and who, apparently, had lost no time in getting out of Ten,' the locked ward. Yes, young Webster was amazingly good looking, he decided. Tall, broad shouldered, with an athlete's waist, as yet unspoiled by the liquor he liked too well. Light brown hair, thick and curling back from a handsome brow. Merry eyes of a clear leaf brown, the whites only slightly bloodshot from last night's spree. Firm fleshed, ruddy cheeks, lightly tanned. A wide mouth, smiling to show splendid teeth.

"Happy is being tactful, Dundee," Archie Webster laughed. "The horrid truth is that I'm a patient just out of Ten,' and it's Happy's job to see that I don't get caught by the Demon Rum. . . . Haven't got a flask on your hip, have you? I could do with a tastier pick me up than the Eno's salts highball they gave me over in Ten' this morning."

"Afraid I haven't," Dundee answered, "but maybe your bootlegger will be around again today."

"My bootlegger?—*again today?*" young Webster repeated, in a puzzled voice. Then he laughed, a frank roar of mirth. "You don't mean to tell me Fatty was a bootlegger, and I—*I!*—didn't tumble! Well, Happy, that's one on me! That pint he slipped me was just a sample, and I didn't realize it–"

"Perhaps I'm the one that was mistaken," Dundee interrupted ruefully. "If so, my apologies to your friend–"

"No friend of mine!" Webster cut in, still laughing. "Never saw him before last night. Don't even know his name. But I don't look a gift horse in the mouth, so when he slipped me what was left of the pint after we'd both had a pull at it, I invited him to see the movies with me, no questions asked. Matter of fact, he was asking enough questions for both of us."

"Curious about the nuts, I guess," Happy Day chuckled. "All visitors are. But who did this chap come to see, if it wasn't you, Archie?"

"Damned if I know," Webster answered, serious for the moment. "I was strolling on the lawn with Enid—that's Miss Rambler, Dundee; the belle of Mayfield—when up walks this fat bird, and Enid runs like a rabbit. Afraid of strangers, the funny kid! Well, he asked me if I'd like a nip, and I said, 'Do I look crazy?' So we had a drink and then he began to ask all sorts of questions about Enid, because she'd run away, I suppose. I wasn't putting out much, but he hung around, and finally we went into the O. T. Shop to see the movies. I guess he'd seen 'Manslaughter' before; anyway, he ducked out before the picture was finished "

"Probably to get better acquainted with Miss Rambler," Dundee suggested.

"Say! That's a thought! Come to think of it, she had left just before that fat bozo ducked! Well, the fat old chaser!" Webster exclaimed in deep disgust. "I'd have hunted him up and socked him one, if I had suspected that was his game."

"As it was, I suppose you just sat tight and enjoyed the show," Dundee suggested craftily.

"Well, no, I ducked, too," Webster confessed, with a rueful grin. "That pint of the best was burning a hole in my hip pocket. Unfortunately, I couldn't find anybody to share it with me, so it landed me in Ten."

"How was that?" Dundee asked sympathetically.

Webster grinned. "When I get likkered up, I get notions in my head. And last night it struck me all of a sudden that Sam Rowan hadn't been behaving exactly like a buddy of mine—not speaking, and all that sort of thing. So I called him for it, and he swung a mean one at my jaw. If I hadn't been staggering already, that old bag o' bones couldn't have even jarred me. As it was, he knocked me flat. And it was me they put in Ten," he added in an injured voice, but with a gleam of mirth in his eyes. "Rowan's all right. My fault. . . . Well, cheerio, old sport! Glad to have you here. Not a bad hole. The Big Doctor's a great guy. . . . And the *little doctor*—Oh, baby!"

"Come along and get your hydro now, Archie," the attendant urged. "See you later, Dundee. . . . Play bridge? Poker?"

"Both," Dundee assured him.

"Then we'll be seeing you," 'Happy' Day promised blithely, linking a chummy arm in that of his patient.

Hardly the type to commit murder, Dundee reflected, as he watched Archie Webster swing jauntily along the driveway. A likeable youngster in spite of, or perhaps because of, his frank weaknesses. But as the detective continued on his way to the second floor of the main building his mind was more engrossed with the problem of the fat unknown, his unexplained visit, his persistent interest in Enid Rambler, and his disappearance. Well, Strawn had an excellent machinery for searching for mysterious strangers. And he could undoubtedly get an accurate description from Webster, when he questioned that unregenerate young man. . . .

"I thought you were never coming!" Justine Harlow scolded from the top landing of the stairway.

"The time seemed long because you're eaten up with curiosity," Dundee scolded in turn. "How about giving me a job here as your assistant? I've already cured one of your patients of a neurosis, and can guarantee to do the same for another."

"You mean Salter—?" she demanded, her gray green eyes widening.

"I mean that Salter heard 'the voice of God,' too," he elucidated. "I mean further that he now knows he was not the only one who heard it, and that it was not the voice of God, but of a devil in human form. . . . Pardon the melodrama, Doctor, but I'm feeling rather strongly on the subject, and I'll be happier when I know that you've taken the same good news to poor Mrs. Morse. ... Of course, in a sense, it is 'too late' for her, since her baby died unbaptized–"

"But he didn't!" she cried, and her voice shook with emotion. "That's why I sent for you. Mr. Morse is here now with his mother in law, Mrs. Prade. Mrs. Prade is a devout Catholic, of course, and it seems that she smuggled a priest into the Morse home and had the little fellow baptized before he died. Mr. Morse didn't know about it. Mrs. Prade thought he'd object, you see–"

"And they're here now?" Dundee interrupted eagerly. "I want a look at Morse. Why are they here so early?"

"I'll let you talk to him," Dr. Harlow offered, and led the way into a small but comfortably furnished office opposite her apartment.

"Mrs. Prade, Mr. Morse, this is Mr. Dundee, of the district attorney's office," the doctor announced, and the detective found himself shaking hands, first with a stout, elderly woman, then with a heavy, middle aged man. Morse, Dundee thought, might have posed for an artist as the typical American business man. Neither handsome nor homely; strong, rather heavy features; shrewd but kindly brown eyes; thick, smoothly brushed gray hair, quietly expensive suit of brown homespun.

"Glad to meet you, Mr. Dundee," Morse said, clipping his words like a busy executive. "The doctor here tells me you've stumbled upon something that closely concerns my wife."

"I'm afraid I have," Dundee admitted seriously. "But first, will you tell me how you happen to be calling so early this morning?"

"For two reasons, sir," Morse answered curtly. "Last night when I visited my wife—the first visit I have had with her since she has become—well, herself again, she began to ask all sorts of questions about the children. On my previous visits she never mentioned them. That was part of her—trouble. She acted as if they did not belong to her, as if she had no responsibility for them."

"I understand," Dundee assured him. "I have heard Dr. Koenig's diagnosis of her trouble."

The big man touched his forehead with a fine linen handkerchief. "It has been pretty bad, sir, but thank God the doctor got at the root of the trouble."

"I always did say–" the mother in law began importantly.

"Yes, Mother, you did," Morse agreed. "Well, last night when she asked about the children I knew she was really cured. But when she wanted to know all about the baby " his voice broke, and his mother in law crossed herself, facile tears springing into her eyes.

"You told her he was dead?" Dundee asked.

"No. I put her off as best I could, but she *sensed* some thing was wrong—mighty wrong," Morse told him, again touching his forehead with the linen square. "She asked me pointblank if he was dead, but I put her off again, told her he was 'asleep that minute.' But I was sure she wasn't fooled. It's hard to fool a mother, sir," he added sententiously. "But for my sake she played the game. Didn't get hysterical or anything like that. But I made up my mind to speak to Koenig and get him to tell her the truth. I thought it best for her to stay here until she'd got over the shock."

"So you called on the doctor last night?" Dundee asked, tense with excitement.

"No. The doctor was in, but I could tell he was busy, and I didn't feel much like waiting," Morse answered. "Besides, I couldn't help hearing and it embarrassed me–"

"Tell me exactly what you heard or saw!" Dundee demanded sternly.

"We—ell, it wasn't anything much," the big man deprecated, flushing, "but that's the second reason I dropped in so early this morning. I thought it just might have something to do with what happened here last night–"

"Go on!" Dundee almost shouted.

"Well, Miss Hunter had told me the doctor was in his office, so I went to the reception room," Morse began reluctantly. "It was then close on to nine o'clock. I was just about to knock when I heard a woman's voice. I thought it was a patient, of course, and I suppose it was. Anyway, she was crying and talking at the same time–"

"Could you distinguish what they said?" Dundee urged, as the narrator paused.

"Not a great deal of it. It seemed like he was trying to get rid of the woman, and she didn't want to go," Morse answered slowly. "I heard her say something like: 'I won't leave you! You can't make me!' And the doctor tried to pacify her. I heard him say, 'But my darling girl!' and then the woman began to carry on pretty bad–" Again Morse's voice dragged to an embarrassed halt.

"Did you hear anything else they said?" Dundee prodded.

"Well, the girl said something about he'd made her love him, and now he hated her, and she could kill him when he looked at her like that," the man continued uncomfortably. "Just the sort of thing a woman will say when she's all worked up, and not mean a thing by it."

Dundee glanced at Justine Harlow. If she had died while the man was talking, her face could not have been more rigid, more ghastly in its pallor.

"And the doctor?" the detective asked dutifully, but his voice was flat and colorless. He was not enjoying his job at that moment. "Did you hear his reply? And did he call the woman by name?"

"No. Or if he did, I did not hear the name," Morse assured him earnestly. "Once he said, "Child! Child!,' as if he was sorry for her and sort of hopeless. And fond of her, too. Then when she began to pound him on the chest with her fists—or that's what it sounded like—I tiptoed out. I was feeling pretty uncomfortable."

"Would you recognize that voice—the woman's voice, I mean—if you heard it again?" Dundee asked, his eyes again resting upon the blighted face of the young doctor.

The man shook his head. He seemed relieved to be able to answer: "I'm afraid I wouldn't, sir. You see, she was crying all the time she was talking, and I'm sure her voice was a lot shriller than it would normally be."

Justine Harlow was not simply relieved. She looked as if she had signed a new lease on life.

"I see," Dundee commented grimly, and relapsed into a thoughtful silence, his blue eyes narrowed to slits.

The mother in law shifted in her chair, which creaked under her weight. "So my son in law dropped in at my house last night, to give me the news of Lora–"

"What time did Mr. Morse arrive at your house?" Dundee roused himself from his reverie to interrupt.

"Why, let me see," the woman ruminated. Then, eagerly: "I know! The Melody Boys were just finishing their program on the radio, and they go on at ten o'clock every night—I wouldn't miss 'em for a farm—so it must have been about twenty minutes after ten when Roland walked in."

"You live in Hamilton?" Dundee asked.

"Oh, yes, sir. On Maple Drive," she confirmed proudly, naming one of the most fashionable streets in the suburbs of the city.

"I drove around for an hour before I called on my mother in law," Roland Morse volunteered, but with no trace of belligerence. "I was pretty badly upset by my visit with Lora—my wife. Afraid the news of the baby's death might unhinge her poor brain again, and yet I realized it couldn't be kept from her any longer–"

"So the poor boy came to talk it over with me," the mother in law cut in. "Of course I was kind of surprised to see him–"

"Then Mr. Morse is not a frequent visitor?" Dundee interrupted swiftly.

The woman flushed and bridled. Morse's heavy cheeks turned a dull red.

"Well, no, sir, things being like they were," Mrs. Prade admitted. "I never have held with mixed marriages, even when a priest performs the ceremony. To my notion Lora and Roland aren't married at all–"

"Then you did not give your consent to the union?" Dundee broke in.

"Certainly not! But there wasn't any stopping Lora, her with her own money and all," the woman answered. "I always did say her grandfather made a terrible mistake, leaving her all that money with no strings tied to it–"

"Then Mrs. Morse is a very rich woman in her own right?" Dundee asked softly.

"Too rich!" Mrs. Morse's mother snapped. "It turned her head–"

"Now, Mother!" Roland Morse pleaded, the flush mounting to his iron gray hair.

"I'm only answering the gentleman's questions," his mother in law retorted acidly. "I said last night I'd for give you, when you and Lora are married in the Church, and I'll stick to it. But I'm no hypocrite. You're too old for Lora, and living in sin with you drove my poor girl crazy–"

Morse shrugged helplessly, and his eyes appealed to Dundee.

"I understand, Mrs. Prade," the detective began, coming briskly to the rescue, "that Mr. Morse called on you last night to tell you that your daughter had been almost miraculously restored to her right mind by Dr. Koenig, but that he feared the effect of the news of the baby's death. Is that right?"

"He wanted me to help him out," the mother in law answered. "And when he said he was more than willing to marry Lora in the Church, I told him that I'd put one over on him by having poor little Rollie baptized by Father Ryan. For a minute he looked pretty mad—yes, you did, Roland Morse!—but it didn't take him a minute to realize that I'd saved Lora from losing her mind all over again, and he was man enough to thank me. I told him I was coming here the first thing this morning and tell my poor girl the truth. A mother's love to comfort her and help her bear—"

"Just say to her," Dundee interrupted, with strange emphasis, his eyes upon Roland Morse, "that it is not *'too late! Too late!'*"

CHAPTER TWELVE

"I FEEL," Dundee told himself, with a rueful grin, as he strolled out of the main building of Mayfield Sanitarium, "like a Boy Scout with a holiday coming to him. Only eight o'clock, and I've already done two good deeds today."

But he paused on the lowest step of the three leading from the porch to the driveway, a frown banishing the grin. Was he giving too much time to the Morse mystery, and thereby neglecting the major mystery of the psychiatrist's murder? But "the voice of God" intrigued and tormented him. Roland Morse had had ample time to wail sepulchrally and disastrously under his wife's windows—and incidentally beneath Howard Salter's windows; pay that first actual or fictitious visit to the reception room; then bide his time until the mysterious and importunate woman visitor had left Koenig's office; then return and–

"But why the devil should he murder the doctor?" Dundee puzzled. "That fiendish wailing was amply sufficient to accomplish his purpose—or would have been, if Salter had not heard the fatal words, too. . . . Motive enough, God knows, if Morse *is* the schemer I'm making him out. A wife rich in her own right, who conveniently goes crazy enough for the courts to adjudge her incompetent and appoint her husband guardian of her person and her property. . . . The old lady let *that* cat out of the bag! . . . But why murder the doctor? Unless, of course, Morse's whole yarn about the sobbing female in Koenig's office is an out and out lie, the truth being that Koenig, on his way to pay a professional call on Mrs. Morse, caught Morse in his wailing act, and–"

But the detective's frown deepened. "That won't wash," he told himself disgustedly. "Leaves too many things unexplained. If Koenig caught Morse in the wailing act, why didn't he immediately reassure Mrs. Morse? And what did Morse do between nine o'clock and nine forty five, when Koenig was killed? Furthermore, would Koenig go on calmly working at his typewriter and let a dangerous man like Morse wander about the office until he maneuvered himself into a position to kill him? . . . No, Bonnie, my lad, *that* won't wash! But I'd wager a fortune, if I had it, that 'the voice of God' is mixed up in this murder—somehow!"

He was about to cross the driveway when he caught sight of a boy in overalls industriously polishing the hood of one of the parked cars—a trim little coupe next to his own roadster, which was sadly in need of the youth's ministrations.

"Neat little car," Dundee remarked idly, as he readied into his pocket for a dollar bill. "How about shining up my boat, young man?"

"Sure thing!" the boy beamed, his eyes on the bill. "Soon as I finish with Dr. Harlow's. ... I like to keep it looking like new–"

"It *is* new, isn't it?" Dundee asked, stepping upon the running board and peering in at the speedometer, which showed a mileage of' 9,066.

"Had it nearly a year, she has," the boy informed him proudly. "I take care of it for her—gasoline, oil, tires, and everything. Had to have the crankcase drained yesterday. *She'd* never remember to, not even with that sticker on the dashboard–"

Suddenly Dundee leaned farther into the car, his eyes fixed incredulously upon the oil change sticker the boy was referring to. He read: "Drain oil at 10,055 miles," and, beneath, the name of the garage which had applied the sticker.

From experience, Dundee knew that a car owner was adjured, by all that was holy in motordom, to drain his crankcase every thousand miles.

"Well, young man, you won't have to worry about that crankcase for another thousand miles," the detective said casually, as he withdrew his head.

The boy peered in his turn, then, grinning at his own conscientiousness, he corrected his new client: "Gotta change again after 989 miles. She's drove eleven miles since yesterday."

"Right you are!" Dundee agreed heartily, but there was no satisfaction or triumph behind the words. "Give my bus a good rub, won't you? I'm afraid you'll have to use a little elbow grease on it."

So the little doctor had been lying when she said she had taken a long drive the night before! That innocent-looking sticker on the dashboard had betrayed her. Eleven miles in two hours!

Dundee's almost stunned brain had hardly begun to wrestle with all the implications of Justine Harlow's lie when he crossed the threshold of Sunflower Court. Lurline Doty looked up from her desk and cocked her hennaed head coquettishly.

"Aren't we the dreat big sheik, though?" she accused him playfully. "A certain booful young lady is just dying to see you. . . . 'Course I haven't breathed a word about who you really are "

"Then don't begin now," Dundee interrupted rather curtly, for his stomach never reacted kindly toward baby talk. "You mean Miss Rambler, I suppose? . . . May I see her now?"

"You may!" The nurse bit off the words and buttoned her mouth into a thin streak of rouge.

"Ni—ize nursie!" Dundee forced himself to say in a coaxing voice as he passed her, and was rewarded by fluttering eyelids and smile curved lips. Silly, he told himself, to antagonize anyone who might be of help. . . .

A jolly looking, black haired little nurse answered his knock upon the patio door of Suite C.

"You're Mr. Dundee, aren't you?" she asked in a low voice, which sank into a whisper after he had admitted his identity. "She doesn't know a thing yet about Dr. Koenig. The poor child's been begging me for an hour to send for him. . . . Yes, Miss Rambler! It's Mr. Dundee. . . ,.. She's been asking for you, too, sir. . . . This way."

The detective led the way into the sitting room—a larger and even more luxurious one than his own, and discreetly disappeared into the bedroom beyond, closing the door softly.

"Do I make a satisfactory picture of an invalid?" the girl stretched upon the big couch demanded.

Dundee cocked his head and an eyebrow as he pretended to give serious consideration to the question, to which there could be but one answer. The girl, laughing, touched fingertips to her gleaming chestnut hair which was parted in the middle and arranged in loose curls that hung to her shoulders and mingled with the white ostrich feather trimming on her peacock blue silk robe—a blue that could not match that of her eyes for brilliance and beauty. The bandaged ankle was hidden beneath a flowered Spanish shawl.

"You'll do," he told her, as if grudgingly. Then: "What are those doing here so soon?" and he pointed to a pair of crutches propped against the foot of the couch.

"Resting quietly, thank you," she smiled at him. "And giving me a warm sense of security. They tell me that I can hobble away, even if I can't run. Sweet old crutches! I wouldn't go to sleep until Miss Lacey dug up a pair for me last night."

"Still feeling fugitive?" Dundee grinned.

"Off and on," she shrugged. Then words came tumbling out, as she raised herself upon an elbow and fixed him with her luminous blue eyes: "Listen, Mr. Dundee! I don't *want* to go! I want to stay right here *forever*, but I may have to go, and I want you to promise to help me–"

"To run away?" Dundee asked gently, ashamed of the role he was forced to play. "Hadn't you better tell me all about it?"

The girl stopped smiling and a wary look came into the deep blue eyes. "Oh!" she shrugged. "Just call it a—complex. A very popular word around here. . . . Tell me! Did you have an interview with Dr. Koenig last night?"

"I saw him," Dundee evaded, watching her intently. "But it was Dr. Harlow who admitted me."

"Isn't she a darling?" Enid Rambler exclaimed enthusiastically. "*She* is my friend. . . . But what did you think of Koenig?"

"A great man, I've been told," Dundee replied care fully. "Do you like him?"

The girl dropped her eyes, her fingers nervously plucking at the ostrich feathers about her throat. "I hardly know him," she said in a low voice, "but he looks—fascinating. And I *thought* he looked kind, but–" Her voice broke, and she was silent for a long minute. Then, lifting her head, the blue eyes met Dundee's bravely through a film of tears. "He isn't kind. He's cruel. He's going to—to have me taken away–"

"But, if you want to leave anyway," Dundee began, when her voice had choked so that she could not go on.

"At least I'd be *free* if I ran away!" the girl interrupted passionately. "I *won't* be locked up—Oh, my God! Who's that?"

Her terror was a sickening thing to see, but before Dundee could find words she was sitting up and clutching at his coat sleeve. "If it's Dr. Koenig, would you mind leaving us alone? I'm going to get down on my knees to him–"

There was the sound of a door opening, footsteps in the little hall. Then into the living room strode Captain Strawn of the Homicide Squad. At sight of his uniform the girl uttered a strangled cry, then collapsed against the pillows, her face as rigid and white as it would be in death.

Dundee turned his back upon the pitiful spectacle, and, winking at his one time chief, demanded indignantly: "What's wrong, Officer? What do you want here?"

Strawn took his cue. "Who are you, sir? . . . One of the patients? . . . Well, then," he commanded sternly, "stay where you are, and answer when you're spoken to. ... Now, young lady! Get a hold of yourself, and speak lively. Your name is Rambler, ain't it?"

The girl's eyes flew open and stared incredulously at the police officer. After a moment she answered, and her voice was stronger than Dundee had expected it to be.

"Yes! Enid Rambler. . . . And who are you?"

"I'm Captain John Strawn, Chief of the Homicide Squad of the Hamilton Police Department," Strawn informed her grimly.

"Homicide?" she breathed, and fell back upon her pillows, her eyelids closing.

"Don't like the sound of that word, eh?" Strawn gibed. "Well, maybe you like the sound of *murder* a little better!"

"I say, Captain!" Dundee protested sincerely, and he did not wink this time. "Miss Rambler is not well, and I beg you "

"All right, all right! Keep your shirt on!" Strawn growled. "Now, young woman, I haven't any time to lose. Dr. Carl Koenig was murdered in his office last night–"

"*Dr. Koenig!*" The words brought the girl upright. Her blue eyes seemed to be starting from her head, but, to Dundee's amazed bewilderment, the expression that slowly dawned in them was relief. "But what—why—I don't see what *I* have to do with it "

"That's what I'm here to find out!" Strawn cut in sternly. "*After* he was murdered last night, *you* ran away from the sanitarium–"

The girl's laugh was hard for Dundee to bear. "And you're here because you think *I—I* killed him?" she cried hysterically. "Why, that's funny! Oh!" And her jangling laughter filled the room.

"Funny as hell!" Strawn agreed grimly. "Come on in, Brede!"

The anemic looking young man who held the job of police stenographer sidled into the room from the little hall, notebook in hand.

"I want a statement from you, young woman," Strawn told the girl, "and I'll warn you that we're already in possession of a good many facts about your movements last night, so you'd better talk fast and talk straight."

"What do you want to know?" Enid Rambler asked, almost coolly.

"Your movements from nine o'clock last night until you were brought back here, *after trying to escape*."

Only then did the girl seem to realize the seriousness of the situation. The flush which had risen with her laughter died out of her cheeks. "From nine o'clock?" she repeated, as if sparring for time. "Why, at nine o'clock I was in the O. T. Shop, attending a motion picture show for the patients. I left when the feature picture was about half finished–"

"Why?" Strawn shot at her.

The girl drew a quick breath. "Because I was—nervous. And I didn't like the picture–"

"Because it was named 'Manslaughter'?" Strawn suggested.

"I didn't like it; that's all!" Enid Rambler retorted crisply. "I'm here for nerves, and I became too nervous to sit still any longer. I left the shop about half past nine, and tried to find someone who had authority to give me a dose of bromide. I got it every night until about a week ago, but Dr. Harlow wants me to try to sleep without it. Miss Caplan wasn't in the chartroom, and I didn't remember until later that she was watching the pictures. I wandered around the hall and living room of the main building for ten or fifteen minutes, then I went upstairs to see if Dr. Harlow was in. She wasn't, so I–"

"Why didn't you ask Koenig?" Strawn suggested sarcastically, as the girl's voice dragged to a pause.

"I—I thought of doing so," Enid told him slowly, reluctantly. "But—I knew he was busy–"

"How did you know that? You saw him, eh?" Strawn pounced.

"I told you I wandered around the hall," the girl answered defiantly. "When I first came into the hall from outside—I left the shop by the back door and walked around the main building—I saw him sitting at his desk. But his back was to the door and he was typing. I thought I could find someone else. Later, after I'd failed to find Dr. Harlow and had tried to walk off my nervousness–"

"Where did you walk?" Strawn cut in.

"Down to the big gates on Willow Creek Drive, and back. I walked slowly till I got to the gates, then I made up my mind to interrupt Dr. Koenig, so I hurried back. , But as soon as I entered the main hall I saw that his door was closed, although the light still showed through the transom."

"That was about what time?" Strawn demanded.

"I don't know," the girl answered, frowning. "Let me think. ... I looked at the clock in hall right after I'd left the picture show, and it was a minute or two after half past nine. I didn't notice the time when I returned to ask Dr. Koenig for the bromide, but it must have been about ten minutes to ten."

"Did you knock on his door?" Strawn asked, skepticism writ large on his face.

"No. I supposed he was interviewing a new patient, or an old one, and I did not dream of disturbing him by knocking."

"Did you *hear* anything to make you think he was busy with a patient?" Strawn asked craftily.

"Why, no—" the girl faltered. "I just saw the door was shut–"

"Come clean, Miss Rambler!" Strawn interrupted with sudden viciousness. "You know damn well the doctor was *dead* at ten minutes to ten–"

"*Dead—then?*" the girl scarcely breathed the words, and Dundee was afraid she had fainted when she fell back upon the couch, her right arm dangling till the lax fingers almost touched the floor.

"Just a minute, Captain!" he pleaded, as he sprang to a table, snatched a sheaf of roses from a vase, and hurried to the couch with the water.

"She's just stalling for time," Strawn muttered, but he waited until Dundee had dabbed at the girl's bluish lips and drawn cheeks with a water soaked handkerchief.

When she spoke at last, without opening her eyes, her voice was a thin thread of sound: "I'm sorry. . . . The shock. ... I didn't know—he was—dead–"

"Then, Miss Rambler!" Strawn almost thundered. "*Why did you run away?*"

The ghost of a laugh came from her pale lips. "There wasn't any reason why I should run away," she said strangely.

"But you did try to escape—and might have got away with it, too, if you hadn't sprained your ankle," Strawn reminded her relentlessly.

"I—can't explain," she answered colorlessly. "I'm a patient here. As Luke Chester says, none of us is here for flat feet. We're all ill, in one way or another. Dr. Harlow will tell you that I'm not—responsible for the way my nerves behave. Last night—" she went on, more strongly, and with a wary, calculating look in her dark blue eyes, "I acted on an uncontrollable impulse—"

"So you're going to frame up the good old 'insanity plea are you?" Strawn cut in brutally. "Well, let me tell you it won't work. Dr. Koenig knew you were stalling—that you didn't have any business to be here–"

"How do you know that?" the girl cried sharply.

"Because Dr. Harlow told me so," Strawn obliged. "Just yesterday she and Koenig had a run in over your case. She contended you were sick, and Koenig said there was nothing the matter with you; that you'd simply pulled the wool over the little lady doctor's eyes, in order to stay on here."

"Did he trouble to tell her why anyone would insist on staying in a place like this, if she was well?" Enid Rambler asked, her voice strangely cold and measured.

"I reckon you know the answer to that question better than Koenig did," Strawn accused. "I can make a pretty good guess myself, young woman. You stayed on here, *biding your time!* Koenig was nobody's fool. He sensed that you had some evil purpose, caught a look of hate in your eyes–"

"What *are* you talking about?" the girl interrupted scornfully. "I scarcely knew Dr. Koenig. I respected him highly, and knew that he did a great work here. Why on earth should *I* kill him?"

"I admit that we've got to find the motive," Strawn told her magnanimously. "Where's your home?"

The girl wilted visibly. "I—have no home. I am—an orphan–"

"Oh, yeah?" Strawn sneered. "Then where were you living before you came here?"

"At the—Randolph Hotel," she answered, but the pause was long enough to convince Dundee as well as Strawn that she was lying.

"And before that?"

The girl's eyelids flickered. "I lived in New York. With friends. The—Hendersons. They are touring in Europe now."

"Yeah?" Strawn was heavily sarcastic. "Got plenty of money, haven't you?" and his eyes swept the luxurious sitting room of Mayfield's most expensive suite.

"Enough," she answered curtly.

"What were you doing in Hamilton?"

"Oh, just breaking my trip to San Francisco," she answered nonchalantly. "I wasn't well, and was going to the Coast by easy stages."

"Yeah?" Strawn's vocabulary of sarcasm was strictly limited. "Now, young fellow!" and he turned abruptly to Dundee. "I hear it was you that found this girl on the roadside. . . . What time was that?"

"About eleven o'clock," Dundee answered easily, keep ing a straight face. "She was unconscious. I revived her and brought her here, since I was on my way to Mayfield anyway."

"How long had you been on the roadside?" Strawn turned again to the girl.

"I can't say exactly how long I was unconscious, if that is what you mean. I decided to run away just after"— she caught her breath sharply and paled—"very soon after I found Dr. Koenig's door closed and thought he was busy. I—just suddenly went to pieces when I couldn't get anyone to give me anything for my nerves. So—I ran away."

"Uh huh. . . . What are *you* here for? . . . Dundee's the name, ain't it?"

"Right!" and the young detctive grinned. "For a rest cure. Been working too hard. I also have occasional trouble with my heart."

"Yeah?" Strawn grinned wryly. "Well, I'm afraid you'll have another attack, if you hang around here," and he cast a meaning glance toward the beautiful girl on the couch. "Come along, Brede. . . . You understand, Miss Rambler, that I'm not through with you yet. And if you try to make another getaway you land in jail! . . . Say, wait a minute, Brede. . . . Miss Rambler, you say you roamed around the place, inside and out, for about twenty minutes, between half past nine and ten minutes to ten, and then lit out for town. . . . See anybody during any of them strolls of yours?"

Color flamed in the girl's cheeks. "You haven't believed a thing I've told you yet, so I don't expect you to believe this: *I saw no one.* No one at all, at any time, except Dr. Koenig sitting in his office at shortly after half past nine." Strawn, who had come close to the couch, was about to wheel toward the door, when he caught sight of the pair of crutches.

"Haven't lost any time, have you?" he grinned at the girl maliciously. "Now, you listen to me, young lady! Either you give me your word of honor that you'll stay right where you are, or I'll station one of my men outside that door to see that you do! Which will it be?"

"I'll make no promise!" Enid Rambler cried, and to Dundee's profound amazement there was a ring of exultation, rather than of defiant anger, in her clear voice. And now there was no fear in her beautiful eyes. . . .

CHAPTER THIRTEEN

"WHEW!" Strawn whistled and mopped his brow, as Dundee joined him on the lawn in front of Sunflower Court. "What a girl! . . . But I didn't think she'd let you go so quick."

"In effect, Miss Rambler told me to run along and roll my hoop," Dundee laughed. "But not until she made sure that you had actually stationed a man outside her door."

"I swear I don't know what to make of that dame," Strawn worried. "First time I ever got mixed up with a bunch of nuts, and they're getting my goat. . . . But I called her bluff. Barney won't even let a mouse get past him."

"Which is exactly what the girl is counting on," Dundee retorted.

"What do you mean?" Strawn scowled.

"Isn't that rather obvious?" Dundee shrugged. "That girl was in a perfect lather of fear that she'd follow Dr. Koenig to the grave—until you kindly offered her the protection of a six foot plainclothes man. She knows some thing she doesn't dare tell, and yet"—he hesitated, his black brows drawn together in perplexity—"and yet, Chief, I'm absolutely convinced Enid Rambler did not know, until you told her, that Carl Koenig had been murdered."

"Then why the hell did she run away?" Strawn demanded angrily.

"Ask Enid Rambler. And she won't tell. ... By the way, I'll feel safer about that girl if you keep a man there day and night until this business is cleared up."

"Wasting a couple of good men, probably," Strawn grumbled.

"Then you don't think Miss Rambler is the murderess?" Dundee smiled.

"Don't ask me what I think!" Strawn growled. "I'm already fit to be tied. Before the day is over I'll have the police commissioner and the mayor and the chief of police, to say nothing of the newspapers, ganged up on me yelping for an arrest. . . . Coming along?"

"What's the program?"

"I'm gonna use a little of this here psychology you high brows are always spieling about," Strawn grinned. "Gonna quiz Rowan and Webster right on the scene of the crime, and see which cracks first. My own money's on Rowan. ... By the way, we checked that Lacey dame's alibi and it's watertight. But I'd still like to know why she's down in the doctor's will for half his estate."

"Then I wonder," Dundee mused, "why she gave a fake alibi the first time."

"Search me!" Strawn shrugged. "But old lady Satterlee and her daughter, Mabel, both swear she got to their house about eight o'clock and did not leave until exactly ten. So that's that. But if you want to hear me go for Rowan and Webster, sneak into Cantrell's office by the back door, and leave the connecting door ajar so's you can hear and not be seen, provided you still want to swank around here as a patient rich enough to afford a suite in Sunflower Court. . . . Here's a morning paper if you haven't seen it."

Automatically Dundee accepted both the invitation and the newspaper, but remained stockstill as Captain Strawn struck off across the lawn, trailed by a couple of his squad and by Brede, the stenographer.

When he did follow, skirting the main building to reach the back door of Cantrell's office, the heaviness of his heart made his feet drag. However much he wanted to, he could no longer dodge coupling the sickening discovery that Justine Harlow had lied with Morse's story of an hysterical woman pleading with Dr. Koenig just before nine o'clock. If that woman had not been Justine

Harlow, then who could she have been? For Enid Rambler, as well as Norah Lacey, had an alibi—as yet uncorroborated except by Nurse Caplan—for the hour and a half between eight and nine thirty. But apparently Norah Lacey, as well as Justine Harlow, had been lying. . . .

"Come in, boy!" It was Strawn, holding the door open for him. "The show hasn't started yet, and I'm fixing you up a reserved seat. . . . See? I've hung this mirror so you can sit behind the connecting door and see what's going on in the other office. Cantrell and the little doctor both insist on listening in, too, to see that the mean old police man don't third degree their precious patients, so you'll have company in here."

The two doctors, who were seated opposite each other at Cantrell's desk, did not smile at or answer the captain's sally. The medical man was wearing a crisp, spotless suit of white linen, and a still bleeding cut on his cheek testified to a recent shave. But that was the extent of his morning freshness. He looked like a man who had not slept for a week, and who feverishly doubted his ability ever to sleep again. Justine Harlow sat grave and still, but to Dundee's quick eyes she seemed less worried than at any time since Dr. Koenig's murder had been discovered.

" 'Bout time for that secretary to show up, ain't it?" Strawn asked.

"Miss Home telephoned about half an hour ago, just after she'd read the morning paper," Dr. Harlow answered. "I told her to report for duty as usual, at nine o'clock."

"Pretty near nine now," Strawn grumbled, as he passed into the dead doctor's office, leaving the door half open.

Dundee took his seat behind it, and unfolded the paper Strawn had given him. "FAMOUS ALIENIST SLAIN" stretched in big, black type across the front page. As he read the story below Dundee mentally blessed

Strawn for his discretion. Not even the exact hour of the doctor's murder, as arrived at by the coroner and Dr. Cantrell, had been given to the reporters. "Some time between eight and ten o'clock last night," the reporter on *The News* had written, "when all his patients who were not bedridden or confined to the locked ward were thrilling to a motion picture melodrama, fittingly entitled 'Manslaughter,' Dr. Carl Koenig, one of the five most famous psychiatrists in the United States, was brutally murdered in his private office in the main building of Mayfield Sanitarium."

And if the murderer had read that account in his morning paper, he must have been dismayed by the fact that his careful, "mad rage" wrecking of the office was not so much as mentioned. But that disappointment had probably been counteracted by the fact that there was also no mention of rubber gloves, and the absence of fingerprints upon the murder weapon.

"Captain John F. Strawn, Chief of the Homicide Squad, is working on a theory that one of the many enemies whom the great alienist made as an expert witness for and against criminals who rely upon the 'insanity plea' "

Dundee lowered his paper and fixed his eyes upon the mirror, for he had heard the door from the reception room open and, simultaneously, a genial, hearty voice calling out:

"Morning, Doctor!"

He saw Strawn swing himself around in the dead doctor's swivel chair, and could imagine the change of expression on the face of the man in the doorway.

"Your name Rowan?"

Dundee could not see the speaker but heard the answer, in a puzzled but still cheerful voice: "Yes, sir. I was told Dr. Koenig wanted to see me–"

"You were told," Strawn corrected grimly, "that you were wanted in Dr. Koenig's office—and you are! . . . Come on in! Sit down!"

The mirror showed a man advancing on slow feet to the chair Strawn was pointing at. Samuel Rowan was thin almost to emaciation, and stooping shoulders minimized his height to a bare average. Thick, slightly curling gray hair was matched in a short, stubby mustache, and contrasted sharply with the sunburned swarthiness of his lean face. Brown eyes, one of them clouded over with a cataract, were shielded by old fashioned, steel rimmed spectacles. His clothes—an old sweater and a pair of gray, baggy trousers, were marked with the unkempt shabbiness of a man who takes no interest in his personal appearance.

Either the man was a consummate actor and had had ample time to prepare himself for the ordeal he was about to endure, or he was genuinely puzzled but not frightened at finding himself face to face with a police captain, Dundee concluded, his eyes riveted upon the mirrored face of Samuel Rowan.

"Well, Rowan!" Strawn snapped. "You know why you're here, don't you?"

"I suppose I do," Rowan answered, surprisingly, "and I guess the sooner we get it over, the better. ... I have to appear in court in person, don't I?"

"You're damned right you do! . . . Pretty cool, ain't you, Rowan? Well, don't kid yourself you're going to sneak out of this on an insanity plea–"

Rowan half rose from his chair, his cheeks flushing darkly. "What the devil are you talking about? I'm as sane as you are–"

"That's swell!" Strawn cut in. "Now, come clean, Rowan! What did you do it for?"

The man sank back into his chair, staring blankly at his questioner. Then suddenly he began to laugh, a harsh, bitter sound that made Dundee's nerves tingle. "I see! Koenig was just stringing me, was he? Didn't believe a word I said. . . . Well! That's a good one on me!" And again that harsh, discordant laughter filled the room. "I keep my mouth shut for two years, and as soon as I open it—to a doctor, mind you!—the police are after me! That's good! That's rich!"

Before Dundee could realize her intention Justine Harlow was out of her chair and half across Cantrell's office. He made no effort to stop her and in a flash she was at Rowan's side, her small white hand closing firmly on his shoulder.

"Dr. Koenig did *not* betray your confidence, Mr. Rowan!" she cried, her eyes blazing upon Strawn. "What ever you said to Dr. Koenig is as safe as if it were still locked in your own brain! Remember that, Mr. Rowan!"

Strawn was on his feet, in a choking rage. "Do you want me to run you in for obstructing justice, young woman?"

"I don't care what you do to me," she blazed, "but have the decency to tell this patient why you are questioning him."

"He knows why! He's as good as confessed," Strawn answered savagely.

"Oh, no, he hasn't! If you have any sense at all, you'd know what he thought you were here for! Tell him, Mr. Rowan."

The man reached up a thin, trembling, brown hand to close over the little doctor's. "I thought—You see, sir, I was adjudged a mental incompetent by the court about eighteen months ago, and was made a ward of the county. Dr. Koenig was in court when my case came up and offered to take care of me here, free of charge. Yesterday I had a long talk with the doctor and when it was over I told him I was cured, and wanted to get out and get to work. He seemed to think I'd better stay on here for a while, to make an adjustment, as he put it, before I tried to take my place in the outside world. But when I saw you here instead of Dr. Koenig I thought he had concluded to let me go, and that you were to take me before the court, in order to have my status as a mentally competent person restored."

"So that's what you thought, eh?" Strawn sneered. "Had a powerful weight on your mind for two years, didn't you, Rowan?"

"I did," the man answered simply.

"Your *conscience* hurt you so bad that people thought you were crazy, didn't it?"

"Yes. I was put in the psychopathic ward of the county hospital for observation because I tried three times to commit suicide."

"And it felt pretty good to spill the beans to Koenig, didn't it?"

"Yes. But it was the fact that Dr. Koenig convinced me that I had nothing to blame myself for that cured me."

"Then why"—and Strawn leaned forward and shook an accusing forefinger in the man's face—"did you have to *kill* Koenig to make sure he'd keep his mouth shut?"

"Kill—Koenig?" the man echoed blankly, and his hand slowly released its clutch of Justine Harlow's fingers.

"You don't mean—?"

"Yeah! Murdered! In this office last night!" Strawn flung the words at the charity patient. "And the man that did it tore up your case history! You weren't taking any chances, were you, Rowan?"

"You mean—you're accusing *me*–?"

"You got me, Rowan! . . . And I've got you!" Strawn assured him grimly.

"But you—you can't " the man stammered, his tanned face turning yellow. "My God! I can't realize these things you're saying—When was the doctor killed?"

"You know damned well when he was killed," Strawn retorted. "And I have to hand it to you, Rowan, for choosing your time well. With everybody, including the night head nurse, shut up in the O. T. Shop watching the movies–"

"But I was there, too," Rowan cut in.

"Oh, sure! You took good care that everybody'd see you and hear you in the shop *before* the lights went off, and that you'd be seen coming out with the rest of the patients when the show was over," Strawn agreed, his voice heavy with sarcasm. "But who can you find to swear you didn't sneak out about half past nine and in again just before ten? Answer me that, Rowan!"

The man's pallor deepened. He seemed incapable of answering.

"Think, Mr. Rowan!" Dr. Harlow urged. "Whom did you sit beside?"

The man turned his head and stared up at her dumbly for a moment. Then he shook his head, and passed his hand across his spectacled eyes.

"Nobody," he admitted lifelessly. "I stood. The shop was crowded. I was talking to some of the patients until the lights went out, and then I couldn't find a seat easily, so I just stood, leaning against the wall."

"Which wall?" Strawn demanded.

"The back wall, near the door," Rowan confessed. "But I swear I did not leave the room between eight o'clock and ten, when the show was over."

"Near the door," Strawn repeated, with satisfaction. "Near the back door that was open all the time. . . . Now, Rowan, I want to know what you told Koenig yesterday."

"I won't tell you!" the patient retorted flatly.

And for ten minutes Dundee had to sit silently in his chair behind the door and listen to Captain Strawn batter at the man's amazing will power. He saw Samuel Rowan reduced to a pitiful, shivering wreck, but he also witnessed the complete defeat of Captain Strawn. Not one syllable regarding his past life would Rowan utter, and there was a flicker of triumph in his exhausted voice as he informed Strawn that he had drifted, an aimless, friendless wanderer, into Hamilton only a few weeks before he had been, made a ward of the county. But as to who he had been before those dark two years, and where he had come from—not one word.

And at last Strawn had been compelled to let him go, followed by a plainclothesman, who was charged with seeing that the suspect did not escape.

"I'll find out what crime he's hiding if I have to send his fingerprints and description to every chief of police in the country," Strawn vowed savagely, as Dundee joined him in the murdered man's office. "He had motive and I'll prove it. Motive and opportunity. That's enough!"

The word "motive" rang a bell in Dundee's mind. He turned to Dr. Harlow: "Do the patients sign for the books they take out of your library?"

"Why, yes."

"Then may I see the library card for *Murder Without Motive*?"

"Miss Home has charge of the library," Dr. Harlow told him. "I'll ask her to bring in the card. I'm sure she's in the reception room now."

"Ring for her!" Strawn commanded. "I want to see that young lady anyway. Chances are she's familiar with Rowan's case history as it was before Koenig made a report on yesterday's session, and can tell us where he came from."

Dundee rose, but Strawn remained sitting when the door opened and a girl hesitated upon the threshold, note book in a hand that was visibly trembling.

She was a pretty thing, Dundee noted with swift appreciation. Plump and dimpled and pink and white as a baby. A chemical blonde, perhaps, but the short, brassy ringlets that rioted all over her round head were in complete harmony with those round, baby blue eyes and that funny little button of a nose. Her soft, too small mouth was quivering like a grief stricken child's.

"What's your full name?" Strawn began with cruel abruptness.

"Maizie Home. ... I mean, it used to be Mary, but I changed it to Maizie "

"All right; Maizie it is," Strawn cut in, grinning slightly. "You know what happened here last night?"

"Yes, sir," she quavered, the blue eyes filling instantly with tears.

"What do you know about it?"

"Nothing! I don't know anything at all about it!" she denied frenziedly, the big eyes rolling an appeal to Dr. Harlow.

"How long have you worked for Dr. Koenig?"

"Nearly five years."

"How old are you?"

"Twenty two—I mean," the girl corrected her automatic lie, flushing scarlet, "I'm twenty four."

"You were here all day yesterday?" Strawn continued.

"From nine o'clock until five," she answered eagerly. "I don't even go out to lunch, except on special occasions. I eat in the staff dining room."

"Did anything unusual happen yesterday? Any mysterious visitors or telephone calls or telegrams, or anything of that sort for the doctor?"

"No, sir."

"Did Dr. Koenig seem to have anything on his mind—anything that worried or upset him?"

"Oh, no, sir! He was awfully busy, but then he always is– was– "

"Has anything at all unusual, anything you did not understand, for instance, happened here since Dr. Koenig returned from his trip Monday?"

"No, sir."

"Now, Miss Home, I want you to give me the name of everyone that came into this office yesterday to see Dr. Koenig."

"Let me think—Do you mean everybody, including the staff?"

"Everybody."

"Well, of course I was in and out all day," the girl began slowly. "And Dr. Harlow and Miss Lacey were in and out, too, and so was Dr. Cantrell. . . . Oh, yes! And Mrs. Cantrell. She came in during the morning to welcome the doctor home from his trip, and to ask him to dinner at her house on Thursday night—why, that would be tonight!" she discovered in awe, and the babyish mouth puckered.

"All right! Who else?" Strawn prodded impatiently.

"Let's see. . . . Oh, yes! Just after we'd finished lunch—that was about half past twelve—old Mr. Powell came to get Clyde's suitcase "

"Powell? Clyde?" Strawn repeated. "Who are they?"

It was Dr. Harlow who answered. "Clyde Powell was a patient here for years. A hopeless case—advanced stages of dementia praecox, with epileptiform seizures. Lately he had required day and night attendants, and his family was unable to pay for them, so they had him transferred Monday to the State Hospital for the Insane. I telephoned his father yesterday to ask him to call for a suitcase full of old clothes and worthless possessions that was not sent on with Clyde."

"And Powell saw Koenig, eh?" Strawn turned back to the secretary. "What was his attitude? Friendly?"

"Why, yes," the girl answered. "Of course he was all cut up over Clyde's having to go to the State Hospital, but he wanted to thank Dr. Koenig for having kept Clyde so long at a reduced rate. They only talked for a few minutes."

"All right. Who else?"

"Well, about one o'clock Dr. Koenig sent for Mrs. Morse, one of the patients," the secretary continued conscientiously. "She stayed about half an hour, and then Archie Webster's father came. Archie is another of the patients, and his father came to see him, and to ask Dr. Koenig how he was getting along–"

"Friendly, was he?" Strawn interrupted.

"Of course!" the girl retorted with some indignation. "Everybody thought the world of Dr. Koenig "

"*One* somebody didn't!" Strawn reminded her grimly. "But go on! How long was Mr. Webster with the doctor?"

"About fifteen minutes. When Mr. Webster left, Dr. Koenig went with him through the reception room where I was working, to the outside door, and I heard Dr. Koenig say, 'Don't worry, old man. She won't be here much longer ' "

" 'She'?" Dundee repeated. "Are you sure Dr. Koenig said 'she,' not 'he,' referring to Archie Webster?"

"I'm positive he said 'she,' because I said to myself, 'If they could see how Enid treats Archie, they wouldn't have any cause to worry about his marrying her.' "

"So you felt sure 'she' was Enid Rambler?" Dundee went on thoughtfully.

"Isn't it quite possible," Dr. Harlow suggested quietly, "that Dr. Koenig was referring to *me?*"

Now why the devil had she brought that up, Dundee wondered. Did she enjoy rubbing salt into the wound caused by the revelation that Dr. Koenig had planned to replace her?

"To *you*, Dr. Harlow?" Maizie Home cried incredulously. "Why, Dr. Koenig thought the sun rose and set in you, and you know it!"

"Then Dr. Koenig said nothing to you yesterday or before then about replacing Dr. Harlow with a male psychiatrist?"

"Of course not! I've heard him say a dozen times he couldn't do without Dr. Harlow!"

Dundee studied the girl through half closed eyes. Apparently she was telling the truth. And what she said merely corroborated the mute but powerful testimony of the doctor's will. But had Justine Harlow introduced the subject cunningly, for the purpose of eliciting this whole hearted corroboration? And what had happened to change Dr. Koenig's heart and mind so suddenly and so completely? For that change of heart had corroboration, too— in the scribbled notation "Sandlin" on the doctor's desk calendar, and in his direct statement to Roger Baldwin. . . . Eleven miles in two hours! . . . The voice of a woman pleading with Carl Koenig not to send her away...

There was something else, a question that had been demanding an answer.

"Miss Home," he asked, "who gave those roses"—and he pointed to the now sadly faded flowers on the dead man's desk—"to Dr. Koenig?"

"Roses?" the secretary repeated blankly. "*I* don't know! They weren't there when I left yesterday afternoon!"

CHAPTER FOURTEEN

AN hour later—a crowded but strangely fruitless hour—Dundee and Captain Strawn parted company temporarily, the chief of the Homicide Squad setting out with his stenographer and Dr. Harlow to make the rounds of those patients who had not yet been questioned, and the younger detective to report in person to the bed ridden district attorney.

But Dr. Cantrell detained Dundee. "My wife wishes very much to speak with you. I'd appreciate it if you would pay her a brief visit. You'll find her in the sun parlor."

"You've discussed the case fully with her, of course?" Dundee asked casually.

"Naturally," the doctor replied curtly. "As I told you, she was asleep when I was summoned here last night, and still asleep when I got home after one o'clock. I did not disturb her, but waited until after she had had her break fast this morning to tell her the bad news. She's very much upset, of course. My wife and I were Dr. Koenig's closest friends—except Dr. Harlow, of course."

There was so much tenseness and constraint in the doctor's jerky, almost defiant words that Dundee was very thoughtful as he took the path that connected the Cantrell home with the main building of the sanitarium.

A middle aged maid, whose eyes were puffed and red with weeping, conducted Dundee into the sun parlor. He found Claire Cantrell seated at a little wicker desk, her great brown eyes staring steadily at a large, leather framed photograph. A beam of sunlight lay in a broad band across her ash blonde hair, making it gleam like pale gold. She was extraordinarily beautiful.

Her voice was slow and deep and rich as she said, with out rising, her eyes still on the photograph of Dr. Carl Koenig: "A great man—pure and above reproach. As wise as Socrates and as gentle as Christ."

And somehow the words did not sound cheaply theatrical to Dundee.

"You were very fond of the doctor, Mrs. Cantrell?" he asked gently.

The sad brown eyes turned their beauty full upon him, but he was quick to note that no color rose to stain the clear creaminess of her cheeks. "I am afraid I almost worshiped Carl," she answered without hesitation. "Not only was he my closest friend, but he, as a doctor, made it possible for me to live fully."

And not even his death, Dundee reflected, had been able to destroy the poise and serenity that the doctor had helped her achieve. He had a sudden, amazing impulse to kiss one of her lovely, quiet hands, as tribute to her grave dignity and beauty.

But he said, almost brusquely professional: "You wished to see me, Mrs. Cantrell? You know something that may help us?"

"What I have to tell you," the slow, rich voice answered, "may have no bearing at all on Carl's death. But it puzzled me at the time, and since Bruce told me what happened so soon afterwards I can't get it out of my mind. ... As my husband told you, I retired at eight o'clock last night, with a severe neuralgic headache. Bruce gave me a dose of aspirin and luminol, and I was dozing before nine. Between our twin beds there is a telephone, or rather two telephones, one an instrument of the inter communicating system of the sanitarium, and the other a straight line out. Both have extensions in the front hall. At nine twenty—I looked at my watch as I picked up the receiver—there came three short buzzes, our call on the sanitarium telephone. It was Carl–"

Dundee was startled into rigid attention. "Why didn't Dr. Cantrell answer the call, since he knew you were asleep?"

"My husband did go to the front hall to answer, but hung up after a moment when it was evident that Carl wished to talk with me, not with him," she answered.

"But Dr. Cantrell made no mention of this call!" Dundee told her sharply.

"I know. He was very wrong, but his sole thought was to protect me from being questioned last night, when I was ill. Bruce—" and there was a throbbing note of tenderness in the rich voice, "is a very devoted and considerate husband, and he did not hear enough of the conversation to attach any significance to it."

"Just what did Dr. Koenig say?" Dundee tried gently to hurry her.

"The first thing he said was, 'Feeling better now, child?' Bruce had told him I had one of my headaches. I answered that I was, and he then asked if Justine was here with me. I told him she was not–"

"Did he say he wanted to see Dr. Harlow in his office?"

"No, but I inferred as much, of course," Mrs. Cantrell answered, with a trace of surprise at the question. "We talked on for a minute or so, idly, as friends do, but his voice seemed strained and tired and worried. I asked him what he was doing, and he said, 'Working on case histories, but not making much headway. The truth is, Claire, something happened this evening to shake my faith in human nature, but just hearing your voice has done a lot to restore it.' . . . I'm proud to say," the girl added, but without a trace of defiance, "that Carl was almost as fond of me as I was of him."

"I can believe that," Dundee assured her gravely. "But did he explain, give you any clew as to what had happened?"

"None at all, and I did not ask any questions. I supposed, naturally, that a patient had made some revelation that had shocked even Carl's understanding and tolerance."

Well, it looked as if Strawn might be right after all, and Rowan the one whose guilty secret must be protected at all costs, Dundee told himself ruefully. But—it was *Justine Harlow* the doctor had wanted to see. . . .

"All this is extremely important, I am sure, Mrs. Cantrell, and I thank you for telling it so freely and clearly–"

"But that is not all, Mr. Dundee," the girl surprised him by interrupting. "We talked on for a minute or so more—he advised me to stay in bed today and cautioned me to take care of myself—when suddenly he interrupted something unimportant I was saying. He cried out, 'Good Lord!,' in a voice I can only describe as horror stricken, and added immediately: 'So that's where I've seen those eyes before!' "

"Yes?" Dundee urged, as the girl paused. "What else? Surely he explained so strange a remark?"

"I asked him what he meant, but he answered evasively," the girl told him. "As nearly as I can remember, he said, 'I've just happened to stumble upon the missing link in a memory chain. . . . But I'll say good night now, my darling girl. I've got a nasty job to do, without wasting a minute's delay.' And he hung up the receiver. I was puzzled and troubled. I started to call Bruce and tell him about it, but my head had begun to throb violently again, and I knew that if I excited myself by talking any more, it would get worse."

"Your husband did not come to inquire what Dr. Koenig wanted?"

"No. Why should he?" Mrs. Cantrell asked. "It was the most natural thing in the world for Carl to call me, to ask how I was feeling."

"Can you recall, Mrs. Cantrell, at just what point in the conversation your husband replaced the receiver of the extension?"

"Not exactly, but very early—as soon as it was obvious that the call was for me only."

"May I ask, Mrs. Cantrell, if you and Dr. Harlow are good friends?"

"The best of friends," she answered emphatically. "I have known and loved Justine ever since I first came to Mayfield for psychoanalysis. She is an utter darling of a girl, and a splendid psychiatrist."

"Then it would be natural for Dr. Koenig to assume that Dr. Harlow would come straight to you, if she were in serious trouble?"

"Quite natural."

"Will you tell me this, Mrs. Cantrell: was Dr. Harlow in love with Dr. Koenig—or he with her?"

"You have no right to ask me that question," she replied with dignity, "but I will answer it. The answer is no. Dr. Harlow worshiped Dr. Koenig, but I am absolutely sure she did not love him, in the usual sense of the word. And Carl loved Justine only as a colleague and as a friend. ... I don't believe Carl was ever in love. He was an almost Christlike ascetic."

"Do you know personally of any woman who was in love with him?"

"I cannot answer that," she said, with dignity. "But I can tell you clumsily what Justine could express much more scientifically. Women patients are prone to fall in love with their analysts, at a certain stage of psychoanalysis. They make what is called a 'transference' of an unhealthy love from its previous object to the doctor. He encourages such a transference, but does not take advantage of it, if he is a reputable analyst. When the cure is completed, the patient is no longer in love with the doctor, but is ready for a normal life. I can assure you that Dr. Koenig was the soul of honor where his women patients were concerned. . . . And in every other respect. For instance, a practicing physician who is financially interested in a sanitarium is exposed to countless temptations–"

"Such as?" Dundee prompted, when the girl paused, as if she feared she was talking too much.

"It would be very easy for a doctor in Carl's position at Mayfield to retard rather than hasten the recovery of rich patients, or even of those who pay for moderately priced accommodations," Mrs. Cantrell explained quietly. "Carl almost leaned backward to escape any such accusation. Many women, and some men, too, find a place like Mayfield a heavenly refuge from life and all its demands and perplexities. After they are really well enough to be out, they want to stay on and on. Carl literally pushed them out, back into the world again. Naturally my husband, financially interested also, as you know, was in complete accord with Carl's principles–"

"But Business Manager Baldwin was not always so cheerful about seeing a well paying patient leave?" Dundee prompted, as she hesitated again.

"Roger Baldwin is not a doctor; he is a business man, and a very good one," Claire Cantrell reminded him. "But I admit that the difference of viewpoint did cause some friction—nothing serious, of course. For instance, Carl was quite upset when I saw him yesterday morning over the fact that poor Clyde Powell, who had been a paying patient for seven years, had been transferred to the State Hospital on Monday, all arrangements having been made before Carl returned. In fact, I am sure that if Carl had got here before Clyde's train left he would have got him back and kept him here as a charity patient."

"I see," Dundee nodded, then asked abruptly: "Did Dr. Koenig say anything at all to you or to your husband about his intention of replacing Dr. Harlow with a male assistant?"

"Not a word!" the girl flashed. "Bruce has told me what Roger Baldwin said, but I am sure Roger misunderstood something Carl said about taking on a second assistant. I am positive Carl had not the remotest intention of dismissing Justine."

"Not even if he discovered yesterday some serious error on her part, in the treatment of a patient?" Dundee persisted.

"He would have condemned the error itself, but not Justine's intentions," the girl assured him warmly. "He knew that Justine's principles were as high as his own."

"Candidly speaking, you believe Roger Baldwin lied?"

"I believe he is mistaken as to just what Carl said," she answered firmly.

"Your friends should prize your loyalty very highly, Mrs. Cantrell," Dundee said, sincerely, as he took her hand.

Her revelation of the telephone conversation had given the young detective so much food for thought that he was scarcely aware of the path he took as he left the Cantrell house. But when he almost stumbled against the footrest of a canopied lawn chair he discovered that he was cutting across a small rose garden which lay between the sanitarium driveway and the Cantrell home.

He was about to apologize for his clumsiness when he saw that the frail old man in the chair was fast asleep, his repose guarded by a white clad male attendant.

"It's Dr. Mayfield, sir," the attendant whispered.

Dundee halted and stared down at the sleeper with intense interest. Every line and contour of the face and head spelled nobility, high intelligence, thoroughbred ancestry and gentleness. But as the detective gazed down upon the old doctor, something like nausea clutched at the pit of his stomach. The unfairness of the tricks that life could play seemed suddenly more than he could bear. Why live decently, finely, cleanly—he asked himself—if at the end life could rob a man of the thing he held most dear, that which distinguished him from the beasts of the field?

"How is he today?" he asked the attendant, whom he beckoned to a safe distance from the sleeper.

"Seems to be in his right mind, when he's awake," the attendant answered. "But something's bothering him. He keeps demanding to see Dr. Koenig, and to humor him, I've told him Doctor's away on a trip."

Dundee nodded and walked on, but his lips silently formed the bitter words, "To humor him." Better a gangster's bullet in *his* spine, he decided, than that he should live on and on, until ultimately a paid caretaker of his body should murmur those words about him. . . .

But the zest for life was again strong within him when he reached the bedside of the pleurisy stricken district attorney.

"Time you were remembering you've got a boss, young fellow," Sanderson chided good naturedly. "What luck so far?"

"Swell luck!" Dundee grinned. "Within twelve hours I've met three of the prettiest women I've ever seen in my life. . . . Unfortunately one of them—and I'm not sure she isn't my favorite—insists on wearing horn rimmed spectacles to add to her dignity–"

"What the devil are you talking about?" Sanderson interrupted.

"Dr. Harlow, naturally—Justine Harlow," Dundee obliged. "A charming name, don't you think? Really, she's the cunningest little trick, especially when she's being the learned doctor–"

"If it won't bore you too much," Sanderson again interrupted acidly, "I'd like to hear a few details about a certain murder you're supposed to be investigating."

"Oh, *that!*" Dundee laughed and shrugged. "The truth is, I know so much about it that I'm afraid I don't know anything at all. . . . Does your doctor hold with having his patients told long, involved mystery stories?"

CHAPTER FIFTEEN

"WAIT a minute, Bonnie. My head's spinning," the district attorney pleaded, three quarters of an hour after Dundee had begun his recital.

"So is mine," Dundee admitted, and stretched prodigiously, his blue eyes twinkling as they rested on his chief's disturbed face.

"If it hadn't been for that damned movie in the what d'ye call it shop–"

"O. T. Shop," Dundee contributed helpfully. "But if it hadn't been for that damned movie, as you call it, think of the fun we'd miss playing 'Button, button, who's got the button?' with a whole squad of suspects. All of the patients would have been peacefully abed, since bedtime at Mayfield is nine o'clock."

"I'm not the glutton for suspects that you are," Sanderson reminded him testily. "Well, get along with it. You'd finished with Rowan, and I'm inclined to agree with Strawn that that bird'll bear checking up on."

"No doubt of that," Dundee agreed cheerfully. "I'm sure his story is an interesting human document, and one that quite possibly would complete a *dossier* in some police department, but–"

"All right, all right! What did Archie Webster have to say for himself when Strawn got hold of him this morning?"

"Oh, he's playing the same sort of game the Rambler girl is up to," Dundee told him. "Knows something he's not telling. But his story is straight enough, believe the story or not. He says he was sitting in the same row of seats at the movie as Enid Rambler, and that he noticed she was getting more and more nervous. Says he passed the word along to her that he had some first class whisky, which was exactly what she needed to brace her up. He says he also sent along the word that he'd be in a sort of little summerhouse in the northwest corner of the grounds, beyond the locked ward cottage. He left, went to the summerhouse, and waited for her to join him. He says she didn't come and he drank the whole pint himself, going back to the main building only in time to see the patients leaving the shop. He says his intention was to ask her to take a turn about the grounds with him before she went to bed, but that, tipsy as he was, he got into the mix up with Rowan, and did not even know she had ever left the movie."

"And I suppose the summerhouse is too far away from the main building for Archie to have seen anything?"

"It is."

"Then what the devil does he know that he's not telling?"

"*I* don't know," Dundee assured him plaintively. "I don't know a lot more than that, if you ask me–"

"And what about that mystery yarn—*Murder Without Motive*, that had the rubber gloves tip in it?" Sanderson asked irritably.

"Another washout. Miss Home, the secretary, says Koenig, who read nearly every mystery he could get his hands on, presented that book to the sanitarium library," Dundee told him. "And the library card shows that practically everyone whose name has been mentioned in the case so far has read the book. And I thought I was lucky to find that hot clew!" he gibed at himself.

"That fat man!" Sanderson ejaculated. "He'd stand a lot of explaining!"

"Strawn's got the 'dragnet,' as the papers call it, out for our fat friend," Dundee assured him. "Description: age, about forty; height approximately five feet five; weight no less than two hundred pounds, mostly under his belt; hair, scant, pepper and salt; eyes blue or gray. But unless he was kidding Archie Webster, the fat man's chief interest was in Enid Rambler, *to whom he did not speak*–"

"Met her outside," Sanderson supplied. "You say your self the girl knows who did it, or has strong suspicions, so strong she's afraid she'll get hers next, and that she won't tell because the murderer has something on her."

"Guess I'm stubborn," Dundee admitted ruefully, "but I can't approve of this mystery story unless the 'voice of God' is tied up nice and tight with the solution of Koenig's murder."

"Oh, don't bother about that voice," Sanderson advised. "Some nut with a religious complex, baying at the moon. Remember the place is full of nuts."

"Ye—es."

"If you want *my* theory, here it is," Sanderson went on, with increasing zest. "Claire Cantrell says—and I think we can bank on what she told you—that the doctor suddenly remembered where he'd seen somebody before, and that he was horrified. Now consider. Get the picture. The doctor's talking over the phone, sitting at his desk. His eyes rove, and light on something. All right! What was that something likely to be?"

"A case history, I suppose," Dundee admitted. "He told her he was working on case histories."

"Sure!" Sanderson was becoming jubilant. "The doctor sees a name—name of a person or a place—that makes his memory click. Now what is his memory most concerned with?"

"His work," Dundee answered dutifully. "And with out your prompting I can deduce that the phase of his work that horrified him most was murder trials, where he testified as to the defendants' sanity. And I agree that if he suddenly realized that one of his patients was an escaped murderer—possibly a homicidal maniac—he'd get busy."

"Correct!" Sanderson snapped. "But remember it's *my* theory! Now what would a doctor do?"

"Send for the patient, verify his suspicion, then put him in the locked ward until he could be returned to the asylum for the criminally insane," Dundee answered promptly, with a grin. "Sorry, Chief, but I'd thought of all that, too, and the fact is that Koenig, so far as we can find out, sent for no patient in the sanitarium last night."

"But what if that patient had already seen him earlier in the day?" Sanderson suggested. "Suppose the patient had had a long powwow with the doctor, but had not told him the real truth. Suppose Koenig said something like this, 'Rowan, I've seen you somewhere before, but I can't place you!' What would you do if you were Rowan? Wouldn't you be tempted to have another chat with the doctor, to tell him some more lies to throw him more off the scent? . . . Well, that's exactly what Rowan does. He slips out of the shop, and into Koenig's office. And he sees Koenig has recognized him at last, and—the jig is up!"

"Sounds good, Chief," Dundee admitted. "But if Rowan *is* a homicidal maniac, why should he have to go to such pains to make the crime look like a maniac's work?"

Sanderson looked nonplussed for a moment, then brightened. "I got it! Rowan *isn't* a homicidal maniac, but a cold blooded murderer whom Koenig recognizes from having seen him before he committed his crime—for which he's a fugitive from justice. He knows Koenig ought to do his duty—turn him over to the authorities. So he kills him, but fixes up his defense *ahead of time.* In case he's caught, there's the evidence of the wrecked room and the fact that he's a patient to prove he had been a homicidal maniac all the time! . . . How's that?"

"Swell!" Dundee applauded feebly. "But—how does Enid Rambler fit into the picture?"

"That's easy!" Sanderson exulted. "She's got onto Rowan's trail. A relative of his first victim, probably. Unknown to Rowan, of course. So she leaves the movie to spill the beans to Koenig. She waits around, thinks he's busy. Then she hears or sees something that scares the wits out of her. Probably Rowan comes out of the doctor's office and she gives herself away to him. He threatens to kill her, and she runs away. Today she learns that Koenig was dead when Rowan came out of Koenig's office, and she knows he meant it when he said he'd kill her."

Dundee shook his head. "I don't believe she'd track down a murderer and then let him scare her off—not even after she found he'd killed Koenig," he said. "But it's the best theory so far, Chief, and I'll work on it."

"Yes, sir! You can't get away from the fact that Rowan's case history was torn up; that he'd had a long talk with Koenig; that no one can swear he didn't sneak out of the O. T. Shop; that he was still wrought up enough at ten o'clock to knock Webster down; and that he won't tell the police a thing concerning his past—doesn't dare tell! . . . And you can't get away from the fact that Koenig didn't consider Enid Rambler a mentally sick girl—thought she was shamming in order to stay on."

"And I also can't get away from the fact that Dr. Harlow believes she *is* sick," Dundee cut in. "My personal conviction is that she is using Mayfield as a hide out, that she has done something which has given her a very real claustrophobia—in other words, that she's afraid of being hauled off to jail. Strawn's trying to get a line on her before she came to Mayfield."

"Poor Bonnie!" Sanderson mocked, not unkindly. "One of his three beauties is married, one is a prospective jail bird, and the bespectacled one tells him a lie that he promptly catches her in!"

"Not only that, but *two* of my beauties have some of the identical roses that the murderer thoughtfully placed at the dead doctor's nose," Dundee admitted gloomily.

"Not—Claire Cantrell?" Sanderson demanded, startled.

"No. Justine Harlow and Enid Rambler. Each had a vase of those roses in her room this morning," Dundee told him. "I checked up with the Mayfield gardener, but he told me they're hothouse roses, a new variety, and very expensive. I'd hoped to find them growing on a hundred bushes about the grounds, but no such luck."

"What's eating on you, my boy, is that you're convinced it was Justine Harlow who paid that tearful visit to Dr. Koenig around nine o'clock last night—and you won't admit it. ... If she had pimples and greasy hair, you'd be a powerful lot quicker at putting two and two together, Bonnie. Face the thing! Koenig had suddenly made up his mind to discharge the little doctor. Why? *Because she was in love with him, and making a nuisance of herself!* He'd been so fond of her that he'd put her down in his will for half his estate, and undoubtedly she had some cause to think he cared for her in a marrying way "

"So now you're suggesting she killed him because he wouldn't marry her?" Dundee asked, in a dangerously calm voice.

"Keep your shirt on, boy!" Sanderson laughed. "I'm suggesting no such thing. All I'm trying to do is to explain why the girl drove only eleven miles in those two hours. You could hardly expect her to admit she'd had that kind of interview with a man who had just been murdered. But I don't believe for a minute she had anything to do with his death."

"That's a help anyway," Dundee admitted, more cheerfully. "Well, I'll be getting on. I intend to be a model 'patient' all afternoon—sit around on the lawn and gossip with all the biddies, male and female. Out of a ton of dirt I may winnow one small nugget of gold. ... By the way, Mr. Sanderson," the young detective added, so casually that it was obvious he had not really half forgotten what he was about to communicate, "I stopped off on my way here to check up on Norah Lacey's alibi. Strawn's man on the same job gave her a clean bill of health, but I wasn't quite satisfied. It seemed odd to me that she should give a fake alibi first, if she really had an airtight one that was true, and one so innocent as spending the evening with friends."

"Yes?" Sanderson prompted impatiently.

"The nurse was there, all right," Dundee said slowly. "She arrived at eight, as she said, and left exactly at ten. The Satterlees are nice people—a sixty year old grand mother, and a fifteen year old granddaughter, name of Mabel. It's a comfortable, but rather humble six room house "

"What are you getting at?"

"One of those six rooms is an extremely well equipped nursery—both beautiful and scientific," Dundee told him reluctantly. "Norah Lacey pays quite a stiff board bill for the three year old youngster that occupies that nursery."

"Whew!" Sanderson whistled thoughtfully. "No wonder she lied!"

"Yes. . . . And Norah Lacey was alone with the little boy, who is quite ill, from a few minutes after eight until ten minutes to ten. It seems that she persuaded the Satterlees to take the evening off and go to a movie. They've been very closely confined to the house on account of the child's illness. Therefore—" and he shrugged, his eyes unhappy.

"Therefore Norah Lacey has no more alibi than a rabbit," Sanderson supplied with some satisfaction.

"No—o. Except that I don't believe she'd leave that sick child alone. Remember she's a nurse, as well as—a mother, perhaps. . . . Funny thing, Mr. Sanderson, but that kid—and a cute brat he is—reminded me of someone. I've seen eyes like his somewhere recently–"

"*Koenig?*" Sanderson cut in sharply.

But Dundee shook his head. "Not Koenig, but–"

"But Koenig left Norah Lacey half of his estate," Sanderson reminded his subordinate grimly.

"I know," Dundee agreed dubiously. "Maybe I'm just a gullible, hero worshiping young fool, but without more positive evidence than we have so far, I'm not going to believe Carl Koenig seduced a nurse in his employ and then refused to 'do right by her.' "

"Got any idea whose baby it is, then?"

"Not the ghost of an idea," Dundee admitted hopelessly. "Another mystery. Just one of the half dozen that are sure to enter into the investigation of any murder. All of us have secrets in our lives, but fortunately most of us don't get mixed up in murders and have to see our secrets dragged into the limelight. . . . No use broadcasting this particular secret, is there, sir?"

"None that I can see so far," Sanderson replied. "No use slinging mud at a dead man, unless it becomes absolutely necessary in clearing up his murder. But bear this in mind, boy. Koenig had some good reason for leaving Norah Lacey—probably a good enough head nurse but easily replaced—one half of all he died possessed."

It was on that somber note that the conversation ended, and Special Investigator Dundee took his seat in his roadster, a well filled suitcase beside him. He began to drive rather slowly, but suddenly his scalp pricked in a way that always presaged disaster, and his foot bore down hard upon the accelerator. . . .

CHAPTER SIXTEEN

"I've been holding back your tray for you, Mr. Dundee," Nurse Lurline Doty told him archly, as he strode, suitcase in hand, into the reception room of Sunflower Court. "I've got a lovely lunch for you—breast of chicken, fresh asparagus, tomato aspic–"

"Thanks!" Dundee interrupted curtly. "Everything quiet?"

"Quiet!" the nurse echoed dramatically. "With all the patients knowing about poor Dr. Koenig, and having hysterics–"

"Has anything serious happened?"

"No one has committed suicide or confessed to the murder, if that's what you mean," she answered, a little sulkily.

In his suite at last, Dundee unpacked his suitcase, made sure that the precious trayful of case history scraps gathered from the floor of the dead doctor's office was still in the drawer where he had placed it, then gave hasty and rather unappreciative attention to his excellent luncheon tray. . . . Was he developing an appropriate neurasthenia, to fit his role of patient? And if not, why the devil should his scalp go on prickling in that way it had of warning him of approaching disaster?

Ready to go out and make the acquaintance of his fellow guests, Dundee suddenly felt a curious reluctance to play the role he had elected. Himself completely sound mentally, he felt a shrinking aversion to contacting those whose brains were warped and whose faces betrayed the disintegration of their minds. There was shame, too, in the fact that he was about to deceive unfortunates who had not the power to match wits with him. But duty was duty. . . .

He found that the largest number of patients out for air and exercise had chosen the wide expanse of lawn that lay between Sunflower Court and the main building. A man and two women were playing croquet, the silly, unprovoked laughter of one—the very fat girl he had seen that morning—shrilling out an almost constant accompaniment to the crack of mallet against ball. Her shots were wild, never making a wicket. . . .

"Play bridge, buddy?" a blithe voice hailed him, and Dundee turned gratefully to accept the invitation of the jolly attendant, Happy Day.

There were two tables of bridge. One foursome was made up of Samuel Rowan; a majestic, white haired woman with protruding eyes, who was introduced as Mrs. Asbury, and who immediately assured Dundee she was at Mayfield merely for a "rest cure"; a silent, homely girl whose name was Helen Rand; and Howard Salter, the writer, who seemed to be completely recovered from his attempted suicide.

"Needed a fourth pretty badly," Happy Day assured the detective, as Dundee took the vacant seat at a table where the attendant, his patient, Archie Webster, and a dignified, thin haired, erect old man were already sitting.

"And this is Mr. Hepple, Dundee," Happy Day concluded the introductions, indicating the elderly man. "Used to be a banker—responsible for the depression, ain't you, old sport?"

The ex banker bowed with grave and exquisite courtesy to acknowledge the introduction. "We are very glad to have you with us, sir. . . . Yes, Mr. Day, it was my sad destiny to bring about this world wide catastrophe, which is euphemistically referred to as the 'depression.' The gigantic scope of my unwise manipulations–"

"Tell him all about it some other time, grandpa," Happy Day interrupted, tossing a merry, significant wink Dundee wards. "Let's cut for deal. . . . Hi! Ace of Spades. And you and me's pardners, Dundee. How's that for a break? . . . Archie, I wish you luck with grandpa."

"My name is Hepple, sir," the gentle old man reminded him, still with beautiful courtesy.

"Excuse me for living!" Happy apologized gleefully. "The old boy doesn't play contract, Dundee, so auction it is, if you can bear it. ... Oh, Lord!"

"Got a pain in your tummy?" Archie Webster asked hopefully.

"Worse'n that," the attendant groaned. "Look who's coming."

Dundee looked, too. Across the driveway and toward them he saw a tall woman striding purposefully, and waving a raffia knitting basket from which trailed yards of purple wool. Her height was accentuated by the Grecian tunic of pale yellow silk which, sleeveless and girdled by a silver snake, hung in voluminous folds from shoulders to ankles. Long curls of gleaming black hair hung below her shoulders, escaping from a floppy leghorn hat weighted down with pink roses. At a distance she looked like a great beauty, but as she drew near Dundee saw before him what could only be called the caricature of a beautiful woman. The lines and coarseness of middle age were smeared over with heavy, theatrical makeup. The once glorious black eyes were thickly mascaraed and deeply shadowed with blue grease paint. Yellowish teeth, some of them false, spoiled the calculated effect of the scarlet Cupid's bow. But Dundee's eyes, after a fleeting summary of her appearance, riveted themselves upon a long stemmed rose that bobbed above the silver girdle. For it was an exact mate of the rare and expensive flower that had adorned the dead doctor's desk, as well as the rooms of both Enid Rambler and Justine Harlow. . . . Did he say *rare*? Why, the damned flower seemed to be an epidemic!

"*Don't* tell me you've already got a fourth!" she sang out, in a vital, throaty voice—the voice of a concert stage contralto. "Why, *hullo*, darling!"

And Dundee was amazed to find that the happily surprised and loving greeting was for him.

"Archie, my own true love, where did this gorgeous male thing come from?" she demanded of young Webster, as she bent to kiss him on the cheek.

"Quit smearing me up with your damned lipstick," Archie commanded ungallantly. "This is Marjorie Merrick, Mr. Dundee. ... At least that's her story and she sticks to it."

"A stage name, darling," Miss Merrick assured Dundee tenderly. "I am the world famous contralto. Of course you've heard of me. . . . What eyes! What a noble brow! What a chin! What a head of hair—" and she suddenly ran her thin fingers through Dundee's crisp black mane.

"In short, what a man!" Archie laughed. "Don't mind her, Dundee–"

"Jealous, my pet?" the odd creature crooned, encircling the young man's neck with a freckled arm. "He simply can't bear to have me pay the slightest attention to another man, darling—Oh! To think I nearly forgot!" and she fixed Archie Webster with glittering black eyes, a red nailed forefinger tapping warningly against her pursed lips. "Not a word, Archie! *For God's sake, not a word!"*

"I'm not saying anything!" the boy almost shouted. "But dry up yourself, Marjie. We want to play bridge."

"Take my place, Miss Merrick," Dundee insisted, rising.

"No, really," as his three table mates protested vigorously, "I'd rather look on."

"Sweet!" Marjorie Merrick breathed, as she slipped into his chair. "*He's head over heels* already, Happy!" she confided in a gusty whisper. "Sit right here by Mama, darling. . . . Well, can you bear it, children? . . . My sweet old Carl—*murdered!*" She turned swiftly to Dundee. "He always called me Marjorie and I called him Carl. . . . Madly, hopelessly in love with me, the poor dear. . . . And now—*now he's dead!* Oh, God, why should I be cursed with this terrible power—But not a word!" and again the forefinger tapped the scarlet mouth.

Again Dundee felt the hair rise pricklingly on his scalp, but this time he knew the cause. Weird and horrible to hear this scatter brained caricature babble on. ...

"I bid two spades—no, I mean I bid three hearts!" she announced triumphantly. "Not my bid? . . . Well, what difference does it make? I'm going to bid three hearts anyway when it gets around to me."

And although she played the hand to a running, rapid accompaniment of relevant and irrelevant chatter, the amazing woman made a little slam in hearts, with a dummy that seemed to promise not a single quick trick.

"That's bridge!" she applauded herself, with justice, her eyes beaming fondly upon Dundee. "Listen, darling! Be a lambkin and run and get Enid Rambler for me. There's something I simply have to tell her–"

"She has a sprained ankle," Dundee told her.

"Then bring her in a wheel chair, idiot!" she commanded imperiously. "Run!"

"I'll go," Happy Day offered. "You take my hand, Dundee."

"No. I'll go along with you," the detective offered, glad of the chance to ask a few urgent questions of one who knew his status. . . . "What a woman!" he breathed, with awe, as the two of them set off across the lawn. "What ails her?"

"She's a manic," Happy Day explained, proud of his knowledge. "Not a *maniac*—a manic. You know—up in the air all the time, happy as hell, and impulsive as a wild mare. Makes her nuts on men, poor girl! But I don't see why we should pity her. *She's* having a swell time—all the time!"

"A nymphomaniac?" Dundee asked interestedly.

"Sure! But not when she's herself. Awful decent sort, really," the attendant assured him, in a suddenly assumed English accent, at which he himself grinned.

"She thinks every man that lays eyes on her is dippy about her. Has a tall story to tell about a man getting a job here as attendant in order to kidnap her. . . . That sort of thing."

"And Archie Webster is her present choice?" Dundee asked.

"Until *you* came along," Happy Day laughed. "Sure! She thinks Archie is insane about her, and only pays attention to Enid to make her jealous. Matter of fact, the kid's honestly dippy over Enid. . . . Swell girl, Enid Rambler. You were the lucky guy that found her last night and brought her back, weren't you?"

"Yes," Dundee assented curtly, for the attendant's blithe familiarity with himself and all the patients did not particularly please the detective.

"Yeah, Archie'd marry her in a minute if she'd have him. But she's not taking on any drunks, thank you kindly."

"Any truth at all in Miss Merrick's story that Koenig was in love with her?" Dundee asked, knowing the question to be a foolish one.

"Hunh! Are *you* crazy, too?" the attendant gibed. "She called him Carl, all right, and he humored her by standing for it. ... Greatest guy that ever lived—Doc Koenig! . . . Wonder what she wants Enid for?"

To Dundee's amazement, the crippled girl readily agreed to be taken out upon the lawn in a wheel chair. And as he lifted her slender body from the couch to place it in the chair he told himself, with a catch at his heart, that here was the real thing—beauty incarnate. She was wearing a sleeveless tennis dress of turquoise crepe de chine and a crocheted silk beret of the same color enchantingly set off the chestnut curls and vivid blue eyes.

"Hello, Precious! Did Muwer's baby hurt its poor little foot?" Majorie Merrick greeted the invalid, her voice rich with real tenderness.

"It did," Enid Rambler laughed. "And did Muvver want to see her baby?"

"God! I'll say I did!" the ex singer breathed fervently, dramatically. "Listen, Enid " and she briskly wheeled the chair to a safe distance, bending low and speaking in an urgent, rapid voice.

"Always cooking up something," Archie Webster laughed. "Enid's an angel to humor her as she does."

"Miss Rambler is indeed an angel of beauty and good ness," the elderly banker intoned solemnly. "But may I again remind you, gentlemen, that Miss Merrick was, in her day, a shining ornament of the concert stage? It was my good fortune to hear her sing, back in 1914–"

"Tell us some other time," Happy Day interrupted rudely, with another wink at Dundee. "Let's shuffle. They're coming back now."

And again Marjorie Merrick took her place at the bridge table, her forefinger tapping a warning of silence to Enid Rambler and Archie Webster alternately.

As the strange, hectic play progressed, Dundee watched the game, first at one table and then at another. Samuel Rowan was a clumsy but thoughtful player, his whole mind apparently upon the game. Mrs. Asbury played a shrewd, pitiless, aggressive game, brooking no conversation and rigidly enforcing the rule, "A touched card is a played card." She was not popular.

"Grand sweep!" Marjorie Merrick announced with loud triumph, as she showed down the last four cards in her hand. Then, with eyes narrowed and voice throatily significant, she asked of the table in general: "Has any one seen Justine? How's she taking it? ... The poor, poor darling! Of course I forgive her, but she never quit trying to keep Carl and me apart."

"Of course we've all seen Dr. Harlow," Archie Webster frowned at her. "She's been as busy as six doctors in a smallpox epidemic. And so has Cantrell. . . . And you'd better bite your tongue to keep it from saying any thing against the little doctor, Marjorie."

"Go roll your hoop!" the strange woman derided him. "As if it wasn't plain enough for a blind man to see that she was simply mad about Carl. To say nothing of Norah Lacey and Rose Caplan–"

"Are you crazy?" Webster cut in angrily.

"Sure! What do you think I'm here for?—ingrown toe nails?" and Marjorie Merrick laughed loudly. "And so are you, you sweet old alcoholic, you! . . . What's the matter with *your* attic, Big Boy?"

"Nothing, I hope," Dundee answered, flushing.

"That's what they all say at first," the woman laughed. "But you'll get so you think it's funny. . . . How's your stomach? Strong?"

"Fair to middlin'," he answered. "Why?"

"Because Jack Hubert's going to throw a fit," she told him calmly, and pointed toward the croquet field.

Dundee looked, then hastily averted his eyes.

"That's nothing," she assured him, almost gleefully. "You ought to have seen Clyde Powell when he was going good. Jack's a true epileptic—can't toss a fit when ever he wants to, but Clyde was a D. P. with epileptiform seizures. Just let him catch sight of anybody he was afraid of or hated, and—pfft! Perfect artist at fits, Clyde was, before he got too bad to come out on the lawn. . . . Have you seen Roy White? Our sleeping sickness exhibit," she explained, and distorted her face and crooked her fingers in a perfect imitation of the paralytic Dundee had seen that morning. "Staggers along as if he can hardly take a step, but one day I saw him run a race with Jack—and win!"

Dundee did not comment, and the ex singer began to shuffle the cards. Suddenly, however, she threw them down and beckoned Webster imperiously. Reluctantly the young man followed her, and another mysterious conversation ensued, Marjorie talking rapidly and earnestly, her finger frequently at her lips, and Webster nodding his head in impatient agreement with everything she said.

To conceal his interest in this by play Dundee strolled to the other table. Mrs. Asbury was announcing in a calm voice, as she reached for pencil and score pad:

"Down three tricks doubled. . . . Sorry, partner. But every cloud has its silver lining, Mr. Rowan. Just because you took that set like a gentleman, and didn't try to show me how a couple of finesses would have saved the game, I'm going to do you a big favor. . . . That stupid police captain thinks you murdered Dr. Koenig, doesn't he?"

Samuel Rowan flushed darkly, but did not answer.

"Well, the next time he has you on the grill, you just tell him that Josephine killed the doctor. She promised me she would kill him if he didn't let me go away with her yesterday."

Before Dundee could speak out of his amazement, Happy Day twisted about in his chair at the other table, clapping his hands. "So Josephine did it, eh, Mrs. Asbury? . . . Good old Josephine! What a load off the captain's mind *that* will be!"

Very calmly, and without a word, Mrs. Asbury rose, overturning her chair. With one sweep of her large right arm she scattered the cards and upset the bridge table. Then, very politely, she bowed to her bridge partner and opponents. "Thank you for a very pleasant game," she said, and strolled off across the lawn.

"Good Lord!" Dundee breathed. "Who *is* Josephine?"

"A lady who exists only in Mrs. Asbury's mind," Happy Day chuckled.

"A poor unfortunate—Mrs. Asbury," the aged Mr. Hepple intoned solemnly. "I should have liked the opportunity to assure her that her beloved and imaginary Josephine did not kill the doctor—but that, to my certain knowledge, he was struck down by the hand of God, as just retribution for keeping me here, when, in one day on the Stock Exchange, I could restore the country to an unparalleled era of prosperity. But he refused to release me, and the hand of God has struck!"

Dundee felt an icy sweat break out upon his brow and upper lip. "The hand of God"—"the voice of God." . . .

"Attaboy, Hepple!" Happy Day applauded. "But I hope *you've* got an alibi, or the bad old police may get you!"

"I?" There was gentle scorn in the old man's voice. "I sat next to Mrs. Asbury during the entire showing of both motion pictures last night."

Slightly sick, Dundee stared at the old man. If there was no one but that insane woman to support his alibi . . . Suddenly a feeling of desperate helplessness swept over the detective. How futile to try to apply sane, normal methods of investigating murder in a place like this! Why, anything—any ghastly thing that a De Quincy could dream of—could happen here! Had he not seen an apparently normal and highly intelligent woman suddenly go to pieces? Had he not heard a fine example of gentleman of the old school babbling matter of factly about the hand of God? In a place where victims of claustrophobia tried to run away, and nymphomaniacs deluded themselves that every man was in love with them

"Someone's calling you, Dundee!" Archie Webster, temporarily free of Marjorie Merrick, reported as he strolled back to the bridge table. "Guess they want to get your case history. Better think up some good complexes and psychoses, to make it interesting reading."

Dundee rose hastily, excused himself, and almost ran across the lawn to where Norah Lacey stood on the steps of the main building. And as he ran a concerted shout of laughter—blending the contralto notes of Marjorie Merrick with the sweet voice of Enid Rambler and the deeper rumbles of the men—followed him mockingly.

He clenched his hands. Had they discovered who he was and plotted this whole mad afternoon to tantalize and confuse him? What—whom—could he believe?

"What's happened?" he panted, as he reached the steps.

The nurse's face was drawn and ashen. "It's Dr. Mayfield. He's dead."

CHAPTER SEVENTEEN

"WELL, thank God, it wasn't murder!" Captain Strawn ejaculated, mopping his heavy, flushed face. "We've got enough trouble on our hands as it is."

"I'll say we have," Dundee agreed gloomily. "No need of an inquest, I suppose?"

The two detectives were temporarily alone in the small sitting room of Dr. Mayfield's suite on the second floor of the main building. Beyond, in the bedroom, with the newly dead body, were Drs. Harlow and Cantrell and Miss Lacey.

"No doubt of its being a natural death, according to Cantrell and the little doctor," Strawn answered. "Just died in a fit–"

"Senile delirium," Dundee corrected. "Best get it right when you tell the reporters. . . . Wonder what's keeping Baldwin? . . . There he is! ... Come in!"

Roger Baldwin, the business manger, stepped into the room, followed by Dr. Mayfield's attendant, who had been sent in search of him.

"Another bad break for the sanitarium," Baldwin commented sourly. "I hope to God the traditional third blow falls quickly, so all three will make the same nine days' wonder."

"You were with Dr. Mayfield when the attack seized him, I believe?" Dundee asked abruptly.

"I was. Granger here asked me to see him, thinking perhaps I could pacify him," Baldwin explained. "He couldn't have made a poorer choice, as it happens. The old doctor hated the sight of me, and 'fired' me every time he saw me. He believed he was still head of Mayfield Sanitarium, and that I was only a salaried cashier."

"How did you happen to call Mr. Baldwin, Granger?" Dundee asked the attendant.

"Gosh! I didn't know what to do," the attendant protested plaintively. "The old doctor was in his right mind, and raising the roof because I wouldn't get Dr. Koenig. He told me flat I was lying when I said he was out of town, because he'd seen Dr. Koenig yesterday and knew he was just back from a trip."

"What did he want of Dr. Koenig?" Strawn cut in.

"I didn't pay much attention," the attendant evaded uncomfortably, "but he kept saying something about that man couldn't stay here another day, that he was a 'menace to Mayfield'–"

"Meaning Mr. Baldwin?" Dundee asked sharply.

"No, sir. It sounded like he meant—like he was referring to Dr. Koenig!" the attendant blurted miserably.

"I got the same impression," Baldwin said drily. "Not that it means a damned thing. The old doctor was always turning against one of us and ordering us off the place–"

"Just what happened when you came up?" Dundee interrupted.

"Granger stayed in this room and I went into the bedroom," Baldwin answered. "I knew it was unwise for me to go, but Granger was afraid to handle the situation alone, and everyone else—Dr. Harlow, Dr. Cantrell and Miss Lacey—was busy with patients. . . . The whole place is at sixes and sevens, now that the patients know about the murder–"

"And Mr. Baldwin is one of the bosses here," Granger justified himself.

"I found Dr. Mayfield in bed," Baldwin went on. "He recognized me and ordered me to get out. Said he wanted Koenig and no one else. I tried to soothe him—told him Koenig was away, but he told me I was lying. Said I was trying to shield Koenig, but that he was still head of this institution, and he'd see that 'that man' didn't stay here another day. But before he finished the sentence the attack came on. I called Granger and then hurried off to find Cantrell or Dr. Harlow. Both were with him when he died—about ten minutes after the attack started. . . . I've been getting off a cable to his daughter, Madame Arnaud, in Paris."

"Do you think she will come?"

"I doubt it. On her last visit she made all arrangements for his funeral, his death having been expected for more than a year."

"Why did Dr. Mayfield hate you, Baldwin?" Strawn asked abruptly.

The business manager shrugged, and grinned wryly. "He got an idea that I was extravagant, wasting the institution's funds. My colleagues accuse me of erring on the other side."

An hour later Dundee was concluding a detailed recital of his own day to Captain Strawn. The two men sat facing each other at the murdered psychiatrist's desk.

"By the way, Captain, when you questioned Hepple and Mrs. Asbury this morning, were you satisfied with their alibis?" Dundee asked, when he had finished his account of the mad bridge games on the lawn.

"The Asbury dame said a friend of hers, name of Josephine, sat in the seat where the old boy, Hepple, swears he was sitting," Strawn grinned.

"Just as I expected," Dundee groaned. "I'll be crazy myself before this case is finished. . . . Come in!"

It was Dr. Harlow. Spectacles could not hide the violet shadows beneath the gray green eyes. But the little doctor scorned to droop with fatigue or to abate one whit her professional briskness.

"Will you tell me if there is to be an inquest upon Dr. Koenig?"

Dundee sprang to his feet and offered his chair. "Captain Strawn and I have talked by telephone with both the district attorney and the police commissioner, and we have all agreed that, under the circumstances—many of the witnesses being psychopathic patients—it would be unwise to hold an inquest. Under the laws of the state, an inquest can be waived, you know."

"Oh!" A tremulous sigh of relief deflated the little doctor's chest and she slumped a bit in her chair. "Thank you—with all my heart."

"Then," Dundee suggested gently, "will you do us a favor in return? Will you tell us frankly and truthfully, Dr. Harlow, where you were last night between eight and ten o'clock? . . . You see, doctor, we know that you traveled only eleven miles in your car after five o'clock yesterday, so I am sure you will want to amend your story that you were driving the two hours between eight and ten."

The small hands clenched to still their trembling, but the tired eyes met Dundee's steadily. "Yes, I did not tell you the whole truth. I was making an unofficial call on a sick person."

"On a three year old little boy?" Dundee asked softly.

The proud shoulders fell then. "Yes."

"On Dr. Koenig's son, in other words?"

She did not flare out at him, as Dundee had half expected. But she shook her head wearily. "I don't know whose child he is."

"Did Miss Lacey ask you to have a look at the child?"

"Yes. She telephoned about eight o'clock that she was worried about Sonny, and not at all satisfied with the doctor the Satterlees had called to attend him. I could not refuse to go, but told her that my visit must be unofficial."

"Then you and Miss Lacey were with the child all evening?"

The girl doctor hesitated, then her eyes met his bravely. "I can't lie again. It would be no use. . . . Norah asked me to stay with Sonny while she went out on an errand."

"When did she leave and how long was she gone?"

"She left about eight thirty and returned at ten minutes to ten. Sonny was asleep, had been asleep for nearly an hour, and I was waiting outside the house in my car, anxious to be back here. The house is set almost flush with the sidewalk and the nursery is a front room, so I should have heard him if the child had cried out. As Norah drove up, I drove off, waiting only to assure her that Sonny was better. I drove home very fast, arriving at ten o'clock, as I said last night."

"Do you know where Miss Lacey was during all that time?"

"I do not," she answered with flat finality, then turned, with obvious relief, as Maizie Home appeared in the doorway from the reception room. "What is it, Maizie?"

"A telegram for you," the secretary said, and handed over the yellow envelope.

The little doctor tore it open and read, then she frowned. "They're in an awful hurry," she said, with the first note of querulous complaint Dundee had heard in her lovely voice. "It's from the State Hospital, asking me to rush them a resume of Clyde Powell's case history. . . . Will you get his history for me, Maizie? I suppose I'll have to attend to it this afternoon."

"Dr. Koenig had a special delivery letter from Dr. Wiggin the first thing yesterday morning, asking for Clyde's history," the secretary explained in a subdued voice as she tiptoed across the room to the file cabinet.

"Then Dr. Koenig must have attended to it, and his letter simply hasn't reached them yet," Dr. Harlow said.

"No, doctor. He had so many interruptions yesterday that he hadn't got to it by five o'clock," the secretary excused her dead employer. "He told me to get the history from the file for him, and I did. I clipped Dr. Wiggin's letter to the folder, so's Dr. Koenig could see just what Dr. Wiggin wanted—Why, it isn't here!" the girl broke off to exclaim.

"*Missing?*" Dundee sprang to his feet.

"It's not in the files," the girl quavered, "but I suppose Dr. Carl hadn't finished with it when he—when he was–"

"Have you sorted out those letters that were scattered over the floor?" Dundee slashed across the girl's hysteria sharply.

"Yes, sir. I smoothed them out and filed those that didn't require an answer–"

"Was Dr. Wiggin's letter among them?"

"No, sir."

"And did you find any letter from Dr. Koenig to Dr. Wiggin?"

"No, sir."

"It seems quite clear, Mr. Dundee," Dr. Harlow interrupted, "that whoever destroyed the other two case histories that are missing tore up Clyde Powell's too."

"Sounds reasonable," Strawn commented. "Convenient to the murderer's hand it must have been, right out here on the doctor's desk. Just more dust in our eyes."

"I've had a hunch all along that the one case history that was a menace to the murderer's safety was not torn up, but completely destroyed later," Dundee told them, his eyes burning with new hope. "What we've got to find out is—which history that was!"

"How?" Strawn demanded, but Dundee, without pausing to excuse himself, dashed out of the office and across the lawn to Sunflower Court.

Within five minutes he was back, carrying the glass tray into which he had piled the precious scraps gathered from the office floor.

"I need help," he announced briskly. "Everybody rally 'round! First, I want to verify my suspicion that only two case histories have been torn up. Begin by sorting the scraps—manila folder scraps in one pile, white paper scraps in another."

He dumped the tray of paper fragments upon the rug, and a moment later four pairs of hands were swiftly busy at the task. When the two piles were complete, Dundee rose from his knees and, his voice crisp with excitement, asked of Dr. Harlow:

"Have you a scales—very delicate and accurate?"

The girl doctor frowned thoughtfully, then nodded. "Gram scales, used in the diet kitchen. I'll get them."

She returned very quickly, carrying a pair of white enamel scales, whose pointer was set at zero.

"Good!" Dundee cried, and, after placing a light wicker letter tray upon the flat top of the scales, he transferred the small pile of cream colored manila scraps from the floor to the tray.

"Hocus pocus!" Strawn growled, as Dundee made a note of the weight of the scraps in grams.

"Yeah?" Dundee grinned. "Now, Miss Home, if you'll be good enough to bring me three manila folders— the exact kind you use for case histories–"

The girl obeyed, wonderingly. From the wicker tray Dundee removed the scraps, replacing them with the three new folders.

"See that?" he cried, pointing to the indicator on the face of the scales. "Three untorn folders weigh exactly *one third more* than these scraps!"

"Proving?" Strawn asked.

Dundee looked at his old chief in amazement. "Proving, Captain, that, while three case histories are" missing from this office, only two have been torn up. The third is completely missing—or at least its folder is, and if you can suggest a single plausible reason why the folder alone should have been removed by the murderer, and the case history torn up–"

"I getcha," Strawn conceded. "But looks like we're no forrader–"

"Down on our knees again!" Dundee cried happily. "What we're looking for now are scraps of paper bearing the typewritten names of Samuel Rowan, Archibald Webster, and Clyde Powell—the whole names or any recognizable part of those names."

It was Maizie Home who made the first discovery, as her nimble fingers picked up and rejected scraps from the sizable heap.

"Here's a scrap that has 'owa' on it!" she exulted. "And I can't think of any word in common use that has those three letters together—except Iowa."

"Neither can I," Dundee assured her approvingly. "Looks as if Sam Rowan's in the clear, doesn't it? But let's try to find more corroboration."

Dr. Harlow announced the next find. "Here's the top left hand comer of page two of Archie's history," she said quietly. "Look!" and she exhibited a scrap that read: # 2—Webs

"That's right!" Maizie Home dapped her hands. "We always put the last name of the patient after the number of each page of his history. I *knew* it wasn't Archie–"

"And here's additional proof that Rowan's history was torn up," Dundee interrupted. "Look, Captain!" and he showed a fragment bearing the letters, "amu." "It's a safe bet that the complete word was Samuel. . . . Well?"

Captain Strawn sat back on his haunches, his heavy face sadly puzzled. "That leaves only the Powell boy's history, Bonnie," he deduced worriedly. "Looks like you've run into a blind alley, boy."

"Clyde Powell," Dundee repeated, frowning.

"*Clyde Powell?*" Dr. Harlow echoed incredulously. "Then the captain's right, Mr. Dundee. We've wasted our time. Clyde was transferred to the State Hospital on Monday, before Dr. Koenig returned. He left here with a guard and a nurse."

"Do you know that he actually arrived at the State Hospital, that he did not escape *en route?*" Dundee asked sharply.

"If anything had happened, I am sure we should have been notified," Dr. Harlow assured him.

The young detective whirled upon Maizie Home. "Did Dr. Wiggin's letter to Dr. Koenig, received yesterday morning, actually state that the patient had arrived?"

The girl's baby blue eyes narrowed in concentration. "I can just *see* the letter, as if I were looking at it now," she answered proudly. "It began, 'Relative to the patient,

Clyde Powell, transferred to this institution on Monday from your private sanitarium—' That proves he really got there, doesn't it?"

"You say you can 'see' the letter," Dundee countered eagerly. "Anything distinctive about it—the paper, I mean?"

"Why, yes, there was," the secretary answered readily. "It was a bright canary yellow, and both the printing and the typing were in green ink!"

"That clinches it!" Dundee struck a fist into a palm. "You say no such letter was found among the crumpled correspondence found on the floor. Well, there's been no such letter torn up, along with the case histories! You can see for yourselves that there are no yellow scraps in the whole lot! Just to make sure, however, that the letter is actually missing, I want you, Miss Home, to search the correspondence files and your own desk, while I go through Dr. Koenig's desk from top to bottom."

Ten minutes later there was no blinking the fact that the canary colored letter from the State Hospital was nowhere in the suite of three offices. Waste baskets had not yet been emptied of their Wednesday accumulation, since the cleaning woman, who did her work here between six and seven in the morning, had been kept out by the plainclothes men on guard. Neither was the letter among the small heap of papers and personal belongings taken from the murdered doctor's pockets.

"So—Clyde Powell's case history is the crux of the whole matter," Dundee said slowly. "The missing letter clinches the thing. The murderer figured it out extremely well. He guessed that the file would be searched for missing case histories of only those patients who are still here. He was right. But it was necessary to *remove* the Wiggin letter, so that no one should be reminded of Clyde Powell's history. If you had not received that telegram from the State Asylum, Dr. Harlow, the fact of the missing history might never have been discovered!"

"But—*Clyde Powell!*" the little doctor protested, in puzzled distress. "He could not have been here last night. Not only is he in a locked ward at the State Hospital, but he is physically and mentally incapable of having committed the crime."

"You're undoubtedly right," Dundee told her, "but—*he has relatives!*"

"By God, boy, you've hit on something!" Strawn ejaculated. "Maizie here says the boy's father paid a visit to the doctor yesterday. It's a cinch the old man was feeling pretty low over his boy's being kicked out just because he couldn't pay Mayfield's big bills any longer–"

"That's absurdly wrong, Captain!" Dr. Harlow cut in angrily. "It was old Mr. Powell who asked that the boy be transferred, and I happen to know from Dr. Koenig himself that he was much upset over our letting Clyde go, and that he assured Mr. Powell yesterday of his eagerness to get the boy back, for as long as he lives—which won't be long—and at the minimum rate, with no charges for attendants. Carl was going to pay the attendants out of his own pocket. And *that's* the reason poor old Mr. Powell had tears in his eyes when he left here yesterday! He had refused the charity—too proud!—but he was touched by Dr. Carl's offer."

Dundee's mind had registered the unconscious slip—the one time she had referred to the dead man by his first name without a prefix, but there was no indication of the fact in his deferential manner as he asked her:

"Dr. Harlow, did Dr. Koenig ever say anything to you about Clyde Powell's reminding him of someone?"

"Why, of course not!"

"Perhaps I'd better put it this way: did Dr. Koenig ever wonder aloud to you 'where he'd seen those eyes before'?"

" 'Those eyes'?" the girl doctor repeated blankly. "Certainly not!"

"I getcha, boy!" Captain Strawn exulted, slapping his thigh. "I knew Mrs. Cantrell's story was the biggest step forward we've made yet. Clear as day, ain't it? The doctor's talking along to the little lady on the phone. His eyes light on Powell's case history, lying open on his desk. Suddenly something clicks in his brain. Funny how the good old memory works, ain't it? . . . Well, he remembers where he has seen Clyde Powell before–"

"He'd seen him here almost daily for five years," Dr. Harlow cut in acidly. "Clyde was here when Dr. Koenig took charge."

"That makes no never mind," Strawn assured her. "He'd been puzzled for five years as to where he'd seen Clyde Powell before, and suddenly he remembers. And he's horror stricken. That's the very word Mrs. Cantrell used to express the way his voice sounded, ain't it, Bonnie?"

"Correct," Dundee agreed.

"All right, then!" Strawn went on vigorously. "It's pretty easy to dope out what happened. The doctor remembers where he'd seen this Clyde Powell before—*and it was in a courtroom!* A boy criminal on trial for some pretty nasty offense—criminal assault or murder. Under some other name, of course. All right! The boy has either been acquitted or has escaped from prison. But Koenig knows that he's dangerous—ought to be in jail, or certainly in the asylum for the criminally insane–"

"And for seven years he was a docile, obedient, harm less patient in this institution," Dr. Harlow reminded him sternly.

"But the Big Doctor knows damned well there ain't no telling when he'll bust out, and there'll be hell to pay," Strawn retorted. "Well, then! He's got to act and act quick. He telephones his lawyer for advice. The lawyer ain't at home. Then the doctor thinks it only fair to warn the Powell family what he's on to and up to. So he telephones Powell to come down for an interview. Old Powell comes, realizes his son is doomed to spend the rest of his days in the asylum for the criminally insane, disgracing not only himself but his family, or that he'll be hauled back to the prison he escaped from. So–" and Strawn shrugged his massive shoulders.

"It fits, all right," Dundee assented, but without joy. A nasty job, this of his—"But before we get out a warrant for Powell senior's arrest, I think we'd better get him and his wife here for questioning."

"Oh, I'm sure you're wrong!" Dr. Harlow wailed, wringing her hands in the first abandonment to distress that she had shown.

"How can we reach Mr. Powell by telephone, doctor?" he asked gently. "I'm going to give him a chance to come without being brought in."

"The Powells own a grocery store on Hubbard Street," she told him, her voice shaking. "The family lives over the store. The initials are J. C."

"Telephone book? . . . Thanks, Miss Home!" and Dundee turned the pages quickly until he found the number.

Seating himself at the murdered doctor's desk, he lifted the combination transmitter and receiver from the French type telephone which still stood on the typewriter table at right angles to the desk. Laying the one piece instrument on the desk, he began to dial. The dialing completed, he reached for the instrument.

But to the watchers' amazement he did not complete the movement which would have settled the receiver against his ear and the transmitter before his mouth. . . .

"What are your eyes popping out at, boy?" Strawn demanded sharply.

Dundee continued to stare at the receiver for some seconds. Then, still without answering, he began to scrape with a finger nail, very carefully and delicately, against the inside surface of the receiver. Moistening another finger on his tongue, he wet the substance under his nail. And then he spoke:

"*One drop of blood!*"

CHAPTER EIGHTEEN

CAPTAIN STRAWN, Dr. Harlow and Maizie Home stared at the young detective in stupefied amazement.

"And now I know," Dundee went on, with deep satisfaction, "how that blood came to be on the corner of the desk, why the murderer had to wipe it away, and—*how the doctor's chin was bruised after death!*"

Captain Strawn was the first to recover the power of speech. "Seems to me like one little drop of blood is doing a powerful sight of talking!" he commented sourly.

"You said it!" Dundee exulted. "Not only has it told me those three vitally important secrets, but—it will eventually send the murderer to the gallows! One drop of blood that he could not see at the time. Oh, he was careful, all right! Look at the inside of that receiver! Wiped clean, probably with the same gauze swab he used to wipe the blood off the corner of the desk. But one drop of blood was hidden from his sight, inside the receiver. The murderer could not see it. But when the receiver was again placed on the prongs, upside down, that betraying drop of blood seeped down until it clogged one of these six tiny holes—a silent witness, waiting to tell its story and, eventually, avenge the man who shed that blood."

"Yeah?" Strawn snorted. "How about a little explanation for them that can't hear blood talk quite so plain?"

"Sorry!" Dundee apologized with a broad grin. "I'm unpardonably melodramatic, but I can't help being excited. . . . Look, Captain! It's plain as day. Dr. Koenig was *not* typing when he was murdered. He was talking over the telephone. That's why he did not see and possibly did not hear the approach of his murderer. Which broadens the scope of our investigation, I admit, since it leaves room for doubt that the murderer was someone privileged to enter this office without knocking. While the doctor is still absorbed in his telephone conversation, the murderer secures the bronze statue and crashes it down upon his head. The doctor is facing the desk, although the base of the telephone is on the typewriter table to his right. As the doctor's head is crashed down, the combination receiver and transmitter is pinned between the head and the desk. As the coroner and Dr. Cantrell assured us, the blow caused a slight hemorrhage from the ear. The blood oozed into the receiver, which must have stayed in that position for several minutes, while the murderer was engaged in faking his stage setting and tearing up case histories–"

"Just a minute," Strawn interrupted. "Why didn't the person the doctor was talking to hear the sound of the blow, and make a fuss when the conversation was cut short?"

"I believe that the murderer pressed down on this bar," Dundee answered, pointing to the telephone base on the typewriter table, "before the blow was struck. It was the work of a second, and his action could not be observed by the doctor, whose back was turned. Dr. Koenig must have thought he was accidentally disconnected, if he heard the resulting buzz above the sound of his own voice, but before he could reach for the dial, he was struck down."

"O. K.!" Strawn grunted.

"Therefore," Dundee continued, "the murderer was safe in leaving the instrument pressed against the doctor's ear and mouth until he had time to remove it—or he thought he was safe to do so. He could not reckon with that one betraying drop of blood. At his leisure, he raised the head and removed the instrument, swabbing out the receiver, which, to his horror, dripped blood upon the blotter, and, as he was carrying it back to its base, upon the corner of the desk. It was natural for the murderer to invert the instrument, before he knew there was blood in the receiver. He did his best. He thought he wiped away all traces of the fact that the doctor had been killed while he was telephoning. Which brings us to the most significant deduction yet. It seems to me that it was vitally important to the murderer that no one ever know the truth—that the doctor was telephoning at the very moment he was killed. . . . Why?"

"Because the telephone conversation concerned the murderer, I presume," Dr. Harlow answered, in a dazed voice.

"Exactly!" Dundee cried eagerly.

"He was telephoning the Powells," Strawn cut in, "and spilling the beans about this Clyde—to the mother, probably. And in walks old man Powell He's reconsidered his refusal to let Koenig get the boy back, and has come to tell the doctor so. But the first thing he hears when he steps into the office is what Koenig is saying to Mrs. Powell about having the boy turned over to the authorities. The old man goes berserk and kills the doctor."

"Please!" Dr. Harlow interrupted, her face pale and drawn with distress. "I'm sure Mr. Dundee is right about the telephone, but I'm absolutely positive you are wrong, Captain, about Clyde Powell."

"It is *his* case history that is missing, the letter concerning *him* that is also missing—not torn up," Dundee reminded her, to Strawn's obvious satisfaction. "Are you familiar with Clyde Powell's case history, doctor?"

"In a general way only," she admitted. "I've read it, and have made additions to it, but I have not gone over it carefully for years. The poor boy's condition was not interesting, psychiatrically. It changed in expected ways, growing steadily worse. He is a dementia praecox, with epileptiform seizures. That is, he is not a true epileptic, but is subject to attacks which resemble epilepsy. For more than a year he has been increasingly helpless. His mind is hopelessly gone."

"Any distinguishing or unusual aspects of his case?" Dundee asked.

"No," she answered. "Like many cases of dementia praecox, he had ideas of persecution, delusions of grandeur, and occasional hallucinations. States of depression and of excitement alternated, sometimes accompanied by epileptiform seizures."

"How long had he been ill?"

"About eleven years, I believe. He came to us from a private sanitarium near Los Angeles, seven years ago—two years before Dr. Koenig and I came to Mayfield."

"Do you remember anything in his case history that would account for its being destroyed by his father or anyone else?"

"Nothing whatever!" she answered emphatically.

"Do you remember whether there was a record of Clyde's having been involved in any serious trouble before he was committed to a sanitarium?"

"There was positively nothing of the sort! He was considered entirely harmless, both because of his past history and because of his behavior here."

"I see," Dundee said slowly.

"Well, *I* don't see, and I'm going to get the Powells here in short order," Strawn declared in no uncertain tones. "Give me that phone!"

"I think it would be wiser if no one else touched this instrument until Dr. Price has had a chance to make an analysis," Dundee suggested. "I'm positive it's blood, but I want official confirmation."

"O. K. Guess it's better to send one of the boys after the Powells, anyway," Strawn agreed, and strode out of the room.

"May I see Miss Lacey, please?" Dundee asked of Dr. Harlow, when the older detective was gone.

"Will you call her, please, Maizie?" Dr. Harlow asked wearily. "Then I'll join you in the reception room. There's work to be done."

When the white faced head nurse arrived, Dundee was grateful for the little doctor's tact which had made it possible for him to conduct the interview privately.

"Please sit down, Miss Lacey," he directed gently. "You've seen the morning paper? You know that Dr. Koenig's will, unless he has changed it without Dr. Cantrell's knowledge, leaves one half of his estate to you and one half to Dr. Harlow?"

"Yes," she quavered, and a thin, work worn hand strayed nervously to her silver threaded black hair. "I was dumfounded–"

"Then you know of no reason why Dr. Koenig should have been so generous to you?"

"No. I couldn't believe my eyes—" she faltered, but those eyes did not meet the detective's.

"Did it not occur to you, Miss Lacey, that Dr. Koenig wanted to help you provide for—Sonny?" Dundee asked, and again he hated his job.

"Sonny?" she repeated, in a voice that was scarcely more than a gasp for breath.

"He's a remarkably handsome little boy," Dundee assured her sincerely. "Whose child is he?" he added with startling abruptness.

Strength came back to her. "He's mine!" she cried passionately. "That's all you need know! He's mine!"

"Did you—give birth to him, Miss Lacey?"

She collapsed again, and Dundee was afraid she was going to faint. "I've said he's mine. That's enough. You can think what you like."

"Then I'm afraid I'll have to think you are his 'natural' mother," Dundee said gently. "Wouldn't it be much wiser and simpler for you to tell me the whole truth about the child?"

"I'd rather die!" she assured him with terrible intensity.

"Again you force me to draw my own conclusions," Dundee told her soberly. "My guess is not a pleasant one, but—here it is. Sonny's father is a man you love more than you love yourself—a man you would the to protect from scandal. Either that, or"—and he shrugged,—"to save yourself now you must protect *him!*"

"What on earth do you mean?" she cried starting up from her chair.

"What is Sonny's name, Miss Lacey?" he countered.

"His name is Lacey!" she cried. "I told you he's mine!"

"What is his first name, Miss Lacey?" he insisted.

Her knees were shaking as she sank back into her chair. "I suppose you'd dig it up somehow," she accused him bitterly, "so I may as well tell you. ... I named Sonny after—after Dr. Koenig. His name is Carl."

"I see. . . . Carl—Lacey. And you wanted him to have the right to be called—Carl Koenig, Jr.?"

She sprang to her feet again, her gray eyes blazing wide. "No, no! That's a lie—a terrible, vicious lie!"

"If it is not true that Dr. Koenig was little Carl's father," Dundee persisted quietly, "will you tell me who the father is?"

"Never! I've told you I'd rather die!"

"I'm sorry. . . . Miss Lacey, last night you were so worried over Sonny's illness that you called Dr. Harlow, begged her to come to see him "

"So *she* told you, did she?" the nurse interrupted bitterly. "I thought I could trust her—of all women!"

Her emphasis and bitterness surprised the detective.

"She told only after I'd learned the truth from a visit to the Satterlees," he assured her. "She obeyed your summons. She went to see Sonny. And almost as soon as she reached the Satterlee house *you* left—on an errand. What was that errand, Miss Lacey? What business was so pressing that it took you away from your desperately sick boy?"

"I refuse to answer!" she cried, shaking as with a chill.

"And I submit, Miss Lacey, that the errand was indeed an important one," Dundee went on inexorably, although his stomach revolted at his own tactics, "that it took you to the child's father!"

She gasped, and her pale lips parted, but she did not or could not find breath to deny the charge.

"Miss Lacey," he went on coldly, but with pity in his heart, "if you had known last night that Dr. Koenig's will left you one half of all he possessed, would you have — behaved differently while you were out on that vital errand?"

"Of course not! Dr. Koenig's will could not help—could not alter—oh, what am I saying? Stop digging at me! I've told you I'd rather die than tell you any more than you've already found out!"

But Dundee considered himself amply answered. He gladly let her go. But when he was alone again there was no triumph in his tired blue eyes. He had uncovered a woman's shame, and his own sense of degradation was the only result. For while he was now fairly sure whose voice had pleaded hysterically with the psychiatrist for a love he could no longer give her, he was equally sure that Norah Lacey had not murdered her betrayer. An ugly word. And a strange word to apply to the austere, almost saintlike Doctor. But human nature—Dundee shrugged. No, the nurse adored him too much to do anything more drastic than reproach him. Women were strange creatures, he reflected tritely. But men, he reminded himself, were no less unaccountable. The "Big Doctor"—so big in every other way—would leave the unwed mother of his child half of his estate, oblivious to the possibility of scandal, but would stubbornly refuse to give their child its rightful heritage of a proud and famous name. But wait! Had Koenig been so oblivious to scandal? Was not that the explanation of the divided estate? If two women were named in his will, to share equally—two respected and capable colleagues—would not the possibility of scandal be reduced to a minimum? But somehow the deduction did not cheer Dundee. He was young enough to be still something of a hero worshiper, and his ideal of Dr. Koenig, whose stature had increased hourly since his murder, was sadly tarnished. . . .

He was still sunk in gloom, still alone, when, ten minutes later, Captain Strawn burst into the room, his heavy face red with excitement.

"Looks like it's all over, boy! Here's a confession. After all this hullaballoo, it was a patient all the time!"

"A patient?" Dundee grinned. "Didn't Dr. Harlow warn us to expect a raft of confessions from upset patients?"

"But this one's no nut," Strawn protested. "The little doctor swears she's legally as sane as you or me—just flighty."

"All right! I bite! Who killed Carl Koenig?" Dundee laughed.

Strawn scowled at his levity, but he shouted the answer triumphantly:

"Marjorie Merrick!"

CHAPTER NINETEEN

GRINNING skeptically, but with delighted anticipation of the lively scene that he was to witness, Dundee took his place behind the door of Dr. Cantrell's office, first making sure that the wall mirror was still so placed that it would reflect what took place at Dr. Koenig's desk.

As he waited for her to appear, the detective re read the "confession" note that Marjorie Merrick had written and sent to Captain Strawn:

"Sir: (it began haughtily, and Dundee chuckled) *Concealment is no longer possible. I can see, feel an invisible net closing—closing, tightening inevitably. Would God that— But remorse cannot interest you. Only THE TRUTH, terrible and shocking though it may be, matters to YOU—representative of the hard hearted police. . . . So, sir, to ease the burden upon my soul, I must tell you that I—I, Majorie Merrick, I ALONE, am responsible for Carl Koenig's death."*

There was no formal signature to the melodramatic note, and again Dundee chuckled. This was going to be fun! What the picture producers called "comedy relief." . . . Well, he could do with a bit of comedy–

A vibrant contralto voice cut across his amused reflections. The mirror was blank for a moment more, then gave him a full sized portrait of the ex singer. With heaven only knew what fantastic notions of propriety, the strange woman had changed from the yellow silk tunic to wide trousered black lace pajamas. Unfortunately, however, for any calculated effect of mourning, the undershirt and shorts she wore beneath the open patterned lace were of vivid scarlet satin. Dundee gasped, and was afraid he had betrayed his hidden presence, but the vital contralto was continuing unchecked:

"We meet again, Captain—Strawn is the name, I believe? ... Thank you! . . . No, no! Don't ask me to sit at *this desk,* where only last night—" and her bony shoulders heaved in terrific shudders.

"Stand then," Strawn told her sourly. "You wish to make a statement, Miss Merrick? . . . Ready, Brede?"

The police stenographer, who was blushing like a schoolboy, fumbled nervously with notebook and pencil.

"Captain!" the woman began, after taking a deep breath, and fixing the Chief of the Homicide Squad with her glittering black eyes, "do you believe that a person who is crazed with drink and mad with love is responsible for his actions?"

"What's that?" Strawn ejaculated. "I thought you said *you* killed Koenig!"

A thin hand went up in a melodramatic gesture, while the other hand settled more firmly the red rose tucked among the too black curls.

"No, Captain! Be accurate, I implore you! I wrote in my note that I and I alone am responsible for Carl Koenig's death!"

"Well, what the devil-?" Strawn sputtered.

"I meant exactly what I said," the vibrant voice pulsed on. "Crazed by drink which some unprincipled stranger gave to him, maddened by love for *me*, driven insane by jealousy which I—*I*, accursed enchantress that I am—"

"Can that stuff!" Strawn exploded angrily. "Listen, lady, I kid easy, but not *that* easy-"

Behind the door, Dundee nearly choked with laughter, but even if he too had exploded he doubted if Marjorie Merrick would have heard him.

"You're insulting, sir!" she stormed. "In good faith, and with a heart heavy laden with grief and remorse, I come to you–"

"All right, all right! Play out the comedy and get it over with!" Strawn interrupted helplessly. "But speed it up, lady! I'm a busy man."

"*Comedy!*" the woman cried bitterly, a black lace hand kerchief dabbing at her mascaraed eyes. "I come to you with the terrible truth of how Carl Koenig was murdered by poor, irresponsible Archie Webster–"

"*Webster?*" Strawn shouted. "Say, begin all over again and tell your story in plain American, without gestures—*if you please!*"

"I find that I must sit after all," the woman gasped weakly, and sank into the chair Strawn had first offered. "I shall try to be brief," she promised, with forlorn dignity.

"Archie Webster loves me madly. That is the secret of his frequent returns to Mayfield. Separated from me, he drinks himself nearly to death, but behind his debauches is the definite plan that they shall land him here again, where he can be with me!"

"Yeah?" Strawn grinned wryly. "I've heard it hinted around that it's the Rambler girl he's stuck on."

"Ah, you know so little of the subtleties of love!" she assured him tragically. "To make me jealous, Archie pretends to be interested in Enid—and a dear, sweet child she is, although God has not seen fit to curse her with the power over men which—"

"Sure! I getcha," Strawn interrupted rudely. "Get along with this yarn of yours."

"Yarn'!" she repeated, more in sorrow than anger; then she shrugged. "Very well! . . . Last night I dropped in on Enid and asked her to forget her fear of crowds and strangers—to go to the movies with me. She consented at last, and, in a burst of affection for me, presented me with a sheaf of lovely roses which, she said, some unknown admirer had sent her. . . . Ah, dear, dead flowers!" she broke off her narrative to croon in a tender voice, and Dundee saw her touch reverently the withered roses on the murdered doctor's desk. "You made *his* last moments sweeter, but you caused his death!"

"What in the name of God are you raving about?" Strawn demanded, mopping his sweat beaded brow.

"I am ahead of my story," she assured him calmly. "Enid and I went to the movies. Of course Archie joined us, but he came with a horrid, fat little man, too late to sit beside me. But they found seats on the same row, and the dear boy and I managed to carry on a conversation of sorts."

"I can imagine how your neighbors enjoyed *that!*"

She ignored his levity superbly. "He asked me where I got the roses," she went on, her voice somber now. "The devil that always lurks just below the surface of my mind whispered an evil plan to me then. I saw how I could repay the foolish boy in his own coin—make him as jealous as he had tried to make me. ... I sent him word that I was taking my roses to my own true love. Of course he asked the name, and I answered—'Carl!' "

"Carl? Pretty fresh with the doctor, weren't you?" Strawn asked, settled now to enjoyment of the comedy.

"Fresh!" she repeated scornfully. "I called him Carl almost from the first. It was as little as I could do, since the poor doctor was hopelessly, madly infatuated with me!"

"Being in love with you seems to be the regular mental disease around here," Strawn chuckled.

"Can I help it if I am cursed with this power over the hearts of men?" she countered with sad reproof. "I was not in love with Carl. The man interested me enormously, but—" and she shrugged. "No sex appeal, if you know what I mean. A great man and a good man, but, except for his passion for me, less man than doctor. . . . But my personal devil sent me to him last night. I went, knowing full well that Archie Webster would follow, would listen, would—Oh, God! No! I did not dream that he would *kill* for my sake–"

"What time did you come to this office last night?" Strawn cut in, thoroughly interested at last.

"Let me think! . . . Ah, my poor head!" She dosed the blue shadowed eyes and suffered visibly. "It was just after the comedy ended, and just before the feature picture, 'Manslaughter,' came on. About ten minutes to nine, I should say–"

"Ah!" Strawn grunted the syllable that was so often breathed by his witness, and behind the door Dundee echoed it with startled amazement. So it was *this* voice that Roland Morse had heard pleading hysterically with the doctor last night! Good bye to his own theory that it was Norah Lacey who, desperate with anxiety for her illegitimate child, had come to plead with Koenig. . . .

"What was Koenig doing? Was he alone?" Strawn asked.

"Alone, yes," the vibrant voice assured him somberly. "And working as always. I shall never forget how swiftly his thin, brown fingers flew over the typewriter keys–"

"Did you see what he was writing?"

"He was working on Sam Rowan's case history," she told him, more matter of factly. "I saw Rowan's name at the top of the paper in his machine. . . . Well, I gave him the roses, then found a vase and filled it with water. As I set the vase of roses before him I heard footsteps—someone entering the reception room. I knew it was Archie, come to spy upon us. Swift as a bird, I sprang to the door leading into the hall and dosed it. Carl told me to open it, but I ignored him. For Archie's benefit I began to babble hysterically to Carl about my great love for him and his love for me. He, the poor dear"— and she broke off to laugh richly—"looked as if he thought I'd gone crazy!"

"I can just imagine!" Strawn assured her.

"Suddenly I forgot I was playing a role. It became real to me. The man's restraint was remarkable — simply incredible! Instead of taking the riches that were offered him, he forced himself to spurn my love. And no man had ever looked at me like that before. ... It did something strange to me, drove me to saying and doing terrible things that I would never have dreamed of doing if he had behaved differently—"

"You accused him of betraying you, of making him love you?" Strawn suggested.

"Ah!" she breathed. "So you knew all the time! I told you I felt the net closing in upon me — and poor Archie! ... As if I were indeed a woman scorned, a woman betrayed, I pleaded with him for his love, charged him, as you've said, with having made me love him, only to spurn me. He tried to soothe me. Once his love broke through, the love professional ethics could not let him show to a patient. He called me his 'darling girl." . . . Ah! I'll never forget that he died loving me!"

"Yeah?"

"But Archie, listening to my wild charges, could not know the truth," she went on mournfully, "that I was only playing an accursed role in a fiendish drama of my own writing! He listened, thought the woman he adored had been foully betrayed. ... Of course he killed him," she added simply.

"Sure!" Strawn agreed. "Guess you hung around and watched him do the deed?"

"Certainly not!" she denied indignantly. "Not then did I realize what a terrible thing I had done. I left Carl, and before I had reached the front porch I was laughing. . . . *I shall never laugh again!*"

"Did you see Webster?" Strawn asked heartlessly.

"No! How could I? He was—in here! I wandered out onto the lawn, waiting for him to join me and protest his undying love and his fierce jealousy. . . . He did not come. After some minutes I realized that I had been crying and that my makeup—I use only a bit of rice powder and the merest brushing of rouge, but—" and she shrugged her thin shoulders. "I did not want the effect of a moonlight reconciliation to be spoiled by a tear streaked face. I went to my room in Aster Cottage, renewed my makeup, changed my frock, wandered about the lawn again, and finally returned to the O. T. Shop, my heart heavy with forebodings. My worst fears were justified. *Archie was not there!*"

"What time did you go back to the shop?" Strawn prodded.

"About half past nine. I came in right in the middle of 'Manslaughter.' I left and returned by the back door of the shop."

"Was Miss Rambler still there when you got back?"

"No. The horrid little fat man, Archie and Enid were all gone. And there I sat, heavy hearted but still not *knowing*–"

"Have you talked with Webster today?" asked Strawn, remembering Dundee's account of Marjorie Merrick's mysterious behavior on the lawn that afternoon.

"Yes!" she cried. "And I don't believe the poor boy *remembers one thing that happened last night!* I warned him not to breathe a word, and he seemed not to know what I was talking about. How could he remember? He was drunk—had gulped down that whole pint of whisky the fat man gave him, to screw up his courage to avenge my betrayal—as he thought!"

"I see," Strawn commented drily.

"Tell me!" she pleaded, clasping her knuckly, thin hands. "Ease the pain in my heart! Tell me that you, too, believe he cannot be held responsible!"

"I don't think Archie will ever be hanged for this murder," Strawn assured her, with a grin he could not suppress.

Clyde Powell's parents, to receive whom Strawn summarily dismissed the ex singer and called in Dundee, were a striking contrast to Marjorie Merrick. They routed melodrama from the dead doctor's office and quietly brought real drama into it. One of those stark tragedies which love to happen to people like the Powells. . . .

Because of the possibility—now looming large—that this man was the murderer, Dundee gave his attention first to John C. Powell, grocer. A small boned, thin old man, who peered diffidently out of pale gray eyes through steel rimmed spectacles. A man whose cadaverous face seemed to Dundee to be the living graveyard of hope and ambition and interest in life. But there was something in it that was not dead—a sort of dogged tenacity, or perhaps it was that pride which had made him refuse charity for his mindless son. Like an ancient and docile child he looked frequently toward his wife—obviously the man of the family. A big, soft fleshed but iron nerved woman, whose brown eyes were stern and uncompromising toward long endured sorrow. . . .

Captain Strawn bridged over the strain of the meeting with two or three routine questions, then, with an almost imperceptible gesture, delivered the couple into Dundee's hands.

"You saw Dr. Koenig yesterday, I believe, Mr. Powell," he began gravely.

"Yes, sir. A great and good man—the doctor. His death is a personal sorrow to the wife and me," Powell answered, in his meek, apologetic voice.

"What was the nature of your interview with the doctor?"

"They had telephoned me to come for a suitcase full of odds and ends that Clyde had left behind when he was transferred Monday to the—the State Hospital," the old man explained, with difficulty. "I got the suitcase and thought I'd like to thank the doctor for all his kindness to our poor boy. The doctor seemed to feel pretty bad over Clyde's transfer—said if he'd been here he'd not have let them take him away. But I explained as how the wife and I couldn't afford the added cost of day and night attendants, and that since the poor boy wouldn't realize much now—" His voice broke and he coughed to hide the shame of his weakness. "Well, the doctor said that, with our permission, he'd try to get Clyde back, and take care of him for the rest of his life, at a nominal cost to the wife and me. I telephoned Susie from the doctor's office–"

"And I said no!" the woman who was incongruously named Susie interrupted emphatically. "Me and John ain't taking charity—not as long as I've got breath to say no. We pay our taxes regular, and we've got a right to take what the State can do for our boy, but charity—no!"

"I understand," Dundee assured her sympathetically. "How long has Clyde been ill, Mrs. Powell?"

"Eleven years come Christmas," she answered promptly. "He was terrible bright in school, was going to be valedictorian of his class when he graduated in June. Just eighteen he was then."

"How did the illness start?"

"Well," the woman hesitated, "he got all wrapped up in religion suddenly, and we all thought it was kinda nice —him wanting to be a preacher and all. Read his Bible all night long many's the night, but on Christmas Day he marched up to the pulpit in church and began to preach something awful—wildlike, and wanting to fight the regular preacher because he wouldn't come out flat footed against kissing and dancing. Couldn't bear the sight of a girl, hardly," she added, and sighed heavily.

"Did he create a very great disturbance then?" Dundee asked.

"It was terrible embarrassing, but the deacons—the deacons overpowered him, and nothing bad happened. Our pastor advised us to put him in the insane asylum then, but we was too proud. We was living in California then and was doing well with our own store out in Glendale. So we put our poor boy in a private sanitarium near Los Angeles—the Good Hope it was called."

"Before you put him in the sanitarium there did he get into any serious trouble?" Dundee persisted.

"Oh, no!" old Mr. Powell assured him earnestly. "We didn't let him out of our sight from Christmas Day till we put him in the sanitarium."

"And while he was at Good Hope?"

"A good biddable patient he was there, except when he got to arguing about religion. He always wanted to fight then, and he got what the doctors call a persecution complex, but of course they watched him too careful for him to hurt anybody," the old man confessed sadly. "Dr. Sandlin used to say the boy had a chance to get well–"

"Sandlin?" Dundee interrupted sharply.

"Yes, sir. A young doctor that worked there," Powell explained. "He was in charge of the mental cases. There wasn't many of 'em; it was a general hospital."

"Then in 1924 we moved to Hamilton," Mrs. Powell took up the story, oblivious to the fact that Dundee was only half listening. "My oldest daughter, Phronsie, married a Hamilton man and she begged us to come here. So we transferred Clyde to Mayfield and opened up a little store here."

Dundee forcibly pulled himself out of a riot of speculations, induced by the name of Sandlin. "Circumstances have arisen, Mr. Powell," he said courteously, "which makes it necessary for us to check up on the movements last evening of every person who came in contact with Dr. Koenig yesterday. A matter of routine, you understand."

"You want our alibis, don't you?" Mrs. Powell demanded, in her downright manner. "I'm glad to see the police are on the job. You don't know us from Adam. Far as you know, me or my husband might have had a grudge against the doctor. Of course we didn't, but you can't know that. . . . Well, Papa and me was in the store all day, except when he come here to see the doctor. I wait on trade, right alongside my husband. After supper my youngest daughter, Belle, was having a little bridge party in our rooms up over the store. I don't play bridge—I used to be quite a shark at 'Forty two' and 'Five Hundred,' but bridge—anyway, I was in and out of the parlor all evening, watching the game and scolding Belle for grouching over bad cards, and fixing a little snack for the party. Downstairs in the store, Papa was fixing up his books—we do a credit business—and writing up bills for our customers. Our youngest boy, Johnny—he's in third year high—was helping his Papa from seven o'clock till ten o'clock, when both of 'em come upstairs for the refreshments. Of course there was customers in and out of the store all evening," she added.

"Thank you, Mrs. Powell," Dundee said, with real admiration. "I wish all witnesses had your gift for telling a straightforward story without resentment."

"You've got your work to do, and I'm not blaming you for doing it, though it's a work I wouldn't choose myself," Mrs. Powell answered frankly.

"It has one advantage," Dundee smiled. "I do get to meet a lot of nice people," and he bowed. "Now, Mr. Powell, one other question: at just what time did Dr. Koenig telephone you last?"

"Telephone *me?*" Powell echoed. "There's a mistake somewhere. The doctor didn't telephone me or the wife last night at all, neither did we phone him."

When they had gone, Strawn turned toward Dundee and shrugged hopelessly. "So that's that! . . . Got it all down, Brede? ... A fat lot of good it'll do. Ain't a doubt in my mind that their alibis will check. . . . An other blind alley, Bonnie boy. I feel like I was lost in a Mirror Maze. . . . What did you think of that Merrick scream's yarn?"

"She was telling the truth, according to her lights," Dundee answered, with a reminiscent twinkle. "Naturally it's all the bunk about Dr. Koenig's being 'madly, hopelessly in love' with her and the same holds true of Archie Webster. I'll lay you a wager it was Archie who sent the roses to Enid Rambler and that she gave some of them to Dr. Harlow as well as to Marjorie Merrick."

"That Rambler baby again!" Strawn caught him up disgustedly. "Whichever way we turn we get back to her, sooner or later. If your hunch is right, Bonnie, and that girl knows who killed the doctor, I'm ready to put the screws on her–"

"Not while she's a patient in this sanitarium!" a lovely voice with a hard edge to it cried from the doorway into the reception room.

"Yeah, Dr. Harlow?" Strawn turned upon her almost savagely. "There's such a thing as conspiring to obstruct justice "

"Then book me on that charge now!" the little doctor challenged defiantly. "For I warn you that if you resort to third degree methods with Enid Rambler, whom I consider to be in a precarious state nervously, I'll put her in "Ten," and nothing short of a troop of militia will get her out of her locked room!"

"Be reasonable, Doctor!" Strawn pleaded, with sudden humility. "The girl's mixed up in this like a fly on fly paper. Not only does she know something about the murder she ain't telling, but she's hiding something pretty smelly in her own past–"

"Bosh!" the girl doctor interrupted inelegantly. "Enid Rambler is as clean and decent and sweet; as–as–"

"As you are," Dundee finished for her, under his breath.

"Well, there's such a thing as striking a bargain," Strawn told them, his eyes grim with purpose. "I'll find out what that young beauty is hiding, and then I'll make her a proposition—immunity in exchange for information about Koenig's murder."

"How are you going about it, Captain?" Dundee asked respectfully.

"First I'm going to find that fat man," Strawn answered. "In my opinion, him and the girl was working in cahoots "

"But according to Archie Webster, the fat man didn't know her name," Dundee objected.

"Ever hear of a hired assassin?" Strawn asked scornfully. "Suppose she'd got cold feet on the idea of murdering the doctor herself, and got in touch somehow with this fat man. She describes herself to him over the phone or in a note, but don't tell her name. . . . All right!

He looks her up. She gives him the high sign during the movie to meet her outside. Both leave about the same time, the girl having fixed it with Webster to be waiting for her some where else—at a safe distance. . . . Check? . . . Sure! Then the deed is done. But the fat man ain't satisfied with the bargain he's made and tries to hold the girl up for five or ten times the amount she'd agreed to pay him— either that or the girl welches. Hasn't had a chance to get hold of the dough she'd promised him. He ain't having none of that—says he'll kill the girl too and make a good night's work of it. The girl runs away, you find her crippled on the highway, Dundee, and today she's holding on to the coat tails of a plainclothesman for dear life! . . . How's that?"

"Very diverting, Captain," Dundee smiled. "But if you honestly believe in that theory, how can you promise her immunity? In the eyes of the law, Enid Rambler would be more guilty than her pot bellied hireling!"

"Aw, go to hell!" Strawn sputtered feebly.

CHAPTER TWENTY

LURLINE DOTY posed, hand on hip, in the doorway, after depositing Dundee's well filled dinner tray upon a table drawn up to his sitting room couch.

"Ain't you the Miracle Man, though?" she kidded, hennaed head tilted, eyebrows arched provocatively.

"And I've just been telling myself that, as a detective, I'm a washout," Dundee retorted wearily, his interest in the food before him rather than in the nurse.

"But, oh boy, as a doctor!" she smiled archly. "Mrs. Morse is so well that Dr. Harlow says she can go home tomorrow—if *you* will let her! And Mr. Salter has borrowed a typewriter from Mr. Baldwin. He told me just now he'd already written five hundred words on the first chapter of a new novel. I asked him if I was going to be in it, and he said yes, and so I said I could tell him a story that would be a best seller, if he'd split fifty fifty–"

"Well—anyway"—the nurse evaded—"it's the most thrilling story you ever heard—all about a girl who goes wrong, and gets 'that way' and dies, and her sister says the baby is *hers*, so her poor little dead kid sister's name won't be disgraced–"

"Un hunh?" Dundee grunted, without interest, knife and fork busy upon the excellent *filet mignon* this silly creature had broiled for him.

"And he snatched at the offer like a starving dog at a bone, I suppose?" Dundee grinned.

"And the beauty of it is, it's a *true* story!" the nurse went on, her voice sinking to a thrilling whisper.

"True?" Dundee repeated, and lost interest in his steak. "Listen, Miss Doty, *does Miss Lacey know you're broadcasting this yarn?*"

"On, I wouldn't tell Mr. Salter the real names, and I'd change the name of the sanitarium, so nobody would recognize the story," the nurse assured him, falling without a thud into the trap the detective had set for her.

"That might be a help," Dundee said very casually, "but unless you've already told Salter, I don't think I'd say anything more about this story, if I were you."

"He wouldn't listen," the nurse admitted. "But I thought I'd write it up myself. I always did want to write, and I've read lots of stories that I know I could write better ones–"

"Not a doubt of it!" Dundee assured her, with a straight face. "You know all the facts personally, of course—not just by hearsay?"

"I'll say I do!" Lurline Doty was delighted with his interest. "Why, me and Colleen Lacey was chums from the time she first started taking Maizie Home's place when Maizie was on her summer vacations. . . . An awful sweet kid—Colleen—even if she did go wrong, and Norah simply worshiped the ground she walked on. Little and cute, with great big blue eyes, and silky black curls, and a dimple in her chin. She looked exactly like a movie actress–"

"And she died when the baby was born?" Dundee interrupted sympathetically.

"Yeah! *And with her lips sealed!*" the nurse whispered with dramatic intensity. "Not even to me would she tell who the man was, although I was with her not five hours before she died. I'd have been right there when the poor kid passed on if Norah hadn't chased me off–"

"Of course Miss Lacey made you promise not to tell the story on her sister?"

"Well, I'm not telling now!" the nurse justified herself aggrievedly. "You already *knew*, and I was going to make up new names when I told Mr. Salter–"

"Of course!" Dundee soothed her for the sake of further information. "And I'll bet you had a good idea who the man was, didn't you? Otherwise," he added craftily, "it wouldn't be much of a story."

"In my story I was going to have it that it was the famous doctor that had betrayed the poor, little innocent stenographer, because that would make it a good story, but I don't think it was *really* Dr. Koenig, although Norah named the baby Carl, and a blind man could see that Doctor thought Colleen was simply the cutest, prettiest, sweetest little thing that ever lived–"

"And why don't you think Dr. Koenig was the man?" Dundee cut in sternly.

"Why, he was too good!" the girl answered simply. "He'd have put out both his eyes rather than let them lust after a virgin–"

Dundee laughed. "I'm afraid you've been reading books that tell more than a young girl ought to know!"

"Oh, I'm old enough to know my way around," she assured him, immensely flattered.

"You're also old enough, Miss Doty," Dundee caught her up grimly, "to realize that the story you've just been telling me should be kept a sacred secret! . . . Don't worry about giving plots to Salter! Keep that story under your white linen cap!"

"You go to the devil!" the nurse cried, in a strangled voice, before fleeing the room in a starchy rustle.

Condemned to the nether regions for the second time that afternoon, Dundee cheerfully concentrated upon his excellent dinner. Perhaps he'd been rather rough on the nurse, he reflected ruefully, as he drained his cup of its superb coffee. True, she was a malicious little scandal monger, but she'd given him valuable information. While he had made no progress toward solving the murder, the nurse had helped him eliminate Norah Lacey from his formidable list of suspects, and had thereby given him a moment of pure pleasure. Swell woman—this Norah Lacey! he told himself with supreme satisfaction. A genuine heroine, right out of the old school of romantic fiction. And a grand guy, this doctor whose murder he was so clumsily trying to avenge. For Dundee now felt sure that Carl Koenig's shining memory need never be tarnished by the breath of scandal. It seemed quite dear. The "Big Doctor" had been devoted to Norah Lacey's unfortunate little sister, in a purely fatherly way. And Norah Lacey, trusting to his love for the girl and his great understanding, had told him the whole story. With his permission, and without ulterior motive, Norah Lacey had given the child the name she loved best, because it was his. And Carl Koenig, regarding himself as a sort of foster father to the "love child," had left Norah Lacey half his estate, so that that child should have a chance in life. . . . Yes, a great guy, Dundee summed up, his impressionable heart swelling. . . .

"But what good can hero worship do the doctor now?" he demanded of himself truculently, and settled down to work. It was slow going without the typewriter to which he was accustomed, but he forced himself to be content with a pad of the sanitarium notepaper and a freshly filled fountain pen.

Things I ought to know and don't, he headed the first sheet of paper. Then, in his sprawling, untidy writ ing, he penned the following questions:

1. To whom was Dr. Koenig talking when he was murdered? (Put paragraph in morning papers, asking such person to come forward.)

2. Whose eyes had puzzled Koenig? Man's or woman's?

3. What had Koenig's own eyes lighted upon, when he was talking with Claire Cantrell over the telephone, causing memory to click? Could that name have been Sandlin, which—as the name of Clyde Powell's doctor at Good Hope Sanitarium—undoubtedly appeared on the first page of Clyde's case history?

4. Why was Clyde Powell's case history completely missing, along with the Wiggin letter?

5. Who was the mysterious fat man? What was his connection with Enid Rambler?

6. What was Enid Rambler concealing? Was she really mentally ill, or shamming, as Koenig believed?

7. Who was the father of Carl Lacey?

8. Where was Maizie Home on Wednesday evening? (Probably unimportant, but should be checked up on.)

9. What had Koenig wanted of his lawyer, that could not wait until morning?

10. Why had Koenig suddenly determined to dismiss Dr. Harlow?

11. Why had Dr. Mayfield demanded, almost with his last breath—and while lucid, according to all evidence—to see Dr. Koenig?

12. Had Dr. Mayfield meant Koenig when he said that "that man" must leave Mayfield? If so, what had Koenig done to incur the old doctor's hatred?

There came a knock on the door, and a woman's white sleeved arm appeared, a newspaper extended.

"Here's the afternoon paper," came a strangled voice from behind the slightly opened door.

"Just a minute, Miss Doty!" Dundee called. "I'll bring you my tray."

"Set it down outside," the choked voice answered.

"No! Please wait!" the contrite young man begged, and sprang toward the door. "I'm terribly sorry I hurt your feelings, Miss Doty. Won't you forgive me?"

The door opened slowly. A tear stained face reproached him "You—you act like I was a leper or something, just because I'm only an attendant, and not a baby doll beauty like Enid Rambler "

"No, no!" Dundee protested, genuinely shocked at the effect of his rudeness. "You've been awfully good to me–"

"I'd do simply *anything* for you, and—and to help you solve the murder," she sobbed. "My boy friend says he's already jealous of you, because I've raved so about you–"

Dundee was acutely embarrassed. "Who is your boy friend?" he asked hastily and without caring in the least what the answer might be.

"Happy—you know, Happy Day," she confided, snuffling miserably. "But we had a tight last night, because a woman had the nerve to call him up at my house, and he had the nerve to leave me flat. . . . And now today he's sore because I've been raving about you—and it wasn't just to make him jealous, either–"

Dundee's cheeks burned. Cooks and policemen—nurse maids and policemen, comic strip combinations. . . . "He's a fine chap! Jolly, and quite the sheik, for a fat

man–"

"He isn't fat!" the nurse flared angrily, and Dundee grinned happily as she snatched his tray and flounced out into the patio with it.

Picking up the paper she had dropped in the doorway, the detective, his work mood broken, scanned the murder story headlines.

"PATIENTS QUIZZED IN SAN MURDER," he read. Smaller head type, pyramided above the two column front page story, announced:

"SECOND DEATH IN 24 HOURS AT MAYFIELD SANITA
RIUM CLAIMS FORMER HEAD; DR. MAYFIELD FOLLOWS
COLLEAGUE TO MORGUE; MURDER THEORY SCOUTED."

The last three words made Dundee smile. "Murder Theory Scouted," indeed! What a blow the coroner's certificate of "Death from natural causes," must have been to the city editors! Not since the double "Murders at Bridge" had Hamilton's newspapers missed so good a chance at front page sensationalism. His eyes swept down the ten point type of the story's opening spread, then on into the smaller single column type. . . .

"Thank God for Strawn's discretion!" he murmured fervently, as he read the story whose skillful padding concealed the paucity of its facts.

But the concluding paragraphs startled him into scowl ing attention:

"Leading physicians of the city, a symposium of whose eulogies of Dr. Carl Koenig appears on Page 2 of this edition, are speculating interestedly upon the question of who will succeed the murdered doctor as psychiatric head of Mayfield Sanitarium, an institution which has brought added lustre to the fair name of Hamilton," wrote the star reporter whose by line topped the story.

"Queried upon this important point, Dr. Bruce Cantrell, head of the medical department, told the writer today that efforts will be made to complete negotiations initiated before his death by Dr. Koenig to bring Dr. Horace Sandlin to Mayfield.

"While Dr. Sandlin is unknown to the local medical fraternity, the fact that Dr. Koenig approached him on his recent stopover in Chicago, in the hope of adding him to the Mayfield staff, is, in the opinion of Drs. Cantrell and Harlow, sufficient guarantee of the psychiatrist's ability.

"Dr. Sandlin, formerly on the staff of the Good Hope Sanitarium of Burbank, California, is at present connected with Howard Memorial Hospital, a private sanitarium for mental diseases located at Evanston, Ill.

"Dr. Justine Harlow, popular young woman psychiatrist and for five years assistant to Dr. Koenig, today handed her resignation to the surviving partners, Dr. Cantrell and Business Manager Roger Baldwin, effective upon the arrival of psychiatrists to take her own and Dr. Koenig's place. Dr. Harlow stated, however, that at this time she has no intention of selling her share of Dr. Koenig's financial interest in Mayfield Sanitarium, bequeathed jointly to herself and Head Nurse Norah Lacey in the famous doctor's last will and testament. No reasons for the resignation were vouchsafed the writer by the charming little doctor, but it is safe to surmise that she wishes the new psychiatric head, whoever he may be, to have a free hand, uninfluenced by the doctor's will, in choosing his assistants. The resignation has not yet been acted upon by Dr. Cantrell and Mr. Baldwin."

"Hell's bells!" Dundee ejaculated, in deep disgust. "That's carrying loyalty a bit too far! If Cantrell and that ass, Baldwin, accept her resignation, they deserve to have Mayfield go bankrupt in a year. . . . And why the devil didn't the little spitfire tell *me* she was going to take such a step?" he grumbled aggrievedly. "Lets me first learn a thing like that from the papers–"

That there was no earthly reason for Justine Harlow to take him into her confidence, in such a personal and heart wrenching matter, did not occur to the indignant young detective.

Those annoying paragraphs completely ruined his evening, which he had intended to devote to a painstaking resume of the Koenig case, from every angle.

"Damn me for a susceptible young fool!" he swore at himself more than once, but his profanity did not prevent his heart's aching for the girl who was undoubtedly tossing upon a sleepless bed, stricken by two grievous blows—the death of the man she had worshiped, and the knowledge that, if he had lived, he would have discharged her. How her pride must be suffering, too, Dundee told himself bitterly. Forced to be a beneficiary under a will which would have been changed if the doctor had lived long enough–

The thought brought to mind that major, unsolved question: To whom was Dr. Koenig telephoning when the murderer's blow struck him down?

Impossible, he mused, sprawling tiredly in a big easy chair, to trace local calls over a dial telephone. But there was an obvious way to ask that question, with some hope of having it answered. He reached for pencil and paper, scribbled a few lines, then lounged out into the reception room of Sunflower Court.

"Telephone?" Miss Hunter, the extremely fat night nurse beamed on him. "There's none closer than the main building. ... By the way, Mr. Dundee, Enid wants you to drop in on her, if you feel like it. She already has company, but she seems to think her little party won't be complete without you."

His fatigue forgotten, Dundee raced across the lawn to the main building, and brushed past Strawn's guard out side the dead doctor's door. A minute later he was talking to the Chief of the Homicide Squad.

"No, nothing new, Captain," he assured Strawn. "But I wish you'd give this paragraph to the newspaper boys when they make their rounds tonight," and he read the few carefully chosen sentences he had scribbled. "Right! We may draw a blank, but it would help a lot if the person Koenig was talking to when he was killed should see this notice and come forward. . . . Yeah, I saw that, and if Baldwin and Cantrell let that girl resign, they're worse nuts than any of their patients. ... By the way, Chief, have you heard from Price? . . . You have? And does he say that was blood in the telephone receiver? . . . Good! Same type as Koenig's, eh? . . . Well, I guess that clinches that! So long, Captain!"

And back Dundee raced to Sunflower Court, his susceptible heart faster than his feet. After all, a man had a right to some relaxation. . . .

He was greeted with a joyous smile from his hostess and an enchanting wave of her beautiful hand, but she did not speak. For, at a baby grand piano which Dundee had scarcely noticed on his earlier visit that day, Marjorie Merrick was playing and singing. Standing on either side of the singer were Archie Webster and Samuel Rowan, the latter an incongruously shabby figure in that luxurious room, the former listening with unconcealed admiration upon his handsome, reckless young face.

But Dundee scarcely saw the men, for, on half of the "love seat" to which Enid Rambler motioned him, a woman was sitting. Exquisitely graceful, Lora Morse sat very still, oblivious to the intrusion, in an attitude of pensive listening. Her beautiful, Madonna like face, framed in smooth dark hair, was sad but not blighted with grief. And in the great black eyes there was a quality of resignation, of hard won serenity, which touched the young detective's heart more profoundly than agonized tears could have done.

"She's well now!" Dundee exulted to himself, and took a mite of credit for her second cure. . . .

A glorious voice, with a rollicking gayety pervading its rich contralto beauty, was dignifying a song that had been popular a couple of years before.

" 'You're the cream in my coffee,' " Marjorie Merrick sang, her black eyes rolling a provocative confirmation to ward Archie Webster, who grinned engagingly, and most respectfully.

"What a voice!" Dundee murmured to Mrs. Morse.

"I'm praying that Marjorie will get well, too," Lora Morse whispered softly.

Enid Rambler lay on the couch, hands clasped behind her shining chestnut curls, her dark blue eyes softly luminous, her lips parted in a smile of happiness.

"Oh, you're so lovely!" Dundee's heart called out to her. "Can any creature as lovely and gentle as you have done any wrong?"

As if she had heard him, Enid Rambler turned her soft, shining gaze upon him, and smiled. . . .

"Well! There's life in the old girl yet, Archie, what the hell!" Marjorie Merrick cried, the instant she had finished her song, and the patness of the quotation from Don Marquis' *Archie and Mehitabel* surprised and delighted Dundee.

"One more, Miss Merrick, please!" Samuel Rowan begged, one of his rough brown hands making an awkward movement toward the singer.

"Gawd! Here's another victim of my accursed charms!" the singer laughed stridently, but her eyes were kind, and her thin fingers fell again upon the piano keys.

"Not till we've had tea, please," Enid Rambler called. "I'm afraid it will be as strong as lye if we don't drink it now. . . . Rally 'round, boys and girls! . . . Oh, Mr. Dundee, it's sweet of you to come! And will you call in my darling plainclothesman? I'm spoiling the man dread fully, but I want to make sure he likes it here and will stay."

"You wouldn't have to feed *me* cakes and tea to keep me around," Dundee assured her gallantly, but sincerely.

"Nor me!" Archie Webster joined in. "Send the dick about his business, Enid, and let me and my attendant watch you—you foul murderess, you!—to see that you don't escape."

Not even the presence of the awkward, blushing plainclothesman and of Webster's sissy looking night attendant—very different from the irrepressible Happy Day— could dampen the gayety of Enid's impromptu tea party. In addition to a pot of tea and a tall, Wedgewood pitcher of chocolate, there was a silver basket heaped with tiny sandwiches, a glass plate overflowing with Viennese *petit fours* of a dozen varieties, and a bonbon dish filled with expensive candies.

"Pretty swell having a Rockefeller Vanderbilt heiress in our midst, *ne c'est pas*, Laddie darling?" Majorie Merrick challenged Dundee, as she cuddled close against him at the tea table. "What a break for us poor nuts that you picked on Mayfield, Enid. For God's sake, don't be in any hurry to get well. We'll be sunk without you."

"I don't think I'll ever have to leave now," Enid answered happily, apparently oblivious to the sinister interpretation which could be put upon the words.

"I feel another song coming on!" Marjorie Merrick set down her cup and strolled toward the piano. "I'm going to warble *Always* this time. . . . Just an old fashioned girl—that's me! And listen, boy friend," she turned threateningly toward Archie Webster, "keep those Don

Juan eyes on me while I'm singing, not on Enid, or I'll smash one of your curly locks clear down into your medulla oblongata."

But not even this threat could keep Archie Webster's eyes off Enid Rambler as the sentimental song soared richly from the singer's throat. And Dundee's own eyes were so occupied in watching lovely Enid Rambler that they almost missed the fact that Samuel Rowan was gazing in the same direction, doglike devotion shining in the brown eye that was not obscured by a cast.

But he did recall that fact later, with a cold chill of shock. In that room that evening were two men—one young, eligible, rich, accustomed to a reckless flouting of the law, the other oldish, life beaten, freshly unburdened of some dreadful secret—two men who, judging by the love that shone from their eyes, would have stopped at nothing to protect Enid Rambler from Dr. Koenig's determination to cast her out of Mayfield against her will.

But that realization came later. As Marjorie Merrick sang. "I'll be loving you always," Dundee's own infatuated eyes scarcely left the young girl. So it was that he saw the storm brewing, from the moment the first quiver passed over her delicate face and the first tear fell from her bronze eyelashes, until she covered her convulsed face with her hands and chokingly begged her guests to leave. . . .

Dazed, the detective stumbled out of the room, his offers of assistance and comfort rejected along with those of all the others.

"Strike me dead for an idiot!" Marjorie Merrick exploded. "I know damned well the poor kid's eating her heart out for some black hearted wretch that's done her dirt, and here I go and babble the sloppiest love song ever written! Kick me, somebody!"

And Archie Webster obeyed, with too much earnestness to suit the singer, who chased him vengefully across the lawn, then embraced him fiercely when she caught him.

Although it was nearly nine o'clock—bedtime for Mayfield Sanitarium—Dundee felt so restless in spite of his fatigue that his extremely comfortable suite in Sunflower Court seemed like a prison cell. There was nothing to read, no more work he could do before morning. . . .

Finally, in desperation, for he felt the need of some thing, anything to lift him out of the slough of despond into which Enid Rambler's tears had plunged him, he gathered up the scattered sheets of the afternoon newspaper. Might as well cast a stony eye over the comics, and dare them to make him laugh

Then he uttered a sharp exclamation as a brief, boxed item on page two leaped at his attention.

MYSTERIOUS MIDNIGHT VISITOR AT MAYFIELD was the two line, italic head over the blackface type of the boxed story. Swearing under his breath the detective began to read:

"Characteristically unable to see farther than the nose on his face, Captain John Strawn, Chief of the Homicide Squad, will first learn from this issue of *The Evening Sun* of a mysterious visitor who arrived shortly before midnight on Tuesday at the cottage shared by Dr. Carl Koenig and Roger Baldwin, Mayfield Sanitarium's business manager, and was closeted for two hours with the psychiatrist who was murdered in cold blood less than twenty four hours later.

"This information was divulged to a reporter for *The Evening Sun* by Mr. Baldwin himself. The business manager, when questioned concerning the murdered doctor's movements since his return from a business and lecture trip, which included New York, Boston, Washington and Chicago, stated that he was awakened by the sound of voices in low toned, earnest conversation. The voices, which undoubtedly came from the cottage living room, according to Mr. Baldwin, and one of which he identified as that of his partner, Dr. Koenig, continued for approximately two hours. Mr. Baldwin says he did not rise to investigate, that he did not see the mysterious visitor, whose voice was unknown to him, and that he did not recall the strange occurrence until the reporter questioned him as to Dr. Koenig's movements on Tuesday. Asked if the doctor and his unknown visitor seemed to be quarreling, Mr. Baldwin said that he got no such impression. On Wednesday morning Dr. Koenig made no mention of his visitor and Mr. Baldwin made no inquiries. Perhaps if he had, the murder of Dr. Carl Koenig might not now be the apparently baffling mystery that it is."

"Hell!" Dundee swore again, as he flung down the paper.

The district attorney's special investigator did not sleep much that night.

CHAPTER TWENTY ONE

KNOWING the enterprise and efficiency of American city editors, Dundee was prepared to find a front page story with a Chicago date line in his Friday morning paper, but *The Star's* revelations were more important than he had guessed they would be. He read as he breakfasted off his tray:

"Chicago, June 4—Dr. Horace Sandlin, when interviewed late today at the Howard Memorial Hospital, where he is a member of the staff, confirmed Hamilton, —, newspapers reports that Dr. Carl Koenig, psychiatric head of Mayneld Sanitarium, who was murdered in his office at that institution Wednesday night, had opened negotiations to bring the Chicago doctor to Mayneld.

" 'I am indeed sorry,' Dr. Sandlin said to this reporter this evening, "that the news of my negotiations with Dr. Koenig had to come to the Howard Memorial Hospital board in this way, but the report is true. On his recent visit to Chicago, for the purpose of delivering a lecture at Northwestern University, Dr. Koenig did me the honor to extend me an invitation to join his staff at Mayfield Sanitarium near Hamilton. It was agreed at that time that I should call upon him at Mayfield, and go further into the question of salary, duties, etc.'

"At this point the psychiatrist laughed ruefully. 'I see by dispatches from Hamilton in the evening papers that 'a mysterious midnight visitor' is likely to be a favorite suspect in this baffling murder mystery. I am sorry to have to furnish so prosaic an explanation of that mysterious midnight visit, but I am glad to be able to clear up this minor point. *I* was the mysterious visitor!

Unable to spare a day from my work at Howard, whose accommodations in my department are taxed to the utmost by patients afflicted mentally by the nation wide depression, I took a six o'clock train from Chicago, arriving in Hamilton at 11:30 P.M. I went immediately to the Sanitarium, or, rather, to Dr. Koenig's cottage on the grounds. There we conferred for about two hours, the interview terminating in time for me to catch a slow local at 2:45, getting me back to my work without loss to the institution I now serve. If the doctor and I had known that Mr. Baldwin was awakened by our voices, we should have taken advantage of the opportunity for me to meet Mayfield's very efficient business manager,' the psychiatrist added with a smile.

"When asked if he was still favorably inclined toward leaving Howard for Mayfield, the psychiatrist said: 'Naturally such a suggestion will now have to come from Dr. Koenig's surviving partners, and must be in line with the agreement already arrived at between Dr. Koenig and my self. For instance, Dr. Koenig was planning to devote most of his time to psychoanalysis, with an office in Hamilton, and to turn over the bulk of his sanitarium work to me, permitting me to choose my own assistant. Since Dr. Koenig is so tragically dead, however, any further negotiations must be instigated by Dr. Cantrell and Mr. Baldwin, his surviving partners."

Dundee lowered the paper, frowning intently. "Meaning," he muttered, "that Sandlin plans to be psychiatric head of Mayfield—or nothing! And that Justine Harlow must go! For who can say now whether Sandlin is lying or not? Koenig is dead and can neither confirm nor deny anything that Sandlin may say. Pretty clever of him to realize that the dead doctor's wishes will be sacred. A golden opportunity, and little Horace—damn his fat face!— seems to be making the most of it!"

He raised the paper and studied the rather indistinct photograph of Dr. Horace Sandlin, relayed to *The Hamil ton Star* by television. A smiling, fat cheeked face, with prominent, pale eyes, a broad nose, and thin hair, either blond or gray. Dundee conceived an instant, unreasoning dislike of the well fed doctor, felt a childish desire to stick his tongue out at those beaming, pale eyes. . . .

Eyes! Could these be the eyes which had puzzled Carl Koenig? Had Koenig suddenly remembered where he had seen Dr. Horace Sandlin before—a memory that called for instant action and brought horror in its wake? Certainly Sandlin's name had been mentioned, probably more than once, in Clyde Powell's case history. And Powell's history had been on the desk under the murdered doctor's eyes. *And*—Powell's history was completely missing. Not a scrap of it remained behind–

His head spinning in the vicious circle, Dundee shrugged and raised his paper again. . . . Yes, there was his own paragraph, prominently featured on the front page in a box to itself, asking all persons to whom Dr. Koenig had telephoned on the night of his murder to come forward for questioning by the police. But the request was worded so tactfully as not to alarm the prospective witness. "Merely to aid the police in fixing the exact time of the doctor's murder," the paragraph concluded.

Fat lot of good it would do, in all likelihood, Dundee prophesied gloomily. But at any rate he would have to await possible developments from that source. . . .

"Come in!" he called, as a knock interrupted his unhappy reflections.

It was Archie Webster, in a purple satin bathrobe and exuding health and vigor.

"Hydros are swell things! You look like you could do with one yourself, old man," the intermittent alcoholic suggested heartily. "So you've seen the bad news, too?" he added, indicating the morning paper. "If that fat slob is going to take charge here, I'm signing the pledge today."

The word "fat" crashed through Dundee's brain. "Have you seen this man before, Webster?" he demanded, his tired eyes suddenly keen with excitement.

"Does look sort of familiar, doesn't he?" Webster agreed. "Might be a composite picture of all the ward politicians–"

"Does he look anything like that fat man who gave you the whisky Wednesday night?" Dundee interrupted sharply.

Webster laughed. "Are you turning amateur detective, too? . . . But, you know, there is a sort of resemblance, at that–"

"Can you identify Sandlin as your uninvited guest?" Dundee persisted.

But Webster shook his head. "That's not a very clear picture, and I'm pretty sure that my fat man was a whole lot fatter–"

"This picture may be an old one," Dundee suggested, loath to relinquish his startling new theory.

"Better leave detecting to the police," Webster suggested with unconscious cruelty, "and come out for a game of peewee golf."

But Dundee excused himself so curtly that Webster quickly took his departure. After a hurried bath and shave the young detective sprinted across the lawn to the main building, cursing the fact that the telephone was so inaccessible.

Having let himself into the dead doctor's office, he dialed a number.

"Hello! Consolidated Ticket Offices? . . . Information, please! . . . Hello! Will you tell me, please, whether there is a train in from Chicago at about half past seven in the evening?" he asked, and waited for two or three minutes. Then: "At seven twenty, you say? . . . Leaving Chicago when?"

When the answer came he thanked the information clerk and slowly replaced the receiver. If it could be proved that Dr. Sandlin had not been on duty at Howard Memorial Hospital on Wednesday afternoon

The telephone rang. Captain Strawn's unmistakable voice came over the wire: "Lemme speak to Mr. Dundee!"

"This is Dundee, Captain," the younger detective answered. "Anything new?"

"Just got a funny telegram from Chicago," Strawn's voice replied. "Listen—and you might make a copy of it if you've got a pencil handy. . . . All right! Here goes:

"PUZZLED BY SANDLIN STORY IN MORNING PAPERS STOP DR. KOENIG MY GUEST WHILE IN CHICAGO ON LECTURE TOUR STOP KOENIG WITH ME CONSTANTLY ENTIRE TWENTY FOUR HOURS HIS VISIT HERE STOP AM POSITIVE HE DID NOT CONFER THIS TRIP WITH SANDLIN RELATIVE MAYFIELD STAFF POSITION STOP DOCTOR DID ASK MY ADVICE REGARDING ASSISTANT PSYCHIATRIST STOP SPOKE HIGHLY OF DR. HARLOW'S WORK WANTED TO FIND YOUNG MALE PSYCHIATRIST WHO WOULD WORK CONGENIALLY WITH HER STOP HAVE NO DESIRE TO INTERFERE BUT AM OFFERING ABOVE IN INTERESTS OF MAYFIELD STOP PLEASE KEEP CONFIDENTIAL.

"Got all that? . . . It's signed Edward Livingstone, Professor of Abnormal Psychology, Northwestern University."

"Whew!" Dundee whistled. "Nigger in the woodpile somewhere, Captain!"

"You said a mouthful," Captain Strawn's voice retorted gloomily. "But what's all this got to do with the price of eggs?"

"Young Webster has halfway identified Sandlin's picture in the paper as that of the fat man who presented him with a pint of whisky Wednesday night," Dundee explained quietly, and it was Strawn's turn to whistle.

When the younger detective again replaced the receiver, he had secured Strawn's promise to check up discreetly on the Chicago doctor's alibi for Wednesday afternoon and evening.

Still he was not satisfied. He sat there in the chair where Carl Koenig had died, and stared gloomily at the telephone which had yielded up the clue from which he, Dundee, had hoped so much. That one drop of blood! How confidently he had banked on it! And yet, according to Strawn, no reader of the morning papers had come for ward so far with the admission that it was to him—or her —that the psychiatrist had been talking when death had cut short the conversation.

Useless to try to trace such a call, if the information was not volunteered, Dundee told himself. Then, with a muttered oath at his own mental laziness, he seized the telephone and dialed 1 1 0.

"Hello! Long distance? . . . Let me speak to the supervisor, please. . . . Hello! District attorney's office speaking. I want to know if there was a toll or long distance call put through over this number—Sheridan 0100—on Wednesday evening."

It was not quite so simple as that, for Dundee had to repeat his request to three different officials before it was finally answered.

And the answer was "No!"

Feeling a little dashed, and that his hunch had betrayed him, the detective absently studied the copy of the telegram Strawn had read to him over the telephone.

"Telegram—telephone" . . . the words seemed to float lazily up from his subconscious mind.

"Lazy idiot!" he apostrophized himself, as he grabbed the instrument and dialed so hastily that the operation had to be repeated.

"Hello! Western Union? . . . Let me speak to the manager, please!"

Five minutes later, not even taking time to get his hat from Sunflower Court, Dundee hurled himself into his roadster, which was still parked in front of the main building. His hurry and excitement were due to no specific in formation which the Western Union manager had given him. He was merely playing a hunch, which, as he had talked with the telegraph manager, had grown to lusty proportions.

He made one brief stop on his way into the business section of Hamilton, a visit which the district attorney vainly tried to prolong. And within twenty minutes after he had hung up the receiver in the murdered doctor's office he was shaking hands with a brisk young man who made no effort to conceal the fact that he was almost as excited as the detective himself.

"I followed your suggestion, Mr. Barrow," Dundee told the Western Union manager. "Here is a note from the district attorney, asking you, as a personal favor to himself and to his office, to waive formalities."

"Well, I hope I shan't get into trouble," the manager smiled, as he accepted the note and read it. "But when it's a case of murder, I believe it is the duty of every citizen to extend whatever aid lies in his power–"

"Absolutely!" Dundee assured him heartily. "Now, you were saying over the telephone, Mr. Barrow, that a file is kept of uncompleted messages–"

"That's right. 'Bust' messages, we call them," the Western Union man explained, with a trace of superiority. "There are several such messages in the course of a day's business here, but not enough of them to file separately. We keep each day's 'bust' messages in a single folder, bearing the date. Naturally, these messages are all received over the telephone. Accidental disconnections are responsible for most of the 'busts,' of course. The client calls back, and is usually pretty sore because he has to repeat the message from the beginning. He does not realize that it would be a truly remarkable coincidence if he should" get the same operator who was taking down his telegram be fore the connection was broken. We have ten girls who do nothing but receive telegrams, night letters, etc., over the telephone."

"Yes, yes, I understand," Dundee fretted, for he had heard all this on the telephone twenty minutes before.

"Now, if you could show me the file of 'bust' messages for Wednesday night "

But the manager hesitated. "I'm afraid I can't do that, not even with this request from the district attorney. But I can read off the names and addresses of those messages–"

"Have you looked through Wednesday's file since I called you?" Dundee interrupted. "I had hoped you might have found one with either the doctor's name or the Mayfield telephone number–"

"In that case, it would not have been a 'bust' message," the manager reminded him, with a smile of superiority. "Consider how a telegram is sent by telephone. You call or dial Western Union. One of our operators answers. You say: 'I want to send a night letter, please'—that is, if you are polite!" and the manager chuckled at his own wit. "The operator's first query is: 'To whom is the night letter going?'—Not, 'What is your telephone number or your name?' "

"Of course!" Dundee acknowledged, a trifle chagrined. "And it is not until the complete message has been taken down by the operator that she asks, 'What is your telephone number, please?' and then, 'In whose name is this telephone listed?' Naturally, if any of this information appeared on the message it would be complete, or so nearly complete that, if the line was disconnected, the operator herself could get the client back on the telephone."

"Correct!" the manager applauded. "And that's exactly why it will be no easy matter to point to a 'bust' message and say with any certainty, 'Dr. Koenig was telephoning this message to Western Union when the line was disconnected.' "

"When he was killed," Dundee corrected grimly. "But if my hunch is right, and Dr. Koenig was sending a telegram at the moment he was murdered, the name of the addressee or the nature of the beginning of the message should be quite sufficient."

"Perhaps you're right," the manager answered, very respectfully. "I'll read the names and addresses of Wednesday's bust messages–"

"Just a moment," Dundee begged. "Have these messages been checked against Wednesday's completed messages? My point, of course, is that *only those which were never completed need concern us.*"

"Completed messages are filed only under the names of the senders," the manager informed him, and he began to read off the names and addresses from a small sheaf of telegraph blanks.

And at each of the first three names Dundee shook his head. For one was the name of a girl whose address was a sorority house at the State University; another belonged to a firm of stockbrokers in New York, and the third "bust" message had been intended for the room reservations clerk of a Detroit hotel.

But the fourth name, even before the address was read off, brought a sharp exclamation of triumph from Bonnie Dundee.

" 'Buron Fitts, District Attorney of Los Angeles County, Los Angeles, California,' " the manager was intoning in his slightly sing song voice.

"That's the one!" Dundee cried. "Surely you will let me see that message? It fits a number of known facts–"

"Very well," and Barrow surrendered the half filled blank.

Dundee read the incomplete night letter avidly:

PLEASE CONSULT YOUR RECORDS YEAR NINETEEN NINETEEN AND WIRE ME COMPLETE DESCRIPTION OF E D I

And there, as if Fate chuckled at the detective's annoyance, the message ended.

CHAPTER TWENTY TWO

BUT Dundee was more than grateful for Fate's small favors when he again reached the bedside of his pleurisy stricken chief.

"Progress, boss!" he exulted, as he flung down a copy of the "bust message."

The district attorney's enthusiasm was slower to kindle. "You're sure this message wasn't being sent by the Chief of Police, to check up on some crook they've picked up on suspicion?"

Dundee laughed. "Thought of that myself! . . . Bright lad—your special investigator! No one at headquarters knows a thing about this highly interesting night letter. And I'll wager my roadster it never reached District Attorney Buron Fitts–"

"I'm concerned with facts, not wagers," Hamilton's district attorney told him cruelly. "Can't the Western Union manager here tell you whether it was finally sent through another operator?"

"I suppose he could, but it would take hours to go through all the files from A to Z, in a blind search for the sender's name," Dundee acknowledged. "The simplest thing is to query Fitts himself. . . . I'll call him long distance–"

"Hold on!" Sanderson stopped him. "While it's half past ten o'clock here, it's only 7:30 A.M. in Los Angeles, and if Fitts and I have anything in common, my fellow district attorney is still in bed at that hour. Send a wire, then prepare to wait at least three hours before you can hope to get an answer. Even so–"

"Don't toss the wet blanket so blithely, Chief," Dundee pleaded. "I tell you I never had a stronger hunch! The way I dope it is this: While he was talking to Claire

Cantrell, Dr. Koenig's gaze happened to light on *something*—a name, probably—that caused his memory to click. Now, that name *must* have appeared in Clyde Powell's case history, because, for no other reason that we can even remotely imagine, Clyde's history is completely missing—not torn up like the others, which were destroyed merely as a blind–"

"Yeah, I know all that," the sick man interrupted peevishly.

"Sorry, Chief," Dundee grinned. "Well, the good old memory suddenly functions, and Dr. Koenig remembers where he has seen those eyes before. *Before*—he said to Claire Cantrell! That means, in my opinion, that the owner of those mysterious eyes was either somewhere about or that the doctor had seen them very recently. Right?"

"Go on," the district attorney agreed obliquely.

"As we've said all along, the doctor's horror was such that he had to get busy without a minute's delay. Why?—Because the owner of those eyes was a possible menace either to himself or to Mayfield Sanitarium. Right?"

Again Sanderson commanded, but less irritably: "Go on!"

"Dr. Koenig calls his lawyer. Whatever it is, it's the sort of mess that the law must deal with. Attorney Forrest isn't at home, and Koenig says he'll have to handle the matter himself. What then? He telegraphs the district attorney of *Los Angeles*–"

"Yeah, I see—where Clyde Powell used to live," Sanderson supplied, as Dundee paused impressively.

"Not only where Clyde Powell lived, but where he was confined in a sanitarium of which *Dr. Horace Sandlin* was psychiatric head!"

"You're off the track there, my lad," Sanderson cut in drily. "In 1919 as well as in 1931 Dr. Sandlin was known as Horace Sandlin—neither part of his name beginning with E d i "

"I'm not saying Sandlin is 'E d i' and hence the murderer," Dundee retorted. "In fact, Strawn has checked up on Sandlin and has found that he has an iron clad alibi for all of Wednesday, day and night. Sandlin was in his office or at work among the patients of Howard Memorial Hospital near Chicago from noon Wednesday until midnight. But I'll wager that same roadster that Sandlin—accidentally, perhaps—is mixed up in this thing somehow."

And Dundee exhibited the copy of the telegram Strawn had received from Professor Livingstone of Northwestern University.

"Professors must be better paid these days," Sanderson chuckled, as he finished reading the long message, which scorned the economy of day letters.

But Dundee was not smiling. "There's something damned queer about Sandlin," he worried. "In my opinion, those last lines of the telegram are the most significant," and he repeated them: 'Am offering above in *interests of Mayfield.* Please keep confidential.' . . . Dr. Livingstone, bless his heart, spares no expense to warn us that Sandlin would be very bad medicine for Mayfield patients, and yet I suppose professional etiquette would seal his lips against any more specific charges. . . . Now why the devil, if there's anything smelly about Sandlin, did *Koenig* practically close negotiations to bring him to Mayfield?"

"Carl Koenig," Sanderson began slowly, "was a very great doctor, but not a particularly good business man. In sudden need of another assistant, Koenig probably listened to the advice of some colleague he met during his trip, and impulsively, without investigating very thoroughly, offered the job to Sandlin."

"But Livingstone wires that no such conference took place while Koenig was in Chicago," Dundee pointed out.

"Livingstone is probably mistaken," Sanderson decided reasonably. "It is unlikely that the good professor was actually with Koenig 'constantly,' as he says in this wire, and even so, the first negotiations might have been made over the telephone, and a personal appointment arranged for Tuesday night. That would explain Sandlin's coming along so soon after Koenig's return."

"Probably you're right," Dundee agreed, but with no conviction. "At any rate, it's pretty obvious that some thing clicked in Koenig's memory on Wednesday night that made him get busy in such a manner that his murder had to take place before that telegram could be finished and on its way to Los Angeles!"

"And what possible connection could there exist between 'E d i' and Sandlin?" the district attorney insisted.

"I don't know," Dundee confessed frankly. "There's this possibility: Koenig, in the role of alienist, served as an expert witness on some case in which Sandlin also testified, as an alienist. The defendant was this 'E d i.' In 1919, let us say, since Koenig himself gives us that year in his wire to the district attorney. 'E d i' has eyes that Koenig remembers, but the rest of his features fade from the doctor's memory. Before him, on Wednesday night, was Clyde Powell's case history, joining Los Angeles with the name of Sandlin. The juxtaposition of the town and the doctor's name brings about one of those freaks of memory. Koenig remembers where he has seen a pair of eyes that have puzzled him. For he and Sandlin, in Los Angeles, both looked upon the owner of those eyes. The whole case flashes back into Koenig's memory. 'E d i' is a dangerous person—and 'E d i' is where Koenig can lay hands on him, if the police still want him."

"Well, who *is* 'E d i'?" Sanderson demanded, irritable again

"I can't read a dead man's mind," Dundee admitted, shrugging. "My guess is that he was either the relative of a patient or a patient at Mayfield."

"Meaning that he may be our mysterious 'fat man,' or Rowan, or Roland Morse," Sanderson deduced. "Or—to change the pronoun, *she* may be—Enid Rambler!"

Dundee flushed, but his hot protest died out before it had made a good beginning.

"Keep your shirt on, boy!" Sanderson advised, paternally. "But you see where idle speculation can lead us. Suppose you put that wild imagination of yours on a leash and keep it there until we've at least had confirmation from Fitts in Los Angeles that that 'bust' message never reached him. If it didn't get through—and I admit that anyone starting a message like that would naturally finish it, in spite of disconnections, if it was humanly possible to do so—we can go on from here. Wire your query to Fitts, then possess your soul with patience until you get an answer."

Rather subdued, Dundee obeyed. But he had better use for the next two hours than to devote them to attaining a Buddha like calm.

CHAPTER TWENTY THREE

ALTHOUGH he was sure that Enid Rambler had lied when she had said she had been staying at the Randolph Hotel before going to Mayfield, Dundee made inquiries there as the first step in his investigation into the girl's "past." The blank he drew there did not at all discourage him.

The city of Hamilton boasted two excellent hotels: the Randolph, the newer and more fashionable—swimming pool, roof garden, radio in every room; and the Hamiltonian, a dignified old house, whose noble spaciousness and graciousness extended beyond the lobby and public rooms into the guests' accommodations. A French chef, who made the only real *croissants* to be found in the city; hospitable and more than efficient service, and an air of leisured dignity seldom found in a Middle West hotel, made the Hamiltonian exactly the sort of temporary home which a girl of Enid's obvious breeding and apparent wealth would have chosen. But faced with the necessity of lying to protect herself, nothing could have been more natural than that she should have given the Randolph as her last address.

The manager of the Hamiltonian was Francis Drake Littleton, an Englishman, who had spent many hours talking London with the young detective, one time holder of a lowly job at Scotland Yard. He received Dundee cordially.

"An interesting case—the Koenig affair," Littleton began, with relish. "Scotland Yard would make short work of it. A great institution, sir—nothing like it in this country. You should have prolonged your training there."

"Oh—we blunder along and find the criminal occasionally," Dundee grinned. "By the way, sir, I need your help–"

"Anything I can do–" the hotel manager assured him, vastly pleased.

"Thanks!—It's just a side issue to the main case, I'm fairly sure, but we can't ignore it," Dundee told him, lighting one of the English cigarettes his host had offered. "There's a devilish pretty girl at Mayfield, who says that, before going to the sanitarium, she was stopping for a few days at the Randolph. My hunch was that she was exactly the sort of young woman who would demand only the best—hence that she was lying; that she really stayed at the Hamiltonian."

The Englishman bowed, and his very mustache registered pleasure in the compliment. "Her name?"

"Oh, she lied about that, too," Dundee laughed. "But I don't think she's at all expert about lying, or really an adept at choosing aliases on the spur of the moment. However, on the off chance that she was not lying, the name she goes under now is Enid Rambler."

The manager shook his white head slowly. "I'm sure no young person of that name has been a guest here, yet it has a vaguely familiar ring to it. ... On what day did she enter Mayfield?"

"The evening of Wednesday, April second," Dundee told him. "May I suggest that you look over the hotel register sheets for a week preceding that day, to see if a Miss E. R. was a guest here."

The manager reached for a telephone and was soon relaying the request to an assistant manager. Within five minutes the seven sheets from the hotel's loose leaf register were in front of the detective, and his quick eyes were racing down the topmost page of legible and illegible, neat and bold signatures.

Not until he reached the third sheet—the register entries for May 31—did he find what he was looking for.

"Here we are!" he cried jubilantly. " 'Miss Edith Ramsey, New York City ' "

"Edith Ramsey!" the manager ejaculated. "Good Lord, Dundee! Are you sure? Is *that girl* at Mayfield Sanitarium?"

"Careful of the good old blood pressure, sir!" Dundee warned. "What's up?"

The manager tried to control himself, but excitement still rode him as he exclaimed: "But this is astounding, sir! Simply amazing! Fearfully ironic, and all that sort of thing! While private detectives scour the country for her Well, well! A bit of a shock, I assure you!"

"Would you mind explaining, Mr. Littleton?" Dundee suggested, his impatience difficult to curb.

"Yes, yes, certainly! But it is *most* amazing, I assure you– Will you describe the young lady who you think may be Miss Ramsey?"

"Perfectly beautiful," Dundee began, with enthusiasm. "Curling chestnut hair, dark blue eyes; quite tall, very slender–"

The manager smiled. "I see that Miss Ramsey has had the same effect on you as she had upon my entire staff—myself included! . . . Yes, I am glad to say there seems to be no doubt that you have discovered the missing heiress."

"Then she ran away from the hotel?" Dundee asked. "Running away seems to be rather a habit of Miss Ramsey's."

But the manager shook his head. "Not exactly. But I'll be glad to tell you all I know. . . . One night—let me think! Yes, it must have been Wednesday evening, April second—Miss Ramsey and the young man of her party–"

"Young man?" Dundee repeated, with a premonitory twinge in his heart.

"Oh, yes!" the manager assured him. "A most estimable young man. One of America's aristocrats, I should say. Family—money–"

"His name?" Dundee interrupted the eulogy.

"Paul Van Twing—the Dutch Van Twings who were among the earliest settlers of New York," the manager answered, with relish. "The young man seems to be the worthy scion of a fine family—distinguished in appearance, with a grace of bearing that one so seldom sees in this–"

"There was a party, you say?"

"Only Mrs. Van Twing, a schoolgirl daughter who was ill, the son Paul, and Miss Ramsey," the hotel manager answered, with a faint air of reproach for these curt interruptions. "It was quite obvious that the young couple were in love. In fact, Mrs. Van Twing confided to me that they were to be married after the party reached California, their objective, toward which they were traveling by easy stages, due to the child's illness. . . . Tuberculosis, I'm afraid."

"And what happened Wednesday night?"

"The young couple went for a drive in one of the cars in which the party was making a luxurious cross country tour," Littleton went on wordily. "Mr. Van Twing dismissed the chauffeur and drove himself. Just before midnight the young man returned alone in quite a dreadful state. I happened to be in the lounge when he arrived. He asked immediately if Miss Ramsey had returned. I said I had not seen her, but made doubly sure by asking the night clerk and by ringing her room. The young man almost collapsed then, and I urged him into my office here and braced him with a spot of brandy. . ,. . Very decent brandy, too! Would you like a sip?"

"No, thanks," Dundee said, sitting on the edge of his chair. "What had happened? Did he tell you?"

"He did—and in the wildest possible way," the manager assured him, smiling. "Young Van Twing begged me to telephone for the police–"

"What?" Dundee shouted.

"For the police," Littleton repeated. "He said he had knocked down a man on the highway and killed him."

"Oh!"

"In a most distressing condition he was, the poor chap. Kept insisting that it was all his fault—and so vehement about it that I deduced"—and the manager smacked his lips over the word—"that it was really Miss Ramsey who was responsible for the accident."

"I see," Dundee said slowly. "I understand a lot of things now–"

"Oh, but it was all what you Americans call a false alarm," the manager assured him. "The poor blighter on the roadside had not been killed at all—was scarcely hurt, in fact. Merely stunned."

"Then why ?" Dundee began.

"Don't you see? Miss Ramsey fled the scene of the accident, believing the man had been killed. Poor Van Twing told her to 'beat it'—as you say over here; that he would assume the entire blame. He thought, naturally, that she would return to the hotel. He telephoned at a filling station for an ambulance and waited until he saw it arriving in the distance, then he 'beat it,' too. . . . Very bad policy, but the poor chap was frightfully upset. His whole thought seems to have been for Miss Ramsey, who, he told me, had become hysterical. He wanted to see her first, reassure her that her name would never be mentioned in the report of the accident, then go to the police and give himself up."

"I saw nothing in the papers about all this," Dundee frowned.

"There wasn't a line," Littleton assured him proudly. "That is, about the accident. I myself went with young Van Twing to the receiving hospital, and there we found that the man was able to leave. Had been stunned, but not seriously injured at all. At my suggestion the young man gave the accident victim a check for five hundred dollars, which made the unfortunate man glad that he'd been bowled over. Of course Van Twing reported the affair to the police, but a word from me kept it out of the papers."

"I see," Dundee repeated, dazedly.

"When we returned to the hotel, Miss Ramsey was still not in her room, and had not telephoned," the manager continued. "Young Van Twing was in a truly pitiable state. I suggested that he tell his mother—a fine, capable lady—and it was Mrs. Van Twing that took charge then and carried on. She telephoned every person with whom the party had become friendly during their brief stay here, but not one of them had seen or heard from Miss Ramsey. And three times during the remainder of the night she made telephone inquiry of every hospital in Hamilton."

"Did she ring up Mayfield Sanitarium?" Dundee asked.

"I rather think not," the manager told him. "Mayfield, you see, is quite remote—at least five miles from the city, I understand. And even if Mrs. Van Twing had inquired, she would have been told that no young person named Ramsey had been received there."

"And so the party shoved off?" Dundee asked.

"Not for several days," Littleton answered. "But the little girl—Alicia, her name is—became worse, and it was necessary finally for the party to move on toward the West, where the child was to be put in a sanitarium. Young Van Twing was in a dreadful state, but he had apparently done all he could, and his mother needed him badly. Mrs. Van Twing, however, did arrange with the society editors of both morning and evening newspapers to display prominently, with headlines, a social note to the effect that the Van Twings were to conclude their visit to Hamilton and go on to California, as soon as Miss Edith Ramsey, a member of their party, had returned from a visit with friends in a near by city. Her hope was that Miss Ramsey would see this item and realize that the coast was clear. But nothing developed. In case Miss Ramsey returned to the hotel, I was to give her a message, and also wire Van Twing in San Francisco."

"You mentioned private detectives, I believe."

"Right you are! A few days ago a person came here, making inquiries about Miss Ramsey. I asked him if he were a private detective—a rather neat deduction as it turned out, for that was exactly what the fellow was," Littleton commended himself. "A rum sort of codger — expert at pumping me, but quite the clam when it came to answering my questions–"

"What did he look like?" Dundee interrupted, but he was sure of the answer before it came.

"Disgustingly fat little bounder," Littleton told him. "Middle aged, fairish sort of hair and light eyes—most ord'n'ry, really."

"Has he been here more than once?"

"No. I particularly asked him to return and relieve my own anxiety, if he discovered Miss Ramsey's whereabouts, but I have not seen him since."

After ten minutes or so, during which the hotel manager plied the detective with questions concerning the Koenig case, which Dundee answered with apparent frankness, the young detective made his escape.

District Attorney Sanderson listened to the story with only an occasional exclamation by way of interruption, his brown flecked gray eyes fixed very intently upon the narrator.

"Hard lines, old man," he said surprisingly, when the narrative was concluded.

Dundee flushed, shrugged, but did not deny the insinuation behind the kindly words.

"I suppose you've wired the Van Twings?" Sanderson asked.

Dundee flushed more darkly. "No. And I asked Littleton not to. There's practically no doubt that Enid Rambler and Edith Ramsey are one and the same, but I can't have her snatched away before the mystery is cleared up. She may be a material witness against the murderer–"

"If your first theory about her is correct," Sanderson asked reasonably, "why don't you simply swap information with her? Tell her it's all a mistake, that she didn't kill any man in an automobile accident, and ten to one she'll be so grateful that she'll tell anything she's been hiding about Koenig's murder."

But Dundee shook his head. "No, Chief, if you don't mind, I'll work this thing out before I try to make use of the girl. Her testimony might be practically worthless if I had no case built up against the murderer. You know how much it takes to convince a jury that a man is a murderer. . . . Besides, the girl may be mistaken. Her story may be entirely worthless, the product of hysteria."

"Wonder why that fat private detective hasn't wired Van Twing?" Sanderson suggested thoughtfully.

"The way I dope it out is this: Fatty saw Enid all right, after she left the movie. Met him on the grounds probably. He made the mistake of spilling the beans first— that he was a detective, I mean. The girl thought he had come to arrest her for manslaughter—we understand now, of course, why the movie of that name scared the poor kid half to death!—and she played her part so well that the fat bloke was completely taken in—thought he had the wrong girl, in spite of the fact that the description tallied. Of course she didn't give him time to tell her what it was all about. . . . Lord! No wonder the blessed little idiot has claustrophobia, and an anxiety neurosis and God knows what else the matter with her poor nerves!"

"Yes, it seems rather obvious that she was running away from the fat man," Sanderson admitted. "And it's entirely possible she doesn't know anything about Koenig's murder."

"Then why is she so damned happy over having a cop to guard her?" Dundee worried.

"Ask me another," Sanderson shrugged. "But here's an answer to one of your questions," and he reached under his pillow for a telegram. "Fitts says no such telegram has been received in his office."

Dundee brightened. "Swell! Mind if I spend a wad of the taxpayers' money, Chief? I'd like to talk to Fitts long distance. If he has a normal amount of curiosity he's already been digging into the 1919 records, and can give me the information I want without delay."

"Hop to it!" Sanderson consented, with only a decent pretense of reluctance. "I'll undoubtedly be 'investigated,' but—I'm curious, too."

To Dundee's amazement—he had never before talked long distance with Los Angeles—it was less than five minutes before the operator's crisp voice informed him: "Ready with Los Angeles, Hamilton!"

There was a moment of disappointment, however, when a man's voice—as clear as if it were coming from a Hamilton telephone—told him: "I'm sorry, but Mr. Fitts is out of the city today." But Dundee's disappointment gave way to exultation when the dear, friendly voice continued, with scarcely a pause:

"This is Assistant District Attorney Boykin speaking. It was I who received and answered your telegram, and I confess it excited my curiosity. . . . May I ask if the matter has any connection with the Koenig murder?"

Dundee grinned and nodded vigorously toward Sanderson, to indicate that all was going well. "I'm pretty sure it has a whale of a lot to do with the Koenig case," he said into the receiver, "and I'm counting on you to help us, Mr. Boykin."

"Delighted, Dundee! We've heard about you, even 'way out here. Better come to the land of sunshine and flowers–"

"Maybe I'll get a vacation on pay if I can clean up this mess," Dundee answered. "Los Angeles is a great town for big time murders, too–"

"Hey!" Sanderson pleaded, in agony. "Cut it short!"

But there was no need for the admonition, since the man at the other end of the wire, the amenities attended to, was swinging whole heartedly into the business at hand.

"Told you I was curious over that wire, Dundee," he said. "I took the trouble to dig into the 1919 files, looking for both first and last names beginning with E d i— "

"Stout fella!" Dundee applauded. "Find anything hot?"

"Plenty!" the genial voice came back clear and strong. "Funny coincidence, too. Dr. Koenig's name figures in *two* separate and distinct cases–"

"What!" Dundee shouted in his excitement. "In *two* cases where the defendants' names begin with 'E d i '?"

"One case never got to the point of the person involved being a defendant," the Los Angeles attorney corrected him. "A flapper by the name of Edith Ramsey–"

"*Edith Ramsey?* . . . My God!" Dundee groaned, and Sanderson jerked upright in bed, regardless of pleurisy.

"Know her? She must be quite a gal by now. I remember seeing her in 1919, when she was only fifteen, but pretty enough then to launch at least a small fleet. . . . Say! She isn't mixed up in this, is she?"

"She's a patient at Mayfield Sanitarium," Dundee answered dully. "What have you got on her?"

"Well, I'll be " the man at the other end of the wire marveled. "Say, I'll sketch her story briefly. It sort of stuck in my mind, but I read up on it a bit, just to refresh my memory, in case I was on the right track about your wire. . . . Here's the dope: Edith Ramsey, daughter of a multi millionaire fruit grower in the Santa Clara valley, was given an automobile on her fifteenth birthday–"

"Another automobile!" Dundee groaned, but not aloud.

"The kid was too young for a license, of course, but her dad pulled wires and she got one—lied about her age, maybe. Anyway, the family had one of their half dozen homes here in Los Angeles, and one day the kid took her parents driving. There was a nasty accident. The kid ran the car smack into a P. E. train, and the mother and father were both killed instantly."

Again Dundee groaned "My God!" and this time the exclamation was wrung from the very depths of his heart.

"Yeah, pretty tough on a fifteen year old kid," Boykin agreed. "Well, Edith simply went nuts—tried to commit suicide two or three times, until they had to put her in the psychopathic ward for observation. Mrs. Ramsey's sister, a Mrs. Henderson, happened to be in Los Angeles at the time, and she was afraid the kid was going stark mad. She called in two or three neurologists, including Dr. William Huntington Edwards, one of our best alienists, and finally got hold of Koenig, who was here on the *other* case I'll tell you about later."

"Whew!" Dundee whistled, and dug into his pocket for a handkerchief with which to wipe the icy sweat from his brow.

"Koenig said it wasn't anything but a nervous break down, although the kid kept insisting she was a murderess, and ought to be hanged by the neck till she was dead. The Hendersons put the girl into a private sanitarium out here–"

"Not the Good Hope, by any chance?" Dundee asked.

"Right!" came the emphatic answer over the wire. "A couple of months out there fixed her up—they said she had what you call 'manic depression,' if you get me–"

"I get you!" Dundee assured him grimly. "I'll be a manic depressive myself if this keeps up. ... Well? How did the girl get into the court records?"

"Merely a guardianship matter," the clear, friendly voice assured him. "She wasn't old enough to come into her parents' money, of course, and this Mrs. Henderson, the girl's maternal aunt, was appointed guardian until the girl was twenty one. I understand the Hendersons took her abroad to finish her education, and that she has lived abroad nearly ever since. At any rate, she's never been back to Los Angeles."

"I see," Dundee said, and used one of the precious minutes that were being marked up against the call to brood hopelessly.

"Don't be so down in the mouth, old man," Boykin, two thousand miles away, advised sympathetically. "After all, what possible motive for murdering the doctor could that kid have?"

"Thanks, Boykin," Dundee answered tonelessly.

"What's the other case?—though I suppose it's useless to look further for the subject of Koenig's inquiry to Fitts."

"I'm not so sure of that," the Los Angeles man retorted over the wire. "I've been saving the hot stuff. . . . Listen to this, young fellow, and get an earful!"

CHAPTER TWENTY FOUR

"SHOOT the works, Boykin, but make it snappy," Dundee advised, a sympathetic eye upon District Attorney Sanderson's distress over the leaping toll bill.

"Right!" heartily agreed the voice of the Los Angeles assistant district attorney. "Sanderson's listening in, is he? —and chewing his nails? . . . Well, tell him there's a bare possibility he can bill Los Angeles County for half this toll call, for it looks to me like Koenig was ready to slip us the dope on one of our own pet fugitives from justice. Have you seen a bad boy by the name of Edinger out at Mayfield?"

"Edinger?" Dundee repeated blankly. "Never heard of him."

"Then I guess Koenig bumped into him on this trip the papers say he'd just returned from when he was murdered," the voice from Los Angeles surmised, with its first trace of gloom. "And Koenig's dead. . . . Too bad!"

"You say the name is 'E d i n g e r'?" Dundee asked.

"Correct!" Boykin assured him. "Wanted to answer to an indictment on charges of conspiracy and misappropriation. Skipped out before the grand jury met, and never been heard from since. In 1919 that was."

"What's the story?" Dundee asked. "Just the bare facts, of course," he added hastily, as Sanderson groaned.

But it was not Boykin's money that was being burned up by telephone wires, and he was not going to have his yarn spoiled. "In 1918, a youngster by the name of Marvin Cooley—only seventeen years old—lied about his age and got into a training camp. He was among the last of our boys to go to France, but he was unlucky enough to be shoved into the front line trenches. He was erroneously reported killed in action. But before the news came, his mother—a widow—had married this guy Edinger, Steven F. Edinger. At least, that's the name he was using out here. Mysterious sort of bird. We knew literally nothing about him before 1918, and mighty little after that. He was in the real estate 'game' when he married the rich widow–"

"But you have a description of him?" Dundee interrupted.

"Oh, yes," came the reassuring words over the wire. "He was then—in 1919, when the blow up came— about 38 years old, medium height, weight about 190 pounds–"

"Good Lord! Another fat man! . . . *Or is it the same one?*" Dundee asked himself, but he said nothing to interrupt the story which was costing the taxpayers a pretty penny per word.

"—eyes brown, hair thick and black—" the voice from Los Angeles went on.

"You're sure of the hair and eyes?" Dundee asked aloud, while he said to himself, "*Not* the same fat man!"

"I'm reading the description from the police circulars," Boykin assured him. "Ruddy complexion, black mustache, pug nose. No scars or disfigurations."

"Fingerprints?"

"Not a one. By the time the police wanted them, Edinger had cleared out, and too many other people had handled his things both in his hotel room and his real estate office," Boykin answered, but added helpfully, "Got a specimen of his handwriting, if that will help."

"It will—if I ever get the ghost of an idea who Edinger is. ... But what was he indicted for?"

"I told you he married a rich widow whose minor son was later reported killed in action," Boykin explained. "Edinger got his paws on the whole fortune by one of the lousiest schemes ever pulled in our fair city. He conspired with a woman who called herself a nurse, although she'd had no training, to get his wife adjudged mentally incompetent–"

"What!" Dundee shouted.

"Stop that, fellow! You'll bust my ear drum," Boykin pleaded. "Didn't I tell you I had a hot tip for you? . . . Well, once she was tucked away in a sanitarium–"

"Good Hope Sanitarium, of course?" Dundee interrupted again.

"How'd you guess it?" Boykin laughed. "As I was say ing, once he'd got her stowed away in Good Hope, he made ducks and drakes of her fortune, or—as everyone believes and no one can prove—he salted most of it away, in a good safe place where it would wait for him if things got too hot for him here—as they did. You see, the kid, Marvin Cooley, blew into town one day, all hot and bothered because his mother, whose name was no longer Cooley, of course, and who had moved from the old Cooley home, hadn't answered his letters. He got on her trail somehow, and found she was supposed to be crazy. He located her at Good Hope, without paying a call on his step papa, and then the fat was in the fire sure enough. The old lady was no more crazy than I am!"

"How did the son find that out?" Dundee asked, a little skeptically.

"Easy!" Boykin retorted over a wire two thousand miles long. "That's where the conspiracy comes in. You see, Edinger had ribbed up the nurse to work a ouija board with the old lady–"

"How old *was* she?"

"Fifty or so," Boykin answered impatiently. "Just the right age to be roped in by a fortune hunter. Well, when she went into a real nervous prostration over the news that her boy was killed in action, Edinger ribbed up the nurse to work the ouija board with her, getting messages for the old lady from the 'Beyond'—supposed to be from the kid, of course. The poor old lady got so she wanted to be at the ouija board all the time. Then Edinger played his trump ace–"

"Not a *voice* from the Beyond?" Dundee interrupted quickly.

"Say! Who's telling this yarn?" Boykin demanded, aggrievedly. "But you're right–"

"Ah!" Dundee breathed, and paid no more attention to Sanderson's agony over the telephone bill.

"Ain't it hot?" Boykin boasted. "The nurse—dame by the name of Whitson—swore it was Edinger that stood under the old lady's window late at night and pretended to be the ghost of the dead boy. She squealed, of course, to save her own hide. . . . But I'm getting ahead of the story. The old lady told everybody how her son not only came to her by way of the ouija board, but that she heard his voice. After that, it was pretty easy to get her adjudged incompetent and put away. 'Auditory hallucinations,' the alienists said, and you've got to remember the poor old lady was pretty well shot, nervously, anyway."

"My God!" Dundee breathed.

"Yeah! Pretty rotten!" Boykin, in Los Angeles, agreed. "Of course the jig was up when the boy returned, safe and sound, and madder'n hell at finding his mother in such a fix. The kid had grown into quite a lad, and he made short work of taking the matter of her 'incompetence' into court. There was a swell battery of alienists lined up on each side, Edinger calling in Dr. Sandlin from Good Hope, along with two or three other big shots, in a desperate effort to make the first ruling stick. But the kid got hold of Dr. Koenig as *his* big gun, along with Dr. Edwards, and finally the nurse squealed, and it was all over. But as I said, before the grand jury could indict or a temporary warrant could be clapped on Edinger, he'd skipped—and hasn't been heard of since."

Another precious minute was consumed by Dundee's thanks and his request that a copy of the grand jury proceedings in the Edinger case be rushed to him by air mail. Then he hung up the receiver and faced his chief.

"What a yam!" he gloated, and himself spun the amazing tale for the district attorney's benefit.

"It ought to be," Sanderson grumbled. "It cost us at least ten cents a word. But as far as I can see, it doesn't butter any parsnips for us."

"You wouldn't kid me, mister, would you?" Dundee pleaded. Then, seriously, "Of course it may be, simply, one of those astounding coincidences that are always popping up in real life. But— Looky, Chief! Koenig was killed when he was telephoning that night letter to Los Angeles, before he could finish spelling a name that begins with 'E d i.' The reason he sent that telegram is that, while talking on the phone to Claire Cantrell, his eyes lit on something on his desk—and we can safely guess it was Clyde Powell's case history—that made him remember where he had seen a certain pair of eyes before. Now, in Powell's case history appeared two names that appear in the Edinger story—Dr. Sandlin's name and the name of Good Hope Sanitarium–"

"Wait a minute!" Sanderson interrupted. "If Koenig was figuring on hiring Sandlin as his assistant at Mayfield, he *knew* Sandlin was formerly connected with Good Hope Sanitarium. Nothing in the juxtaposition of those two names to make him have a brain wave. And no reason that I can see why this chap, Edinger, would have to destroy Powell's case history, just because Sandlin's name and the name of the Los Angeles sanitarium were in it."

"You're right!" Dundee assured him eagerly. "I admit there's a missing link—something else in Clyde Powell's case history that, *connected with those two names*, fired off a bomb in Koenig's brain. Can't you guess what that missing link was?"

"Edinger's name, I suppose," Sanderson obliged sourly. "But what in the name of heaven should it be doing in *Powell's* case history?"

Dundee considered for a long moment. "Both Powell and Mrs. Edinger were patients at Good Hope during 1919, but I admit I can see no reason why either

Edinger's or Mrs. Edinger's name should get into Powell's history.

. . . Wait a minute!" he cried suddenly, and reached for the telephone.

"Another Los Angeles call?" Sanderson moaned.

But Dundee was dialing the number of Mayfield Sanitarium. Fortunately it was the staff's luncheon hour, and it was only a matter of seconds before Dr. Harlow's lovely treble came over the wire.

"Listen, Doctor!" Dundee urged. "Try hard to remember something for me, won't you? . . . Thanks! Did Clyde Powell have delusions of persecution against real or imaginary people?"

"Both," she answered promptly.

"Were the names of his 'persecutors' recorded in his case history?" Dundee continued eagerly.

"Clyde had a pet imaginary enemy whom he called 'Frank,' " she told him. " 'Frank' was responsible for nearly everything bad that happened to Clyde, and some times he shadow boxed with his imaginary foe, or held long, abusive conversations with him. But I can't remember any other names."

"Was the name of—*Edinger* among them?" Dundee asked tensely. "E d i n g e r?"

"Edinger?" came the slow, sweet voice very thought fully. "No, I'm positive it was not."

"That's tough," Dundee admitted, out of the depths of his disappointment. "Miss Home is familiar with the history, I believe. Will you ask her if the name of Edinger appeared in it, in any connection whatever?"

"Hold the line," Dr. Harlow directed.

As Dundee waited, Sanderson spoke, frowningly:

"Even if Powell got a persecution complex against this Edinger, through meeting him at Good Hope, when he was visiting his wife, I don't see why it was so damned necessary for Edinger—supposing he was the murderer—to destroy the case history. The history had been on hand at May field for years, and it's hardly likely his name occurring in the early pages of it would have meant a thing to anyone but Koenig."

"You forget that the first three letters of that name were spelled out in Koenig's wire," Dundee reminded him, his hand cupping the transmitter of the telephone. "This murderer was the most cautious, cold blooded, farseeing bloke I ever heard of. He left absolutely nothing to chance—except that one hidden drop of blood! He foresaw that there was a bare possibility that the 'bust' message would be traced to Dr. Koenig. Any scrap of paper left in Koenig's possession, which would give the remaining letters of the name, Edinger, had to be destroyed. He couldn't simply file Powell's case history, in the hope that it would not be read again, for there was the letter attached, from the State Hospital, asking for excerpts from it. ... See? . . . Hello! Yes, Dr. Harlow?"

He listened for a moment, thanked the little doctor, and slowly replaced the receiver.

"No luck," he admitted gloomily. "Miss Home is as positive as Dr. Harlow that the name of Edinger was not in Clyde Powell's history. She says she skimmed through it when she got it out of the files for Dr. Koenig on Wednesday, and had handled it several times before, when additions were made to the record."

"Too bad," Sanderson sympathized. "Looks like an other blind alley."

"No. I'll swear we're on the right track," Dundee insisted stubbornly. "The key to the whole mystery lies in Clyde Powell's case history, which, undoubtedly, has been thoroughly destroyed by this time, and Steven Edinger is the murderer. The question is: who is Edinger?"

"The answer to that, to put it obliquely," Sanderson grinned, "is that Edinger isn't Edinger. A fugitive from justice doesn't parade a name under which he has been indicted."

"That's a foregone conclusion," Dundee agreed, a little curtly. Did his chief think he was that dumb? . . . "The question remains: who is Edinger—whatever name he may be using now? Have we had the pleasure of his acquaintance? In other words, is he Samuel Rowan, or the mysterious fat man, or—Roland Morse?"

"In the order of their probability, eh?" Sanderson suggested. "But why the mysterious fat man? I thought he was accounted for—as a private detective hired by Van Twing to find Enid Rambler, or, I should say, Edith Ramsey."

"I was willing to write him off, too, until I remembered that Littleton, the manager of the Hamiltonian, took it for granted that the fat man was a private detective, when he turned up at the hotel asking for Edith Ramsey. In fact, Littleton asked him if that was his job, and of course, whether it was true or not, the fat man said yes. But we can't blink the fact that somehow, innocently or not, Edith Ramsey is mixed up in this case. Otherwise, we've got a most amazing web of coincidence. Edith Ramsey was in Los Angeles in 1919. Koenig was called in on her case. Also, in 1919, she, as well as Mrs. Edinger and Clyde Powell, was a patient at Good Hope Sanitarium, where Dr. Horace Sandlin was employed as psychiatrist. We have the further coincidence that Koenig was called as an alienist by Marvin Cooley in the suit to restore his mother's status as a competent person. I tell you, sir, there's a solution to this case which will explain and include all these apparent coincidences, leaving only the coincidence that Edith Ramsey, under the name of Enid Rambler, was a patient at Mayfield at the time Edinger turned up to murder Dr. Koenig. An unlucky coincidence for her, poor girl, for it puts her in danger of her life."

"Then we'd better make sure that her guard isn't a victim of sleeping sickness," Sanderson said grimly.

"Right!" Dundee agreed heartily. "And I'll rest easier tonight if I know our friend, Roland Morse, is also under the watchful eye of an uninvited guest."

"How does he fit into Edinger's description?" Sanderson asked.

"Fairly well," the special investigator answered. "He's heavy, rather than fat, but diet and a medicine ball could have taken care of that. I'd say he's a couple of inches over the average in height, but police descriptions are not apt to be astonishingly accurate, especially when they concern the height of a very fat man. You've noticed that a wide girth apparently takes inches off a man's height. Morse's eyes are brown, all right, but I wouldn't call his nose pug. It's quite a nose, in fact, but the nostrils are rather noticeably wide. And it is an easy enough matter to change one's nose, plastic surgeons being what they are today. Morse's hair is pepper and salt, Edinger's was black in 1919. In fact, Morse fits the bill so well that I'd very much like to know exactly where he was during the latter half of 1918 and the first half of 1919."

"Odd, isn't it, how a criminal repeats himself," Sanderson mused with satisfaction. "The voice of a 'dead' son offering ghostly comfort to his mother in 1919, the voice of God wailing 'too late!' under a bereaved mother's window in 1931—with the same fiendish purpose: that of driving a rich wife crazy."

"Yes," Dundee agreed soberly. "And by a criminal's repetitions ye shall know him—and hang him!"

CHAPTER TWENTY FIVE

IT was a very thoughtful young detective who, after a lengthy conference with Captain Strawn of the Homicide Squad, drove slowly the five miles from Hamilton to Mayfield Sanitarium.

One question, which seemed rather irrelevant, persisted in annoying Special Investigator Dundee: Why had Dr. Koenig, so outstanding a man in his field, planned to bring Dr. Horace Sandlin to Mayfield, if, as Professor Livingstone of Northwestern University broadly hinted in his telegram, Sandlin had a none too flattering reputation among his colleagues? Certainly Koenig had had first hand opportunity for judging Sandlin, since the two psychiatrists had been opposing expert witnesses in the Edinger case.

The twin to that question also buzzed like a persistent gnat at his ear: Why had Koenig determined, quite suddenly, it seemed, to dismiss Justine Harlow, who had served him so faithfully and so well that he had willed her half of his estate?

Even if Morse should prove to be Edinger—and who else came anywhere near fitting that description, except possibly Samuel Rowan?—how should he ever learn the answer to those two questions? And Dundee wanted them answered. A solution with loose ends was no solution, to his type of mind. . . .

Mayfield's lawn looked like the pleasure grounds of a fashionable resort hotel, as Dundee drove in and parked near the main building. In the warm late afternoon sun, patients were playing croquet, miniature golf, and bridge. There was even a horseshoe pitching contest, Night watch man Whalen as champion challenging all comers. Archie Webster and his attendant, Happy Day, were proving to be unexpectedly formidable opponents as Dundee strolled by. He refused an invitation to join in the sport, and continued his apparently aimless stroll.

A bridge game was being held up while Marjorie Merrick checked a small heap of parcels which Business Manager Baldwin had evidently been delegated to purchase for her.

"My God, Roger!" the singer was exclaiming in a tragic voice. "You didn't get that perfume! I told you I simply couldn't live another day without it–"

"They didn't have it, Marjie," Roger Baldwin answered conciliatingly. "I tried the best drug stores and department stores–"

"Cheap hicks!" she dismissed all of Hamilton scornfully. "Wire Chicago to send me some, Roger—there's a lamb."

Dundee was about to stroll on when a sudden thought halted him.

"May I speak with you a moment when you're at leisure, Mr. Baldwin?"

"You can have him, darling!" Marjorie Merrick called out stridently. "As a personal shopping bureau, he's a bust, although he did bring me a box of candy—the pet!"

"The pet" flushed darkly as he backed hastily away from the bridge table and joined Dundee.

"Good business—that's all," Baldwin muttered, as if he were afraid Dundee might give him credit for a kindly impulse. "This shopping for the patients is the devil's own nuisance," he grumbled. "Just let the word get out that I'm going into town and I've got to bring back everything from face powder to pink silk step ins. ... If you wanted to see me about the rates on your suite, there isn't going to be any bill," he added gruffly.

"You're very kind," Dundee smiled, knowing that Baldwin would hate the soft impeachment. "But I wanted to speak to you about something else. . . . You handle all checks that are given in payment of bills here, don't you, Mr. Baldwin?"

"Not all; in fact, not many of them," Baldwin denied. "The cashier attends to that phase of the routine here. . . . No, I'll amend that statement somewhat," the business manager interrupted himself conscientiously. "Before the checks go to the bank, I see that their amounts tally with the deposit slip the cashier has written up. And I usually attend to the banking myself."

"Then I wonder if you have ever received a check here signed with the name 'Edith Ramsey'?" Dundee asked.

The business manager frowned, knit his brows. Then his face cleared. "Thought that name sounded familiar!" he exclaimed with mild triumph. "We haven't had a patient here by that name, but another patient, Enid Rambler—funny coincidence, the initials being the same, isn't it?—endorsed over to us a New York check made out to her and signed by the name of Edith Ramsey. That was the first week she was here, and the amount of the check was nearly a hundred dollars more than her bill."

"And you took a chance on the check's being good? Handed the change over to her?" Dundee marveled, knowing the business manager as he believed he did.

But Baldwin grinned wryly. "No. I issued a credit on her next week's bill, and by the time it was due, the check had cleared O. K."

"Did she pay by 'Edith Ramsey' checks after that?"

"No. After that first time, she gave us checks on a Hamilton bank."

"Signed 'Enid Rambler'?" Dundee asked.

"Certainly!"

"Did it occur to you, Mr. Baldwin, that Edith Ramsey and Enid Rambler were one and the same person?" Dundee asked.

"No! Why should it?"

"Was the handwriting similar?"

"Not similar enough to attract my attention, certainly!" Baldwin retorted. "Let me think. I'm pretty good at remembering details of that sort. . . . I've got it now! The Edith Ramsey check was written in a bold, large hand, that slanted sharply toward the right. Miss Rambler's signature is always written in a very round back hand."

"Exactly what I should have expected," Dundee murmured.

"Look here, Dundee!" Baldwin commanded sharply. "I don't know what you're driving at, but if you've got any wild notion that that girl is mixed up in Carl's murder, you're crazier than any patient we've got here. She's as fine and straight a girl as I ever met—and I'm not speaking now as Mayfield's business manager, out to protect a rich patient from scandal. If, for some reason of her own, Miss Rambler is here under an assumed name, I'd stake my life that it's an innocent reason."

"I'm sure you're right, Mr. Baldwin," Dundee assured him, and again set off across the lawn toward Sunflower Court.

It was obvious, he reflected, that Enid Rambler—as he still called her to himself—had managed to open a bank account in Hamilton, by mail. Easy enough to send in a large check, made out to Enid Rambler, signed by the name of Edith Ramsey, and endorsed by Enid Rambler, with a request that the money be deposited, when collected, to the account of Enid Rambler. Even if a handwriting expert had detected that payor and payee were the same person, it was no legal offense to open a bank account in an assumed name. But that first check, given to Baldwin, had wiped out the last vestige of doubt that Enid Rambler was Edith Ramsey. In this business, Dundee congratulated himself, it paid to be *sure*—not "practically certain."

"Yes, Enid's in her rooms," Miss Doty assured him, when he entered the reception room of Sunflower Court. "Now, don't blush! I just knew that was what you were going to ask!"

Having given up hope for herself, the day nurse had apparently decided magnanimously to sponsor a romance between this handsome young detective and the girl she had previously acknowledged as a formidable rival. Though what all the men saw in her, beyond the fact that she was pretty "in a way," Lurline Doty for the life of her could not say. . . .

Barney Flynn, the plainclothesman on duty outside the door that led from Enid Rambler's suite into the patio, showed a grateful inclination to talk when Dundee paused to greet him.

"Yep! Everything's swell!" Flynn told him enthusiastically. "Say, Dundee, I don't care if you never solve this here murder. It's the softest job I've struck in a coon's age."

"No trouble at all, I take it?" Dundee asked, smiling.

"You mean, does she try to make a get away?" Flynn asked. "Not that baby! She peeps out a dozen times a day just to make sure I *am* here—cautions me not to budge an inch. Pretty as paint, ain't she? . . . And sweet? Umm!" and the plainclothesman smacked his lips. "But at that, I'm kinda sorry for the poor little thing. Acts gay and chipper all the time, but she's scared, Dundee —scared stiff. Why, today she made Miss Lacey, the head nurse, have a set of heavy, barred screens put before all her windows. Seems like they keep sets of 'em on hand, to stick 'em in the windows of patients that suddenly go off their nuts."

"Is anyone with her now?"

"Sure! They's always somebody running in and out," Flynn assured him. "That baby could win a beauty and popularity prize in a Ziegfeld chorus. Rowan it is now. Been there about fifteen minutes. And I'll bet she's making that moth eaten old bozo feel like he's the Prince of Wales."

"Yes, that's a gift of hers," Dundee agreed, grinning, as he opened the door.

He was treated to a sample of Enid Rambler's gentle and exquisite courtesy as soon as he entered the girl's sitting room. She was lying on the couch, her injured foot resting on a pillow, and, in a chair drawn close, sat

Samuel Rowan. The shabby charity patient was freshly and closely shaved; the coarse gray hairs had been plucked from his nostrils, and somewhere Rowan had found a not too dingy tie and a frayed but very clean white shirt.

The man's meek brown eyes—one clouded with a cataract—peered upward at Dundee with just a hint of disappointment at the interruption, but his greeting was respectful and friendly.

"So glad to see you, Mr. Dundee," Enid Rambler told him, and motioned toward a chair with one hand. In the other she held a small, limp leather book. "Mr. Rowan's trying to cheer me up," she continued, and there was gentle gravity in her eyes as they rested on the little book. "Isn't it dear of him to bring me this book—*The Casting Out of Fear?* ... If only there were no fear in the world, what a wonderful place it would be to live in!"

Rowan flushed, and turned his hat slowly in awkward hands. "It's a real good book," he said humbly. "It helped me a lot. In fact, that little book and Dr. Koenig have given me a new lease on life."

"I'm sure it's wonderful," the girl said warmly, but in the dark blue eyes which flicked a quick glance toward Dundee there was no hope.

"I'd like to read it myself," Dundee lied politely.

"There's nothing like it, if you've got something preying on your mind and haunting your dreams, night in and night out, like I had," Rowan told them, sincerity vibrating in his uncultured voice. "Mr. Baldwin gave me that little book, not dreaming what a miracle it would work in me–"

"But I'm sure he said it was 'good business' to give it to you!" Enid laughed, but Dundee's quick ear caught a note of hysteria in her voice. Probably old Rowan had been boring her intolerably. . . .

"Then I reckon he'd be right," Rowan told her, in nowise offended by her laughter. "Good business for the sanitarium to get rid of a charity patient, and good business in a larger sense to set a man on his feet and put him back into the world."

"You really want to go back into the world, don't you?" Enid asked softly. "I envy you, Mr. Rowan. But I'm afraid I–"

"Afraid! Afraid!" the old man repeated solemnly. "If *I* can get rid of that 'Old Man of the Sea'—that's what the little book calls Fear—a young girl like you, with every grace that God ever endowed a woman with "

"But you don't *know!*" Enid interrupted, and tears filled her eyes.

"If there's anything I do know, it's what fear can do to a body," Rowan corrected her gently. "That big police man has been pestering me to tell him my story, but I don't see no call to tell it to people it wouldn't help–"

He paused uncertainly, and Dundee cut in, gravely, without too much eagerness: "I think you're right, Mr. Rowan, but I'm sure both Miss Rambler and I would be greatly helped by your experience."

"Of course we should, Mr. Rowan," Enid agreed kindly, and Dundee saw that not even the prospect of being bored could dim the fine luster of her courtesy.

The older man settled himself a bit more easily in his chair, and Dundee waited, scarcely daring to breathe.

"Young people like you," Rowan began, "with the world before you and your hearts full of romance and hope, don't have no idea what life looks like to people who're getting old and never have had the good things you two take for granted. . . . Now, me and my wife," he began again, less sententiously, "was in love with each other, in a manner of speaking, when we got married in a little town down in Texas. She was a peart, high stepping girl, and I had my health and the sight of both eyes."

Unexpectedly, Dundee felt his heart contract with pity, not asked for by that quiet voice.

"We got hitched, and things went pretty well for a time," Rowan went on. "Then, somehow, I didn't seem to be turning out no great shakes as a money maker. My wife, Melcie, got pretty much disgusted with me, and her tongue got to be sharp as a razor. Long about '28—when our third child followed his two little sisters to the graveyard—Melcie got it into her head that California was the Promised Land. Nothing would do her but I should pull up stakes and light out for California. I had a few acres of land that got so all it could raise was boll weavils and mortgages, so when cotton picking was over that fall I give in. Sold out for what I could get and bought a Ford. . . . Well, me and Melcie had a pretty good time the first week, seeing new country and spinning yarns with the neighborly sort of folks we met in the auto camps. Her brother, Curtis, was along, and it was him buttin' in that turned a little spat between me and Melcie into what you might call a first class row. At one of them auto camps it was, and I needn't bother you folks with telling you what it was all about. Maybe I was a mite jealous the way Melcie carried on with that barber fellow at the camp, her being old enough to behave herself–"

He stopped abruptly to brood, and Dundee and the girl exchanged pitying glances.

"Well, Curtis butted in and I told him he'd better hitch hike the rest of the way, if he wanted to get to California," Rowan went on. "Melcie was pretty sore, but Curtis stayed behind, and we hit the trail alone the next morning. Come night, I didn't feel much like mingling with the folks in an auto camp, so we struck camp by our selves in a ravine among some of the biggest mountains in Colorado. I didn't sleep so good that night. I'd et a big mess o' canned beans, and I reckon they didn't set so well on my stummick. Anyways, I had a nightmare. I dreamed the whole side of the mountain was tumbling down on me and Melcie, sleeping there by our camp fire."

Again the slow, uncultured, flat voice dragged to a stop. In the intensity of his interest, Dundee was gripping the arms of his chair. Enid Rambler's blue eyes were wide and dark with premonition of tragedy.

"Well, sir," Rowan went on, with no intention of excluding the girl. "Till this day I can't say where the dream left off and the real thing begun. All I know is, whether it was in the dream I saw it or whether I was actually awake by then, I saw a big rock come sliding and crashing down the mountain side–"

"A landslide?" Dundee interrupted.

"No, sir," Rowan denied. "Except for some trash that it brought along with it, that big rock was the only thing that fell. Likely some animal brushed against it and tipped it over. . . . Well, there it come and there I laid, watching it, but no more power to move a hand or a leg than if I'd been paralyzed. ... It hit my wife. It killed her."

The awful suddenness of the conclusion struck both his hearers dumb. While Dundee's hair was still prickling on his scalp, Enid Rambler found her voice, brought it out in little, quivering gasps:

"Oh! But you—*you* couldn't help it, Mr. Rowan!"

The old man drew a deep breath and brought his hand down heavily on the arm of his chair. "No! I couldn't help it, child! . . . But for more'n two years I've called myself a murderer, and lots of other people think I'm a murderer, too. That little book there, and Dr. Koenig "

"But I don't understand!" the girl protested hotly. "It was simply a terrible accident!"

"You see, little girl," Rowan told her gently, and with no hint of familiarity, "if I'd acted soon as I saw that rock coming down the mountain side, I could have saved Melcie. And the rock would have killed me."

"But you *couldn't*—one can't *think* as quickly as all that–" she cried brokenly, and Dundee knew that her defense of Rowan was also a defense of herself.

"Melcie's brother, Curtis, found us there next morning," the quiet voice went on. "I'd waited till dawn, not knowing what to do—half crazy–"

"Of course!" the girl agreed passionately.

"Well, Curtis told the folks he was with—a couple giving him a hitch—all about the quarrel between me and

Melcie," Rowan continued very quietly. "The three of 'em got their heads together and Curtis didn't have much trouble making 'em believe I'd pitched the rock down on my wife. They took me in to the nearest town in the county, and turned me over to the sheriff."

"Oh! Oh!" the girl moaned.

"I didn't much care what happened to me," Rowan comforted her obliquely. "I stayed in jail till the grand jury met, but they refused to indict, for lack of evidence."

"I should think they would!" Enid cried.

"They might as well a hung me," Rowan said soberly. "I knowed I was the biggest coward that ever–"

"No! No!"

"They let me go, but I didn't seem to take no interest in living," Rowan went on. "Finally, by the grace of God, I got sent to Mayfield. Wednesday, after I'd read that little book about casting out fear, I felt like I owed it to Dr. Koenig, being as how he was so good to me, to put the thing up to him fair and square. He asked me if, deep down in my heart, I wanted my wife to be killed by that rock. And I said no, she's been a good wife to me, and I didn't bear no malice after that tiff we had at the auto camp. Then he asked me—and there he hit the nail on the head—whether I'd ruther it would a been her than me. And I told him, God being my witness, I'd ruther a thousand times that rock had cracked my own skull wide open than to a seen it hit Melcie."

"Of course you would!" Enid championed him almost hysterically.

"Then he asked me what was eatin' on me," Rowan went on. "I said I couldn't get over it that I'd been a coward—laying there like a lump o' mud and letting it hit her. Then he told me that the way I'd 'reacted,' as he called it, was exactly what a psychiatrist would have expected. 'Suspended between the dream world and the real world,' he said, my brain refused to 'differentiate' between them. He said I'd been locked in a paralysis of horror, just as real as if I'd been actually paralyzed. He said I couldn't a moved to a saved my own life. He said I wasn't to blame," Rowan summed up simply.

"Oh, he *was* good!" Enid Rambler sobbed, hiding her face behind convulsed hands.

"I just thought I might help you to get a new light on your own little troubles," Rowan said awkwardly, and bent to touch one of her clenched hands. "I don't want to see *you* old before your time, child. . . . How old would you take me to be?"

The girl dropped her hands and stared blankly at Rowan with drowned eyes. Then her beautiful courtesy asserted itself.

"Why—why, I wouldn't take you to be a day over fifty five," she quavered.

"I'll be forty three years old, come August," Samuel Rowan said simply, and again Enid Rambler's face hid itself behind her hands.

Rowan was gone before Dundee realized his intention.

It was not often that the young detective found himself at a complete loss. Now, every instinct of his susceptible heart prompted him to soothe and console this girl whose grief was certainly as much for herself as for the poor devil who had tried to help her. But, equally, every instinct of his professional nature urged him to press his advantage, until the girl's own unhappy story should come tumbling out.

Enid seemed to realize that they two were alone. A thin, exhausted voice came from behind her sheltering hands.

"Please! I'm sorry, but—would you mind—? I can't talk now–"

The gentleman rather than the detective rose to his feet, hastily. "Certainly!" Dundee ejaculated. But it was the detective who paused in the doorway to ask, in a carefully casual voice:

"By the way, Miss Rambler, do you know a chap named *Edinger*?'

CHAPTER TWENTY SIX

As Dundee left Sunflower Court he told himself ruefully that he now knew how a navigator must feel when, steering confidently into port, he finds himself in a strange harbor hundreds of miles off his course.

It was simply no use telling himself that Enid Rambler had lied. Caught with her defenses down, called upon to answer a question which should have been the exact touch needed to bring on an attack of hysteria during which anything or everything might have been revealed, that question had, perversely, served to steady her nerves. Because it was obviously so irrelevant, so meaningless to her!

"Edinger?" she had repeated blankly, her eyes meeting Dundee's candidly but with a sort of hurt wonder that he should try, at a time like that, to strengthen the slight bond between them by discovering a mutual acquaintance. "I don't recall. . . . Edinger? ... I met a writer by that name in London. . . . No! *His* name was Edington. . . . *Edinger!* . . . The name does sound vaguely familiar, but I can't think—I'm really awfully tired," she had pleaded pitifully.

And he had left her, believing she had spoken the absolute truth. At first the acuteness of his disappointment made him feel lost, almost physically ill. For his whole case against Edinger began with and rested upon the hypothesis that Enid Rambler, or Edith Ramsey as he should call her, was not only innocently involved but actually possessed proof of his guilt, if she could be persuaded to furnish it. And now Dundee would stake his life on the conviction that the name, Edinger, meant nothing to the girl.

But a few minutes' reflection served to assuage the detective's disappointment. That Edith Ramsey had not recognized Edinger did not really affect the case against the unknown murderer in the least, except that it eliminated the possibility of an easy and quick solution. Edinger, whether a casual visitor to or an inmate of Mayfield Sanitarium, had seen and recognized Edith Ramsey in Enid Rambler. That had been almost inevitable. In 1919 Edinger's pathetically persecuted wife had been an inmate of the same sanitarium near Los Angeles which had sheltered Edith Ramsey after the tragic accident in which her parents had been killed. Undoubtedly the girl's pictures had been featured in the newspapers for many days, not only because of the shocking accident, but because of her great wealth and her efforts to commit suicide. Dreadfully conspicuous, even in Good Hope Sanitarium, she had been gazed upon by all visitors, among them the then unnoteworthy Edinger, calling to see the wife whom he had driven to the verge of insanity. Of course Edinger would remember her, and use his knowledge of her pitiful past to terrify her into silence now when she had inadvertently stumbled upon proof of his guilt. And that proof, Dundee believed, consisted in nothing more than that Edith Ramsey, hysterically seeking medical aid on the murder night, had seen Edinger—an unknown and meaningless figure in her eyes—leaving Dr. Koenig's office.

Dundee frowned mightily as he reconstructed that hypothetical scene. Edinger—whoever he was—had recognized the girl, had terrified her by calling her "Miss Ramsey." Entirely ignorant that a murder had been committed, but sure that, now she was recognized as the heiress who had not only killed her parents in an accident but had recently killed another man in a traffic accident, Mayfield Sanitarium could no longer serve her as a hiding place. And so she had fled, only to be brought back, crippled, by Dundee himself. And not until the next morning, when Strawn, in an effort to heckle her into a confession, had brutally broken the news of the murder, had she had the faintest inkling as to what had happened, nor that her flight, if it had been successful, would have been a God send to the unknown who had accosted her.

And why had she not told, when the truth burst upon her? For the very simple reason that she believed her own liberty was at stake. If—she must be reasoning in her overwrought, always slightly hysterical mind—she "told on" Edinger—whom she did not know by that name, and possibly did not know by name at all—he would "tell on" her—tell that she was Edith Ramsey, wanted for manslaughter. For Edith Ramsey undoubtedly believed, with every terrified cell in her brain, that she was a fugitive from such a charge. In her unbalanced condition, she must be telling herself that the 1919 accident would be brought into the new case against her, making conviction and imprisonment doubly sure.

Dundee's heart throbbed heavily with pity for the girl. His almost overwhelming impulse was to go to the girl and say to her:

"You are not guilty of manslaughter. I know who you are. You are Edith Ramsey. The man your car struck on the night of April second did not die. He was only stunned. Now—whom are you shielding?"

But the inevitable consequence of that revelation instantly presented itself. Edith Ramsey now feared not only arrest on a charge of manslaughter, but she feared death at the hands of the unknown, if she told what she knew. And not even Dundee's adroitness could conceal from her the fact that the murderer's identity, beyond a name and a description that was eleven years old, was unknown to him. *She* could furnish a description, of course—probably an inaccurate or hazy one, registered upon an hysterical mind—but, she would ask herself, did she dare take the chance of telling what she knew when the murderer was still at large? In her opinion, would even a squad of plainclothesmen serve to guard her against his rage, and his supreme need to remove from earth the one witness who could actually connect him with the scene of the crime?

If—Dundee prided himself—he had one gift, it was the ability to *be* another person mentally. And now for five minutes he had been Edith Ramsey, thinking her thoughts in her own hysterical fashion.

No, he decided. It was not through Edith Ramsey—*yet*—that Edinger, whoever he was, could be brought to justice. How, then? Just as Dundee felt himself slumping into baffled weariness one tiny bit of information, scarcely noted at the time, came crashing through his brain like a streak of lightning.

Regardless of the fact that it was almost time for his dinner tray and that he was very hungry, the young detective sprinted across the lawn to the main building.

He found Dr. Harlow in Dr. Koenig's office, which had finally been turned back to the sanitarium by the police. With her was the secretary, Maizie Home, taking dictation.

Without preliminary, Dundee began:

"Wednesday night, Dr. Harlow, you said something about old Dr. Mayfield's habit of interviewing patients, during his lucid intervals. Tell me: did he remember Clyde Powell, and occasionally send for him?"

The little doctor's look of dignified annoyance at the interruption gave place to vivid interest.

"Why, yes! He did—frequently!" she answered eagerly. "You see, Clyde was a patient of Dr. Mayfield's for two years before the old doctor became incompetent to carry on his work. He was fond of Clyde, as we all were, and whenever Dr. Mayfield asked for a patient who was either dead or no longer with us, we made a practice of sending for Clyde, so that the old doctor's love of continuing with his profession might have an outlet."

"Dr. Mayfield made notes of his interviews with the patients, to add to their case histories, I suppose?"

Dundee asked, excitement making his blue eyes bright as diamonds.

"No," Dr. Harlow answered, and Dundee's heart sank. "When he was in active practice it was his theory that note taking embarrassed and impeded a patient. But"—and Dundee's hopes skyrocketed—"Dr. Mayfield had used a dictaphone for years. As soon as he had dismissed a patient, he dictated a record of the interview and his comments upon it, into the dictaphone. Naturally he continued the habit until his death."

If Dundee had been seven years old instead of twenty seven, he would have clapped his hands with joy.

"That's great!" he cried, instead. "May I see the transcriptions of all the records dealing with Clyde Powell's case?"

Dr. Harlow smiled pityingly. "Transcriptions? You forget, Mr. Dundee, that Dr. Mayfield was—not himself, that, while some of his comments on patients might have been very valuable "

"Then that hunch is a washout!" Dundee interrupted, so like a deflated, forlorn small boy that the little doctor took pity on him.

"I don't know exactly what your hunch is, Mr. Dundee," she said gently, "but there's a chance that it is not a 'washout.' "

"You mean there were actual records in the dictaphone?" Dundee pounced happily.

"Exactly! . . . Everything possible was done to make Dr. Mayfield happy, to foster his delusion that he was still head of the sanitarium. Not only were there actual records in the machine, but they were all kept—every record he dictated during the five years since his retirement," Dr. Harlow assured him. "Such a precaution was necessary, since Dr. Mayfield's memory was very erratic. A year after he had dictated his comments on an interview with a patient he might demand a transcription of the record, sure that the interview had taken place only the day before."

Maizie Home spoke up. "Sometimes I'd have a simply terrible time finding the one he wanted," she said indulgently. "But I always humored him—no matter how busy I was. Then maybe after all my trouble he'd have forgot all about it by the time I handed him the typed copy."

"Did you keep these occasional transcriptions that Dr. Mayfield asked for?" Dundee asked the secretary.

"Oh, yes. In a folder all by themselves," Maizie Home told him.

Two minutes later Dundee was in possession of the small collection. It was a pitiful exhibit. Crisply phrased, masterly commentaries on all sorts of psychopathic cases either ended abruptly, on an unfinished note, or trailed off into incoherencies that were, in themselves, indisputable evidence of the writer's own mental condition. Not only was Dundee disappointed to find nothing referring to Clyde Powell, but he was inexpressibly saddened.

That feeling of rebellious sadness continued with him after the young and mentally proud detective was admitted to the old doctor's private apartment on the second floor —primly neat now that its puttering old occupant was dead—and left alone with the dictaphone and the huge box of wax cylinders.

Dr. Mayfield had kept his dictaphone on a table beside his bed. Resting there after the fatigue of interviewing his "patients," he had recorded those facts and opinions so important in his own eyes and so worthless in the eyes of all others.

Now Dundee sat beside that table, listening to the record which contained the last words Dr. Cyrus Mayfield had ever dictated. The wax of that cylinder had not been called upon to immortalize a great many of Dr. Mayfield's last utterances, but as Dundee listened to that reedy, quavering, but dignified old voice, the hair stirred on his scalp. During the last hours of his life the old doctor had tried valiantly to get an audience with a man he did not know was dead, and now Dundee was to know what Dr. Mayfield had died trying to tell.

"Memorandum for Dr. Carl Koenig," announced the thin voice in his ear. "It has just come to my memory, which I am afraid is not so good as it once was, Carl, that I am by accident in possession of certain facts which require immediate attention."

Dundee held his breath as the record, blank for a few revolutions, spun in silence. Then:

"A few nights ago when my attendant, 'Happy' Day—and let me here register another protest against the useless expense to my establishment of having attendants idling about me—I repeat, when my attendant, Day, believed me to be asleep he was visited in the sitting room of my apartment by a young woman whom he called—ah—ah— Mavourneen. . . . No, another Irish word—Ah! Colleen! That's it! Colleen! The old man's memory is pretty good after all, eh, Carl?"

And while the ghostly chuckle spun the wax cylinder, Dundee whistled softly in awe and astonishment. "A few nights ago!" Good Lord! Colleen Lacey had been dead three years!

"Without eavesdropping intentionally I learned that the young woman, whose voice I recognized as belonging to the stenographer who takes Miss Home's place occasionally, is about to become a mother. She demanded of Day that he keep his promise to her to marry her, but he told her that he was already married to a Catholic who would not divorce him.

"It was my intention to inform you of this state of affairs the next morning, and have you attend to dismissing the man immediately, but it temporarily slipped my mind. All day today I have tried to see you and have failed. Please see that Day goes immediately. He is a disgrace to Mayfield. And do what you can for the poor child he deceived. Cyrus Mayfield."

That was all. But Dundee, as he slowly removed the last record Dr. Mayfield had ever dictated, felt that, doubly futile though that memorandum had been, it constituted a rather fine monument to the founder of Mayfield Sanitarium. And it was not wholly useless after all, for it removed the one possible shadow from Carl Koenig's name. Not, Dundee assured himself, that he had ever seriously suspected that Norah Lacey's adopted child was Koenig's. . . .

But—and Dundee braced himself to an arduous task— he had not found what he was looking for. Shrugging at the hopelessness of trying to apply any system to his task, the detective selected a cylinder at random, fitted it into the machine, and began to listen.

Although he ran the machine at its maximum speed he was discouraged and very tired when at the end of an hour he was no wiser, so far as his quest was concerned. His knowledge of abnormal psychology and of the treatment of mental diseases was enormously enlarged, and, specifically, he learned a great deal about the advance stages of *dementia pracox*, as exemplified in Clyde Powell. But in all the many dictated additions to Clyde Powell's case history to which Dundee listened over the dictaphone, he could discover no single conceivable reason why Edinger or anyone else should have destroyed it.

And yet that reason had to exist! Otherwise the murder of Dr. Carl Koenig was as stupid and insane as its perpetrator had tried to make it appear. Regardless of hunger and weariness, Dundee kept on at his task.

When the clew did come the detective was so weary, so nearly asleep, lulled by the dignified cadences of that reedy old voice, that he almost missed it.

"—identifying him with his delusional persecutor, "Frank,' and being subject to epileptiform seizures whenever he encounters him," was the conclusion of the sentence which finally aroused Dundee, and made him, with frantic haste, turn the machine back so that he could again hear and this time take in the opening words.

When the voice of the dead doctor had obediently repeated the words which, to Dundee, seemed the most brilliant ever uttered by a doctor, the detective sat in stunned silence for a long minute. And as he sat, effort less, every fact, like a well trained soldier, marched forward and took its place, forming a perfect "British square" before which Dr. Carl Koenig's murderer would have not the slightest defense when the battle was joined.

But it was not in military terms that Dundee sounded the battle cry when, having plunged downstairs to the murdered man's office, he got Captain Strawn on the telephone. The office was temporarily deserted, the staff being at dinner. But Dundee had taken the precaution to close the door into the hall, and his voice, while jubilant, was little more than a whisper.

"How soon can you get here, Captain?" he demanded urgently. Then he added the words which had announced the end of the chase in every murder mystery upon which he had worked in Hamilton:

"Got a pot on to boil, Captain!"

CHAPTER TWENTY SEVEN

TWENTY minutes later, Captain Strawn, Chief of the Homicide Squad; Brede, the police stenographer, and James F. Dundee, Special Investigator attached to the district attorney's office, entered the reception room of Sunflower Court.

Fat Miss Hunter, the night nurse, looked up from her work at the chart table with her usual beaming smile, which became rather strained as she realized who her visitors were.

"Is Miss Rambler in her room, Miss Hunter?" Dundee asked, unsmiling and without greeting.

"I—I think she's in the patio, down near the back gate," the nurse stammered, her florid face turning very pale.

"Thanks, Miss Hunter. . . . No, don't call her!" and Dundee turned to whisper instructions to the older detective.

In silence the three men crossed the room, passed through the little hall and stepped out upon the stone porch that bounded three sides of the patio.

Luck was with them. The girl who was known to Mayfield Sanitarium as Enid Rambler was seated at a table near the iron fence which stretched across the rear end of the patio. She was alone, and her head was bowed upon her crossed arms, which rested on the table. A pair of crutches propped beside her told how she had achieved this solitary outing. Nearby, stationed outside the door of her suite, the plainclothesman who had been detailed to guard her at night watched her stolidly. In the twilight he looked something like a faithful mastiff, watching the suffering of an adored mistress with dumb sympathy.

Dundee remained where he was until Strawn and Brede, as noiselessly as Indians, had reached the guarded door of Enid Rambler's suite. He saw them pass in, the greased hinges of the door making no sound. Then, walking normally, the young detective crossed the patio.

"Is there anything I can do, Miss Rambler?" he asked softly, when he had reached her side.

The girl raised her head, then strained away from him, cowering as if she expected him to strike her.

"Go away!" she panted. "I can't talk to you—I mean " Her hoarse whisper tripped over a terrible fear that blighted her beauty. "I mean," she repeated, "I don't feel well. I don't feel like talking to anyone."

"You mean," Dundee corrected her gently, "that some one has just told you who I am—why I am here."

"You—want me?" she said, and the words scarcely moved her white lips.

For a dreadful moment Dundee thought she was going to faint, and that his carefully planned climax would have to be delayed. But after that moment she opened her dark blue eyes and looked at him with a hopeless sort of courage that tore at his heart.

"I want to talk with you—yes," Dundee again corrected her, very gently. "Shall we go into your sitting room? . . . Let me help you!"

"No, thank you!" she refused his offer, struggling with her crutches.

And Dundee, although his heart was nearly bursting with pity for her, noted with keen satisfaction that, as she swung herself painfully ahead of him, awkwardly manipulating the crutches, her eyes darted terrified glances in every direction, as if her supreme fear now was that she be seen in his company.

Still preceding him, and avoiding even an accidental contact with him as if he were a leper, the girl passed through the little hall of her suite and on into the sitting room. Dundee, following her, glanced quickly toward the bedroom door. It was slightly ajar, but no carelessly planted boot or protruding elbow hinted at the presence of Strawn and Brede, who, he knew, were stationed in the bedroom, impatiently awaiting developments.

In spite of the girl's repugnance Dundee drew up a chair and relieved her of her crutches.

"I don't want to sit down!" she told him, bracing her self against the arm of the chair. "There's no need to talk. . . . Shall we—go now?"

"Go where?" Dundee asked, as if great surprise.

"To jail, of course!" she cried passionately, scornfully. "There's no use pretending any longer–"

"Really, Miss Rambler, there's no reason in the world why I should take you to jail," Dundee assured her, in a reasonable, soothing voice. "Of course, *material witnesses*"—he stressed the words, and paused to let them sink in,—"are frequently held in technical custody, but in this case–"

"Wait!" she cried, and sank weakly into her chair.

And Dundee knew that, as he waited obediently, she was trying to adjust herself to an incredible hope.

When she began, it was with a smile, a ghastly but gallant smile. "I—I thought you were going to arrest me for —for Dr. Koenig's murder, which would have been ridiculous, of course," she babbled. "But detectives do make the most absurd mistakes–" Her voice broke on a sob of relief, and again Dundee waited patiently for her to go on. "I see now that you merely think I know something about the murder that I've been concealing. *I don't know anything!*" She concluded in a suddenly loud and ringing voice.

"Is that so?" Dundee asked mildly, his face and voice giving no sign that he understood for whose benefit that loud declaration had been made. Not that he was in the least afraid that person had heard her and been reassured. . . . "Then it looks as if I've been wasting my time, Miss Ramsey."

At that casual use of her real name the girl's face be came like a death mask. Not even the eyes which stared at him in fixed horror looked as if they had any life left in them.

"I'm very sorry you had to learn from someone else that I am a detective, Miss Ramsey," Dundee remarked, in an easy, conversational tone, to give her time to recover from the shock. His very attitude, as he lounged in the chair he had drawn close to hers, was one calculated to reassure. "Please believe that my purpose in calling on you this evening was to tell you the truth, and to bring you a bit of good news."

"Good news?" she repeated blankly, with stiff lips.

"Yes—good news, but of course there, too, I may be wrong—blundering simpleton of a detective that I am," and he grinned at her companionably. "You see, I've had the impression all along that you were burdened with a very real terror, a fear that once you left this sanctuary you would—lose your liberty."

"Yes," the girl whispered.

"So, being a detective, and disliking all unsolved mysteries, I did some work on your behalf," he went on easily.

"On—my *behalf?*" she repeated, incredulously, but life was coming back into her frozen face.

"And, you know, Miss Ramsey—strange as it may seem —I believe you still don't know what actually happened on the night of Wednesday, April second!"

"Oh, don't I?" she shuddered, and covered her face with shaking hands, as if to shut forever from sight a picture she could not bear to look upon. But hands could not shut it out, and from behind them she moaned, "I'll never forget it! Never! If I could only die! . . . One minute he was walking, his whole body swinging as if he were so glad to be alive, and the next—Oh, my God!"

"You thought you had killed him, didn't you?" Dundee asked.

"Why are you torturing me like this?" she dropped her hands to demand wildly. "I admit it! I killed him! It was all my fault! I was simply paralyzed when he stepped in front of the car. I didn't know what to do—I didn't realize what I was doing when I let Paul persuade me to run away. And I don't *really* blame him for telling the truth–" But her crucified love rose up to choke her, even as she lied for it.

"Miss Ramsey, how do you know your sweetheart betrayed you?" Dundee asked softly.

"Why should he stand trial, when it was *I* that killed the poor man?" the girl defended her man passionately. "But I know he wouldn't have told the police if he hadn't thought I was safe—somewhere!"

"Paul Van Twing is a lucky devil," Dundee remarked, with just a hint of ruefulness. Then, because all his unspoken questions had already been answered, he could deny her relief no longer. "Miss Ramsey, I'm terribly glad to be the one to tell you that—you are not guilty of manslaughter!"

"Not—guilty?" she gasped. "You mean—oh, please!"

"I mean that the man your car struck was only stunned, not seriously injured; that his injuries were so slight that Paul Van Twing was able to adjust the matter without a charge being entered against him."

"But—But–" she gasped, and struggled to her feet, the sprained ankle forgotten.

"Miss Ramsey, who told you that you were guilty of manslaughter?"

"Who told me?" she repeated, and suddenly her body was electrified with the most terrible anger Dundee had ever seen.

He did not try to restrain her as she snatched up her crutches, let her swing herself strongly, head high and eyes blazing, from the room. For she was carrying out the part he had devised for her as exactly as if she had read the lines.

"No! Don't come in yet!" Dundee called in a low voice to Strawn, who was edging into the room. "But have your gun out—and ready!"

He himself waited in the sitting room until he heard the tapping of crutches in the little hall. Then, noiselessly, he joined Strawn and Brede in the sitting room.

"There's one difficulty," Dundee whispered to the older detective. "She may be terrified to face him alone, when he gets here."

"You're pretty sure she telephoned him, ain't you?" Strawn asked skeptically. "But don't worry about her being afraid! She's so damned sore she'd face him if he was a man eating tiger."

And he was right. The girl was still in such a towering rage that she did not seem even to notice that Dundee was no longer there. She did not sit down, but stood, swung between her crutches, her blazing eyes fixed upon the door which Dundee confidently expected the murderer of Dr. Koenig to open. For if the murderer did not come of his own accord, after receiving that telephone message, Dundee had made sure that he would be brought forcibly. . . .

The sounds of an arrival came, however, before Dundee expected them. How had he got here so soon?

With their eyes at the door crack Dundee and Strawn heard the knock upon that other door, heard the girl's ringing "Come in!" saw the door flung wide and a man's figure framed for an instant before it leaped forward.

"Who's that?" Strawn hissed into Dundee's ear.

And Dundee muttered, blankly, "I don't know!"

But he knew in the next instant, for the newcomer, far from assaulting the girl who, her crutches dropped, was swaying toward him, was sweeping her off the floor into his arms.

"Oh, Paul!" Edith Ramsey gasped. "Paul, Paul! I thought you didn't love me any more–"

The blond, six foot two young giant laughed exultingly, and Dundee gave him time to kiss the girl once before he stepped into the room.

There was scant time for explanations, and the young detective ruthlessly brushed aside the astounded new comer's protests.

"Come with me, Van Twing! Explanations later!" he ordered curtly. "Miss Ramsey is expecting another—guest. Quick, I say! . . . Don't be afraid, Miss Ramsey! Captain Strawn is in the bedroom, too–"

"Afraid!" she laughed, and anger returned, in nowise diminished by her joy at Van Twing's arrival. "Do as he says, Paul! Quick!"

The bewildered young man obeyed, even chuckled. "I say! What sport!" he gloated. "The hounds and the fox, eh?"

"Fox is right!" Dundee assured him grimly, but he felt that he was going to like this wholesome, handsome young giant, when he had time to think about him. "Stand back, Van Twing! . . . Ready, Captain?"

"Look! Is Edith in danger?" the young man protested, at sight of Strawn's leveled gun, and started for the door.

"Stand back, I tell you, Van Twing!" Dundee commanded savagely. "We are all delighted to see you, but I'll be damned if you spoil everything now! . . . Shut up!"

And Van Twing subsided just in time, for again the door from the hall was opening, and this time it framed no unfamiliar figure.

Roger Baldwin stepped into the room.

CHAPTER TWENTY EIGHT

"WHAT do you want?"

From his place of concealment behind Edith Ramsey's bedroom door Dundee's very flesh felt the blight of the quiet, deadly coldness of Roger Baldwin's voice.

But apparently it had no power to chill the girl's terrific anger. She was magnificent as she faced him, head high, blue eyes blazing, her crutches forgotten.

"I want the joy of seeing your face when I tell you that I am going to have you arrested for the murder of Dr. Koenig!" she told him, her voice vibrating with a terrible exultation.

Roger Baldwin smiled, but no light gleamed in the strangely cold opaqueness of his brown eyes. Weird eyes they were! No wonder Dr. Koenig had been haunted by the certainty that he had seen them somewhere before. . .

Braced upon Dundee's shoulder, its muzzle thrust into the crack of the partly opened door, was Captain Strawn's revolver, and behind it was Captain Strawn's steady trigger finger and steadier eye. Otherwise the young detective would have been in a sweat of fear as the business manager of Mayfield Sanitarium walked slowly, but with deadly purposefulness to where the girl stood.

"You are insane, Miss Rambler," Baldwin said unemotionally. "You are suffering from a suicidal mania–"

"Suicidal?" she laughed scornfully. "You *know* I saw you come out of Dr. Koenig's office! You *know* I heard you tearing up papers–"

"—from a suicidal mania," Baldwin repeated, in his flat, unemphatic voice. "It will always be a great grief to me that I arrived too late to prevent you from shooting yourself with your own automatic. I struggled with you, but–"

But the shot that shattered the moment of silence which followed Baldwin's calm words did not come from the small automatic which he had lifted to press against the girl's right temple. . . .

"Won't be much of a job for you, will it, Doc?" Captain Strawn asked regretfully two or three minutes later. "I'd have liked to plug the devil through the heart–"

"I'm afraid this right hand will never be much use to him again," Dr. Cantrell answered. "But since he seems to be ambidextrous, the inconvenience won't be very great."

"That baby's not going to need either hand very long," Strawn gloated, but not even then did Roger Baldwin's opaque eyes, fixed on Strawn in an unwinking stare, register any emotion.

The murderer lay on Edith Ramsey's couch, where unsympathetic hands had placed him after his one spasm of fury had been subdued. Bending over him, silent and white faced, administering to his wound as carefully as if he had been any other patient, was little Dr. Harlow. Dr. Cantrell's rubber gloved hands were selecting instruments silently handed to him by Norah Lacey. For Dundee's preparations for the boiling over of his pot, as he called it, had been prophetically complete. Close upon Baldwin's unsuspecting heels had walked the little procession of the business manager's associates, half informed of what they might expect.

When all that they could do for the not seriously wounded man had been done by the doctors and nurse, Dundee took Dr. Harlow's place in front of the couch.

Solemnly but very quietly, in the deep hush, he spoke the dread words:

"Steven Francis Edinger, sometimes known as Frank Edinger, alias Roger Baldwin, I arrest you for the murder of Dr. Carl Koenig, and it is my duty to warn you that anything you say may be used against you."

The silence was profound for a long minute. Baldwin closed his eyes in token that Dundee's warning was superfluous.

"Won't you please take him away now, out of my rooms?" Edith Ramsey broke the silence, her voice sounding very small and pitiful, but there was no hysteria in it. Paul Van Twing's arms were around her. . .

"I'm sorry, Miss Ramsey," Dundee answered sincerely, "but I want to submit you to one more ordeal. I want you to tell your story in this man's presence."

Brede, the police stenographer, automatically opened his notebook.

"I shall be glad to!" the girl cried, righteous anger returning to give her strength. "I've been sure for two days —ever since Captain Strawn talked to me Thursday morn ing—that I was shielding Dr. Koenig's murderer, but I didn't dare—Oh, I can never forgive him for making me hate myself so!"

"Will you begin by telling how you happened to come to this sanitarium, Miss Ramsey?" Dundee suggested soothingly.

"Paul and I were driving on a lonely road. A man stepped from the bushes right into the path of the car," she answered obediently. "I was driving. The suddenness of it paralyzed me. I—it's happened to me before. ... I couldn't think, I couldn't act. I—hit him. Paul and I both thought he was dead. I seemed to go crazy. I *must* have been crazy, or I shouldn't have run away when Paul, who understood me, told me to. He said he would take all the blame, that no one need ever know I'd been in the car. I was a coward. I ran away. But I took my own automatic that I've always carried on motor tours. It was in the pocket of the car. Paul didn't know I took it. I meant to commit suicide before I'd let them take me to jail. The thought of a cell–"

Dundee's sympathy cut across her shuddering sobs. "We understand, Miss Ramsey. You have not really been your self since you were fifteen years old. . . . But bow did you happen to come to Mayfield?"

"I didn't know what to do. I had quite a lot of money with me, and Paul had told me to walk for a mile or so, then telephone for a taxi from a filling station, and go on back to the hotel But I—couldn't. I remembered meeting Mr. Baldwin on Main Street in Hamilton. He came up to me and said, 'How do you do, Miss Ramsey? . . . Don't you remember me?' I said I didn't, and he said he had known my father in California. Then he told me he was business manager of Mayfield Sanitarium now. He said again, "You're sure you don't remember seeing me before?' and I thought it was odd, but Daddy had so many friends mat I only met casually–"

"Baldwin was glad of the chance to test the completeness of his changed appearance," Dundee interrupted to explain. "You *had* met Baldwin, or had seen him but he was no friend of your father's. He was the husband of Mrs. Edinger, a patient at Good Hope Sanitarium at the time you were there."

"Oh!" Edith Ramsey breamed. "So that's why the name seemed vaguely familiar. . . . She was awfully sweet, so gentle, so good to everyone. I remember how devoted one poor boy was to her. . . . And that's an odd coincidence!" she discovered. "The boy was Clyde Powell, who was a patient here until Monday, I believe. I recognized him, but he didn't remember me at all. I was afraid at first that he might–"

"You distinctly remember, however, that Clyde Powell and Mrs. Edinger were friends?" Dundee interrupted eagerly.

"Oh, yes!" the girl cried. "Clyde simply adored Mrs. Edinger. And because she blamed 'Frank,' as she called her husband, for putting her in the sanitarium, Clyde adopted 'Frank' as his own persecutor—hating and fearing him exactly as Mrs. Edinger did."

"Thank you, Miss Ramsey," Dundee said triumphantly, though her statement only confirmed his own deductions. "So—in your extremity—you thought of this friend of your father's, business manager of a sanitarium?"

"Yes. Ever since 1919 I've thought of a sanitarium like this as a haven of refuge," she confessed. "And I believed no one would think of looking for me here. If they did find me, my record as a 'psychopathic patient' would keep me from being sent to jail. ... So I telephoned Mr. Baldwin from a filling station. He came for me in his own car. I told him the dreadful thing I'd done, and he said he'd hide me—*for ten thousand dollars!*"

"Good God!" Paul Van Twing ejaculated, and started up from the "love seat" he was occupying with Edith Ramsey.

"Sit down, Van Twing!" Dundee ordered curtly, but not unkindly. "I sympathize with your reactions, but Baldwin, or Edinger, is going to be amply punished for his crimes. . . . Go on, Miss Ramsey!"

"I gave him a check on my New York bank, and he explained to me how I could open a bank account here, in the name of Enid Rambler. He chose the name for me himself, because it fit the monogram on my handbag and the gun, and everything."

"He took the gun away from you?" Dundee asked.

"Yes. He said I must not think of committing suicide, that he'd protect me. . . . And all the time," she added, "he was planning to kill me with it if I told on him. These last two days, after I knew he had killed Dr. Koenig, I knew what he could do to me. Being the business manager here, he could walk into my suite any time he chose, and the plainclothesman on guard would not dream of trying to prevent him. And I couldn't tell a soul—I couldn't even say that Mr. Baldwin was to be kept out of my rooms–"

"My poor darling!" Van Twing said huskily, and tightened his arms about her. "I don't see how you kept from going crazy!"

"That's what he planned!" she cried, with passionate anger. "All the time I was here he knew I hadn't killed that man. But not only did he remind me somehow, almost every day, that I was a murderess and a coward, he made me believe you had turned against me, Paul, that from information you had given there was a warrant for my arrest–"

"But didn't you see the papers?" Paul Van Twing interrupted.

It was Dr. Harlow who explained, bleakly: "That is our fault, I am afraid. New patients, in Miss Ramsey's condition, are not permitted to see newspapers, for fear the stories of suicide will influence them."

"But Mr. Baldwin saw the papers!" the girl cried. "He knew! ... Of course, after he had got all the money he could out of me, his plan was to drive me crazy, so that nothing I said against him could be believed—and so that I'd never get out of here and learn the truth! ... I gave him thirty five thousand dollars altogether," she added, "but if he'd only told me the truth—that I was innocent of manslaughter and that Paul had not betrayed me, I'd have gladly given him every cent I had in the world, out of sheer gratitude!"

"Now, as to Wednesday night, Miss Ramsey?" Dundee hurried her gently.

The girl sank back into the shelter of her sweetheart's arms.

"I'd never gone to any of the entertainments in the O.T. Shop," she said quietly. "I was always terrified of strangers—afraid someone would recognize me and inform the police. But Wednesday evening, just before seven, Mr. Baldwin came to my suite and told me to go to the movie. He said I'd enjoy it particularly. He didn't tell me the name of the picture, said it would be a 'pleasant surprise.' I knew it was a command I did not dare disobey, so I went, along with Marjorie Merrick. It was—'Manslaughter,' " she added, in a horrified whisper. "He'd got it because he knew what effect it would have on me.

It's about a girl who kills a traffic policeman, and is put in prison. I couldn't bear it. I thought I was really going crazy. It was horrible. . . . But I meant to tell you some thing else he said to me when he ordered me to go to the movie," she interrupted herself. "He said Dr. Koenig was 'suspicious,' that the doctor didn't believe there was any real reason why I should be here. Of course I was terrified at the thought of leaving my 'sanctuary.' I didn't know that Mr. Baldwin had got the picture with the express purpose of making me so hysterical that Dr. Koenig would let me stay on."

Her voice shuddered to a pause, and Dundee took advantage of the opportunity to glance at the girl's audience. Little Dr. Harlow sat very still and very straight, her eyes disks of horror set in the chalky whiteness of her face. Dr. Cantrell was listening with head bowed and shoulders slumped, the image of despondency. Norah Lacey was weeping silently and apparently unconscious of the tears that trickled down her thin, freckled cheeks. Only Roger Baldwin seemed unmoved by the girl's story of an incredible inquisition.

"So you left the movie, Miss Ramsey?" Dundee prodded gently.

"Yes. About half past nine. As I told you, I was in a terrible state. I tried to find someone to give me a bromide. Finally I went to Dr. Koenig's door off the main hall, but it was closed. So I decided to wait until he was not busy. I sat down in the reception room. I heard some strange noises, but they were not loud at all. Then I heard someone—I thought it was Dr. Koenig—tearing up paper. That sound went on and on. I was about to knock, because I couldn't hear him talking to anyone, but the door opened and Mr. Baldwin came out."

Dundee drew a deep breath of triumph. Strawn slapped a thigh in mighty exultation.

"He looked terribly queer when he saw me there," the girl went on tonelessly. "Then he bent over me and whispered, as if he was afraid Dr. Koenig would hear him. He said the doctor had just telephoned the police to come and get me, that he'd found out somehow who I was. And then Mr. Baldwin told me to run away. I started to run, and he stopped me. He gripped my shoulders and whispered: 'Run along the highway, my girl, and if you happen to get hit by a car, remember it's a quick, easy way to die. You ought to know. *You've killed three people that way yourself!*'"

"I'll be damned if I sit here and–"

But Dundee sprang toward Van Twing and forced him back into his seat.

"He's right, Paul," the girl soothed her sweetheart. "I'm really safe now, and we're going to be happy. I'm well now—I'm *well!*"

But Dr. Harlow must have thought otherwise, for during the interruption she had slipped from the room. Now she was back, and silently offering a sedative to the girl.

"I don't think Miss Ramsey need talk any more now," Dundee said soberly. "We know the rest of her story. We know that she tried to carry out Baldwin's diabolic suggestion, but that she sprang out of the path of a car in time, suffering no more than a sprained ankle as she stumbled into the ditch."

The girl nodded mutely, and Dundee went on:

"As the district attorney's representative, Miss Ramsey, I thank you with all my heart for the aid you will render to the state in this man's trial for murder."

"But I'm still in a fog, boy," Strawn protested. "I know all about Edinger, and the mess he got into back in 1919, but why the devil is he here, and why in the name of God did he want to murder Koenig?"

"I'd like to know the answer to those questions myself," Dr. Cantrell said heavily.

"I know nothing of Edinger's story between 1919 and 1926, when he ingratiated himself with Dr. Mayfield's party on board ship," Dundee acknowledged. "From the looks of the man—and I judge he has not changed much during the last five years, I should say Edinger, who had adopted the name of Baldwin, had gone through some devastating illness. At any rate, he had lost so much weight and aged so drastically that scarcely any other disguise was needed to make him unrecognizable to those who had known him as Edinger."

"Amebic dysentery. Picked it up in China," the murderer astounded them by explaining in his emotionless voice.

"Thanks, Edinger," Dundee said drily. "As for the nose, a plastic surgeon would make nothing of the job of converting a short, stubby nose into a Roman beak. . . . At any rate, Baldwin felt safe when his enemy of the Los Angeles courtroom, Dr. Carl Koenig, met him and failed to recognize him. Baldwin did not know that his eyes haunted Koenig, nagging at his memory. The partnership was formed—*suggested by Baldwin*, who had had good opportunity to gauge the chances of fraud in a private institution for the treatment of mental diseases.

"Koenig was, of course, a severe check to Baldwin's schemes. But he found Mayfield to be a profitable field, in a perfectly legitimate way. If he had not been a born crook, he would have been satisfied with the profits which Dr. Koenig's skill and reputation made possible. It is possible that he was almost satisfied, until he chanced to meet Edith Ramsey, and later found the girl flinging herself at him for protection. The temptation was too great. Possibly there have been other patients here whose recovery Baldwin has cunningly retarded. Certainly we know of one other. . . . But let that rest for the moment.

"Tonight, after I was sure that Edinger was Baldwin, I asked Dr. Harlow if Baldwin had been away on a business trip recently. She told me that he had been to Chicago, to confer with architects, during the month of May. I knew, then, that the Sandlin mystery was solved."

"Sandlin?" Cantrell echoed incredulously, and Dr. Harlow lifted her eyes, which seemed suddenly to come alive again.

"Of course it was Baldwin who negotiated with Dr. Sandlin," Dundee assured them impatiently. "I feel sure that Baldwin ran into Sandlin by accident, when looking over the Howard Memorial buildings with an architect. Sandlin recognized Baldwin. And Sandlin, being as big a crook if not so clever a one as Baldwin, threatened exposure, if a suitable price for his silence was not forthcoming. Baldwin could not face trial on the Edinger indictment in Los Angeles, and he was much averse to turning over hard cash to the man who had helped him in his scheme against his wife. But he could—and would—pay another price."

"Get Sandlin into Mayfield and split the crooked profits with him," Strawn deduced happily.

"Right!" Dundee smiled. "But Koenig, when Baldwin broached the subject to him, was not having any Sandlin, thank you. That doctor wasn't good enough for Mayfield! Baldwin, who had had a long conference in his own cottage with Sandlin on Tuesday night—for of course it was Baldwin and not Koenig whom Sandlin came to Hamilton to visit—could see no way out. He insisted, as a partner, on Koenig's considering Sandlin as an assistant psychiatrist. Koenig made a note of the name on his desk calendar, intending, no doubt, to investigate Sandlin thoroughly enough to convince the business manager. I think it was probably true that Dr. Koenig intended to devote most of his time in the future to psychoanalysis. The two crooks would have had practically a clear field here—except for the annoying fact that Dr. Harlow, as straight and incorruptible as Koenig himself—would still be here!"

"Oh!" the little doctor breathed, and light began to shine through the horror in her eyes.

"On Wednesday afternoon," Dundee went on, "Dr. Koenig told the business manager that Mrs. Morse would be leaving in a day or two—cured. That was a severe blow to Baldwin's cupidity. Mrs. Morse's monthly bill here was well over a thousand dollars, a sum Baldwin could not bear to lose, if human—or inhuman—ingenuity could prevent it. But first he protested to Dr. Koenig, or so I firmly believe. Koenig was astounded at Baldwin's suggestion that the woman be kept on indefinitely, on the chance that she was not really cured. Something of Baldwin's true nature must have betrayed itself to the psychiatrist at that moment. Not only did Baldwin want Mrs. Morse to be detained, but he argued against 'Enid Rambler's' being sent away, although Dr. Koenig was convinced she was not a definite psychopathic case, and that such an atmosphere was harmful to her."

He paused, and the silence which awaited his further revelations was electric with suspense.

"Picture to yourself, as I have tried to picture it, Koenig's state of mind in regard to Baldwin. The business manager, he suddenly realized, was becoming a definite menace to Mayfield. Not only was he opposed to patients being cured, but he wanted to add to the staff a doctor against whom Koenig had heard vague but sinister insinuations, and Koenig must have remembered his impression of Sandlin's insincerity at Mrs. Edinger's sanity hearing.

"Koenig was troubled, but there was nothing definite— yet. He worked all evening, unconscious of the fact that Baldwin had slipped out of his own office just before nine o'clock, and had staged that dreadful 'Voice of God' farce beneath Mrs. Morse's windows.

"Shortly before half past nine Dr. Koenig remembered that Mrs. Cantrell was not well. He interrupted his work of typing the excerpts from Clyde Powell's case history, wanted by the State Hospital doctors, and telephoned Mrs. Cantrell. As he talked, his eyes roamed idly. Then they were arrested by a line in Clyde Powell's history that had seemed unimportant before. That line was to the effect that, *at the sight of Roger Baldwin, the patient showed fear, and suffered epileptiform seizures.*"

"Has the case history been found?" Dr. Harlow asked.

"No, it must have been completely destroyed," Dundee assured her. "But Baldwin did not know that a senile, feeble old man had recorded the same interesting fact."

"Did that doddering old fool–?" Baldwin began, then his lips snapped to.

"Exactly," Dundee assured him. "It would have been 'good business' to clean out Dr. Mayfield's rooms thoroughly, wouldn't it, Baldwin? . . . But possibly you were saving those useless old dictaphone records of his, planning to have them shaved for future use?"

Baldwin did not reply.

"But how did that sentence in Powell's case history tip the doctor off?" Strawn demanded, sorely puzzled. "It wouldn't have meant anything to us if we'd seen it!"

"Right you are!" Dundee agreed triumphantly. "Baldwin's guilty conscience made him a little too far sighted. Without the fact of that completely destroyed case history But to answer your question. The sentence concerning Baldwin would have meant little to Koenig, even troubled as he was about Baldwin's attitude toward the sanitarium, if it had not occurred on the same page with two other names—Good Hope Sanitarium and Dr. Horace Sandlin. Those three names leaping into his vision almost simultaneously caused something to click in Koenig's memory. Suddenly he knew where he had seen Baldwin before! I am sure the whole picture of that Los Angeles courtroom flashed into Koenig's mind. Baldwin was 'placed' at last. And Baldwin was Steven Francis Edinger, 'wanted' in Los Angeles!"

"So Koenig tried to put the matter in his lawyer's hands," Strawn supplied with satisfaction.

"Yes," Dundee agreed. "After all, Baldwin, or Edinger, was connected with Mayfield, and the doctor must have planned to avoid publicity as much as possible. But when he could not reach Forrest, he acted. He was killed in the very act of dictating a night letter to the district attorney in Los Angeles."

For the benefit of Dr. Harlow and Dr. Cantrell, and partly, it is just possible, to let Baldwin know how his undoing had come about, Dundee told briefly the story of the "bust message," which had ended with the three letters, "E d i ."

Then he turned to the quiet, apparently uninterested man on the couch.

"You congratulated yourself on your luck in having entered Dr. Koenig's office just in time to prevent that message being completed, didn't you, Edinger?"

The murderer scorned to answer.

"And as you busily 'dressed the set' to make it look like murder committed by a homicidal maniac, you boasted to yourself of your coolness and far sightedness, didn't you, Edinger?"

There was still no answer, but Dundee expected none.

"Yes, you were clever, Edinger," the young detective went on relentlessly. "Damned clever! But—just a little too clever! You made three very bad errors, which–"

That drew fire. "Three!" the murderer snorted. "I didn't overlook anything—except that single damned drop of blood."

Dundee smiled. Brede was taking down everything in shorthand.

"I admit, Edinger, that that one drop of blood was in dispensable to us—that it led directly to your undoing. But you made two other serious errors. Not being a psychiatrist, Edinger, and having had only one really original idea in your life, you chose to repeat. *But Mrs. Morse does not hear voices.* She is not, and never was, that type of psychopathic case."

"The third error, Bonnie," Strawn reminded him. "What was that?"

"He told a lie," Dundee answered simply.

"Guess he's done a lot of lying these last three days," Strawn retorted, puzzled.

"Not much," Dundee corrected, in all fairness. "But he told one lie that has stood out like a signpost from the first hour of this investigation. He said that Dr. Koenig told *him* he was going to dismiss Dr. Harlow. . . . Very bad, Edinger! . . . Now, it was just conceivable that Dr. Koenig might have come to the conclusion that the little doctor was too credulous, too soft hearted for her job, even though he thought enough of her to put her down in his will for one half of his estate. But—Koenig would never in this world have told Roger Baldwin, whom he did not like particularly, of his intention to dismiss a woman who had served him faithfully and devotedly. With the utmost tact and gentleness he might have broken the news to the little doctor herself, but he would never have told anyone else *first*. And of all people, he would not have told you, Edinger! . . . And the more fool I, that I didn't follow that signpost more quickly!"

"I'm glad you made a detour," Edith Ramsey said softly.

"By the way, Van Twing," and Dundee turned to the young man who had arrived so opportunely, "I presume your fat private detective, who, incidentally, almost succeeded in getting himself suspected of murder, notified you of Miss Ramsey's presence here, incognito."

"Fat, is he?" Van Twing grinned, but without amusement. "He's fat mentally, too, it seems, for in his regular night letter report to me of his activities I was informed on Thursday morning that he—Fuller is his name—had located a girl strongly resembling Miss Ramsey, at Mayfield Sanitarium, but that the business manager had convinced him of his mistake. Naturally, when the newspapers blazoned forth the news of Dr. Koenig's murder, I was intensely interested. Late Thursday editions carried a paragraph describing 'Enid Rambler,' as one of the patients who had been 'quizzed,' and I was so positive it was Edith that I took a plane as soon as I could charter one. . . . There is some excuse for Fuller, however. The photograph he has of Edith shows her with bobbed hair, and considerably plumper than she is now. She has let her hair grow since I saw her last."

"I see," Dundee commented, and was silent for a long minute. Then, very soberly, he turned toward Dr. Harlow.

"For those who are grieving for Dr. Koenig," he said, almost apologetically, "I am presumptuous enough to offer this bit of consolation: Dr. Koenig did not die in vain. His tragic death saved Edith Ramsey. For this girl was doomed. Edinger would never have permitted her to leave this place until she was dead or hopelessly insane. Dr. Koenig would have given his life to save her. . . . And he did!"

THE END

More Mysteries by Anne Austin

Murder at Bridge

When an afternoon bridge party attended by some of Hamilton's leading citizens ends with the hostess being murdered in her boudoir, Special Investigator Dundee of the District Attorney's office is called in. But one of the attendees is guilty? There are plenty of suspects: the victim's former lover, her current suitor, the retired judge who is being blackmailed, the victim's maid who had been horribly disfigured accidentally by the murdered woman, or any of the women who's husbands had flirted with the victim. Or was she murdered by an outsider whose motive had nothing to do with the town of Hamilton. Find the answer in . . . **Murder at Bridge**

One Drop of Blood

When Dr. Koenig, head of Mayfield Sanitarium is murdered, the District Attorney's Special Investigator, "Bonnie" Dundee must go undercover to find the killer. Were any of the inmates of the asylum insane enough to have committed the crime? Or, was it one of the staff, motivated by jealousy? And what was is the secret in the murdered man's past. Find the answer in . . . **One Drop of Blood**

AVAILABLE FROM RESURRECTED PRESS!

GEMS OF MYSTERY LOST JEWELS FROM A MORE ELEGANT AGE

Three wonderful tales of mystery from some of the best known writers of the period before the First World War —

A foggy London night, a Russian princess who steals jewels, a corpse; a mysterious murder, an opera singer, and stolen pearls; two young people who crash a masked ball only to find themselves caught up in a daring theft of jewels; these are the subjects of this collection of entertaining tales of love, jewels, and mystery. This collection includes:

- In the Fog - by Richard Harding Davis's
- The Affair at the Hotel Semiramis - by A.E.W. Mason
- Hearts and Masks - Harold MacGrath

AVAILABLE FROM RESURRECTED PRESS!

THE EDWARDIAN DETECTIVES
LITERARY SLEUTHS OF THE EDWARDIAN ERA

The exploits of the great Victorian Detectives, Poe's C. Auguste Dupin, Gaboriau's Lecoq, and most famously, Arthur Conan Doyle's Sherlock Holmes, are well known. But what of those fictional detectives that came after, those of the Edwardian Age? The period between the death of Queen Victoria and the First World War had been called the Golden Age of the detective short story, but how familiar is the modern reader with the sleuths of this era? And such an extraordinary group they were, including in their numbers an unassuming English priest, a blind man, a master of disguises, a lecturer in medical jurisprudence, a noble woman working for Scotland Yard, and a savant so brilliant he was known as "The Thinking Machine."

To introduce readers to these detectives, Resurrected Press has assembled a collection of stories featuring these and other remarkable sleuths in The Edwardian Detectives.

- The Case of Laker, Absconded by Arthur Morrison
- The Fenchurch Street Mystery by Baroness Orczy
- The Crime of the French Café by Nick Carter
- The Man with Nailed Shoes by R Austin Freeman
- The Blue Cross by G. K. Chesterton
- The Case of the Pocket Diary Found in the Snow by Augusta Groner
- The Ninescore Mystery by Baroness Orczy
- The Riddle of the Ninth Finger by Thomas W. Hanshew
- The Knight's Cross Signal Problem by Ernest Bramah

- The Problem of Cell 13 by Jacques Futrelle
- The Conundrum of the Golf Links by Percy James Brebner
- The Silkworms of Florence by Clifford Ashdown
- The Gateway of the Monster by William Hope Hodgson
- The Affair at the Semiramis Hotel by A. E. W. Mason
- The Affair of the Avalanche Bicycle & Tyre Co., LTD by Arthur Morrison

RESURRECTED PRESS CLASSIC MYSTERY CATALOGUE

Journeys into Mystery
Travel and Mystery in a More Elegant Time

The Edwardian Detectives
Literary Sleuths of the Edwardian Era

Gems of Mystery
Lost Jewels from a More Elegant Age

E. C. Bentley
Trent's Last Case: The Woman in Black

Ernest Bramah
Max Carrados Resurrected:
The Detective Stories of Max Carrados

Agatha Christie
The Secret Adversary
The Mysterious Affair at Styles

Octavus Roy Cohen
Midnight

Freeman Wills Croft
The Ponson Case
The Pit Prop Syndicate

J. S. Fletcher
The Herapath Property
The Rayner-Slade Amalgamation
The Chestermarke Instinct
The Paradise Mystery
Dead Men's Money

The Middle of Things
Ravensdene Court
Scarhaven Keep
The Orange-Yellow Diamond
The Middle Temple Murder
The Tallyrand Maxim
The Borough Treasurer
In the Mayor's Parlour
The Saftey Pin

R. Austin Freeman
The Mystery of 31 New Inn from the Dr. Thorndyke Series
John Thorndyke's Cases from the Dr. Thorndyke Series
The Red Thumb Mark from The Dr. Thorndyke Series
The Eye of Osiris from The Dr. Thorndyke Series
A Silent Witness from the Dr. John Thorndyke Series
The Cat's Eye from the Dr. John Thorndyke Series
Helen Vardon's Confession: A Dr. John Thorndyke Story
As a Thief in the Night: A Dr. John Thorndyke Story
Mr. Pottermack's Oversight: A Dr. John Thorndyke Story
Dr. Thorndyke Intervenes: A Dr. John Thorndyke Story
The Singing Bone: The Adventures of Dr. Thorndyke
The Stoneware Monkey: A Dr. John Thorndyke Story
The Great Portrait Mystery, and Other Stories: A Collection of Dr. John Thorndyke and Other Stories
The Penrose Mystery: A Dr. John Thorndyke Story
The Uttermost Farthing: A Savant's Vendetta

Arthur Griffiths
The Passenger From Calais
The Rome Express

Fergus Hume
The Mystery of a Hansom Cab
The Green Mummy
The Silent House
The Secret Passage

Edgar Jepson
The Loudwater Mystery

A. E. W. Mason
At the Villa Rose

A. A. Milne
The Red House Mystery
Baroness Emma Orczy
The Old Man in the Corner

Edgar Allan Poe
The Detective Stories of Edgar Allan Poe

Arthur J. Rees
The Hampstead Mystery
The Shrieking Pit
The Hand In The Dark
The Moon Rock
The Mystery of the Downs

Mary Roberts Rinehart
Sight Unseen and The Confession

Dorothy L. Sayers
Whose Body?

Sir William Magnay
The Hunt Ball Mystery

Mabel and Paul Thorne
The Sheridan Road Mystery

Louis Tracy

The Strange Case of Mortimer Fenley
The Albert Gate Mystery
The Bartlett Mystery
The Postmaster's Daughter
The House of Peril
The Sandling Case: What Would You Have Done?
Charles Edmonds Walk
The Paternoster Ruby

John R. Watson

The Mystery of the Downs
The Hampstead Mystery

Edgar Wallace

The Daffodil Mystery
The Crimson Circle

Carolyn Wells

Vicky Van
The Man Who Fell Through the Earth
In the Onyx Lobby
Raspberry Jam
The Clue
The Room with the Tassels
The Vanishing of Betty Varian
The Mystery Girl
The White Alley
The Curved Blades
Anybody but Anne
The Bride of a Moment
Faulkner's Folly
The Diamond Pin
The Gold Bag
The Mystery of the Sycamore
The Come Backy

Raoul Whitfield
Death in a Bowl

And much more!
Visit ResurrectedPress.com
for our complete catalogue

About Resurrected Press

A division of Intrepid Ink, LLC, Resurrected Press is dedicated to bringing high quality, vintage books back into publication. See our entire catalogue and find out more at www.ResurrectedPress.com.

About Intrepid Ink, LLC

Intrepid Ink, LLC provides full publishing services to authors of fiction and non-fiction books, eBooks and websites. From editing to formatting, from publishing to marketing, Intrepid Ink gets your creative works into the hands of the people who want to read them. Find out more at www.IntrepidInk.com.

www.ingramcontent.com/pod-product-compliance
Lightning Source LLC
LaVergne TN
LVHW010051110826
845155LV00028B/294

* 9 7 8 1 9 3 7 0 2 2 5 3 2 *